# THE KILLING FILES

# THE KILLING FILES

## NIKKI OWEN

**BLACKSTONE**
PUBLISHING

Printed in the United States of America
ISBN: 978-1-5047-8065-0

1 3 5 7 9 10 8 6 4 2

CIP data for this book is available from
the Library of Congress

Blackstone Publishing
31 Mistletoe Rd.
Ashland, OR 97520
www.BlackstonePublishing.com

To Brian—this one's for you, Mr. Blue Sky

# CHAPTER 1

**UNDISCLOSED CONFINEMENT LOCATION**

*Present Day*

The room is dark, damp. I cannot see properly. I have been caught, that much I know, but by whom? The Project? MI5? Someone else? I don't know how I got here. I don't know how I am going to escape.

I lift my head, but it feels heavy, a sack loaded with potatoes. I inch it back. My breathing is hot, the air a woolen blanket on my face, thick and scratchy, and as my sight begins to adjust to the dark, slowly, like a curtain being lifted on a stage, I start to see small slivers of solid items. Where am I?

A room. I think that is what this is, but I am unsure. Then what? A cell? Prison confinement again? But I was found innocent. I am free, I tell myself. I am not guilty, have not killed anyone, yet even when I say the words to myself, for some reason they don't seem right, instead feel out of place, a code reassembled in the middle.

One breath, two. My eyes begin to adjust to the gloom, and my sight registers small globules of shapes. The corner of a wall, the faint rectangle of a window—snapshots only of a whole picture. There is a seat of some sort, a table perhaps, but beyond that, nothing. The air is too black for me to take an inventory, the atmosphere sticky tar turning all the soft daylight into hot, putrid night as adrenaline starts to spurt out into my blood, creating short, sharp alerts. I am not safe here.

It is then I hear it: the rustle of movement.

"Who is there?" My voice clicks with a cotton-swab dryness, and I wonder how long it is since I last drank water, as my brain rapidly tries to calculate timings and bearings and any scrap of geolocation memory it can cling to.

"Who is there?" I repeat, yet there is no answer, only darkness. A worry rises inside me, but I press it back, not wanting to panic, not wanting to melt down here and now.

Focus. Breathing. I can hear someone breathing, there, on the whisper of the air. I inch my eyes left, sensing what exists but not wanting to acknowledge it. Have I put them there, whoever it is? Is that what this is—a hit? Did I try to kill them? I didn't murder the priest, but I doubted myself then, at the trial. And then a horrific thought strikes. What if I have been on an operation for the Project and this is the result? A body on the floor beside me, injured by me and waiting to die. A killing I may later have no memory of.

I keep my torso as rigid as possible, not daring to move. How did I get here? I think hard, connect my cognitive thoughts, but no matter how much I try, nothing shakes, as if my memory has been erased.

As if who I am doesn't really exist.

The person's breathing is shallow now, graveled and raspy. I know what bleeding out sounds like—the sharp, slicing quality of inhalation—but this is not it. And yet, there is an urgency to the breath, a desperation that I cannot place, but it makes no sense why. I am a doctor, so I should know the signs, but still I cannot place them. What is wrong with me?

I blink three times and try hard to concentrate, to return my brain to function mode, focusing again on the room for clues. The edges. They are shrouded in black, but the window above affords a slip of light that plops in a puddle to my left. It is then I see it—an arm—and a gasp slips from my mouth.

I track the limb, milky-white skin on a long, limp wrist. Different from my own arms, my muscled, tanned ones with bitten nails and dirt in the creases. Even in this murky room, I can tell that this arm is clean, scrubbed.

I keep all my attention on the body part and again try asking who this is, instinctively counting the time as I wait. The numbers soothe me as seconds rack up in twos, the action slowing—at least for the moment—the anxiety that is building inside, but when I ask again who is there and no one answers, a moan slips from my mouth. The urine-colored light has all but disappeared, yet somehow I start to see something slithering into view. A long T-shirted torso. An elegant white neck. A skull.

A face.

A scream pierces the air, and I am shocked to realize it is mine. I catch my breath, frantically slap my hands up and down, straining to thrash my body forward from the seat, but still my pulse flies. Because there is a face staring back at me, a face I know. Shaven scalp, sharp cheekbones, gapped teeth, and pool-blue eyes—eyes that, even in this tar-black air, shine. My hearts races; my chest tightens. How can she be here? How have I let this happen? We are all in danger now, all of us.

"Doc." The voice comes from the head on the floor.

I slam my eyes shut, not wanting to believe what is here, reciting an algorithm in a vain attempt to calm myself.

"Doc, it's okay." The voice is a cotton sheet flapping in the breeze, a rustle of green grass. "Doc, I'm okay."

My eyes open. One millimeter, then two, gradually allowing my sight to do the work my brain does not want to understand. My friend is here. My only friend in the world is lying crumpled on the floor beside me.

"Patricia?" I say, testing out the word. "You are out of Gold-mouth prison."

"Yes, I got out on parole, remember? Two months after you."

Confusion, worry. They spin around fast in my head. "You are here. Why are you here?"

"Because they have us," she says, the Irish lilt to her voice still there as I remember, but scratched now, torn. "The Project has caught up with us. You can't hide from them anymore."

The Project has found me—that's why I have woken up here in this room. They have entrapped us, and there is only one way it will end: someone will die.

"We have to get out. Tell me your status—are you injured?" I listen for her reply, but there is only silence.

"Patricia?" Still there is no answer, no words back to me as I continue to repeat her name over and over again in the gloom. When I finally stop calling for her, I flop back, flooded with fear— fear of myself, of who I am. Because it's me—I have done this. I have caused this to happen. I slam my head back and back again, crying out, yelling into the thick, black air. Why can't I recall how I got here? Why don't I recognize where I am? Why?

Why?

One solitary fat tear slides down my cheek. "Do not die." The words slip out, silent, unbidden. "Please, do not die."

My eyes search for Patricia's body, for an arm or a head— anything that can reassure me she is okay, that my friend is okay.

"I am sorry," I say. "I am sorry. I am sorry. I am sorry."

I stop, haul in oxygen, listen for signs of life, but in the ten long seconds that next pass, the only sound audible in the thick, foul air is the rasp of my own breath.


## SALAMANCAN MOUNTAINS, SPAIN
*34 Hours and 59 Minutes to Confinement*

The sun is blinding me. I kick off my running shoes, prop my hand on my forehead, and, squinting toward the distance, listen to the morning as the mountains wake up. Clicking cicadas, dry summer grass rustling in the breeze, pregnant lemon and orange trees groaning under the weight of fat fruit spritzing citrus into the air, the distant bleat of a mountain goat—all the sounds that are now familiar to me, part of my daily routine. The security camera lights surrounding my hidden villa glow green—six lenses in total, covering every angle of the property. The Salamancan earth is slowly rising.

I pick up my coffee cup, drain it, then pad inside, counting my steps where the terra-cotta tiles are cold on my soles.

*One, two, three*, my feet move forward until twenty-four arrives and I halt at the sink, my eyes watching everything. I set down my cup, pick up a white cloth, and dry last night's dishes: one plate, one knife and fork, and one small wineglass. Opening a metal cupboard, I put the crockery away, all of it fitting easily, the only occupants in the large, spotless space.

I scan the rest of the kitchen, returning everything to its place. One pan, one white jug with a scratch seven millimeters long on the inside of the handle, one metal pot, small, for milk to warm at night when the sun rests and the night blanket covers the sky where the stars switch on and glow until morning. I count them all and document them in my head and, satisfied all is correct and present, close all the cupboards, and, stretching up my arms high into the air, recite the words I have spoken now every day since I came here to hide from the Project and MI5.

"I am Dr. Maria Martinez. I am thirty-three years old." My fingers ripple in the warm air, a gentle wisp of a breeze drifting in through the small open window, its wooden frame cracked yet solid. "I am innocent of murder. I am free."

I stretch my hands farther into the void, my muscles elongating into the empty space around me as I go through my routine to remind myself who I am, because if I did not tell myself, I fear I would be lost entirely. My hands fan out and my muscles are taut and strong, and when I twist toward the glass door of the oven, my reflection stares back, green contact lenses patched over brown eyes, black hair dyed platinum and sewn in clumps to my small skull, the flesh on my face and limbs deep and sun brown, lines thick and grooved and ingrained into my worn skin and elbows and ankles and knees.

"I am Dr. Maria Martinez. I am thirty-three years old," I repeat, inhaling, my back arching downward and my arms reaching forward so my palms flatten on the floor, the tiles cold on my skin, tiny sharp jolts reminding me I'm alive. "I am innocent of murder. I am free."

The yellow morning rays shine warm on my face. I close my eyes and I breathe it all in, moving, exhaling, saluting the sun, feeling my body work as one with my mind as I repeat my chant over and over, losing my thoughts to the repetitive medicine of it, allowing my brain to soften itself of the millions of cognitive connections automatically made every second of the day and night. I bend my knees now, toughened skin touching down on the terra-cotta as I crease my spine up toward the ceiling, eyes still closed as I battle in my head with the pictures that sway before it—pictures of the loud, excrement-filled prison I was kept in, of the court trial and the beatings and the discovery of the Project entire, the shredded, sordid secrecy. I breathe, try to let the thoughts pass by me as my spine curves inward now. Rippling the muscles of my torso up and down, I feel them creak and stretch after the running outside, shorts riding up and itching my skin, vest top stuck to me with sweat, and even though the irritation of it is sharp, I continue focusing, letting my brain be even a little bit at ease with who I am, all the while chanting, reminding, never ever forgetting, because without conscious thought, what would we be?

Ten minutes pass in the early morning sun of my movements across the tiles and in the empty air, and when I am ready and complete, I stand, exhale, and open my eyes. The sun shines into them and I blink as my sight adjusts to the hazy film of the day that yawns out ahead of me, my mind registering with a glow of satisfaction that there are no people to attempt to converse with, no social games for me to decipher how to play. I turn to the sink. I extract one small glass from the cupboard to my left and, filling it with water, drain the contents and, mouth refreshed, rinse out the glass and return it to its home.

When I am certain that all is in its place, I wipe dry my palms on the back of my running shorts and pad toward the lounge, grateful for my daily routine, for each phase of it I have created. Every day since I left prison and came here to hide from the Project and MI5, after my morning run and yoga, I spend three hours tracking and documenting the latest news stories on the US National Security Agency Prism scandal and any terrorist crimes or cybersecurity threats that I think the Project may be involved in.

I am just entering the lounge past the wooden crates on the floor when, today, it happens. I don't know if it's the thought of analyzing the latest news on the NSA that has triggered it, or if it is because I slept badly last night, nightmares of prison waking me up in sweat-soaked fits, but the memory arrives, fast and bright—not the hazy part of clouds that normally occurs when such recollections float to the surface, but this time quick, a Taser prod, switching my mind from what is in front of me to what is inside, to a distant drug-hazed memory.

"No!" The sound of my solitary voice rings loud in the silence, sending the birds in the orange trees outside scattering in random directions.

I grip the kitchen sink. This process, this feeling, it is now familiar, so many times over the years has it passed, but still there is a fear as my brain is thrown into recalling something locked deep within my subconscious.

Something from my past.

# CHAPTER 2

Suddenly, I am not standing in my Salamanca kitchen but instead am in a white clinical room, a room that now, from my dreams, from my nightmares, I know well.

I am fifteen years old, limbs long and thin, jutting out at awkward Bambi angles. I am sitting robot-straight in a metal bed, and my long, matted rope of thick black hair is uncut and wild and resting on a white hospital gown where freckles puncture plump, sun-kissed skin, cashmere soft, no lines yet of a longer life lived. ECG probes sit glued to my small rib cage and concave abdomen, and in the background the *pit-put* of a heart rate monitor hums.

I turn my head and see him. The man. I intake a sharp breath, but there is no surprise in it, no immediate concern, as if I have been expecting him, as if this, here, is a routine that offers me some strange, warped comfort.

"Your vital signs are good," the man says. His voice has a Scottish edge, each word a slice of a knife, a slow turn of a screw. "Can you tell me who I am?"

"Dr. Carr." My voice is a feather, a butterfly wing. I shiver.

He smiles and when he does, his lips slice thin and it makes me think of a cut on my arm. "And you have a special name for me, don't you, Maria? What is it?"

"Black Eyes."

I can feel my nerves tense, and so I scan the room as a distraction. The walls are white, and by them stand three stainless steel seats and two cream Formica tables. There are no pictures or soft materials, just brown plastic blinds and two officers guarding the doors, with handguns hanging by their sides. I don't like it and so start to jig my leg.

"Maria, look at me. Can you look at me?"

"No." *Jig, jig.* "I want to go home."

His smile slips, and without warning, his arm whips out and slaps my leg still. "Stop stimming and look at me."

A sting like one hundred needle points pricks my skin. My leg drops still. I want to scream at him, jolted by the feel of his touch, but am too scared because I know he could shout and the noise would bother me too much, and so instead I attempt to do as he says so he won't touch me again.

He rolls his fingers into his palm and withdraws his hand to his lap. "I'm sorry for that," he says. "We are on a tight deadline today."

I strain my eyelids, force my sight to stare straight at him, but it is hard, hurts, almost in an uncomfortable way, as if opening my eyes to his, to anyone's, would allow them to see into me, see into my thoughts. In the end, I manage to make contact for only two seconds, then have to look away, exhausted.

He inhales. "For the next few hours, I want you to practice making eye contact for half a conversation. This will help you slip more seamlessly into a regular situation if you ever go operational. Make you appear more ... normal. Yes?" He smiles and I think I see tiny eye creases crinkle out on the corners of his face, but I am unsure. "Yes, Maria?"

"Yes," I respond on autopilot.

"Good. Look at me." I do. "One second longer, that's it. Two, three, four ... Good. You can lower your eyes now."

I drop my gaze, shattered, as he takes notes in green ink on a yellow page. Behind him, a woman walks over, petite, a tattoo of a cross on her brown neck, hair cropped so closely her scalp shines through it. The woman stops and whispers in Black Eyes' ear. I cannot hear them, so I bend forward a little; yet, when I look down at my thin, gowned body, the probes sticking out, it is merely crumpled, having barely moved at all. Beside me, the heart rate monitor beeps faster.

My body shifts on the bed. Black Eyes is nodding now to the woman who has appeared in the room, and at first the words they whisper fade into the squashed air, but after two then three seconds, their sentences filter through as, slowly, my ears switch fully on.

"The program is showing her skills are improving, Dr. Carr," the woman whispers. "Her handler at the church is communicating very positive results."

"Such as?"

"He gave her a complex code to crack, and she did it within thirteen seconds."

"Good. Good. What else?"

She consults her notes. "The subject's IQ is exceptionally high, photographic memory sharp—she is obsessed with classical composers, tracks all their family details, their names, all their pieces—"

"Has she learned to play the piano yet?"

"Yes. Self-taught, Trinity College London, grade eight standard within three weeks. Further information: the way in which she can sense acute sounds and scents is exceptional—I know you were concerned about that."

"Hmmm."

"And her dexterity skills, her technical assimilation—it's getting faster. She can take apart and reassemble a clock radio, for example, within three minutes now. Last time it was five. Her handler at the school recorded that."

There is a nod from Black Eyes as he turns and provides me

with a narrow stare. "We have been operating for twenty years now, and this is our breakthrough. She's the only one the conditioning appears to be working on."

"Yes."

He looks to her. "MI5 will want to hear about this."

The woman hands him a slip of white paper. "Done. Here are the results we sent over to our contact there."

Black Eyes scans the data, pinching the page, each finger a spindled vine of pale flesh. "All these people we have conditioned and tested, and none of them are quite like this test child, this Maria Martinez. What is her confirmed subject number?"

"Three-seven-five."

"Subject 375. Yes." He taps the paper. "We have some scenarios I would like to use her for, see what she can do. MI5 are pressing us to assist them with unusual security threats—cyber elements, computers, et cetera. Let's see how she can help us."

His head dips, and without warning, his skeletal fingers creep forward and skim my calf. I flinch, but he doesn't appear to notice, instead seems in some kind of trance. "It's okay," he tells me. "It's okay." Then he turns to the woman. "She is strong, but not yet old enough to fight. Soon, though …" He lifts his hand, knuckles and flesh hovering in the air, and the thought occurs to me that he may hit me. "While she is here, we will ask her what she knows."

The woman frowns. "But won't that stay in her memory? The covert details are just that: covert. What if she recites them when she's back in her normal environment?"

He shakes his head. "We will give her Versed as we always have, administered before she's dispatched home to Spain. It's worked well so far." He looks to me. "It will wipe her immediate mind so no secrets are divulged—she will simply believe she has visited the specialist clinic with her mother because of her Asperger's." He hands the woman the paper. "The Versed drug means she will be unable to recall fully what she has or has not done, but enough remains in the subconscious for her to be useful until she reaches an age where she can be fully operational. It is important that you learn this." He folds his arms. "The subject may recall things, facts, but they will be hazy, like dreams. But we need that. We need this data, this training we give her, to remain stored in her brain somewhere so we can use it when the time is right."

"Maria?" He is talking straight to me now. A rush of heat prickles my entire body, and I don't know what to do. My eyes search for a way out, but there are no exits anywhere. "Maria," he says, voice unusually soft, low, "where are we?"

But nerves rack me, and instead of speaking, I press my back into the bed, the cold cotton of the gown skimming my knees, goosebumps popping out.

"I want to go home."

"You will. But first—that's it, look at me, good—answer me: Where are we?"

I look between the woman and Black Eyes. When I open my mouth, my voice trembles. "I am in a Project facility."

"And who are the Project?"

"It is a covert group linked to MI5."

"And what do we do?"

Despite myself, despite my resistance, the words trip from my mouth, as if they are preset, robotic. "The Project is a covert program formed in response to a global threat of terrorism, specifically cyber-terrorism. It trains people with Asperger's to use their unique skills at pattern recognition to combat security threats. Only MI5 knows that the organization exists."

"And the UK government?" he asks. "What of them? Do they know who we are?"

"Negative. They have no knowledge of the Project's existence."

"Good." A smile snakes onto his face. "Good."

The woman nods once to Black Eyes, then leaves through a door that has no handles or hinges. Black Eyes waits for her to exit, then perches himself on the end of the bed. I grip the sheets tight. At first, he does not speak, but then, after one and a half seconds, he opens his mouth and speaks in a precise, metallic voice.

"You will not remember being here, Maria. You won't recall this conversation or the details of the tests we carry out on you. But know that we are always watching you, are always ... here for you. We are everywhere." He leans to the side and picks up a loaded syringe from a metal trolley.

My heart rate rockets.

"You are at school now, yes?"

I swallow, confused. "No. I am not at school now. Now I am here."

He pauses one second, two, three, his teeth appearing to clench. "Your teacher next year," he says finally, exhaling. "He will be working for us, helping us to watch you. These people you see nearly every day—they are your handlers. Even your family priest. But of course, you won't"—his mouth emits a strange, mewling laugh—"you won't remember." He sighs. "I cannot believe I am telling you this now. You'll only forget. But Father Reznik, your friendly Catholic priest—he's one of us." My eyes go wide. The priest? But I saw him kissing Mama. "Oh, the big brown eyes! Maria, I am growing to know you well now. You do remind me of my own daughter ..." He drifts off, momentarily looking downward, the needle resting in his fingers. I glance to the door and wish I could run. "Anyway," he says after a moment, "don't worry. When you go on to university and work, we will have our people there, too, Project people like me and you, people who will watch over what you do, even though you won't, at the time, know they are with us." He flicks the needle with a finger. Sweat beads all over my face. "Oh, there's no need to fret," he says now, leaning in, studying the sheen on my forehead. "We are friends, aren't we?"

I recoil. "I do not have any friends."

He halts, tilting his skull. "No. No, I don't suppose you do." He drifts off again for a second, then, checking the needle, shackles my wrist with his fingers and pulls my arm toward him. "Your mother, Ines—lovely woman, isn't she?"

I say nothing, instead watching his eyes narrow as they inspect the vial for air bubbles. Bile wells in the base of my throat.

"Shame she is on her own now after Alarico died. Loneliness is a terrible thing. Car crash, wasn't it?"

Alarico, my papa. Hearing his name makes my head spin a little, my heart ache. The vomit rumbles.

"Still," Black Eyes says now, his Scottish lilt dancing on the cold air, "she's a strong woman, your mother—a lawyer like your father, but, well, more forthright. She'll make a good politician when she hits the Spanish parliament, after she's got over her little … illness. Your brother, too—Ramon, isn't it? Seems like he's following in their legal footsteps, what with his fondness for debate club. Quite the family. And family, Maria, is important. It keeps us together."

Black Eyes is leaning into me so close now, I can see the faint shadow of stubble on his chin, feel the hot garlic and tobacco of his breath on my neck. I want to scream. I want to run a million miles away, but no matter how hard I try, I cannot make myself move, and even if I did run, where would I go? Where would I ever go?

"You, though, Maria," Black Eyes says now. "My—our—test child. For you we have plans. We would like you to become a doctor. Try and press that into your subconscious, hmm? Even though this will make all of today fade away. A plastic surgeon, specifically. We need to test your dexterity skills, hone them so they can one day be of use to us. Study in Madrid at the university hospital there—that's where one of our handlers resides." He smiles, a flash of crooked tombstones. "Do you understand?"

I nod.

"With words."

"I understand."

"Good. Because you are the one our conditioning is working

on, and we wouldn't want all these trips your mother takes you on to be wasted, now, would we?"

"Mama believes she is taking me to an autism clinic," I say, an unexpected flash of defiance streaking through me. "She does not know what you really do. You are lying to her."

He stares at me. He levels his black, bottomless eyes at me and delivers a look so chilling that even with my emotionally challenged brain, I get a shiver of fright.

"We have a bit of terrorism to fight out there," he continues now, as if I had never spoken. "Pesky little terrorists trying to break into our computer networks, into our global infrastructures. But now"—Black Eyes taps my arm, lowers the needle to my skin—"now, my dear, sweet Maria, now you will forget ..."

# CHAPTER 3

**SALAMANCAN MOUNTAINS, SPAIN**

*34 Hours and 53 Minutes to Confinement*

I come to. I tumble into the present day, sucking in a sharp gulp of oxygen, falling against the kitchen table, sweat pouring from my brow and arms and bare, wobbly legs. I go to haul myself up, blinking furiously, desperate for water, but almost instantly another subconscious recollection arrives, dragging me back into a deeper, stronger dream. More lucid and glaring.

This time, I see myself sitting at a desk in a Project tech lab. The walls are regulation white, and around the bottom are long strips of brushed steel, all bases for sockets with red and green flashing bulbs that are controlled from a panel to the left. Computers sit in pre-allocated slots, with controlled acoustics used to minimize background sounds for the subjects, subjects like me, who inhabit the zone. There is spatial sequencing, and lights and levels that are all compartmentalized to define their use. Everything routine, expected.

My fingers tap a keyboard, and I notice they are older now, not fifteen this time, but tanned, longer—the fingers of my stronger twenty-year-old self. I am writing detailed notes from memory into an online file classified "Top Secret," scores of numbers and times and geolocations going directly from my brain to the computer. On the screen is a photograph of a woman with caramel skin, wearing a hijab draped around pink-rose cheeks. She has a prominent aquiline nose, and eyes so brown they look as if they were of pure liquid. Her picture is superimposed on the file, and as I type I record details of this woman I have known for two years but who has now caused problems for the Project. My informant, my asset in the field, whom I have code-named Raven, a bird symbolizing good omens, yet also the keeper of deception, of tragedy.

A beep sounds, and I stand, quick, lithe, the colt now fully formed. Turning to the right, I march out of the door, to the main corridor warren of the covert Project facility. Scanning the area, I proceed straight to room six, where I enter through the thick metal door, shut it, and turn.

Raven lies on the floor. She is spattered in blood, and her black veil lies splayed out, torn down to her neck, exposing cut, charred skin and deep, gaunt eyes. Gone is the rose tint of her cheeks, replaced now by two hollows. When I look at her, I know she is the enemy, and yet, for some reason, a lump forms in the base of my throat and I have to swallow it away.

A Project officer, younger, walks over to me. He wears a gray shirt of soft cotton fabric, and beneath the front of the right-hand shoulder is the letter "H," followed by a three-digit number.

"I was called here," I say. "What do you require?"

He turns to me but makes no eye contact. "You need to guard the detainee. I have been asked to go to the control center. I will be back in three minutes and thirty seconds."

He turns and exits, and I do not move. My eyes stay ahead, my body now defined, muscles strong, hands nimble, dexterous from the medical school training.

"M-Maria?"

The woman lifts her head from where she lies slumped on the floor. She has raised her gaze to me, but I do not look at her. The lump in my throat tightens.

"Detainees are not permitted to talk," I say, eyes front.

"It is you, isn't it? Maria? You … you cut your hair." She coughs, and blood speckles the white tiles. Her eyes dart left and right and then settle back on me. "I know you think I am the enemy, but I am not. That's just what they made you believe." She heaves in oxygen. "They set me up, Maria—you have to believe me. They'll do it to you, too, if they have to. I'm not a terrorist." She coughs again, wipes her mouth. "They'll be back soon, so you must listen. There … there is a file. It's encrypted." She licks her cracked lips. "It's on a file within a computer that's not … that's not attached to anything—a stand-alone device. No server is linked to it, but it contains a file that you created—a hidden file, away from the Project. Do you understand? Do you understand what that means?"

"Detainees are not permitted to talk." I strain not to look at her. She is the enemy, and yet her words, her injured presence—they bother me.

"It has details, this file," she continues, "ones they cannot track. It will give you what you need: confidential data, who the Project has tested on, the files and names of who they've killed. What they're doing is wrong, Maria. They can't treat people like this. They can't act like gods of the world, and yet that's what they do. Give man power and I give you an eternity of pain." She spits out some blood, and I fight the urge to wipe it away because, for some reason, I feel connected to this woman. But I don't know why.

"Maria?"

"Detainees are not permitted to …" I trail off, confused, unsure which side she is really on.

"You are struggling, I know," she says now, her speech low, labored, "struggling with who I am. But we were in the field together. Maria, I helped you and you helped me. They'll mess with your memory after they've done with me, like they always do. The file will give you what you need, tell you what you've done—the truth! Find out who you really are, Maria! I know you, I do. We were … we were friends."

My eyes briefly flicker to her. Then, snapping back into position, I look away. "I have no friends."

The door bolts open, and the officer with the "H" on his shirt returns, accompanied by two higher-ranking officers. They stride over to Raven, haul her up, but as they pull her away, she digs her feet in. "The file," she whispers. "Find it!"

As they yank her forward, she shouts, "They will make you complete it, Maria! 'Prepare,' they told us. 'Wait. Engage! Eliminate the threat.' They will make you kill me! You know this, Maria. I know you do. Fight it," she says, her feet leaving long smears of blood in their wake. "Fight the Project! Help!"

But I do nothing, just watch her go. And as she is dragged screaming away, past the cold, pale doors along the Project walkways, what bothers me about her so much comes to me, slapping me hard in the face.

"I never knew your name," I say aloud to the now empty room, the words echoing in a void that can never be filled. "I never knew your name."

The image begins to swirl away, gently at first, then faster downward as a noise vibrates in my ears and I realize it's the radio alarm clock clicking on, blasting a newscaster's voice into the kitchen.

My eyes fly open, taking in a woozy, hazy view of my warm, sun-drenched kitchen. I touch my head with a shaking hand and, lurching forward, grab a glass, fill it from the tap, and drain the water until it is sliding down my chin, liquid fangs on my shocked skin. I slap the glass down, slam back into the wall, smear my lips with the back of my hand, and try to steady my breath. The memory, the subconscious dream still fresh in my mind—these have happened before, but never this strong, never with her so vividly in them. I throw my hand to the side, feel my way forward, the image of the hijab throwing me off center. What she said about the files—was that true? Did she store a data file at the Project? Did that actually happen? I spin around, brain firing left and right. My notebook. I need my notebook, need to write it all down, record it so I can track it and try to make sense of what is hidden in my head.

The news piece on the radio is talking about the American National Security Agency, how Edward Snowden has revealed more information and is in hiding now. I try to pay attention. I try to press it all to my mind so I can lose myself and record it all on my wall, but the words are too much, the noise all too loud, and I can't think straight, the dream of the woman and her screams still lingering in my mind even in the bright glare of the summer sun. A dull moan slips from my mouth, and I slap my hand down on the radio, silencing it as I count my stumbling steps into the lounge.

My eyes automatically scan the solitary armchair, the old brown piano with its back against the wall, the towers of books that skyscrape their way almost to the ceiling, the thousands of newspaper articles plastered to the wall, covered in scrawled notes and pushpins and sketches of blank faces I don't remember. I look at it all, my sight hazy, struggling to focus until, finally, I spot my notebook on the cabinet island by the far wall.

I go straight to it, flip past the pages of algorithms and codes and sketches of Project facility buildings, all vague memories of events and details, and scratch out what I have just seen. Done, I slam the book shut. I stare at the cracked brown leather cover that curls at the corners. My memories, my nightmares, are in there, the ones I don't know about, the details and facts I cannot even recall having occurred although, somehow, they are in my head. Somehow, despite the drugs, I recall them. But why?

I think of Raven. What if there is a file? What if, despite the drugs that Black Eyes gave me, I have just recalled something that happened a decade ago? If the file the woman stowed away was at the Project, does that mean it is still there, now, after all these years? I hold out my hands, look at my fingers—long, slim, trained plastic surgeon's hands that reconstruct faces and skin ravaged by injuries, and a mix of disgust and sadness hits me. The Project made me become a doctor. It was not my choice or conscious will; it was a foregone conclusion, a fait accompli. But what are we when we are not in control of our own choices and lives? What does that eventually do to us? And what do we eventually do as a result?

I stare again at my fingers and skin and bitten-to-the-quick nails. I am Dr. Maria Martinez. Raven said they would make me kill her.

Did I?

They have made me believe I have killed before. They even got me convicted of the murder of a priest because they—MI5—wanted me hidden and out of the way when the NSA Prism scandal broke out, just so the Project would not be uncovered. They framed me to suit their own ends, but even then I doubted myself, because if the Project has decided and directed who I am and what I do in life, if they have drugged me all along, how will I know with any certainty what really happened?

And who it happened to?

I reopen my notebook. Perhaps, if I scan the pages again, if I link my thoughts here to the wall and the research and the faces and facts, I can make some connections between what I know and what I have just seen. I can lose myself in my thoughts and record everything that swims to the surface of my memory, linking it if I can to the NSA, to MI5 and the Project, find some comfort purely in the challenge and routine and order of it all, safe in the knowledge that I won't take it any further, that I don't ever want to leave here and the sanctuary it provides, and if they don't find me, I can remain hidden in my villa forever.

I look up at my wall. I study the multiple news articles and anonymous faces and facts and arrowed figures, and just as I am about to reach forward and readjust a pinned article so that it sits neat and straight and in order next to the others, the emergency cell phone shrills into the calm morning silence.

And everything stops.

# CHAPTER 4

**SALAMANCAN MOUNTAINS, SPAIN**

*34 Hours and 46 Minutes to Confinement*

I pick up the cell, slamming down the button so the shrillness will stop hammering into my head.

"Who is this?"

"Maria, it's Balthus."

"You are speaking on the emergency cell," I say, fast. "Is there an urgent situation?"

"What? No."

"Then why are you calling me?"

"You haven't contacted me for three days, and I was worried."

The ring of the cell still echoes in my head. I shake it. "Four days."

"What?"

"I have not called you for four days." My eyes catch the sunshine dancing a waltz along the curves of the glass panes. I focus on it, and gradually, my head calms down. "You said three."

There's a pause. "Maria, we agreed when we split up in London, you'd stay in touch, contact me every day. I got worried when you didn't call."

"Why?"

"Because I care for you. Because I promised your father before he died I'd look out for you."

"Oh. Okay." The glass panes twinkle in the daylight. "I had another memory today."

"What? When?"

"At zero-six-twelve hours this morning."

I pick up my notebook and proceed to tell him what happened. He listens. This is what he does, Balthus Ochoa. I talk and he listens. When he was the governor at Goldmouth Prison in London, where I was incarcerated, his listening led me to find an encrypted file that uncovered the Project and my subsequent involvement in it. He has always told me how he promised my papa that he would be there for me, tells me he cares for me, and I catch myself feeling what must be gratitude toward him, but I never know how to express it, don't understand how people say what they feel inside.

"That's odd," Balthus says now, his voice a layer of gravel, a boulder on a mountain.

"What is odd?"

"Well … Okay, so it may be nothing, but there's something bugging me about the stand-alone computer the woman in your flash mentioned, but I can't figure out why it bothers me. Maria, the memory with the woman, with Raven—do you remember which Project facility that happened in?"

"No. I only recall the facility with Black Eyes when I was younger. That was in Scotland. That is the facility Kurt brought me to. Do you not remember this?"

"Jesus, how could I forget? I bloody well suggested you see that therapist after you were acquitted—and he turned out to be working for MI5."

"He was working for the Project."

"That's what I said."

"No. You said MI5. When Kurt—although his real name is Daniel, a Hebrew name meaning 'God is my judge'—when he was meeting with me, he was only working for the Project. By then—"

"By then the NSA Prism scandal had been exposed, and MI5

wanted to ditch the whole Project because they were scared of a similar blowup."

My eyes rest on the wall, on my drawings and newspaper articles and lines of connections and notes.

Balthus sighs. "I don't know, I just … What they did. I still can't believe the Project framed you for the murder of that priest just to get you in prison and out of the way, so they could then get rid of you."

"So they could kill me to eradicate any connection to the Project."

"Yes." He pauses. "Yes."

The window in the lounge is open, and in the breeze the muslin curtain drifts in and out, the white cotton veil of it brushing the tiled floor.

"Anyway, look, Maria," Balthus says after a while, clearing his throat. "The other reason I wanted to call was just to let you know there's been no sighting or word from the MI5 officer who posed as our prison psychiatrist—Dr. Andersson. You were asking about her."

Dr. Andersson. Her face springs into my mind.

Swedish-blond hair, ice-blue eyes, freckled pale skin. A vision of her making me take apart laptops, timing me to complete a Rubik's cube— all the tasks she was doing to monitor me without my knowledge. I shiver. "She has not approached you or any of Harry's family?"

"No. No, I don't think so. But, Maria, listen. How are you about Harry now, since his death? It's been six months since Dr. Andersson shot him on the court steps when she was aiming to kill you. Harry wasn't just your barrister or even simply your papa's old friend—I know you had a soft spot for him." He pauses, three silent seconds passing. "I just worry about you. It's a lot for *any* of us to process, never mind for you."

I am stuck for words as a strange tightness presses against my chest. "The Kübler-Ross grief model says I should be at the acceptance stage now."

"And are you at that stage, Maria? Do you accept Harry's death? He cared for you a lot." I can hear him swallow. "We both did—do."

I swallow and clench my jaw as conflicting feelings of anger and sadness wash through me. A tear escapes. I reach up, smear my cheek dry.

"Dr. Andersson killed Harry. MI5 killed Harry."

"Yes."

Over on the window ledge, a small bird with golden-brown feathers lands on the white wood. It dips its head once, then, going very still, it looks up, free, and flies away. For a few seconds, I watch the now empty, open space where the bird stood. Inhaling, I look back to the cell phone.

"Did Patricia get parole?"

"Yes," Balthus replies. There is a rustle of paper on the line. "I told her you were okay, in hiding from the Project, let her know what you did—sending the texts to MI5 and the Project on Kurt's phone in London so they both thought you were dead. She understands you're hiding, that you can't contact her."

"And Dr. Andersson has not been trailing her?"

"No. I'm in touch with Patricia; all seems well. You two struck up a good friendship in Goldmouth. I'm glad, I'm …" He stops. "You need friends, Maria. I hate the thought of you being entirely on your own."

My eyes catch the room. The solitary chair, the bare white-washed walls, the cell phone lying on the upturned crate, with Balthus' voice trapped inside.

"Look, Maria," Balthus says after two seconds, "I don't know why, but something about this Raven memory of yours … Well, I know I mentioned it just before, but it … well, there's something about it that rings a bell, but I don't know what."

"Is it a recent recollection?"

"I don't know. I …" He trails off. "It's just, well, something Ines told me when she called me when you were in prison. I don't know if it even means anything, but it was weird."

"The word 'weird' means a suggestion of something supernatural."

"What? No, no, I didn't ..."

"'Weird' can also mean connected to fate, to a person's destiny."

"Okay. Well, anyway, she was specific, Ines was, about talking to me, about calling me and telling me what she did."

"When exactly was this?"

"It was before the retrial."

"What date?"

"I don't know."

"Why not?"

"Maria, my memory's not as accurate as yours. But, look, it was strange. We hadn't spoken for years—since Alarico's death, in fact—and then, after her visit to you in Goldmouth, she calls out of the blue, talking about ... God, what was it? Something about secrets. Damn it. I can't remember. I just know she was acting odd." He breathes out. "It's probably irrelevant anyway."

"How did you know she was acting odd?"

"What? Oh, I don't know; her tone of voice, perhaps? It was like she was under pressure or something, as if there was someone there, maybe. In danger? I really couldn't say for sure."

I go quiet, not understanding how a simple tone in a voice can lead to so many unconfirmed conclusions.

I pick up a book, one of many on computer coding and language—a routine, orderly subject—and place it on a tower of other research, then turn to my board. The faces containing different expressions, different photographs of people I know, sketches of those I vaguely recall from hazy, drug-filled dreams. Ines, my mama, sits there, a photo taken from her Spanish parliament file, her face sculptured and clean, coiffured black hair, gold jewelry, shoulder pads, rouge. Beside her, my brother, Ramon, thirty-five now, tanned, lean, a slick of tar-black hair above defined cheekbones, the black suit he wears to his legal firm, tailored to perfection. And then my papa, an aged, more lined photograph, yet still I can see very visibly his eye creases, his lined skin, his crisp white linen shirt, and by his side, me, my hair long and dark, with Papa's arm over my shoulder, holding me—back then, the only person I would allow to touch me without instantly jumping or yelling. I close my eyes. I can still smell him—the spice cologne, the ink from his quill where he used to write in his study. I open my eyes and look at an image pinned to the right—a fading picture of Balthus, Harry, and me taken just after we won the retrial and I was acquitted. My fingers trace Harry's face. His skin is plump and black, and when he smiles, he, too, like my papa, has eye creases that crinkle outward, his tortoiseshell spectacles perched almost on the tip of his shiny round nose. Next to him is Balthus. Balthazar Ochoa. Name meaning "lone wolf." In his picture he is tall, athletic even for his fifty-plus years, his skin washed with the Mediterranean sun, his black hair silver at the tips, his face dominated by two brown pools of eyes. But while Harry's and Balthus' bodies are relaxed and smiling, mine, in contrast, is rigid and tight, flinching at close group contact, my olive skin pale from months of incarceration, hair dark and sawn into a jagged cut that grazes my temple and neck, eyes and cheeks hollow. I touch my neck. The Salamancan sun has drenched my skin now into a deep golden hue, my dark pixie cut is bleached blond, and my brown eyes are disguised by green contacts. A fake look for a fake world.

"Maria? Are you still there? Look, I was thinking. The flashback you had, the one with that woman—I think you need to understand where that facility is, and get to it. I can help you. If there is information there, it could mean we can put a stop to all this madness. Maria, it could end the Project!"

Heat rushes to my head, accompanied by a clear, frosted image of Black Eyes and his smile of tombstones. My eyes go to my villa, safe and hidden. "No."

"What?"

"I said no. I do not want to understand where the facility is."

"But, Maria, why track all the NSA stuff in connection to MI5, the explosion of it all, if not to get at the Project?" He pauses. "Look, you're not on your own. I know you think you are, but you're not. You have me. You have Patricia. Jesus, you even have your mother and brother. Maybe they can even help. Ines knows a lot of people high up in the Spanish government—she's minister of justice now."

Black Eyes. Raven. My tortured, sweat-drenched nightmares that keep me awake in the middle of the night when there is no one to soothe me. I glance to their scrawled sketches on the wall. "No."

He sighs. "Please. Just consider it. If you could, say, connect what I can hopefully remember from a conversation with Ines, to what you have told me about this woman Raven, it may help you know where the memory is coming from. If you know the facility, it will lead you to the file."

I open my mouth to tell him no, then hesitate, though I do not understand why.

"This woman," Balthus says, pressing on, "she said the file she loaded up will give you what you need to know, tell you what you've done—that it will help you know who you really are. Why note down all the dreams you recall, want to know how it's all connected, if you don't want to find out how to put an end to it all?"

I look down, confused. I thought the answer was obvious.

"I have my notebook. I like to record information. That is why I require the details. I just record the data, all of it." I glance to my coding books, to the comforting structure and formality of them.

"But this woman said the files could help you. Don't you want to know who she is, find the file? Don't …" There is a pause, and when he speaks again, his voice is oddly lower, quieter. "Don't you want to know who you really are?"

I look at Balthus' photo on the board, stare at all the unframed images and notes and encryptions and news articles, and after a second, they all start to blur into one solid image of color. I switch, glance to the turrets of books in neat, multiple piles, to the solitary seat, the makeshift wooden crates for tables, the single toothbrush that lies on the shelf. I walk three steps to the worn piano by the wall, gently press my finger down on a key, the smooth ivory cold beneath my skin. E-sharp tolls out.

"I know who I am," I say after a moment. "I am Dr. Maria Martinez, a plastic surgeon, born in Salamanca, Spain. I want to remain hidden. I do not want to go back to the Project or to their files or to anyone from there. It is too chaotic. I will record what memories appear, but no more. I do not want to endanger my family." I glance to the image of Harry. "I do not want to endanger you and Patricia."

"I understand that, I do. I really do," he says. "But they'll find you, Maria. You know that; I know you do. I worry about you there on your own with no one. You need answers. I can help you. I have a contact. I sent you an e-mail about him. He's called Chris. He's a hacker, used to be in Goldmouth. He can—"

An alarm sounds, high, war-siren sharp. My head jerks up. "Maria? Maria, what's wrong?"

I sprint to the laptop, head dipped at the noise, but my feet are so sweaty, I slip on the tiles, toppling into the crate, knocking the computer clean off the upturned box.

"Maria?"

I shake myself off, wincing at the scream of the siren, dragging the laptop over to me, scanning it fast.

"Maria? Shit. Can you hear me? Maria? What's happening?"

Leaning forward, keeping my fingers strong, steady, I click the icon flashing on the screen.

"Someone is on my property."

# CHAPTER 5

**UNDISCLOSED CONFINEMENT LOCATION**

*Present Day*

I don't know how much time has passed. I blacked out, coming to only now as, somewhere in the room, a noise clicks high in the air: *one, two, three, four.*

My body instinctively bends forward as my brain attempts to gauge the level of danger, and then I remember: Patricia.

I call her name, yell into the abyss of black. There is a click, another trip of light mixed with darkness, and then, finally, a voice, singular, pure.

"Doc? Doc? Are you there?"

She's okay! "Patricia?"

"Doc!"

"What is your status? Are you injured?"

"No. No, I don't think so, but my leg—it hurts. Help me, Doc."

I open my mouth to ask her specific diagnostics, but the air is so black and hot, so suddenly suffocating, that it feels as if a palm were being pressed into my nose and mouth, giving off an acrid taste of metal. I struggle hard against it. I have to know where we are, and yet nothing here seems to make sense, but I do it. My conditioning, my training, despite my horror at it, kicks in and I begin to function on cognitive thought.

"Doc! Doc, where are we?"

*Click.* The sound, there again on the surface of the room. It makes me halt.

"Doc, what was that?"

*Tap, tap, tap.* My heart rate rockets. "Patricia, stay still." I listen. It's like the beak of a robin on a windowpane.

"Who is there?" I ask the thick, dark stench of the room. *Click, tap. Click, tap.* My breathing becomes fast, shallow. "Who is there?"

But no answer comes back. I slap away the fear and strain my neck, try to catch sight of something, anything, but just as my eyes clear, just as they begin to see through the haze, the click sounds again and something happens inside me.

A heat, a surge of liquid in my veins, burns its way through me, scalding one second then freezing the next, and an ice blade of pain stabs me. I cry out.

"Doc! Doc, what is it?"

My mouth opens to yell, but I am mute, a primal fear taking over, a tsunami of fight or flight, the words *"You are in danger! You are in danger!"* screaming over and over in my head, and I must be moaning, groaning, because I can hear Patricia shouting at me to stay awake.

My eyelids vibrate, brain attempts to calibrate a connection, find an answer to what is happening to me, but the codes, numbers, solutions that instinctively inhabit my head are all jumbled up, as if I had been shaken like some unwanted toy and discarded on the ground and kicked under a bed to gather dust and wither.

"Patricia," I gasp, my chest ready to explode. "Escape. I need you to escape."

"I don't … My leg aches, Doc, but I think I can …" A grunt, a scrape. "My hand—it's free."

"Does that mean …?" The searing pain burns so hot in my chest now, I have to force myself to concentrate once more on my eyes. "If your hand is free, does that mean you can be mobile?" And then I spot something: a lick of light.

There! In the corner.

"Doc, it won't … I don't know. Oh, God. My leg feels numb."

The single sliver of light disappears, and I try to reach out, grab where it was, but nothing moves. A hazy gray film is slowly bleeding over my lenses.

"Something is happening to me." I swallow. "Drugged," I slur. "I must be drugged."

"Does that mean we're at the Project? At their facility?" There is a shake in her voice, a tremor.

And then I hear it: water. A trickle of water, a rush of liquid. I shake as a terrifying thought tears into me: we are drowning. We are not actually in a room or a cell or a locked-away facility, but we are drowning, almost dead already, and this haze, this gray film, this distant cry of Patricia's Irish voice that I can only just detect is the last twisted hemorrhage of my lie of a life. The Project has found me and intends to kill me, and now, finally, this is it, here: death.

"Can you feel any water around you?"

"What? I … Wait." A scream, a gurgled cry. "Doc, I'm hurt!"

Panic wells up. "Drag yourself free. Quick!"

"I don't want to die!"

"Stay awake!"

"I … can't breathe."

I struggle to cough. I try anything: a lick of my lips, a last gulp of oxygen—anything to dismantle the rolling tide as, to my side, Patricia groans.

"Pull your arms up!" I shout. "See if there is anything you can grip on to."

"There's nothing! Only a … Oh, Jesus, help! It hurts! Doc, help, please."

Her voice stops abruptly, a radio being switched off. "Patricia?" Nothing.

"Patricia! Patricia, shout to me that you are …" I stop breathing.

My hands form two fists, knuckles white, chest bursting, ribs ready to crack, as my mind prepares, because this is it.

The final seconds of me, of my life. Dr. Maria Martinez. Gone.

## SALAMANCAN MOUNTAINS, SPAIN
*34 Hours and 32 Minutes to Confinement*

I shut down the alarm and haul in a breath.

"What's going on, Maria?"

"Wait." My eyes remain locked on the computer screen, but my vest has become sweaty and it itches my skin. I scratch my stomach, up down, unable to stop as the nerves seep out.

"Maria, for God's sake, what's happening?"

"The red icon is flashing."

My skin flushes, feels as if it's burning, nerve endings so sensitive to the change in the fabric that it's too much to bear.

I rip off my vest, throw it to the floor. The relief is almost overwhelming.

"Anyone on the cameras?" Balthus says now.

I flip open the surveillance program, then pause. The reality of what could happen slams me in the face, and I recount Abel's binomial theorem to focus my mind.

No matter how many times I scan the CCTV film, it comes back blank, eight square gray live pictures of the fields and walls around the villa. No trespassers, no intelligence officers, just everything as it was before I stepped inside the house.

"The cameras are displaying no signs of intruders."

My body leans back as my mind attempts to get a handle on what is happening, already planning ahead on what I may need to do. As I think, a whip of wind lashes at a funnel of cypress trees outside, sending a swarm of starlings scurrying into the sky, and it is so sudden, so fast and loud, that I jump, slapping my hand to my chest.

"Maria, is everything all right? Talk to me."

The starlings rush away, their swarm temporarily blackening the sky.

"Birds," I say.

"What?"

The last remaining starling flies into a cotton candy cloud.

"I was frightened by a murmuration of birds."

"A mumur—what?"

Wiping the sweat from my face, I stare at the now empty branches outside. The air is static. For a moment, I swear a shadow glides over the sand-colored earth, its hazy contours rippling over the deep green cypress giants that guard the perimeter of the villa, but when I blink and rub my eyes, it is instead the tall, scorched grass reeds I see, their long shadows swaying innocently in the morning air. Each movement of the reeds vibrates in my eardrums. I bang the heels of my palms against the sides of my head to try to dislodge the sound.

"Maria?"

One more hit, and the reed rush will be gone.

"Maria? Maria, answer me."

Bang. Done. "What?"

"Did you install the trip-wire system I told you about?"

"Yes."

"And it's not flagging anything up?"

"Negative."

"Then what could have triggered the surveillance? Could there have been a system error?"

I consider this but am unconvinced. The CCTV shows no trespass entry, so why the alarm? My mind scans through every tiny detail yet still concludes that all is as before. The fields are empty for several kilometers, the long gravel drive is free of foreign vehicles, and the only car is an old black truck I use on the rare occasions I need to drive into the village in the fading evening sunlight for supplies. So why did the alarm sound? A colony of nerves collect in a lump in my stomach, and my thumb taps my forefinger.

"Maria, do you think you are in danger?"

My eyes flicker to the window then return to the red icon that still flashes on the laptop. "I cannot say with certainty until I run a complete check. But …"

Another shadow creeps across the cypresses again, this time more distinct, more clear.

More human.

A bolt of electricity shoots down my spine. "Someone is here."

"What?"

I grab my notebook, hide it behind a stack of books, and run to the window, adrenaline immediately spiking as I press my back against the wall and count to three.

"Maria, have you seen someone?" Balthus calls out, but I ignore him because if I shout now, if I utter one single word, whoever is out there will know my location.

Another shadow passes by. I track it. Breath heavy, heart rate way beyond acceptable, I count my steps as I drop to the ground, crawling to the opposite side of the window. I stand again, acutely aware that I am unarmed, and yet, I know what to do. It scares me, always has. It scares me that if someone should come in now, I am trained not to even need a gun to kill them.

Slowly, I inch my head up to the window ledge, one millimeter, two, three, until I reach the edge where the citrus scent from the groves beyond drifts in. If someone is standing by the outside of the wall, then, if I move one centimeter more, they will detect my presence. My cortisol peaks. Sliding one bare foot forward, I raise my hands and step left, maneuvering my body so it slips almost invisibly to the side, my brain instructing me, from some hidden tactical manual, what to do. *Prepare, wait, engage.* For some reason, the phrase flicks into my mind. *Prepare, wait, engage.* And I realize, with a feeling of revulsion, that I am recalling something the Project must have trained me on.

Despite my disgust, I do it. I track the area, I pause, listen to every minute sound, to each tweet, rustle, bleat, and creak, creating a complete map of the scene before me, until I am ready. After preparing and waiting, I am ready to engage.

I exhale long, deep into my diaphragm, as the sunlight shimmers across my eyelids, cheeks, onto my forehead, my neck, onto my bare shoulders as, gradually, a millimeter at a time, I peer over the edge to the glazed window.

There is a face staring right back at me.

# CHAPTER 6

**SALAMANCA, SPAIN**

*34 Hours and 28 Minutes to Confinement*

Dr. Andersson stares straight back at me.

I yell out her name, alerting Balthus, who is still on the phone, as Dr. Andersson ducks out of sight. She is running toward the far entrance, where the kitchen yawns wide open, exposed to the fields and beyond.

"Maria," Balthus whispers, "where is she?"

Panic and chaos rise in me as I look to the cell phone. I need it, but I cannot have any noise giving away my location. Checking left and right, I count to three, drop down on all fours, and, darting forward, snatch the cell and scamper back. I squeeze into a corner hidden by a tower of books and the smashed wooden crates, planks, and splinters strewn about the room.

I catch my breath, try to think.

"Maria? Talk to me."

I gulp down saliva. "She is here," I whisper. "Dr. Andersson."

"Oh, shit. Oh, shit. She's with MI5, and they want the Project gone. That can mean only one thing, right?"

"She is here to kill me." The words hang in the air like a foul stench, jarring against the fragrant green grass of the fields beyond. For a moment, I freeze, not wanting to acknowledge that my peaceful retreat, my quiet hideaway, has been shattered.

"MI5 want all connections to the Project to disappear," Balthus says. "Kurt—Daniel—he said that to you, right? That's why he wanted you to stay with him. The Project did not want to disappear; they broke away and wanted you with them; MI5 wanted you gone. Maria, you're right. Oh, Jesus. She'll kill you—she's a trained officer."

I scan the kitchen door. Nothing. Yet. "I am trained, also."

"Yes, but she … well, she's not like you. She won't hesitate to do what she's been told."

I start to say something, then stop as the image of Raven floats to my mind. *They will make you kill me.* I have no recollection of what I actually did to her, no tangible evidence of whether I ever hurt the woman, no real idea of who I am or what I am capable of.

I glance to the window. It is open. Another bird sits there now on the wooden ledge, head jerking right and left. I can see its feathers, soft and shining even from here, brown and black, shimmering in the morning sun.

"There is no sign of her," I say, turning to the phone. "She may have a map of the dwelling."

"How did they find you?"

"What?"

"MI5," Balthus whispers. "How the hell did they find you? You've been off radar."

I think for a moment, uncomfortable. Have I made a mistake in my encrypted file tracking? In my proxy ISP e-mails? "It is possible they may have infiltrated some files if they have the right technical people to carry out the hack." My eyes glance to the laptop open on the crate. "I need to hide my notebook."

"What? Maria, get out of there!"

A clatter outside, a shattering of glass. I freeze.

"What was that?" Balthus whispers.

I dart my eyes to the side. Every part of me is on fire, desperately pressing back the visceral fear that surges upward. I need to move now—get to the laptop and get out—but if I go right, I'll have to open the door to the bedroom where my bag is stored, yet if I turn left and head past the kitchen, where Dr. Andersson may be, then I have no chance of grabbing the laptop and notebook.

My instinct is to go into meltdown, to curl up into a ball and squeeze my eyes shut and plead for this all to go away. Yet even as my brain shouts at me to run, something else is happening: gradually, like a rainbow appearing on a stormy day, something happens. A change, a composed, butter-colored difference. A coolness crackles over me as an instinctive knowledge takes control, and over and over in my mind, three words shoot across the shadows of my thoughts: *prepare, wait, engage.*

Up ahead, the kitchen door, closed earlier, is now swinging open. My hairs stand on end. "She's here."

The phone crackles, Balthus' voice dipping in and out of audio.

I grip the cell phone tight, telling myself that if I do so, maybe, somehow, I won't be on my own.

Every muscle in me is ready. Suddenly not caring about the illegal methods the Project has trained me in, I want to remember every tiny detail of what I was taught, because it may save me.

My eyes land on the solitary toothbrush on the shelf by the wall.

The phone flickers again.

"Maria? Maria, are you okay? Are you there?"

Balthus. For some reason, the sound of his voice, the familiar curve of it, floods me with relief.

"I am here," I whisper. Creaking sounds drift in from the kitchen. *Prepare.*

I do a rapid assessment. I am wearing my running gear. I am fast, fit, but even when I calculate the speed at which I can sprint, I know that if Dr. Andersson has a gun and surveillance of her own, I will never escape unless I can get to the bedroom.

"Can you get out?" Balthus says.

"The bedroom door opens onto the shed where the truck is parked. It is my only safe route out."

"Good! Can you get to the door?"

I look to the kitchen, calculate angles. "I cannot determine if I can be seen."

"Well, is there another way?"

I think fast when my eyes, scanning the area for Dr. Andersson's face, see something long, thick, rusty—solid.

A two-foot iron bar, used for the fire pit outside, leans against the cabinet; I must have discarded it while obsessing yesterday evening over every tiny detail about the NSA scandal.

The kitchen door suddenly sways, a waltz, one, two, three, one, two, three, dancing in and out of the room. Is she here? I look to the iron bar then back to the door, and even though it screeches when it swings, too loud for my senses, I slap aside the aggravation because that unbearable noise offers me something I need: it offers me cover.

Dropping flat to the floor, I scurry along the tiles so fast that by the time the second creak sounds, my fingers are wrapped around the iron bar. On the third creak, I am crawling back with it to the window.

Balthus' voice trickles in from the cell phone.

"Where are you?"

"Home."

"No, I mean … Oh, it doesn't matter. Have you got the laptop and book?"

"No."

"But you can get them?"

"Yes." I glance to where they still sit on the crate. Right now it is all a matter of timing.

*Wait …*

Squatting, I rest my back for a moment against the coolness of the wall and listen. My hands squeeze the iron bar as I assess where the danger source is, scanning my memory, determining what I should do next. For some reason, after two, three seconds pass, I find myself slowly coming to my feet. The move surprises me, but still I do it, slipping the cell phone into the band pocket of my shorts, watching as my feet glide, ghostlike, engaged, and before I can order my body to halt its course, I am holding the iron bar ready, tiptoeing to the kitchen door.

*Eliminate the threat.*

"Maria," Balthus says, "have you left yet?"

"No."

"Why?"

"I can eliminate the threat."

"What! No. Just get the laptop and notebook and run."

"Negative. The best course of action is to—" I see her. There, in the glass door of the cabinet, a waterfall of blond hair reflecting in the panes. My chest tightens as the fear rises. "She is here."

"What? Christ, Maria, move!"

I go to run, to dart out of the way, but before I do, before my feet flip fast enough, the window behind me shatters, a clap of thunder in the silence. Shards of glass rain down onto my bare neck, shoulders, arms and legs, scissor splinters tearing apart the warm suede air of the summer sun.

A bag is thrust over my head, plunging me into a sudden frightening, claustrophobic darkness. Frantic to get out, I thrash about, and as I lift my arms to rip the bag off my head, the iron bar slips from my grasp and clatters on the tiles.

"Maria? Maria!"

The bag becomes tighter and tighter, and Balthus' voice echoes from the phone, the sound of him reduced to just lost, helpless words drifting alone into the ripped, fractured room.

# CHAPTER 7

UNDISCLOSED CONFINEMENT LOCATION
*Present Day*

I wake up once more to find myself still alive.

Woozy, weary, my eyelids flicker, and I peer out into the black stench. My muscles ache and throb, and a searing pain shoots from my head down my neck, all the way to the base of my spine, and stays there, pulsating, a globe of pins pricking my skin and bones. I curl my fingers into fists. The hallucination, the memory of it, all floods back: the water, the feeling of drowning all fresh in my mind as if the shore were still at my feet.

"Patricia?" I croak. "Can you hear me?"

There is a cough. "D-Doc?"

"Patricia?" Hearing her voice makes me happy for one solitary, exquisite second, and I let out a small whoop. "What is your status?"

A laugh ripples out—weak, vanilla, but there. "I love how ..." She halts, hacks up something from her throat. "I love how even in a shithole like this, you're still so formal." She gags, then hauls in a breath. "My leg's killing me."

"Your leg is killing you?" I say, alarmed. "How can your leg kill you?"

"No, no it's not ..." She laughs again, but it does not sound like her, as if it were altered somehow, down an octave. "Doc, it's a figure of speech. Remember those? I taught you about them in prison. My leg's not *actually* killing me; it just means it really hurts."

"Oh."

Some time passes, but I don't know how much. I drift in and out of consciousness, the blackness of the room throwing a blanket over everything, rendering each line of vision I try to establish useless. Slowly, though, after a while, a degree of lucidity begins to return. It is small, the tide of it, the clarity that trickles back toward the shore, toward the solid certainty of land in my mind, but it is there, and for the first time since I awoke in this room, I feel a core of strength inside me.

"Doc, where are we?"

I let out a breath, one controlled exhalation, and think. Location, logistics. How did we get here? If there are drugs in my system, how were they administered, and why? To transport me? But from where? And if so, does that mean Patricia was drugged, too?

For the next few moments, we remain silent. Patricia sings some sort of Irish lullaby, a song about the sea, and for ten seconds I become calm, listening only to her melody, all whipped vanilla cream and light chocolate soufflé. I know it is wrong. I know that for her to be here, trapped in this room with me, means danger. And yet, as she sings, as her voice dances through the air, gliding through the gloom, I feel a sliver of gratitude, of selfish thankfulness that my friend is near me.

"Hey, Doc," Patricia says after the serene song has faded into the dark air, "do you remember when we first met?"

"Oh. Yes. It was a Tuesday."

"Was it?"

"Yes."

"Cool. And do you remember what you said to me?"

The image of the scene flashes in my mind. Patricia, tattoos of the Virgin Mary and a blackbird on her arm, me bending forward to analyze them without saying anything at all to Patricia until she spoke again to me, telling me I was "getting a little close." "The first words I spoke to you were about your name," I say. "Patricia. It is the female form of Patrick. Patrick means—"

"Means 'nobleman.'" She laughs, joining in the end of my sentence. There is a small, mewed sigh, and I find myself breathing more easily at the sound. "Your face was all bruised, Doc. Do you remember?"

"Yes." A flash comes to me, a blurred fist coming at my face. I swallow.

"Doc, I'm so sorry I brought it up. Are you … are you okay?"

"Why do people think I am a freak?"

"Huh?"

"Why do they call me weird?"

She wheezes into the air. "I don't know, Doc. People are idiots. They don't always see that it's okay just to be who we are. Last time I looked, we were all, by our very human nature, I guess, different to each other. At what point does 'different' turn into 'weird'? Who the hell knows? My answer? It doesn't. We just are who we are, and the quicker the world accepts that, the better a place it will be."

I sit and think about my friend's words and about how, when I am confused, she seems to cut through the bewilderment, and the clouds in my head part a little sooner, and the cage that surrounds me feels just a little less isolating.

After a few moments, Patricia coughs. "She worked for MI5, that Michaela, right?"

"Yes. She did."

"Jesus, it's fucked-up shit." She pauses, the blackness of the room pressing down on us. "I'm glad I met you, Doc. Even though we're locked up now in God knows where, I'm glad I met you. Without you, I wouldn't have got out on parole so fast. That

Harry lawyer of yours helped me, before he … well, you know." She inhales. "I still think about my mum, how she was in pain. It was the right thing to do to, you know, to end her life. I'd do the prison sentence all over again if I had to, just so she wouldn't have to suffer."

"Euthanasia. That is what you did."

"Yep." A sniff. "Yep."

"I am sorry you are sad," I say after a moment.

"Thanks, Doc. Thanks."

We sit, the two of us, in silence and thoughts, the blackness of the room covering us. My muscles ache. I try to roll my shoulders to move the blood in them, but when I do, each bone creaks and my neck at the back tightens up.

"Er, Doc, you there?"

"Yes. Of course."

"I can see something."

I forget my sore neck and jerk forward. "What?"

"On your hand there—some light."

I look down. She's right. I can see my hand for the first time, illuminated by a globule of buttered light. Adrenaline shoots through my bloodstream as, inch by inch, a rash of light spreads from my hand to my wrist, shining on the rope that ties me down, then continues up my arm to the well inside my elbow, until it shows me something that I did not register until now.

"Doc, what is it?"

I blink, check once more, but there is no denying it, because I am a doctor—I have seen thousands of them.

"Doc! What?"

I start to shake. "The drugs are in my cubital vein."

"The cubital … Wait, what?"

"The cubital vein resides in the antecubital area."

"What? Doc, you'll have to explain in words I can understand, because you—"

The light shines bright. My panic intensifies. "There is a needle in my arm!"

## SALAMANCAN MOUNTAINS, SPAIN
*34 Hours and 20 Minutes to Confinement*

The hood over my head has blacked everything out, and all I can see through the pinprick gaps in the weave are shards of sunlight and shadows of shapes. I try to get a handle on where Dr. Andersson is, but the bag is so scratchy on my face that it is becoming distracting, and the urge to yank it off, claw at my face over and over until the heat subsides, is almost overwhelming, but when I reach up with my free hand, someone slaps it back down.

"Move."

I gulp in buckets of breath, sucking on the hood as she pushes me forward, the tiles sliding under my bare feet. Then we stop. For a moment, there is complete quiet. I jerk left and right, disoriented as I try to pinpoint where Dr. Andersson is, willing her to utter one more clipped syllable of a word, but all I can hear is my own breath rushing in my ears. I don't move. My muscles scream out at me, itching in agony where Dr. Andersson pinches my wrists and shoulders. And all the while, my cell phone sits hidden in the band of my shorts.

There is a click of a phone, but it is not mine.

"It's me," Dr. Andersson says, her voice a basket of plums, a rich slate board of cured meats. There is a tug on my wrist. "Stay still!" I wince. "Her hair's blond now and she's skinnier, but it's still Martinez. We still on plan? … Good. We have to put an end to the Project. And she's it."

My mind races. *She's it. She's it.* The fear rises in me, immediate, urgent, but the will to survive, to forge something that will get me out of this situation, is stronger than even my urge to curl up moaning in a ball and hide.

"You cannot kill me," I say, spitting out fluff and fibers.

She slides a plastic tie around my wrists, pulls it tight, and walks away, her boots slapping the tiles. "I'm sorry," she says, and there is utter silence as she seems to go into another room. Where? The kitchen? I whip my head left and right to determine where Dr. Andersson is. Staggering back a little, I count in my head. The numbers not only sooth me; they also allow me to analyze the time frame and get a slice of clarity. I reach thirty and listen. Nothing. Just the starlings on the cypress trees in the fields, and the light tidal rush of grass in the wind. My body relaxes a little, shoulders softening, and then I remember my cell phone.

"Balthus," I whisper.

There is a scratch of static and then one word. "Maria?"

His voice is low, quiet, but hearing it, knowing he is there, makes the heat of the bag, the confusing disorientation of it all, easier to bear.

"Maria, are you okay? My God, she's going to kill you. You have to get out. Can you?"

"I do not know." I blink, try to gauge any shapes from behind the fabric. I sniff the air. "Chanel Number Five."

"What?"

"It is Dr. Andersson's scent, and I can smell it. The scent was stronger before. Judging by the distance now of the perfume, it means she is not in the room, yet she remains on the property."

"Well, get to another room, then! Move out of there."

He is right. It is a risk, but if I can get to the bedroom, I can run.

I begin to raise my arms, slowly at first, the plastic ties digging in, then fast, projecting in the dark the direction my body will need to crawl, when the scent of perfume suddenly becomes so strong it feels as if my head will explode from the sensory assault.

"Where do you think you're going?"

She's here! I go to grab the bag with my tied hands, desperate to run, but Dr. Andersson hauls me back and slams my arms down.

"No!" I yell.

"Just stop fighting. God, Maria."

I kick out, but Dr. Andersson's grip on me is tight and she thrusts her elbow into my ribs. My torso folds in like a pack of cards, my eyes watering, lungs burning as I suck the bag so hard into my mouth that I begin to suffocate. I get a fierce kick to the shin. It catches me right on the bone, sending fire up my leg, and the fabric blows out of my mouth, letting air in. I lash out with my tied fists, but she bangs my head, pinning me against the wall.

"How long have you been tracking the NSA?"

"Let me go."

She exhales hard and shakes her head. "I'm tired," she says. "I've come a long way and my family are at home and I'm missing my daughter's third birthday for you, for *this*, so just do"—she shoves me hard against the wall, then loosens her grip—"as I say, Maria. Jesus."

I hear her stalk away, and I catch short sips of air, listening, a wild animal caught in a trap. There is a tearing of paper.

"What are you doing?"

"Finishing what I was supposed to do when you were in Goldmouth."

The tearing restarts, and I realize she is at my wall of news articles and images, ripping them off from the plaster, tracking the data I have traced. I toss my head left and right, shout out, but another kick hits my shin, harder this time, knocking me to the floor, where a fist catches me in the solar plexus. Yelling, I curl up as a stab of heat shoots through my whole body. Amid all this, the cell phone slips farther down, and all I can think about is not the pain that roars through me, but the cell phone and whether Dr. Andersson has seen it.

I have to do something quick. Taking in a fractured breath, I roll to my left and hit a crate. I go rigid.

"She has everything here: news articles, the lot."

She's talking somewhere on her cell phone again. Eyes blinking as fast as wings, I listen for a clue, for anything. Is Balthus listening, too?

"There's CCTV all over the place," Dr. Andersson continues. "We'll have to destroy all evidence. When I'm done, I'll meet you at the agreed rendezvous point. Surveillance still pulled back so no ops can be tracked? … Okay. Good. See you when it's over."

A rendezvous point—does that mean her team is near? I try to think it through, but my brain is so overloaded by the hood and the adrenaline that it is almost impossible to be coherent, and if I …

There is a crash. Things breaking, drawers yanked out, towers of books crashing to the tiles—she is tearing apart my villa. I try to think fast what to do, and then I remember my notebook.

Some time passes. I try to count the seconds, track the minutes, but pain from the kicks comes in waves, swelling then rolling back. After a while, the noise stops and I hear her footsteps toward where I think the kitchen is. I take my chance.

"Balthus?"

A second, two, then: "Oh, thank God. What's happening?" I tell him fast, then blink, trying to see something through the weave of the hood.

"Maria, have you slipped the ties from your wrists?"

"What? No. I have tried, but it is secured with some type of—" A smash of crockery. I wait, swallow. "With some type of hard plastic that I am unfamiliar with."

"Hang on. Can you feel it, the plastic?"

I touch it with my fingertips. "Yes. Why?"

"How small are the grooves?"

I feel. "One millimeter in depth."

"I think I know which type it is. If it's just a millimeter, sounds like it's the new restraints we sometimes used at the prison."

A flicker of hope begins to burn. "Do you know how I can untie it?"

"I think so."

Another smash from the kitchen. "Then tell me. Fast."

After three, perhaps four minutes, Dr. Andersson returns. Her boots sound lighter now on the tiles, as if she has changed shoes, and the drift of her perfume is softer, weaker. She marches up to me and halts. The hood scratches at my face, but I bite my lip, keep my back against the wall, and wait.

For a moment, nothing moves. She is crouching in front of me—I can just make out the shape of her body. But more than this, it is the heat of her, of another person, that catches me off guard. Oddly, the thought strikes me that this is the first time in six months that I have encountered, in such close physical proximity, another human being.

"Right," she says finally, "let's do this, shall we? The day is getting on and so is time."

The hood is whipped from my head, and my skin, slapped by sunlight, stings as my eyes blink over and over. And for the first time, I get a complete look at Dr. Andersson as she looms in front of me. Her blond hair is tied back in a ponytail that slides down her back and rests against her spine all the way to her hip bones. Her forehead is high and sharp and peppered with freckles, nose straight, cheekbones high and sharply defined. I choke, spitting out fibers from my mouth and throat.

"What do you want?"

She offers me a smile, the one I remember from Goldmouth, with white teeth and scarlet, plumped lips. "I want to do my job and get home. I understand you're on the harsh end of this, I really do, but MI5 wants the Project to end, which means I have to deal with you, end you." She pulls a pistol from her waistband. "I'm really very sorry, Maria. I always rather liked you."

And then she shoots me in the leg.

# CHAPTER 8

**UNDISCLOSED CONFINEMENT LOCATION**

*Present Day*

"Doc, you sure there's a needle? Can you see it?"

"Yes. But the light is fading again."

The blackness has reclaimed the air, but now I know the needle is there. I will my arm to move as much as it can, wriggling my fingers in an attempt to feel the point of the metal inserted into my veins. At first, nothing shifts, and I feel so thirsty, am so desperately weak and tired that my mind begins to think it has imagined the entire thing.

And then it moves, there, the needle in the crease of my elbow. Just one pull at my skin and veins.

"Can you see it now?" Patricia says.

"No. I can feel it."

"Doc, you know what this means, right?"

I go to speak the words *they are drugging me again*, but instead clam up. An instinct to yell out, to cry as loud and deep as possible, wells up inside me. This was not supposed to happen again. No, no, no, no.

"Doc, are you still there?"

"I ran away from them," I say after a moment, catching a short, shallow breath. "I hid. The Project and MI5 thought I was dead after prison. I thought I had escaped it all."

"Oh, Doc. Doc, I'm so sorry."

For a moment, in the blackness, it feels as if everything has stopped, as if here, now, all I have is collapsing on me, folding inward never to push out again. It feels hopeless. I sit there silent, scared, until there is a rush of something on the moist, murky air.

"Doc? Doc, you're groaning. What's the matter?"

I squint as hard as I can, frantically forcing my eyes to see something, anything, in the dank, suffocating space. The rush sounds again, distinct now, a click licking the air as what must be a liquid begins its gentle whoosh. It is only when I hear again that my groggy brain engages in the intricacies of the noises around me, and I realize, with stabbing clarity, what is actually happening and what it means to me—what it means to us both.

"What if they are drugging me so they can transport me to another facility somewhere? If they do that, what will happen to you?"

"I'll be okay, Doc."

"What if they are intending to kill you? That is what the Project does: it kills those I love." My breathing begins to speed up in short, rapid inhalations as the worry inside me escalates.

"Doc, I can't get to you, so look, it's going to happen either way, so try to breathe through it. There, that's it …"

I try so hard to focus on her voice, jerk my arms against the rope on my wrists, desperate to run, to hide, because what is charging forward like a pack of hungry wolves makes my heart stop, makes every pore of my skin scream out in fear. A hallucination.

"Breathe, Doc. Keep breathing. Keep listening to me."

A body with multiple heads, each one spinning 360 degrees, hurtles toward me. I scream. My nails scratch the wood of the chair, legs kick out, but it does no good, and I know it must be the liquid shooting inside my veins, but there is nothing I can do. I am trapped.

The monster is on me now, here in this room. I yell out my friend's name, hear the distant scream of her voice, but I can't reach her. The heads in the image sway, thorns in the breeze, and I hear a voice screech and realize it's mine, because the faces on the heads are Mama and Ramon. My mother and brother.

"Patricia, where are you?" I yell.

"I'm here, Doc. It'll be over soon. Keep calm, okay? Keep breathing."

I try to scramble back, tell myself that none of this is real, but still they come, the heads grotesque, twisted out of shape, all images in a fairground mirror, their mouths and eyes huge, both of them laughing over and over like two sick clowns. "*Freak! She doesn't understand,*" they sing. "*She doesn't understand, the freak.*" Children run beside them, children I recall from my school days, and they skip and they chant, "*Weirdo, weirdo, stinky nerdy weirdo.*" I ask them what they mean, scream at them to tell me what is happening, but the heads—all of them: family, children—simply look at me, at each other. And then, just as I think they're going to disappear, they let out one roar of a laugh and, merging together, morph into a gun as tall as a car and shoot me point-blank in the head.

My eyes fly open. I choke, gasp for air, as I look down at myself and out into the black room.

"Patricia, the drugs …"

"*Sssh. Sssh.*"

I stutter, voice cracking, and it takes a full minute for my body to settle, for the nightmare image of my mama and brother to slowly subside.

"Doc, I'm here. It's okay. It's over."

I hear my friend, cling on to her voice as if I were sinking and she were my life raft in the sea. My brain recalibrates itself, but it is taking its time, and each movement of my eyes and hands and limbs makes the room sway and soar and churn up nausea in my stomach.

After a moment, after the heat has subsided, Patricia checks on me, then asks me a question.

"Doc, you know these are hallucinations, right?"

"Y-yes."

"Well, why's it only happening now?"

My head throbs, throat runs red, raw. Everything in the room still fades into black. "What do you mean?"

"Well, if this needle, yeah, this drug, is permanently in your vein, why's it not causing you to trip all the time?"

I begin to think. What she is saying, what she talks about. My brain finally starts to shrug off the drug effects and engage, calculate.

"Doc, I guess what I mean is, what's making the drug only come out in doses?"

And in the foul, moldy darkness, I sit and I think and I try to understand what is happening. And how to make it all stop.

## SALAMANCAN MOUNTAINS, SPAIN
*34 Hours and 11 Minutes to Confinement*

A searing heat explodes in my thigh.

The room begins to sway, the white sun from the window blinding me, mixing with the pain, slow at first, then faster. When I look at Dr. Andersson, her smile appears distorted, as if someone had taken an ax to her head and sliced it clean down the middle. Fear grows as blood wells from the wound.

I force myself to keep my hands where they are, fixed in position behind my back, despite the instinctive urge to throw my arms forward and attend to the wound.

As the pain rips into me, I focus on the cell phone, still hidden behind me, knowing that Balthus has listened to everything that is happening. Sweat drains down my face. Ahead, Dr. Andersson proceeds to tear apart my laptop, pocketing my USB sticks, disabling every part of my surveillance system, all that I have been unable to hide now being destroyed, and it hurts me, every smash, every rip and pilferage. What she is doing, the way in which she is creating pure chaos out of my routine and order, feels as if it is physically hurting me.

If she is destroying evidence, the point will soon come when she finds my notebook.

I have to stall for time. "I need to stem the blood flow from my leg," I say. "I need to press my hands into it. Untie me."

She throws me a glance, hesitating for a moment, her eyes on my wound, and I think she may come to assist me. But then she checks her watch, shakes her head, and returns to pulling apart my data.

My body is getting weaker. The blood from the wound is slowing a little but still oozing, and if I don't get pressure on it soon, I may lose consciousness. My eyes spot the iron bar—it is still on the floor where it fell.

Dr. Andersson comes over and crouches by me. "Maria? Can you hear me? I need you to tell me something. Is the Project still functioning?"

"You are MI5," I say, wincing at a new stab of pain. "You should have the intelligence for that answer."

She sighs. "I'm looking for a file."

My ears prick up. "What file?"

She glances around at the mess. My teeth clench at the chaotic sight. "There is a file that was hidden by a woman you knew, an asset in the field some time ago, when the Project was more … useful. Do you know where the file is?"

Sweat trickles past my eyes. Raven, the dream. Does she know? "What is the woman's name?"

"Ah, now, wouldn't that be easy if we had a name?" She wipes her cheek dry of sweat. "I'm afraid that's what I was rather hoping you could provide." I shift, careful not to dislodge the cell phone. "Do you know where the file is, Maria?"

"No."

She stands. "Then I'm sorry, but …" She gives one swift kick to my wounded thigh. I cry out in agony.

"B-but …" My speech slurs. I must be losing more blood than I thought.

"Where's the file, Maria? Please, just tell me." She pastes on a quick smile. "Let's just get this done as fast as we can, okay? I really don't want to hurt you any more than I have to before, well ... Just help me out here."

My eyes narrow as I muster every ounce of energy that is left in me, every scrap of anger and fear and pain and loss, straight at her. "Bitch."

Her smile and shoulders drop. She reaches into her pocket and pulls out a knife, black handled, solid. My brain fires into red alert mode as she slides off a leather sheath to reveal a small, sharp blade seven centimeters long. The sleek silver of it shines in the summer sun, a gentle light dancing warm and carefree on the glide of the metal.

"I'm sorry I have to do this, but you were supposed to die months ago." She kicks aside a piece of computer casing. "You evaded our officers then, even dodged my bullet for you outside the court, but not now. I'm afraid we can't risk the service being exposed. You understand; it's this NSA scandal. MI5 don't want the Project blowing up like NSA's Prism program did. The Project was good while it lasted, but it has to end. The file I need—we'll find it. I hear there's been a run of break-ins and knife crime in this remote area." She glances to the upended room. "I'm afraid this will have to look like a burglary gone bad."

Panting, I look at my leg. The limb is damaged, but the blood loss is finally slowing. I can move my toes, but I don't know if I can mobilize my body at all. My hands are still behind my back, and for now, I need to keep them there. I start to count.

*One.*

Dr. Andersson takes a step forward.

*Two.*

She grips the knife tight in her fist, eyes downturned.

*Three.*

I glance to the iron bar nearby on the floor.

*Four.*

Dr. Andersson lunges forward. "I'm so sorry ..." *Five.*

I unleash my hands, the wrist ties gone thanks to Balthus' expert instruction. And despite the blood loss, despite the odds stacked against me, and the chaos and fear and sheer sensory onslaught of the entire situation, I come at Dr. Andersson with every drop of force I can muster.

# CHAPTER 9

**SALAMANCAN MOUNTAINS, SPAIN**

*34 Hours and 7 Minutes to Confinement*

I ram my shoulder hard into Dr. Andersson's abdomen.

She yells out and totters to the left, the knife slipping from her grip and sliding onto the floor. "Maria, stop! Please, don't …"

She steadies herself, and I think she is going to recover. Her hand reaches behind her for the gun under her jacket, and, faster than I can even process the thought, I head-butt her in the face.

I feel the crack and crunch, and my left fist is already arcing around with a hammer blow to the temple. As she reels back, blood spurting from her smashed nose, the half-drawn pistol hits the floor and slides under a table.

I move fast, my wounded leg throbbing.

"Maria!" Balthus calls from the cell. "What's happening?"

I survey the damage, the slump of Dr. Andersson's slight body, the skewed limbs.

"She is alive," I say. "Injured."

"I don't give a damn about her. Just get the hell out of there! Grab your notebook and bag and run!"

But my eyes catch sight of my ordered articles and photographs and sketches, ripped on the floor and crumpled under Dr. Andersson's inert body. For a moment, an eerie silence prevails, as the summer sun through the windows shines warm and serene on the devastation in my villa. I slap the wall to steady myself. Everything is spinning a little as I will my brain not to melt down at the chaos. *One-two-three, one-two-three* … Playing out a waltz of numbers in my head, I draw in a long breath, look up, and see the notebook. Then I stagger past Dr. Andersson's splayed limbs, toward the fallen gun.

Balthus' voice crackles on the line. "Are you on the move?"

"Yes."

I step over a broken laptop and stop. A torn photograph of my papa lies discarded amid a pile of books and eviscerated sofa cushions. It is the one of him with his arm around me, except that the picture now shows only me with Papa's arm on my shoulder. The sight instantly bothers me.

"Papa …" I scan the floor, frantic. "Where is the rest of you?"

"What?"

"The photograph of Papa," I say to Balthus, crouching down despite the searing pain in my leg and clawing through the tattered paper and kapok that litters the floor.

"She tore it in two. Papa is missing."

"Maria, you've no time for this."

But I keep looking, ignoring Balthus, ignoring the sting in my leg, led on by the urge to stay connected to my father in any way I can. I lift up a heap of shredded news clippings and drop them, confetti bits floating in the sun. "He taught me not to flinch," I say to myself. "Papa."

"Maria? Maria, I know this is hard for you, but you don't have time for this. If MI5 don't hear from Dr. Andersson, they'll come to the villa. And if they know where you live, chances are, the Project do, too."

It's as if his words had no meaning. I can only obsess on Papa's picture.

"Maria!"

I lift up files. I throw torn shreds of NSA articles and images around until the air becomes thick with paper, and no matter how hard I try, no matter how much I tell myself to leave, I can't go without Papa, not without seeing him with his arm around me. Not without me safe, secure, knowing I'm not on my own, because I don't want to be on my own, not really, not like this for the rest of my life. And then, as I turn, there among the broken pieces of laptop plastic, I see him, Papa, his eyes shining bright as if he were still alive, warm, breathing next to me.

"Maria, have you got it?"

"Yes!"

I grab the picture and thrust it to my chest, so happy to have him close to me, even if it's only like this.

"Good. Okay, Maria. Now you need to run. Run now, yes?"

"Yes. Yes."

I turn, checking the room, glancing to Dr. Andersson's body on the floor. Then, grabbing my notebook from where it lay half hidden by a pile of toppled books, I hobble to my bedroom, to the hidden floor compartment containing my emergency bag. But as I reach the door, a shriek fills the room, piercing my ears.

Dr. Andersson flies at me. "No!"

She smacks me against the wall, and the picture of Papa floats from my fingertips, notebook flying to the left. Slammed to the wall again, I feel the blood flowing once more from my thigh. She throws me down and digs her knee into my chest, pinning me, but my right arm breaks free, and I turn and punch her face. Her head spins back as blood spurts anew from her nose and, now, her upper lip.

I shift faster now, heart racing, counting all the while to focus, my body rolling away, quicker now, Balthus' thin voice shouting at me from the cell phone, over and over again, to get to the door, to get out. But before I do, I feel a new and excruciating pain in my thigh.

I look down. Dr. Andersson has dug her nails into my skin, clawing at the wound as she tries to get at my cell phone.

"Just ... Maria, don't do this ..."

Heat rockets up my leg and I scream out, stumbling forward,

trying to stand, but my knees wobble and I topple forward, slicing my scalp on the corner of a chair.

Blood runs down into both eyes, blinding me for an instant. Wiping at my eyes in the frantic effort to see, I wobble away, but Dr. Andersson gets to me before I take three steps. The blood from my scalp wound has found a new path, and I can see, but now she has an arm locked around my neck, and her other hand is grasping for my cell phone.

"Who are you speaking to?" she yells. "*Who?*"

I smack her hands away and then, spinning around, see it: her gun, under the far edge of the table.

And now her eyes are on it, too.

Quick and slick, she throws me to the side, lurching for the weapon. My shoulder slams onto the stone floor. She kicks me hard in the stomach, and I reel back, engulfed in pain.

"Jesus Christ, Maria, *why?* Stay fucking still!" She spits out some blood, looking around for the gun. "I didn't want to fucking do it like this."

But I can't let her get the gun, can't let her get to my cell and, through it, to Balthus. And then I spot my torn photograph of Papa, lying with the ripped sketches of Mama, Ramon, Patricia, and Harry, and a sudden rage courses through me. Again those three words lodge in my mind: *prepare, wait, engage.*

I glance once more to the photographs, and then I fly. I punch Dr. Andersson in the throat, straight on the windpipe, and her whole body collapses with a strange gurgle. I scramble up, eyes scanning the floor. The gun. Where is the gun?

"Stop!"

Dr. Andersson jumps onto my back. I reel under the load, horrified that she is on me, touching me. I hit out, kicking at her shins, but it does no good.

Her ankles hook both my lower legs, and as I topple forward, the cell phone almost slips from my grasp.

"Maria!" Balthus yells.

My face smacks the floor, and I roll onto my back, but her full weight lands on my chest, and her knees pin my arms. Air shoots out, and it feels as if I were drowning, as if every molecule of oxygen were wheezing from my lungs.

"So it's the governor you're in touch with," she says, spitting blood onto the floor. "I know his voice. Maria, it's over. Don't drag *everyone* into this."

She shifts to her right, blowing her sweat-damp ponytail off her face. And as I try to jerk my head out of her way, I see it. The iron bar.

I whip my right hand out to my side, stretch, and grab the bar. Continuing the motion, I swing, catching Dr. Andersson with a glancing blow to the side of the head.

Her fingers go slack, and with a low moan, she slips to the side. Pushing her off me, I scramble away on all fours. My eyes dart to the gun lying under the table, against the wall. Chest heaving, I grab it and lurch to my feet, pointing it at her.

"My baby," she croaks. "It's ... her birthday." The blood loops around her ear now, pooling in the canal, and she drifts out of consciousness.

I pause at the sight of her, my brain stuck, torn between helping and running.

"Maria?" Balthus. "Are you okay?"

"She is injured. I should help her."

"What? No. No! Is she down?"

"Yes."

"Then go. Go!"

Swallowing, unsure what to do but knowing that Balthus is right, I grab the cell phone. Then, sparing one last glance at Dr. Andersson's broken body, I hobble away as fast as I can. But as I am dragging myself across the room, somehow Dr. Andersson crawls up and grips me by the ankle. "Give me ... the gun," she rasps.

I fall, and she is on me again, fingers finding my throat and squeezing hard. I gasp for air. My arms stretch out as far as they can go, the gun still in my fingers but only barely. My legs thrash as I try to wrench her off me, but she presses harder, her other hand nearly at my fingers now.

"I'm so sorry. I hate doing this."

I feel myself begin to asphyxiate, and it is hard to keep a grip on anything at all. The room is swaying, my eyes bulging as if they might explode. I look around at the torn news articles on the floor, at the images of the friends and family that, though I have never told them, I do love. I thrash and yell, but Dr. Andersson's fingers just dig in harder, her strength coming from somewhere, her blue eyes fixed on mine. The sun is shining on us, and I feel its warmth, and my mind goes to Papa, to his face and his eye creases and his complete, unquestioning acceptance of me for who I am.

I have almost no oxygen reserves left.

"*Shhh*," Dr. Andersson says to me now. "It will all be over soon. *Shhh*."

A warmth spreads over me, tentative at first, then rushing in as, one after another, faces swim before me: Balthus, Patricia, Harry, Ramon, Mama. And seeing them, watching the contours on their expressions, the grooves and lines, I start to believe that when I die, I will no longer be lonely and awkward and hunted down, but happy and free and regarded as normal.

"Maria? Maria, fight her!"

Balthus? His voice swims into my head.

"Maria," he shouts, "don't let the bastards win!" Hearing his voice sparks something that feeds the last flicker of a flame inside me. My fingers wriggle. Slowly, then picking up speed, I summon up from somewhere a fight, a hidden strength. And instead of letting the pistol slip from my hand, I clutch it and flick the safety off. "*Prepare, wait*," the words whisper in my head. "*Engage*."

I force myself to look straight at Dr. Andersson and I make

myself focus, make myself do what, to my dismay, I've been trained to do, what I must do to survive.

"No!" Dr. Andersson yells, eyes wide, staring at the muzzle. "No. No … Her … her name is Briony. She's three today. Three. I … I can't let you get away. Can't let you stop me." And then she presses down harder on my throat.

I shoot.

# CHAPTER 10

Patricia is singing again. The song drifts in and out of my head as if in a dream, its melody and lyrics soothing, rocking me into a state of peace and calm as I think about the drug coming in through my arm, the hallucinations.

The heat in the room appears to have increased. Sweat drips off me, and while I know I am clothed, for the first time I begin to think about what I am wearing. Can I rip any of it off to cool me down?

"Can you see me?" I ask Patricia. "I want you to tell me what I am wearing."

She stops singing and sighs. "Doc, you know I can't see you. You know, really, that's impossible."

"It is not impossible."

"Yep. I'm afraid it is."

Unsure what she means, I look to my arm and to the needle, to my body, my clothes. I can see nothing. The weak light that was there before has gone, leaving dark, dripping heat in its place, and every movement of my muscles is heavy with fatigue.

We remain this way for a while. Now and then Patricia will talk about how we may have arrived here, where the Project is, if they are watching us, but each time one of us attempts to conjure any significant recollection of our journey here, our minds come up blank.

Four, perhaps five minutes of silence have passed when there is a sudden sound, the first we have heard at higher volume since we awoke in this dank, foul place.

"Hey, Doc, can you hear that?"

"Yes."

It is there in the air, a ticking, a soft *put, put.*

"That sounds like the stand thing, you know, the drip they had me hooked up to when I was in the hospital ward at Goldmouth."

I listen to her words. The drip. The one she was hooked up to after she tried to kill herself in prison. *Put, put, put, put.* She is right. My brain begins to tick, firing now at the slender hope of some kind of answer.

"How close do you calculate you are to the sound?" I ask, alert now.

"Dunno. I'm not as hot on this math stuff as you are. Say, a meter away, something like that?"

"No. That cannot be correct. That would mean that you are closer to the sound than I am."

"Well, yeah. Of course."

"That does not make sense."

"Doc, nothing makes sense in here."

*Put, put.*

"There!" Patricia says. "I hear it again."

The clicking sound hovers in the air now, hanging near us. "Doc, do you think, like, it's got something to do with your arm, that sound?"

"No. It is not ..." I stop, think. She is right—of course she is right. The needle. A drip. I whip my head to the side. "Have you got your bracelet on?"

"Huh? Yeah, my mam's. Why?"

"Twist your wrist."

"Uh, okay."

"Are you doing it?"

"Yes. Hold your horses."

"Horses?"

Patricia moves her wrist, and at first nothing happens but then, slowly, a tiny shaft of light appears.

"There must be some small bit of light. It is now reflecting on your bracelet. Keep moving your wrist."

The bracelet reflection affords a shred of brightness across my body, and I begin to look. At first, nothing appears, only a snapshot of my limbs, my knees, legs, but then, as Patricia's arm moves some more, it happens. Inch by inch, upward, light slithering toward my arm.

"Can you see anything yet, Doc?"

There is a glint where the needle pierces my vein; then it fades. "Move your arm again."

"This is hurting now, Doc."

As the weak light returns, the glint comes again, stronger this time, and gradually, like clouds parting in the sky, what lies beneath is revealed.

I gasp.

"What, Doc? What is it?"

I shut my eyes and open them, but it is still there.

"Huh? What? What can you see?"

Sweat slices my head—confusion, deep-rooted fear. "There is a drip." I narrow my eyes, desperate to see anything I can.

"It is … It is hooked up to a metal medical stand."

"I told you."

"There is a tube and it is … it is linked to the drip bag."

"That must contain the drugs."

"Yes, and …" I stop, every muscle in my body freezing rigid.

"Doc?"

Suddenly, everything makes sense. The *put, put* sound. Why the hallucinations only come in phases. Why I cannot move my arms.

"There is a timer," I say after a moment.

"What?"

I look back to the device, to the stand and the drug bag. "The drugs are being administered through a controlled, preset timer."

## SALAMANCAN MOUNTAINS, SPAIN

*33 Hours and 54 Minutes to Confinement*

Andersson's body slumps sideways.

I push her leg off me, and for some reason I notice that her fingernails are painted crimson.

I stare at them and cannot pull my eyes away. I rub at my chafed and aching throat, and a moan escapes my lips.

"Maria?" Balthus yells. "What's happening?"

Staring at Dr. Andersson and her fingernails, and I moan again and again, rocking gently back and forth. She is lying on her right side. In her forehead is a small round hole, a centimeter in diameter. A thin trickle of blood, the same color as her nails, runs down from it into her hairline.

"She is dead," I say to Balthus.

"Oh, Jesus."

A damp spot the size of a dinner plate spreads across Dr. Andersson's blouse and onto the tiles, painting them red. At first, paralyzed by the sight, I cannot understand why there is a hole in her head when it's her shirt that oozes blood. Finally, I drag my eyes away from the growing stain on her chest as, slowly, the reality of what I have done begins to sink in.

"I shot her twice."

"Maria, it's okay. Maria?"

The deep-red stain emanates from a second hole, in the center of her chest.

"No," I say—a whisper at first, then louder. "No, no, no!" I shout as my hands grope Dr. Andersson's torso, desperate to stem the bleeding, to close up the wounds.

"Maria? Maria, talk to me."

"I killed her."

"Okay. Okay, I know, I know, but it's okay."

I look at her breathless body, at my hands soaked in her blood. "No. It is not. Killing is not okay. It was her daughter's birthday today. Oh my God, oh my God, oh my God."

Then, barely realizing what I am doing or why, I find myself slapping Dr. Andersson's face, rattling her shoulders, frantic for her to open her eyes, to wake up.

"Who else has the Project trained?" I yell at her. "Who was Raven? Who was she? Why did you not just refuse to come here? Then you would still be alive! You would still see your daughter! Daughters need their mothers." Fat tears roll down my face. "They need their mothers."

"Maria!" Balthus yells. "Stop!"

But I shake Dr. Andersson's dead body again and again, an anger I don't understand surging inside me, gripping me tight in the chest, making me pant, making my eyes blur and my head drop. I give her body another shake, her head flopping to the side, when something falls out of the inside of her jacket.

I pick it up. It is a piece of paper, pink, letter size. Slumping back, I wipe snot from my face and peel open the paper. What I see shocks me to the core. "It … it is my family."

"What?"

I slap the paper down on the floor and smooth it out as what I see sinks in. "There is a file containing pictures of you, Mama, Ramon, and Patricia."

"Where was it? With Dr. Andersson?"

"Yes." My hands shake.

"What does it say?"

I scan it all, not believing what I see: that they would do this, say this, believe this is right. "There is one word next to your name and to Patricia's name," I say after a moment.

"What?"

My eyes swim; head struggles to accept it. But finally, I say it aloud. "Locate."

I drop the paper to the floor. "They are looking for you. They know you are both my friends and that you know about the Project."

"And MI5 want all connections to the Project eliminated." Balthus exhales hard and heavy, and when he next speaks, his words are low and slow. "Look, Maria, I know this is not a good situation. But right now, you have to focus. You heard what Dr. Andersson said before. She was looking for a file. It could be the same file you remembered in your flashback."

Slowly I pick up the paper again, eyes glancing to the blood and the crimson nail-polished fingers. I open up the paper and force myself to look at it again. "They want to monitor you all."

"Okay, hang on a second," Balthus says. Let's look at this one step at a time. First off, we have to get you out of there. The Project will locate you anytime. And if you go now, maybe you could find the file, figure out where it is. Maria, that file, what's in it—it could stop all this."

He halts now, just his breathing drifting on the phone line. I think about his words and look again at the images of the people I love. My jaw clenches. "You are all in danger because of me."

"No," Balthus says immediately. "No. This is because of the Project, because of MI5. But you can do something." He pauses. "Maria, you can stop it. You find the file, you end the Project. You end MI5's involvement in it—you end it all."

I rub my eyes. Is he right? Can I really end it all? Should I? *Eliminate.* The word swirls around my head, mixing with the image of Raven, with her voice, with her caramel skin and her cries for help. Why can I not remember everything? Where is that file? Papa has died. Harry has died. The thought of it, how it makes me feel—it drags me in, creates something inside me that I do not fully understand. An anger. A deep-rooted belief that what is happening—what has happened—is wrong. *Wrong. Wrong. Wrong.*

Disregarding the limp body of a woman I myself have killed, and the lives beyond hers that I have just changed forever, I pat down Dr. Andersson's chest and arms and legs until I find what I am looking for: her cell phone.

I grab the pink paper and stand up. Flipping Dr. Andersson's blood-smeared cell phone over in my hand, I pop open the back and unclip the SIM. Then I locate a tiny black device, lift it out, and drop it on the floor. Then I pick up the iron bar and bring it down hard.

Noise splinters the air, and the device shatters into tiny pieces.

"Maria? What's going on?"

With one bare foot, I sweep the shards away. "I am destroying the GPS tracker in Dr. Andersson's phone."

"Won't that alert MI5?"

"Yes. I estimate I have approximately eight minutes to vacate the villa. I have her SIM card."

"Shit. Shit, shit, shit."

Next, I limp over to the crate and dig through the mess till I find the box of matches. Lighting one, I put the flame to the pink paper until nothing remains but charred black flakes.

"Maria, what are you doing? Where are you going now?"

I pick up the two halves of the photograph of Papa and, hobbling across to the only two stacks of books still upright in the corner, I take out my hidden notebook and shuffle toward the bedroom door, the phone to my ear.

"I am going to take the bullet out of my leg."

# CHAPTER 11

*33 Hours and 48 Minutes to Confinement*

Pushing open the door, almost screaming from the pain in my thigh, I jam my hip against the bed's wooden frame and shove it into the middle of the room and nearly collapse on the floor. I drag myself over to the trapdoor. A wire, transparent and barely visible to the naked eye, still stretches across the opening. To my relief, the latch has not been tampered with.

"How much time remaining before MI5 get there?" Balthus asks.

"At least seven minutes and forty seconds," I say, consulting only the clock that ticks in my head. I scour my bedroom. The walls are white and bare. There is only one glass by the bed, one pillow, one small set of drawers, and one book by Jean-Paul Sartre, entitled *Nausea*.

From the space beneath the trapdoor, I pull out a rucksack, unzip it, and check the contents. A USB thumb drive with all the encrypted Project data I have found so far, ten energy bars, chips, four liters of water, three pay-as-you-go cell phones. I add my notebook and the torn picture of Papa and me. The sun peeking in between the muslin curtains shines on Papa's image as I zip the bag. I haul myself up and stagger toward the bathroom.

Scorching heat sears my thigh, all the walking having worsened the wound. Bending down, I study it. Blood is oozing out from a hole perhaps a quarter inch in diameter. I deliberate what to do. If I leave the wound unattended, then no matter how far I want to run, I will not make it. The bullet has to come out.

"Maria," Balthus says. "Time left?"

"Seven minutes."

Staggering across to the bathroom, I slap open the door. My sight is a little blurred—lowered blood pressure from the gunshot wound—but I manage to sway into the small windowless room. My leg brushes the white enamel bath, painting a broad, curving stripe, and my eyes take in my reflection in the mirror above the sink. The sight shocks me. I have small cuts on my cheek and neck from broken glass, and where Dr. Andersson tried to suffocate me, purplish bruises are starting to form in the shape of her small fingers. My spiky blond hair is damp with my sweat and Dr. Andersson's blood from the head butting. The eyes are dark and heavy, and when I stare in closer, my cheeks that only a year ago were rounded now look sunken.

Clenching my jaw at the pain, I set down the cell phone and the SIM card and ease myself down on the edge of the bathtub. The pain feels almost unbearably bright and loud. From the medicine chest just right of the bathtub, I pull out some bandages, tape, surgical scissors, a suture kit, a bottle of isopropyl alcohol, and ... where are they? I rifle through both drawers before finding the hemostats. Dunking them in the alcohol bottle, I leave them for now.

"Maria? Are you okay?"

I had almost forgotten that Balthus is still on the line. "I am in pain."

"Oh ... Is there anything I can do?"

I wince. "No. You are one thousand, two hundred forty-six kilometers away."

Sweating, I search for a washcloth. One is draped over the sink. I roll it up and put it between my jaws. Pulling the hemostats from the alcohol, I lay them on a newly opened sterile pad, then pour alcohol into my palm and rub it over both hands, wetting the entire surface of each finger. I bite down on the washcloth, counting to four, and tip the alcohol onto the wound.

I scream into the cloth. Five long seconds pass before I can pick up the hemostats.

Swallowing hard, I take out the suture kit and lay out what I need. It is time. I have to do it now.

"How long now?" says the tinny voice on the cell phone.

"Six minutes."

Routine, I tell myself. To complete this task, I simply need to follow routine, so I bite down hard on the washcloth and push the hemostats into the wound. Almost an inch and a half in, I feel the tip hit something hard: the bullet, resting against the femur. Screaming again as I open the stainless steel jaws inside my flesh, I get them around the lump of lead and carefully withdraw my prize.

After another minute and twenty seconds have passed, the wound is closed with three sutures and covered with a sterile dressing and surgical tape.

I drop my head. My thigh is made of pain now, but the bullet is sitting there in the soap well on the sink. Splashes and streaks of red color the white enamel bowl, where scrunched-up antiseptic pads lie discarded like roadside rubbish. I look at it all and feel a sudden stab of nausea and worry. The mess, the disorder. It takes every shred of willpower in me to grab the cell phone and the SIM card and stagger away from it and back into the bedroom.

"How's the leg?" Balthus asks.

I grunt a reply.

The time on the clock by the crate next to the bed reads 07:01. I stop and listen for any sounds of entry. When all appears clear, gasping at the pain, I grab some clothes from the splintered drawers, pausing to grit my teeth as a fresh wave of heat from the wound rips through me and then ripples away. Black jeans, fresh gray tank top, a checked shirt and a black cotton bomber jacket. I get them on, groaning when the denim skims over the dressed wound. "Maria, I'm worried about you," Balthus says, though I don't know why. "How much time left now?"

A slice, a sting, shoots through me. "Four minutes remaining."

I shove my feet into a pair of biker boots and put on a baseball cap and some clear, nonprescription glasses with thick black frames. Then, grabbing my cell and Dr. Andersson's SIM card, I turn. This may be the last time I see my villa. I stand still for three seconds, taking a picture of it all in my mind. The silence of the sunshine on my face, the gentle flutter of the morning birds outside, the slow sway of the orange trees. The air is warm and fragrant, a fresh, light wisp of heated earth that wanders in through open windows, through unfilled nooks and corner crevices, catching me by surprise. A wave of sadness hits me. I have been happy here. No social rules to follow, no chitchat to make, no confusing body signals to decipher.

I put the cell phone to my ear. "You said you had a contact, a hacker I can go to."

"Yes," Balthus says. "His name is Chris. American, but he used to be an inmate here."

"Can you trust him?" I step back into the living area, shuffle past the torn newspapers and the splinters of computers and crates, biting down hard on my lip, pressing back the urge to shout out loud that I can't cope with all the chaos.

"Yes, I trust him. One hundred percent," Balthus says now. "I got to know him well; he's a good sort. He lives near Barcelona, in a village up by Montserrat. I'll text you his address."

"No, do not text me. It may not be safe. Tell me now. I will remember it."

Holding Dr. Andersson's SIM card in my hand, I reach into my rucksack and open my notebook.

"How much time left now?" Balthus asks.

"Three and a half minutes."

"You'd better go."

I hold out the SIM card at arm's length in the sunshine. "I have one more thing to do first."

Wiping a bead of sweat from my forehead, I take out one of the burner cell phones from my bag and slip the SIM card into it, tapping the keypad fast to check for data.

"You still there?"

I keep my eyes on the phone. "Yes."

"What are you doing?"

"Checking Dr. Andersson's SIM for data."

"Jesus," he mutters. "Hurry."

My eyes scan for numbers, codes, anything that may help. At first, there appears to be nothing. The card is clear, the data apparently corrupted, but something niggles. Unsure, I turn to my notebook and start flicking pages. My brain registers every word, every sketch and algorithm I have ever recorded from my dreams and flashbacks, until I arrive at a series of numbers that looks familiar. *Think.* Where are they from? Who gave them to me? The configuration is short yet complicated, and somehow I know it could be of use, could hold an answer. I begin working through it, methodically, efficiently. After seven seconds, I crack it.

"It is a SIM code override," I say aloud, amazed that I know this. Who taught me to use this code?

"What?"

Locked on to my task, I ignore Balthus as, one by one, my fingers tap in the decoded key.

"Maria, what's going on?"

Data flashes up, one followed by two short, sharp lines of it. But then something scrolls up, something new. Something significant. I look again to be sure. Can it be …?

My pulse starts to ramp up.

"It is a subject number."

"What?"

Again I analyze the information in front of me, knowing what it is but not wanting to say aloud what is true.

"Maria, what can you see?"

"I see a subject number similar to the one on the MI5 report I hacked into from your office." I track the number, say it in my head, trying to make it true. Sweat beads below my cap brim as I look. "This one is number one fifteen."

"What? But you are subject number—"

"Three seventy-five."

We both go silent. The lemon trees rustle, and within them sit fifty starlings, their heads bobbing up and down in the sunshine.

"It means there are others," Balthus says after a few seconds. "If that's a different subject number, it means that somewhere else, others like you may still be alive. Jesus …"

Balthus' words pinball in my skull. Others. Like me.

"Could it be connected to the file, to the woman you remembered?"

"Raven."

"Yes."

The thought arrests me. The flap of her veil in the breeze, the memory of her invisible face, the smell of the heat and the sand, the secrecy, the hush of some deep, dark void, and her long, loud pleas. I glance again to the subject number. Could this be, as Balthus says, connected to her?

I shake my head and look again at the phone, scrolling down, then stop. "There is something else next to the number."

"What?"

I check again. "It is a grid reference number."

"You sure?"

"Yes."

"Do you think they are related?"

My mind instantly starts trying to determine the location of the map point, trying to forge any connection that may be there.

"Maria," Balthus says. "How much time's left now?"

"Two minutes."

"Damn it, you have to go. You can't wait any longer. I'm on my way to the airport now. Can you keep the SIM card data safe? Take it with you?"

I drag my brain away from fact tracking and take one more look at the information on the screen. A subject number. A grid reference. Data. How do they connect? If there are others like me out there, then is there a chance I can end all this? Stop the danger? I want to know who I am. I don't want to be pressing my nose up to the window of life anymore.

"I am going to find the file," I say after a moment.

"Really?"

"I do not want MI5 or the Project to harm you or Patricia or Mama or Ramon. If the file can provide information on the Project that will put a stop to the entire program—information on others like me—then I have to find it. Dr. Andersson came for me today. It will be someone else tomorrow. It will never stop. And you—and my family—will always be in danger. Therefore, I am going try to find the file by locating the facility my flashback originated in."

"Okay," Balthus says. "Good, good, but look, let me help you. I know you can handle yourself, but still. Get to Chris' place and I'll fly over there now. We can figure out together what to do next."

"They will be watching you if you come to me."

"Then I'll be careful. I have contacts who can help me slip out."

I look at the ripped images and faces that lie on my villa floor. "What about Patricia?"

"I'll get her, too. Okay? She'll be safe."

"Okay."

"Good. Then, go. Please, please, go."

I drop everything into the rucksack—the SIM card, the extra cell, all of it—then pause. Dr. Andersson's body lies lifeless and broken on the floor. Her blood is already drying in the cemented cracks in the tiles. My eyes are on her belly, where a tiny baby girl once was. Pale, stretch-marked skin glistening in the morning sun. I look at her one more time. Then, fighting back an emotion I do not want to feel, I turn, settle the rucksack on my shoulders, and hobble away, bandaged leg throbbing in time with my footsteps.

I open the back door of the villa and am greeted by a blast of warmth and sun. For a second, I let it sink into my skin as I blink at the images of the distant Salamancan mountains, the birds and olive trees and groves upon groves of fragrant citrus fruit. I breathe it all in as, directly in front of me, a Carbonell's wall lizard—rare, endangered—slides onto the fire pit. Its scales are yellow broken by curved edges of black, and when its tail moves, it whips around, long, thin, and fast, its hind legs two stabilizers on the bricks. It hovers there for three seconds, tongue flicking out; then, one second gone, it scurries away.

"Time?" Balthus says.

His voice from the phone makes me jump. "Two minutes."

"Christ."

I throw my rucksack into the truck, turn on the ignition, look to the cell. "I am switching off now." I go to hit the red button.

"Wait!"

I pause.

"You mean a lot to me, Maria. Just remember that, yes? No matter what happens."

I sit, unsure what he means or what I am required to say.

"You still there?"

"Yes. The time remaining is one minute and fifty-two seconds."

"Oh, Jesus. Right, yes, yes, go. Go. Oh, and Maria? Please look after your—"

I switch off the cell—there's no time left. I put the truck into gear, check all around me for anyone arriving, then pull away.

As the truck speeds off, dust billowing in the air, I slip one last glance in the rearview mirror.

My villa fades away until nothing of it is left.

# CHAPTER 12

**UNDISCLOSED CONFINEMENT LOCATION**

*Present Day*

Straining my neck, I get a glint of the timer again. Patricia has been quiet, falling asleep at the exertion of moving her arm, so I use the silence to see whatever I can.

It is difficult at first, the room swathed in darkness, a stench of dirty water saturating the air, pricking my nostrils, but it is there, the timer, I know it is, and despite my head pulsing a pain that shoots like steel through to my shoulder blades, I force my neck backward as, slowly, a sliver of light appears.

"Patricia? Can you see the timer?"

But she remains quiet, and while worry bubbles, I calm myself. She is okay. She's just sleeping.

My eyes scan the area before the light slips away. The timer is on a clock rotation device. It is small, compact, like a shiny penny, and is connected directly to a tube that leads to a drug bag hung on a spiked metal medical stand, long and thin. While I have seen devices similar to it before, this one is unlike any other. Its size is unusual, being so small. The timers I am familiar with are more substantial, as big as the base of a coffee mug, but this … I squint, strain my whole torso. This device is so condensed that it appears unreal, made up, somehow, by a child, not actually functional, rather, decorative, for play. As if this were some sort of game.

"Patricia," I whisper, "I think I can see the details of it now."

I track the circumference of the timer, trace the outskirts of its mechanism so I can gauge when it's set to go off next, but what little light comes through the window is fading now and it is becoming impossible to see. My body slumps back, exhausted. My neck unable to sustain the twisted position any longer, I am forced back into a front-facing position.

"Patricia, you must now wake up." When there is no reply, I get concerned. "I need to check your status. You are injured. Wake up."

There is a sudden, sharp clunk. I freeze. My fingers grip the chair, and my feet curl into the dirt floor beneath.

"Patricia?"

*Clunk.* It sounds again, once, then twice. My whole body goes rigid. "Who is there?"

My voice echoes in the blackness, but no reply comes back.

The rope digging into my skin, heart banging against my rib cage, my eyes track the room, straining to see something, anything that will give me a clue to what is happening.

"Patricia, is that you? Can you move now?"

Steps ring out, there on the air, soles of shoes on stone. My fingers instinctively form fists.

There are more steps, louder now, nearer, and I count them. *One, two …* Closer. I swallow. *Three, four …* They sound like shoes, smooth soles, not boots. *Five, six …* I sniff the air and smell after-shave, spiced, heavy. A man?

Two more steps echo, advancing now. Sweat streaking past my cheeks and mouth. I try to spit it away.

*Seven, eight, nine …*

The steps are near now, and I can hear breathing, low and gruff, and the spiced aftershave scent is so strong it makes me feel sick.

*Ten.*

The steps halt.

"Hello, Maria."

My breathing stops, hands grip still. Because someone stands there now, in this room-size coffin, and even though it is dark, even though the drugs have distorted my lucidity, I know this person. I know the voice, the Spanish inflection. I know the face.

The person looking at me right now.

It is my brother. Ramon.

## MONTSERRAT MOUNTAIN VALLEY, NEAR BARCELONA
*26 Hours and 54 Minutes to Confinement*

By the time I reach the town at the foot of Montserrat Mountain, the sun is beginning to fade. I swing the truck to a halt and pull the hand brake as sweat drips past my eyes despite the open window.

I pull out my cell phone, then pause. The seven-hour journey around the cities of Valladolid and Zaragoza was hot, dusty, taking longer than normal because I stuck only to dirt roads, back routes, staying off grid and out of sight. A breeze brushes my face, and I lean against the window frame now for a moment, let my head rest, my brain recalibrate. I have not stopped. Not to eat, not to drink. Too scared, too worried that at any point, MI5 will discover what I have done, catch up with me. Kill me. Kill my family and friends. The image of Dr. Andersson's limp, lifeless body flashes across my mind, mixing with Raven's face, but instead of sadness or upset, a flame of anger whips up inside me, and my brain lands on one thought: the file.

I look up now and get my first view of Montserrat Mountain ahead. What strikes me most is the color of the serrated, mist-shrouded mass rising up on the horizon. It is deep pink. It has a dusky hue to its sharp, unforgiving surface that pierces a clear blue sky tinged with the orange glow of the afternoon sun. The mountain is majestic against the canopies of white pines, of sweet maples and scented lime trees, of hollies and oaks and yews that thrive in its dense undergrowth, and the rocks, when I track them, jut in jagged blades that stick up tall into the air like broken glass bottles glued together, clusters of red clay boulders millions of years in the making. I track the sawtooth edges, counting every single one. They would slice a falling body like a sharp knife through an onion.

I look now to the area where I am parked. The street is empty for siesta. Each house in the town is sand in color, its windows now closed with white wooden shutters that sometimes swing a little in the breeze, rippling small echoed creaks through the empty narrow roads. To my right is a small moped, rusty and blue, and turning my head, I see an old barrel on its side, with a gaunt black cat curled up asleep on top of it.

Running my hands through my hot, sweaty hair, I catch sight of myself in the truck mirror and lean in. Minute blond curls lick my brow, black roots are painted along my part, and my cheeks and chin are dusted with a gray and brown film of dirt and sun. The bruises around my mouth and cheeks are deeper now, crops of small black-currant buds smeared on, tiny thorns of cuts welded into my bone and skin. I look beat and tired.

I reach over to the passenger seat for a water bottle and drain the whole liter. Then, grabbing my cell, I wind down the window, a wall of heat blasting in, and dial Balthus. I fan my face, prop one hand above my eyes, until finally the dialing tone clicks.

"I have arrived," I say when Balthus picks up.

"Nice of you to say hello."

"I didn't. What is your location?"

"I'm in Spain."

I check my watch. He is on time. My leg throbs. I scratch it.

"Are you close to Chris' house yet?" he asks.

I glance down the street. "I am approximately 1.76 kilometers from my destination."

"Okay. I'll be with you soon. Get to Chris. Oh, and, Maria?"

"What?"

"Be friendly."

"Friendly," I say. "'Friendly' is an adjective that means to be kind and pleasant, or, in British terms, can be a noun used to describe a match or game that does not constitute part of a point-scoring competition. Which one do you require of me?"

"Oh, Jesus."

We say our goodbyes, and I switch off the cell and begin walking to my destination. I have gone one meter and fifty-five centimeters when, ahead, an old woman, hair crowned on her head and deep grooves etched into her cheeks, shuffles into the dusty alleyway and halts. She stares at me, stooping, eyes squinting, two cloth bags swinging from her fingers, her body shawled in a tent of black lace. She stays there, one second, two, her eyes locked on mine. My skin prickles. Why is she gazing at me? Is she with them? With the Project? Her eyes appear glazed over, cloudy, and at first I don't connect what it is—the unusual appearance, the arresting fear stopping me from concluding the answer. I hold my breath when her head suddenly turns, slowly, millimeter by millimeter, then stops, and I finally understand what I am looking at.

Her eyeballs. They are completely white.

No black pupil, no iris, just the milky-white sclera. She shuffles away and I stand for a moment, shiver despite the heat, then, head down, not wanting to glance at her again, move on as fast as I can.

When I arrive at the villa of Balthus' contact, I count to thirteen and stop. My heart is racing. My shirt is damp with sweat, and when I sniff my arms I smell of body odor. I don't feel comfortable here. Friendly, Balthus said. Be friendly. Does that require making social conversation?

I force my eyes upward and observe the villa door. It is small, square, two meters in height and creaking. Blue paint peels from the edges like cracked skin on the soles of aging feet, torn, ripped, and when I scan the inner ridge, splinters protrude. I listen. There is a hiss somewhere, a grass snake sliding unbidden, free among the long rushes that sway drunk on my left. I watch, on alert, yet see nothing amid the grass but an old stone fountain, cracked and forgotten.

Nerves rising, I recite a mathematical theorem, then look again to the door. There is no bell, no buzzer, just an iron ring to bang on the wood, and when I sniff the air, I smell beets and jam and old, damp wood. I scan the area once, then twice, and tell myself that I have to do this. I have to speak to a stranger. And so, counting to three, I knock on the door and wait until, eventually, it creaks open and a man stands there before me.

"Are you Maria?"

The first thing that strikes me about him is that he is tall. His shoulders are broad and his frame appears to fill the entire entrance area, and when I open my mouth to speak, I find that I am uncertain what to do. Remember, I tell myself, Balthus said *friendly*.

"I am Dr. Maria Martinez," I say. "Balthus sent me—you know him." I track the man's frame. "You are 187.9 centimeters in height. Your muscles are defined, which signifies that you must lift weights regularly."

"Rrrright." His accent is American, a low, vibrating twang.

Unsure what else to do, I thrust out my hand as I have seen others do.

He shakes my hand. "I'm Chris."

I expect his skin to be rough as the stubble that shadows his cheeks and chin, but his palms are soft and warm, reminding me of the freshly baked bread Papa used to buy from the local bakery when I was young. A broad smile now spreads across this man's face, and the effect of it takes me by surprise: it is like the white foam of a wave trickling onto a beach, gently soaking into fine sand. I swallow. I feel a strange flip inside my stomach.

"Balthus told me a bit about you," he says. "It's okay. You can trust me." A slick of hair flops into his face, and when he flicks it away, I notice his eyes are sunken, so much so that it is almost impossible, at first, to see the blue waters of his retinas. He scans the area behind me. "You'd best come in."

And yet, I wait, uncertain, my leg beginning to jig. If I go in, it is harder to protect myself if he is not who he says he is—if he is someone I cannot trust.

"Your name is Chris," I say, "short for Christopher, yes?"

"Er, yeah."

I stare past him into the hallway and see mustard-colored walls and dark mahogany scraps of furniture leading to a rusty old kitchen with one stove burner and a scratched enamel sink.

"Chris is short for Christopher," I say, looking to him. "Christopher derives from the late Greek name Christophoros, which means 'to bear or carry Christ.' It is ranked the twenty-sixth most popular boy's name in the United States of America and has been used as a first name since the early tenth century."

He laughs. It is light, a ripple of water glistening in sunlight.

"You're funny."

I don't know what he means, but right then I make a decision.

"I am hungry," I say, counting up in fives and walking straight in. "Do you have food?"

Chris presses his lips together and shakes his head, then, closing the door, gestures toward the hallway. "Well, please, come on in."

# CHAPTER 13

"Ramon?" I croak.

My brother leans forward and moves his arm, but instead of touching me, he reaches out and flicks a switch, sending straw-colored light seesawing into the room. I blink, the sudden brightness burning my eyes that have been accustomed only to darkness. A corncob bulb swings in the air above.

I immediately panic. "They have got you! Ramon, are you hurt? Have they hurt you?" Worried, I look around fast. "Where are we?"

As my eyes adjust to the light, I realize we are in a room with brick walls. The dirt-brown masonry is smeared with tar-like paint, and when I look closer I see that some of the bricks are not flat or solid but raised and soft, padded with some kind of fabric or filler. I crane my neck to the side and see the timer and the medical stand and the drip bag of drugs, and a lump sticks in my throat, a feeling of dread growing in my stomach.

"Where is Patricia?" My eyes roam the soot-covered floor, but there is no sign of her.

"Who are you talking about?"

My brother's voice is rippled like bark. Confusion spills over as I examine him, his tall frame, broad shoulders, lean, taut limbs, a glowing face that has never looked three years older than mine. He appears, Ramon, as he always has: his silk tan, his almost plastic features, hair a perfect round of slick black. To my relief, he seems okay, uninjured, and still something bothers me, something I cannot yet pinpoint.

"Are you … safe?"

He nods. "Yes. Of course I am."

I look around. The door is shut, but Ramon is with me, at least, and even though I am tied up, there may still be some chance I can keep him safe. But where is Patricia?

"Does the Project have you, too?" I say, the words tumbling out as I try to assess the level of danger. "What did they say to you before they sent you in here?"

He tilts his head the way he used to when we were young.

"M, who is 'they'?"

"Do they have Mama, too?"

"Mama is safe."

"Is she still ill?

"Yes, but stable. The cancer's not spread."

Air billows from my lungs, yet my chest immediately tightens as I try to think it all through. We must be at a Project facility—that has to be the answer—and somehow, they have captured my brother and put him in here now with me. The Project doesn't have Mama, at least, and her condition is steady, and yet, why does that information not calm me?

My brother reaches forward and flicks another switch, and the room is bathed in more light—another, smaller bulb this time, casting a tepid sepia sheen in front of me, illuminating my wrists now. I blink at them and see blue plastic rope that ties not just my arms to the chair, but also, as I look farther down, my ankles to the base.

I strain forward. "Where is Patricia?"

"Your friend from prison?" Ramon drops his head, shaking it. "M, she's not here. Did you think she was?"

I look around, agitated now, the light scratching my eyes and brain. "Yes. She is in here somewhere," I say, searching the room. "She is very ill. You have to help her." Then I stop, feeling confused, suddenly not aware of what I am saying or why. "Why are you here? Where is Patricia?"

"M, I don't know what you are taking about." He raises his hand, slicks back a stray lock of hair, then adjusts the collar on a white linen shirt that has tiny thread lines of blue cotton woven into the fabric.

"Patricia was in this room," I say, scanning again for any sight of her, worry rising fast. "You must be able to see her. Or she may have been moved. Did you see her when you came in? Did the Project take her out? Is she safe?"

I raise my head, searching the illuminated ground, but there is nothing, no sign of Patricia's long frame slumped on the floor, or her shaved head—only dirt and maggot-size bits of white cotton string and the fallen dust from the brickwork on the wall. "She was talking to me not ..." I try to calculate the time but find I can't. "... not long ago."

My brother looks at me for three seconds, and for some reason I shiver, goose pimples popping out all over my skin. He walks to the dark corner on the far right and returns with a wooden crate. He sets it flat in front of me and takes out a white handkerchief from his pocket, brushes off some dust, and sits, crossing his legs, lacing his fingers on his knees.

"M, I'm sorry this has had to happen."

I barely move, because even though he is my brother, I find that I am suddenly scared. "What has had to happen, Ramon?"

He glances to the timer. "Who you think you've seen—it's all just a hallucination. It's ... it's all just a side effect of the drugs. She was never really here." He points now to the medical stand behind me, to the timer that still ticks like a hammer in my ear.

I look back to my brother, and a deep, raw fear rears up now, juggernauting forward, reaching my throat, until finally I make myself ask the question I dread the answer to.

"Who was never really here?"

He sighs. "Your ex-cellmate. Patricia."

## MONTSERRAT MOUNTAIN VALLEY, NEAR BARCELONA
*26 Hours and 44 Minutes to Confinement*

Chris has led me to a room on the right side of the house. He said he would be back in a minute with food. That was thirty-seven seconds ago.

I wring my hands together, squint my eyes in the sun, and wait. To keep myself calm, I scan the room for details, automatically searching for a focus. Dimensions, corners, curves, grooves. Late afternoon light streams in through a locked window decorated with gray, ripped netting, and the stagnant, warm air feels thick and pungent on my face, with a faint smell of feet.

The room is small, six meters square. There are seven pieces of furniture slotted against four fading walls decorated with pale-green paint, and inside broken wooden picture frames are three old photographs. I step forward and examine them. Three grainy faces stare back. The eldest is a man with white hair. He is stooped and wearing a chewed straw hat, and by his side is a woman of similar old age, an apron squeezed around a balloon waist, eyes dark, wrinkled mouth downturned. Next to her is a small boy, eleven maybe, head bowed, but with eyes that light up. In his hand is a tennis racket, and by his foot lies a small yellow ball, white shorts on his legs, a gray long-sleeved jumper on his torso. Who are they? Why are they here? Do they mean something? Or are they simply pictures of people forgotten in time, never to be recalled or recounted, slipping by silently, invisibly, as we do from present to past?

Agitated, I turn my attention to the corner of the room where a computer sits, and walk toward it. Sliding my rucksack from my back, I dig out my USB stick and Dr. Andersson's SIM card and, listening for any signs of this man Chris returning, switch on the computer.

I call Balthus. "I am here." I settle into a small, splintered seat and fix my clothes so the fabric does not itch me.

"Maria? Oh, thank goodness. You're at Chris'?"

"Yes."

I peer at the computer. I need it to find out some information, but when I turn it on, the connection is slow, and no matter how much I tap my finger, it will not speed up.

"Is Chris okay?" Balthus says. "Is he there now?"

"He is fetching food."

"Oh, right. What are you doing?"

I place the SIM card and my USB stick on the dark wooden table where the computer sits. "I am switching on Chris' computer to see if I can access any information that will tell me which Project facility the flashback was from."

"Oh, right. Okay. So soon? How are you going to do that? Use the grid reference you found?"

"Yes."

I do not need to check the reference number from Dr. Andersson's phone, since it is already in my head, but it is frustrating. I am ready to search, but the computer is still loading.

"Will Chris be back soon?"

"He said he would be one minute." I check the time, tap my foot. "He is late."

When Chris does finally enter the room two minutes and thirteen seconds later, he is carrying a tray containing bread cut into rough chunks, a block of sliced Manchego cheese on a white plate with blue swirls, and two steaming mugs of coffee in black cups.

He sets the tray down on the table to the right and puts his fists to his hips. "Er, like, what the hell are you doing?"

"I am using your computer," I say. "Balthus is on the cell."

"Oh," Chris says. "Hi, Balthus."

"Chris! Good to hear you. Thanks for this."

Chris picks up the cell and puts it to his ear, and I desperately want to grab it from him, not wanting anyone else's scent on it, but I see the bread Chris has brought, and realize it has been several hours since I ate, and my stomach is rumbling. Reaching across, I grab a chunk of bread, take a slice of Manchego, and shove it all in at once. The food instantly expands in my mouth like soaked cotton balls.

"You have been three minutes and thirty-seven seconds," I say to Chris. Crumbs spit out.

He lowers the phone and just stares at me. "What?"

I swallow the food. "You said you would be one minute. You were not. You were three minutes and thirty-seven seconds." Taking the cup, I swig a gulp of coffee. It tastes good—hot, bitter. I start to thaw out, a little less tired, a little less worn.

"What are you discussing with Balthus?"

Chris' eyes follow me. "Do you have *any* manners?"

"I did not hear you."

"I said, do you have any manners?"

"Oh." I pause, think. "No." I look at my phone at his ear, think of his skin touching it, his smell all over it. I can't stand it any longer. Standing, I unhook the cell from his hand, put it back onto speaker mode, and place it on the table.

"What the …?"

"Did she just take the phone from you?" Balthus says to Chris.

"Uh, like, yeah."

"Don't take it personally. She does that kind of thing to everyone."

Chris shakes his head, stares at me a little again, then eventually picks up the other cup and, taking a small sip, nods to the computer. "Why do you need to use my stuff?"

"Stuff?" I frown. Is he referring to the computer? I conclude that he must be. "I have some confidential files to access. Your computer takes a long time to boot. What modem are you using?" I drink more coffee.

"What?"

"You say 'what' with reasonable frequency."

Balthus laughs.

Chris' mouth hangs open, and it seems I should speak some more, but I don't know what to say. The uncertainty of the social situation makes me want to hum, but I know that may seem strange, so instead I divert my anxiety by counting the pixels on the screen while the modem loads to the connection.

"I have to go," Balthus says. "Just about to go through customs. Chris, you have the rendezvous location, right? It's not far from you."

"Yep. Got it."

"Good." He pauses. "Look after each other."

Chris throws me a glance. "I think it might be me that'll need looking after."

Balthus laughs again, and I lower my head, listening, unsure what could be funny. "Okay," he says. "See you soon. Stay low."

"Will do."

I switch off the cell, and Chris blows out a breath, then pulls up a stool and sits. "So," he says after a moment, "you know Balthus from prison, right?"

"Yes." I have counted one hundred and twenty-three pixels, and that's in just the far right corner. I grab my cell, pull it close, sniff it, and scrunch my nose, unhappy: it smells of this Chris now, of deodorant and baked bread.

"How long were you inside for?" he asks now.

"What is this 'inside'?"

"You know, prison."

I pause my counting. What do I say to his question? The truth?

"It's okay," Chris says, "I know your deal."

"Did we have a deal?"

"What?"

"You said 'what' again."

"What?" He slaps his forehead. "Jesus. No. I mean I know about your conviction, you being in jail. I don't mind."

Four hundred and three pixels. "If you know about my conviction, why did you ask what I was in prison for?"

"Um, I was just … making conversation."

"Oh." I don't know what to say. "Okay."

He taps his coffee cup now, watches the screen as the modem fires. "So, whereabouts in Spain are you from?"

I swivel my head so I can see him. "Salamanca," I say, unsure whether to tell him, and yet finding my lips automatically wanting to speak, as if they had a mind of their own. I look at him in more detail. There is a small rip on the sleeve of his marble-gray T-shirt, which is half tucked into dirty light-blue jeans, baggy in the legs. I lean in and sniff the air. This close, he smells slightly different—raw cake mix spritzed with musk cologne.

I sit back. "You smell good."

A laugh spurts out. "What?"

"I said you smell good. Why are you laughing?"

"I know what you said, it's just that …" He stifles a cough, moves back a little, rubbing his chin, and I find myself becoming concerned at how I may have acted.

"Balthus told me to be friendly," I say after a second, looking down. "But sometimes I … say things that people … that people do not like." My cheeks flush. I spin back to the safety of pixel counting on the computer, feeling exhausted by the short exchange. Five hundred and two pixels.

For a small while, Chris does not speak, but after a small while, he leans in—not too much, just a little—and says, "You smell good, too, by the way."

Finally, after a while, the computer sputters to life, and the screen I was awaiting pops up. I whip around immediately, ready to search for the map reference.

Chris points to the screen. "You're going to use a proxy, right?"

My fingers suspend themselves above the keyboard. "You are a criminal hacker. I thought this would be a secure line."

He shakes his head. "No. Well, yes, it is, but I like to make sure everything's like, well, supersecure, you know?"

He looks at me, waiting. For what? "Oh. Yes," I say, though not sure why.

He smiles. "Cool. So, you need to use a proxy. I can't have anyone finding me. Finding you." He tuts. "Us. Sorry—I promised Balthus."

"How do I know if I can trust you?"

He shrugs. "You don't. You just have to, I don't know, take my word for it, I guess."

A shot of adrenaline charges through me. I look at this man, the black hairs on his arms, his nut-brown skin chalked with tiny scars. The body can tell a thousand stories, Papa used to say to me. You just have to figure out the plot.

Over by the window, the shutter outside swings forward then back silently in the breeze. I look back to Chris. I trust Balthus, and Balthus trusts Chris.

"I need to perform a search," I say finally.

"No problem. Want me to sort the proxy and stuff?"

I hesitate. "Yes."

He delivers me a wide grin. "Cool." Then he takes the keyboard and, tapping in a code, sets up what I need to begin.

To calm my nerves, I start reciting in my head all the famous people I can think of with "Chris" as a forename.

# CHAPTER 14

I try to understand what Ramon is saying, but it does not make sense.

"But Patricia was here," I say, searching the floor, the light weaker now, a single shaft of it projecting forward as, in my head, doubt begins to mushroom.

"No, M, she wasn't."

"She was there," I say, nodding forward to the spot where I assumed my friend was, but all my sight catches now is an empty space of black dirt floor, dust floating in the shaft of light that slants into the room. "I heard her," I find myself saying. "I did." My breath is short, sharp, and I struggle to understand what is happening.

Ramon shifts on the crate and delivers me a long stare. He clasps his hands together, folds one knee on top of the other, and juts out his chin. "M, it was the drugs. What you saw, heard—it wasn't real."

His voice is cotton soft, and I try to focus on it, cling to the life buoy of the sound, but all I can think of is Patricia, and when I blink in the gloom, my eyes sting and a wetness prickles out onto the red-hot flush of my cheeks. I close my eyes.

"Is she safe?" I say after a moment. "Does the Project have her?"

"I don't know."

"Why do you not know?" I open my eyes. I can feel my chest tighten as my sight becomes singular and funneled.

"M, I don't know anything about Patricia, but what I do know is that it was the drugs you're being given that made you see your friend." He pauses. "I'm sorry."

"Then you have to help me," I say, an anger, a hint of fire, burning up inside me at the confusion, at the fear. "You have to help me escape."

His head drops. "No."

A shiver from somewhere runs over me. "Yes. You must."

He lifts his head now, and when he directs his eyes to me, I see they are tinted with light pools of wetness.

I don't speak. I am confused. Nothing here makes sense, and even though my brother is with me now, he is not helping me escape.

"M, you have to talk to me."

I force myself to look at him. He is pristine. The crate upturned, he is sitting one leg swung over the other as if he were posing for a catalog shoot on the deck of a yacht. His hair, when the light catches it, is wet with gel, not a strand out of place, and when he opens his mouth, I see his teeth are straight and glowing, and his clothes, when he moves, are starched and pressed where his muscles flex long and lean from years of early morning swimming.

"M? M, are you okay?"

"You have not called me M since I was twenty-one," I say.

"We grew up."

"Why are you here?"

He hesitates. He opens his mouth, then closes it and scratches his chin with his index finger and thumb. I glance around the room. The place still does not look familiar.

"I am here," Ramon says after a few seconds, "because I want to help you."

"Did they send you?"

"Did who send me, M?"

"The Project."

He stares at me. He says nothing in reply and keeps his gaze on me, on my torso and limbs, and when I turn my head away, unable to bear the intensity of the attention, he scrapes the crate forward and moves closer to me. My breath quickens. I can smell him now, my brother. I can smell his washed skin scrubbed with soap, the lemon cologne, and when I raise my nose I get mold and damp from the black of the room, and all the scents mix together to create a bucket of aromas that smack a punch in my nose. I gag.

"M," Ramon says, moving in nearer, "what's the matter?"

"The smells," I say, pressing my head back as far as it will go against the damp wood of the chair I presume I am sitting on.

"Oh, sorry." He moves back, fixing the crate to its original position and running a hand along his slacks. I breathe out and allow myself a glance left and right, then straight ahead toward Ramon. I shake off the scents, try not to let them engulf me.

"Tell me …" I stop, shake my head away from the smell of mold that remains in my nose. "Tell me why you are here. They have not hurt you, so what have they asked you to do?"

"I … I cannot answer that."

"Why?"

But he does not respond.

"I asked you why."

His eyes rise, but they are not sparkling as usual, are instead dulled and washed out, as if the person behind them is not really there, and for the first time I start to wonder whether he will hurt me.

"Ramon, who tied me up?" My voice rises with my fear. "Who connected me to the timer and the drug?"

Ramon's eyes flicker upward, toward where the timer now begins to click a little louder, a little more *pit, pat, put* into the room.

My eyes dart to the drugs and back. "The timer is set to go off at intervals," I say, words tripping out. "The Project has either forced you to be here or convinced you that they are good. They are not. Untie me and we can escape together."

He hesitates. "I can't. I … can't help you escape."

"You can. It is simple." I jerk to the timer. The fluid is rushing faster now. "You need to untether me. I can take out the needle."

He fleetingly closes his eyes, inhales a long breath. "Maria, what do you think is happening?"

The needle starts to dig farther into my skin, the liquid building pressure in the vial. Fear flies up. Why isn't Ramon helping me? Why? And then I stop, suddenly understanding the situation. "They are watching us."

"What? Who?"

Hair matting to my head, sweat dripping, I scan the room for any recording devices. "They have used fake spiders before to covertly record me, so what are they using now?"

"M, you sound crazy. You're worrying me."

My eyes land on a hole in the wall, tiny, black, barely visible in the murk, but there, real. "The hole one meter to your left. That could be a recording device."

He spends two seconds staring at it, then, shaking his head, returns his attention to me. "M, do you know what is happening?"

A thought slaps me right on the cheekbone, cold and stark.

"Are you a hallucination?"

At first, he does not utter a word, and then he does something odd and unusual. And frightening.

Unexpected, unprompted, he shoots up to his feet and screams.

The noise ricochets around the walls. It bangs around my ears and against my skull, and even though the padding on the brickwork smothers some of the sound, my brain feels as if it will explode, the force is that great. I cower. Ramon kicks the crate, and I can't move, cannot get out of his way, because my hands are still tied and the timer still ticks.

After two, perhaps three seconds pass, he finally comes to a stop and heaves in three gulps of breath. The corncob bulb swings above us. I say and do nothing, too confused to try. Ramon takes one look at me and, withdrawing a handkerchief from his pocket, wipes spit from his mouth, dabs his lips at the corners, then, sliding the white cotton cloth back to its home, clears his throat.

"I apologize for my outburst."

I don't know what to do. I stay as still as I can and try to assess the situation. What is happening? What has the Project told him? How have they brainwashed him? My pulse is charging through my wrist as I think to myself what I can do, think through the next steps, and tell myself that no matter what happens, it will be okay. Because no matter what the Project has said to him, Ramon is my brother and he wouldn't hurt me.

Would he?

## MONTSERRAT MOUNTAIN VALLEY, NEAR BARCELONA
*26 Hours and 40 Minutes to Confinement*

Chris taps the screen and sets up the proxy. He creates the information he needs to ensure a secure line, and while he waits for the next stage, he stretches his arms high above his head and yawns.

"So," he says, yawn over, "how was prison?"

"It was a large brick place constructed in the British Victorian era."

He drops his arms and looks to me. I face the computer.

"The proxy is ready," I say.

"Oh. Right." He leans into the screen and taps the keyboard in the next required part of the process. His fingers work fast and carefully, and I find myself enjoying watching the movement of them as they work, lost in the rhythm of their dance.

"Hey, you know, your conviction was bigger than mine," he says after a moment, still working the keyboard. "I don't know if I can trust you." He turns, grins.

"Why are you smiling?"

"Huh? I was just—"

"I was acquitted of murder in a retrial. You were in prison for hacking government websites. You were not acquitted."

A laugh spurts from his mouth.

I watch him, curious. "That was funny?"

He leans back in his chair and lengthens his arms outward, this time toward each wall, and when he does, I see the dark shadow of the hair under the pit of his shoulders.

He looks at me and smiles. "I like you," he says.

"How can you make that assessment? You do not know me. I do not know you."

He nods. "Okay. Okay, sure, sure." His arms drop and he turns his torso to me. "You seem like an oddball, but that's kind of cool with me, and you know Balthus, so I'm going to tell you who I really am."

I glance to the door. I can be out of it in two seconds and through the main house door in under eight.

"I'm a hacker," he says. "I'm from Idaho. I'm thirty-one years old, and when I was twenty-three I got my first hacking conviction, for smashing open some shit firewall of a defense behind a government military facility." He exhales. "Anyway, by the time I reached the prison Balthus was at, the one he was at before Goldmouth, I'd been inside twice more. I was supposed to be extradited to the US from the UK, but it didn't happen. Balthus—he was good to me, helped me with my case."

Chris folds his arms across his chest, and his T-shirt tightens over his rib cage and abdomen, making each muscle and bone jut out, and I watch him, finding myself uncertain, not sure what to think.

"So," he says, grinning. "Now you know me at least a little more." He moves aside, points to the computer. "It's all ready. What do you want to search?"

Hesitating, I pull my chair toward the computer and, calling up a search engine, tap in the grid reference number from Dr. Andersson's phone. After three seconds, the answer flashes up.

"Switzerland?"

I ignore Chris and look to the screen. LAKE GENEVA, SWITZERLAND, blinks in front of me in straight, formed letters, round and clear. I scan my memory for any connection, but I cannot find one that lights anything up, and even though I have been fed and am not now as tired as before, still my mind runs blank. Is it a place I have been before with the Project and cannot recall? Is it the location of the Project facility where Raven was held?

"Hey," Chris says, "this yours?"

He is holding the SIM card from Dr. Andersson's phone.

I snatch it back.

"Whoa, okay, okay. I was just looking because it's odd."

I am sliding away the card, then stop. "What is odd?"

He leans in a little. I lean back. "It's just that, well, it's not a standard SIM card."

Despite my best efforts, my curiosity is piqued. "Tell me why."

"Um, well, do you mind?"

"What?"

He points to the card. "Can I … If I could have it, I can show you."

I hesitate as the issue of trust flags again in my brain. But then I think of Balthus, and I find myself slowly handing over the SIM.

"Thanks. Okay, so this groove here, see?"

I bend in, squint. "Yes. I see."

"Well, it's computer-linked."

"What do you mean?"

"It's, like, compatible with a computer. But"—he shakes his head—"not in an ordinary way. See, the groove is specially made—customized, really."

Neurons fire in my head now, back and forth. "Is it compatible with *this* computer?"

He shrugs. "I guess so. Want me to try?"

"Yes." I then pause, remember what Balthus told me. "Please."

He smiles. "Okay, then."

He slots in the SIM card to a slit no more than 1.5 centimeters long on the side of the computer. He takes the keyboard toward him and, tapping in a series of numbers and figures, leans into the screen and waits. His leg is jigging, and on his face, his cheeks flush as the late afternoon heat beats in the window where the shutter outside has come loose.

"Ah, fuck."

"What?"

He rubs his chin. "Well, this bit's encrypted."

I look. He is right. The access to whatever data is on the card is locked, enshrined in a code that is so long, my brain plays catch-up with following it.

"I can access this code," I start to say, "however—"

"Oh, I can do it."

"What?"

"The code. I can hack it. Seen this kind of thing before."

I suddenly become concerned. "How?"

"Er, duh? Hello, I'm a hacker. I hacked the US government. They have the highest level of security. Which means, actually, this is high-level stuff, too." He pauses, looks at me.

I look away, uncomfortable, unsure how to respond. "Can you access the SIM?"

"Huh? Oh, yeah. Sure. I don't know what all this is about, but if Balthus is part of it, I trust you."

Chris starts the process at speed. I take out my notebook and write down what he does, the sensation strange—I do not recall learning from someone else like this before, learning coding and decryptions in such a way. Yes, the Project has taught me a lot, but that, I have no real recollection of. Watching Chris, gaining knowledge from him—it makes me feel ... happy, as if I'm not on my own, not the only one living in a head like mine.

"Okay, so," Chris says after less than thirty seconds have passed, "I've brought up the next phase. I'm gonna try moving the cursor over everything."

On the screen is a ticker tape of numbers that snake in a line across the glass, where a file of black and white sits. "Look out for an icon structure," he says.

"What type of structure specifically?"

"Black. Square."

I stop. A black square structure. Heat rises to my head as I connect two elements. "When I was in Balthus' office," I say, fast, "I hacked into a confidential website through a black square."

"Cool. Well, let's see what we can find."

At first when we search, there is nothing, but then, after one, two seconds, everything changes. The screen flickers once, twice, and the numbers switch to flat green lines that crackle across the glass and peak into mountaintops, then dip to the bottom of the file. Neither of us moves.

Chris wipes his mouth. "What the fuck …?"

"What is happening? Is it a loose connection or a faulty wire?"

"No." He stops. The screen has begun to pixelate fast, out of control as, slowly, something flashes across the glass.

"Holy shit!" Chris says. "What was that?"

My chest goes tight, and my fists scrunch to two tight, nervous balls. "I do not know."

The screen goes black. Chris drags his chair toward the computer. "This isn't right."

I open my mouth to attempt to explain something, anything, of what is occurring, when I stop.

Because there on the screen is an eye.

Yet it is not static, not an image or a photograph, but real, moving, blinking.

A silent scream slips from my mouth as the eye stares straight back at me. Someone has accessed this computer.

Someone knows where I am.

Someone is watching me.

The eye blinks; then, as quickly as it appeared, it vanishes from the screen, without a trace.

# CHAPTER 15

*26 Hours and 26 Minutes to Confinement*

"Holy shit! Holy shit! What was that?" Chris jumps up from his seat, hands scouring through his hair. "What the fuck was that?"

"Black Eyes." I say the words. I say his name and expect to feel fear, yet instead experience a strange stillness, my emotions landing like sediment at the bottom of a glass.

"Black Eyes? What …" He shakes his head. "What's that? I mean, what is …"

His voice fades, and he is pointing to the screen now. I look. The eye is gone and has been replaced with a series of words and numbers. I grab my notebook and lean in.

Chris quits pacing and looks. "That says 'Black Eyes.' Why does that say 'Black September'?" His voice is higher than normal.

I analyze what Chris is staring at, an urgency building up fast. He is right. Black September and the year 1973 are listed.

And something else.

Subject number 115.

It is the number from my flashback in the villa. The same subject number that was on Dr. Andersson's cell phone.

Chris stares at it all. "Holy shit. It's got your name on this. And your age. And … What the …? Is that a clock?"

I look down. There on the bottom of the file is my subject number, 375, and my name, plus my age, thirty-three, and by it is a yellow-flagged box that clicks away each second, minute, hour, day, month, and year.

"Is that . . ." Chris whistles. "Is that thing counting down your age?"

I try to think. How is it all connected?

I look up. "It says September is Black. What does that mean?"

"Seriously? You don't know? Who are you involved with? Shit." He paces. "Black September—they were the gang responsible for terrorist attacks in the seventies." He points to the screen. September fifth, 1972—that's when it all kicked off. But look, that age thing."

"It must be tracking me."

"But how? Why?" He rakes a hand through his hair. "Whoever this data belongs to, how old you are is a big deal."

"It *is?*" I turn back to the screen and scroll down and feel a wave of pain in my stomach. How can all this be linked? How can the woman, Raven, be part of whatever information is on Dr. Andersson's SIM—be part of how old I am?

I look at Chris. "You say this Black September organization were terrorists."

"Yeah. Big-time, serious shit." He shakes his head. "You know, it all went underground, the response to it. There was a load of us hackers way back who got wind of some unit that was set up in response to that kind of terrorism, to a shift in approach, but . . . Hey, you don't think that's connected to whatever you're involved in, do you?"

I hesitate, think about what he has said. Balthus trusts this man. I decide to take a risk and tell him. "The group that is tracking me—it is called the Project. They are unknown to the government. They are, as you say, underground."

He blows out a breath. "Jesus."

I look back to the screen, back to the data and the facts. If all this is linked, then why? And what is the significance?

"We need to get out of here," Chris says. "Like, now."

I turn. He is right. If Black Eyes is watching, they could track our location. I pick up my USB stick, start to download the files.

"What are you doing?"

"Saving the file."

Chris shakes his head. "It's protected. I set up a shield. Let me do it."

"Oh." I thrust the USB stick out to Chris. He takes it.

"You have heard of the word 'please,' right?"

"Of course." I hold the USB stick out farther toward him. "I need you to download it all."

"Christ." He takes the stick and, fingers flying fast, he downloads the files.

"Can you retrieve the last section, where it says 'critical' next to my age?"

"Yeah, hang on." He taps the keys, but the screen suddenly starts to fade fast. "Shit. This isn't right."

"What is the problem?"

"I don't know. It's just all disappearing."

Chris sets up the download, but still the data pixelates until all that is left is a pinprick dot, minute, black. Then nothing.

"Shit, is that big eye coming back?"

I stare at the empty screen, an urgency surging forward, expecting to see Black Eyes reappear. "Did you secure the download?"

"I don't know, maybe, but I do know that if I don't pull this now, we're screwed."

Dropping to his knees, Chris wrenches the table away and crawls underneath and starts ripping out the wires, dragging away lines of cables, and as he does, they all spill out onto the floor, rolls of intestines gathering on the tiles. Done, he crawls back out, catching his breath. My USB stick is still in his hand.

"I have been here"—he swallows, hair dropping forward—"for six months now and not once, *not once*, has anyone found me. And then you show up and a fucking Cyclops springs onto the screen and a bomb flashes up with a whole heap of intelligence data."

I try to focus on what he says, but my mind races, thoughts screeching around my brain, adding, subtracting. What does Switzerland and Geneva refer to? Why would the Project be connected to Black September?

"Well?" Chris says now.

I snatch the USB and turn. "I am sorry. I may have put you in danger."

He stares at me, and at first I think he is going to leave, going to walk away from me and the chaos I have brought upon him. But then, slowly, he does something that surprises me: he smiles and sighs.

"D'you think this is the first time I've been in trouble?"

"Oh." I think. "No."

"Correct." He turns, pulls one last cable from the wall, and then, snapping back the pictures of the old people from the wall, he clicks a button, and a small metal safe door swings out to reveal a bunch of passports, money, keys, and cell phones. "Handy how the past," he says, tapping the photographs hanging in midair, "can mask the present."

He grabs a duffel bag from a cupboard, fills it with the safe's contents, then turns and checks his watch.

"Look," he says, "I don't know what you're mixed up in, but I like you. And I like Balthus, and he'll be on his way now and I promised him I'd get you to him. You ready to go before whoever you're involved with finds us?"

I glance around the room, at the ripped computer, at the screen where Black Eyes was. "Yes."

"Good. Then, let's go."

I gather the SIM card, my USB stick, and my notebook, and go to walk ... but find that I don't move. For a moment, I can't, as all the information I've just seen, all the events of the past ten hours, swamp my mind. I don't know who I am. I suddenly want to scream. I want to run back to my villa and hide away forever and never deal with anything or anyone again.

Chris stops, looks to me. "You okay?" He dips his head, smiling again, creases crinkling at his eyes. "You ready?"

I look at him, at his eye crinkles. Balthus knows him, I tell myself; he trusts him, and his smile is good. I know it is good.

"I am ready to go," I say after a moment, gripping the strap of my rucksack.

"Great."

We walk through the back of the house, past a broken blue door and two rusty metal tubs of water, to a small black car with splashy tires, parked in the shaded alleyway, hidden from the sun. We both get in, Chris driving, and pull away fast.

The dust on the road flies up as the car speeds along a warren of clay-colored roads that wind up toward the first stage of the huge, jagged mountain range beyond. As we drive, my mind turns to facts and data and to the people I know. If the Project is flashing up on a screen in a house in Montserrat, then they could be anywhere. They could be with anyone.

Glancing to Chris and watching the route we are taking, I pull out my cell and text my brother and check that he and Mama are safe.

## UNDISCLOSED CONFINEMENT LOCATION
*Present Day*

The timer ticks in the room and my panic rises. I look to my brother. His face is bathed in a streak of light, and when the bulb above his head swings, his cheeks move in and out of darkness.

"Turn off the timer," I say, but my brother does not move. "The Project is not who they say they are. They lied to Mama when I was young, and they are lying to you now. Whatever they are making you do, stop."

Ramon remains solid and does not shift, not even one inch,

as, drop by drop, the liquid begins to work its way toward the needle in my arm.

Panic floods me. It will trip soon. "Ramon, take it out. Now."

"They voted you 'worst girl in school.' Do you remember that?"

"What?" *Drop, drop.* "Why are you saying this?" The timer is ticking faster now. I count the seconds as they speed by, and know that at any moment the drug will enter my vein. "Take out the needle. I know they will be watching us, you, but you need to do it."

"You cried," he says now, as if I had never spoken. "I know you remember. You cried all night in your room after they voted you worst girl. I slept on the floor because you didn't want to be alone. Five years after Papa died, and you still struggled without him."

His words make me hold my breath. School. It was like a living nightmare. I never understood the rules, and as I got older, the teenage games everyone seemed to be playing, especially the girls, baffled me, especially the way they would be with boys. Why couldn't you say someone looked awful if they did, in fact, look awful? Especially if they asked you?

I feel suddenly tired, weak, and when I speak, my voice is cracked. "The boys used to laugh at me. You used to laugh, too."

He stays silent. For a moment, his chest remains so still that it appears as if he were not breathing at all, even though the air around us is damp and loaded. When he does eventually talk, his voice is chalky, ripped.

"I didn't know what to do."

I say nothing. The timer ticks.

"You have no idea what it was like." He sucks in a breath. "Everyone thought you were odd. The girls laughed at me when you did your odd things, and I couldn't even get a girlfriend because of it."

"That does not make logical sense."

"That's what I mean! You were my sister, but oh, my God, it was a pain having you trailing after me."

He briefly shuts his eyes, and confusion swamps me. I don't understand what my brother is talking about or why it exhausts me; trying to figure it out, trying to decipher the social connections—it wears me out. I lick my lips. They are dry. A heat is rising in the room, and it feels as if it is closing in on us, as if the walls are surging forward almost, the only space the immediate air around our faces. When Ramon finally opens his eyes and speaks, it is about a different subject.

"We are in a city, do you know that?"

I look around. Is he lying? I try to detect clues. There is a window, but it is thick and heavy with some kind of black soot, and when I track the frame, I cannot see any latch or distinct opening, as if the entire thing had been fused shut some time ago.

"The Project does not have any facilities based in cities." But then I stop, because, in truth, I cannot be completely certain of this statement. I cannot be completely certain of anything.

My eyes land on the brickwork ahead. "The walls are padded, Ramon," I say. "Why?"

"For your own safety."

Fear, right then, deep, shakes within me. What have they told him to make him believe that all this is acceptable, that this is the right thing to do?

"Okay," he says, "so it's time for you to have your medicine now." He goes to leave.

"No!" Panic hits, and I thrust forward but am slammed to a halt by the ropes. "Wait!"

He stops, turns, and as I catch the side of his face unshadowed by the weak light, for a fleeting second I see the face of the brother I knew when I went to school: skin soft and unmarked, no stubble or sharp bones, just plump red cheeks, wide eyes, and a deep summer outdoor tan. A small lump swells in my throat.

"Why are you keeping me here?" I say. "Why are you not freeing me from them? Freeing us?" My voice is quiet, broken.

Ramon hangs his head, and when he raises it again, when he lifts his face to mine, his eyes are wet and his mouth is downturned.

"Because I love you."

The timer clicks, and with one loud rush, the drug enters my blood.

# CHAPTER 16

## MONTSERRAT MOUNTAIN ROAD, NEAR BARCELONA
*25 Hours and 59 Minutes to Confinement*

The woman code-named Raven floats into view beneath the sunlight. I observe her face. Her eyes are deep liquid pools, and when she flickers her lids, her lashes are as fine and exquisite as threads of silk. The Middle Eastern sun beats down and bakes our skin covered in cloth and gauze.

She ushers me to move. The woman's hand now beckons me, fingers thin, nails round and smooth at the edges, long, elegant bones on the end of her palms gliding toward me, and as they do, something happens: I begin to float along, an apparition, a ghost.

We move together simultaneously, the woman and I. She is talking to me fast in Arabic, and to my surprise, I understand her, even talk back to her, as if it were a language I was born with, had always spoken. We are discussing an operation, a target. She has stopped, the woman, now, here, the desert hot, sticky, sweet honey drops of heat sliding down our skin, and as I look around, there is only a sprinkle of uninhabited sand-colored buildings nearby. Taking out a computer tablet, the woman shows me something, and I peer in. It is a series of algorithms, of equations and numbers, and I understand it all, every single part of it, yet there is a connection missing, a link, though I cannot say what.

The woman slips her hand into a pocket and unfolds a piece of paper. She points to it, holds it near me, and I see a code, a complex code on how to hack a social network website. She speaks now again, fast, and mentions the CIA. She talks about how difficult their system is to penetrate, but not impossible, that who I am, my age, is vital, and I listen, not because I want to join in her hacking, but for another reason, a reason that somewhere inside me feels infected, wrong. I watch myself as I reach into my pocket and switch something on. What? A phone? A tracker? It is unclear, but what I am certain of is that this woman knows me, trusts me, yet I know in my head that I will betray her. The feeling is so strong, so powerful, that a pain radiates across my chest, and though I try to fight it, an unfamiliar part of my brain tells me that it is the right action to take, the only action—that it is for the greater good. For the Project, I am going to betray her. I am going to hurt her.

I am going to kill her.

Static appears, and the mirage of the woman escapes to the sky. She hovers, a bright firefly, beautiful, mesmerizing, impossible to catch, and I try to grab the mirage, try to keep it locked in my consciousness, stowed away, but it flutters off, flapping left and right until its wings rotate and it disappears from my view entirely.

I wake up and intake a sharp breath.

"Hey. Hey, are you okay?"

I jump. Chris is to my left, driving. I had forgotten he was here at all. The sky has become darker, sudden deep gray swirls of clouds threatening to open.

"Where are we?" I rub my eyes. The memory of Raven lingers, a warm fug of freshly tumble-dried linen.

"We're on the road, far away from Montserrat now. You've been out of it a while. You okay?"

"I …" I shake my head and pull myself up straight. "How long have we been driving?"

He shrugs. "Dunno. Twenty-five, maybe thirty minutes?"

I rub my shoulders where they have become cemented stiff from a lolling head. I fell asleep. I must have been more tired than I realized. I smooth my hands through my hair, think about the woman I have just seen. Was it just a dream? Was what I felt real, something that has actually happened? I reach for my rucksack on the backseat, scrambling for my notepad. I have to write it all down.

I scratch pen to paper and record everything I have just recollected, and glance over to Chris. "Has anyone followed us?"

"Huh? Oh. No." His eyes remain on the road. "It's hot. There's some water in there if you want it."

I look to where he's pointing, where a plastic bottle peeks out from a shelf under the dashboard. I set down my pen, unscrew the bottle cap, and gulp down all the liquid, Chris throwing me sideways glances the entire time.

"It's all right. I didn't want any."

I drain the bottle, wipe my chin with the back of my hand. "Okay."

We drive. The clouds have swallowed the sun now, transforming the sky to a thundering wash of orange and gray that gathers in a soup of broken marble in the air, thick and looming, and when I breathe in I smell a faint aroma of peat and vegetation and burnt tarmac. I roll down the window a little, and the outside ushers itself in through the gap. Rosemary saturates the air, pungent and fragrant, its delicate fragrance mixed with the heavier, muggy odor of rich, rocky moss. I feel a warm breeze on my face, and when I look up, the turrets of the mountain loom ahead, raised and rigid, at the summit of the gods. A world ruled by a nature we will never truly understand. I give the turrets one more look, then, turning back to my notebook, finish writing what I recall about my dream.

"What music do you like?"

I look up. "Why are you asking me that?" I close my notebook and slip it into my rucksack.

"Just thought it'd be nice to talk, you know?" He shrugs. "Break up the journey."

I stare at him. "Oh. Okay."

"Well?"

"Well what?"

"What sort of music do you like?"

I hesitate. Is this a trick question? There was no intonation that I traced in his voice, but I am never entirely certain. "Classical," I finally say. "I like classical music."

"Oh, yeah? Cool. You like Mozart?"

"Mozart died on December fifth, 1791. I never knew Mozart, therefore, I cannot say whether I like him or not. I do, however, appreciate his music."

Chris' mouth is hanging open. I take my gaze to the mountains rolling past, satisfied that I have given a sufficiently social answer and the conversation is closed.

"Aren't you going to ask me what music I like?"

So we are doing this. I clench my jaw. "Why?"

"Because that's what people do."

I face him and try very hard to make an effort. "Christopher, what sort of music do you like?"

"It's Chris. Just Chris." He smiles, and for some reason I think of Goofy in the Disney movies that my brother used to put on for me the year Papa died. "Grunge," he says. "Nirvana, that kind of thing; you know, Kurt Cobain."

He looks at me. Is he awaiting a response? "Okay," I decide to say. It must satisfy him, possibly, because he keeps talking.

"And don't tell anyone, but I kinda like Taylor Swift."

"Do you know her?"

"What?"

He says "what" a lot.

"No." He laughs, eyes flitting between me and the road. "No. I mean, I like her music. You know, 'Red,' 'Twenty-Two,' 'Shake It Off.' You've heard of them, the songs, right?"

"No."

"What? You must be, like, the only person on the planet who hasn't heard of her. What, you don't even know 'Shake It Off'?"

"No." I can feel my irritation rising, and start to tap my foot, when Chris does something unexpected and strange: he sings.

"This is 'Shake It Off,'" he says before relaying to me what I assume is the musical song he refers to.

I watch him closely. He appears to be enjoying himself, I think: smiling, his head shaking and bobbing so much that I am surprised he can keep track of the road at all.

"Your singing and movement is endangering the car and therefore us," I say.

He ceases singing, and I think that is the end of it, but he simply continues to talk. A vague tiredness at the effort required of me in order to cope with the interaction starts to form in the base of my body and work its way to my head.

"See," he says now, shifting down a gear as we swerve around a sharp bend that takes us farther up the mountain and into the looming clouds. "What I love about Taylor is that she's a country singer at heart. I love a little country. I mean, sure"—another gear drop as we rise—"I like grunge and stuff, but country?" He whistles. "That's where it's at. Gets to your heart and soul, you know?"

I don't—at all—but, unsure why, I reply, "Yes."

"My mama loved country." He trails off, and for a moment I think I can see tears in his eyes. I think of my own mama back in Madrid and wonder if she is safe.

Chris drives for twenty, perhaps thirty seconds more, and we sit in silence. For me, it helps. The exhaustion that was bubbling from having to converse is subsiding slightly now, and the headache at the front of my forehead is slowly fading away. I keep the window down and let the air fan my face, all the while keeping my eyes directed not just to the front of the car, but also to the back so, if anyone is following us, I will know.

"I told you I was from Idaho," Chris suddenly says after he negotiates a sharp left bend.

I don't reply. Initially, I am unsure what reaction he expects me to give, but then, after a second, he talks on and I begin to realize, with relief, that when Chris chats, he doesn't always expect a response.

"Mom and Pop are from Idaho, too. Pa still lives there. Remarried." He shakes his head. "That's why I got into computers, you know? I hated his new wife. I was young and they had a new baby, and so …" He swallows, pushes back a stray hair. "I threw myself into the tech world, and voilà!" He smiles. "You got yours truly: a word-class hacker."

His knuckles are white on the steering wheel, and when I observe him in more detail, I see that his cheeks are streaked with rogue tears that leave dirty tracks on his sun-washed skin, and sweat trickles down his temples at anarchic angles.

"What is your mother's name?" I ask.

"Huh?" He turns the car to the right. "It's … it *was* Janet."

"Janet. The name Janet is the feminine form of John. It means 'God has been gracious.'"

"Okay."

"Your father's name—what is that?"

"What?"

"You said 'what' again."

"Oh, right, yeah, sorry. It's …" He clears his throat. "Jack. My pop's name is Jack."

"The meaning of the name Jack originates from Jakin, which is a medieval diminutive of the name John. In the Middle Ages, it was a slang name that meant 'man.' Jack is considered now an American baby name. Do you have siblings?"

"Huh?"

"Do you have siblings?"

"Er, yeah. A sister."

"Name?"

He lets out a small trickle of a laugh. "Sarah. Her name's Sarah."

"Sarah means 'princess.' In the Bible, she was the wife of Abraham. What are your hobbies?"

He laughs again. "What is this, an interview?"

"Yes."

The laugh drops. "Oh. Oh, right."

"I like you," I say. "I am interviewing you to see if we are compatible."

"Compatible?" There is a curve in the road up ahead that creates a blind spot in the rearview mirror.

I look to Chris. "Compatible. Yes. That is what I said."

"I know, I know, but …" He shrugs. "Okay. You want to know my hobbies? I like computer games. *Dungeons and Dragons*. That's my hobby. As well as hacking."

"And listening to Taylor Swift."

He laughs out loud now. Flecks of spit from his mouth pepper the window, but there are tears in his eyes.

I become concerned. "You are crying. Are you sad? Have I upset you?"

"Wh—*no*. No, you're just …" He sighs, sinks back into his seat. "You're just so funny."

"I am?"

He nods. "With a capital *F*."

We sit in silence, and I am suddenly very aware of the heat from his body. It is warm, hot, like coals of a fire, and I begin to wonder if I have said the right thing, if I have talked as I should. If I have been adequately friendly.

"Okay," Chris says after several seconds have passed, "since you got to interview me, how about you?" He shifts to face me. "I like you, so what can you tell me about you? You got family?"

"Yes. Everyone does."

"Brothers? Sisters?"

I pause. "I have a brother."

"That's cool."

"Cool." I try the word out as if it were a hat or a new jacket. "Yes. Cool."

The road behind us goes straight, restoring my view behind us, where dark clouds bulge with rain.

"And are you close, you and your brother?" he asks.

"Close?"

"You know, do you love each other?"

"He loves me very much," I say. I stop, not wanting to continue, unsure what to say, then remember Balthus' advice to me and so I carry on.

"When my papa died, I was ten. My brother's name is Ramon, which means 'protector.' He looked after me after the death of my papa."

"Your papa was … he was nice?"

"Yes," I say. "He was nice. And when I was eight and I wet my pants in my bedroom because I wouldn't stop writing about composers and medical procedures, Papa cleaned me up and hid all the dirty linen from my mama and the housekeeper. My brother Ramon often had to do the same for me. Sometimes, because the girls at school wouldn't talk to me, my brother used to put on Disney movies and dress up as Mickey Mouse. I used to get depressed, at least twice a month, because no one would talk to me and because I couldn't understand how to talk to them. Sometimes, I would forget moments of time entirely. I recorded two hundred episodes of complete memory lapse between the ages of eleven and twenty-one."

I stop, satisfied that Chris now has information to process, facts for his interview of friendship. But Chris just stares at me. Not just glances, but stares straight out, eyes not on the road at all, but fixed on me as if he were blinking into a pool or a lake.

"I want you to stop looking at me now," I say, suddenly nervous. "Please."

"Huh? What? Oh, yes, of course. Sorry. Sorry."

We take another blind bend and the car swerves, and I slide

in the seat. I dart upward, check the mirrors. "What was that?"

"Nothing. Just a rock in the road. I think." He scratches his scalp. "Sorry, I should have been watching, but you …"

As he trails off, I crane my head backward and scan the tracks behind. The rock is there, the one Chris mentioned, about sixty centimeters in diameter, but something else is, too. "Slow down."

"What? Why?"

There is a black van, and it's getting nearer. Adrenaline shoots straight through me, head to toe. I slip back into my seat. "Someone is following us."

Chris leans into the rearview mirror. "Where?"

"Is there another route to where we're traveling?"

"Shit. Yes. No. I think so."

I glance behind us. The van is approaching faster now. "Quick. Do you know another route?"

"What? Fuck. Yes, yes." He jerks the steering wheel to the left and we veer down a side road, dirt flying through the air like shrapnel.

He slams his foot on the gas pedal, and the car screeches away. The van starts to disappear, slow at first, then faster, until it is barely there at all. My fingers grip the seat as the air whips in through the open windows, sending Chris' hair flapping in the wind.

I allow my shoulders to soften a little. "This road will take us to Balthus still, yes?"

"Yes. Yes." He gulps, and when he grips the wheel, the veins in his forearms bulge. "Jesus, that was scary." Sweat steams from his brow. "Who in the hell are you?"

"I told you. I am Dr. Maria Martinez. I know the governor—"

"Okay! Please. It's just that I'm not used to this and you are so calm and—" There is a loud crack. "Fuck!'

A spider web has suddenly appeared around a small hole in the rear window. I jerk my head toward it.

Chris has been shot.

# CHAPTER 17

**MONTSERRAT MOUNTAIN VILLAGE, NEAR BARCELONA**
*25 Hours and 45 Minutes to Confinement*
"Oh, God. It hurts, it hurts, it fucking hurts!"

I check the mirror. There are no vehicles in the background, no other cars on the road, and even though I scour the area for any sign of the black van, there is still no evidence of it anywhere.

Chris cries out. I whip around to him now and crane to get a view of his wound. He is bleeding from his right shoulder.

"Stop the car."

"What? No." His hand slips from the wheel, and we slide across the road. The car skids, spinning in a complete circle, Chris screaming, and at first I think we will stop, but then, on the final turn, the vehicle veers to the right and the car lurches forward and nose-dives and we skid to a halt.

"Oh, Jesus!"

I ignore Chris and peer over through the windshield and stop dead.

The entire car is dipping forward, and below is a sharp drop of perhaps three thousand feet into the valley below.

"Fuck!" Chris shouts. "Fuck!"

"Shouting will not help," I say. I inch my torso forward, instinctively checking for the angle and pivot point of the car as it rests on the road's edge, while outside, starlings flit and fly and goats watch from a hilltop ahead.

"What are you doing?" His voice is high, screeching.

I turn to him. "We are currently stuck on ..." I glance through the window to confirm my suspicion. "... a metal guardrail. That is the only thing preventing us from falling down the mountain."

"What? Oh, fucking great."

"You said 'what' again, and no, this is not fucking great. This is a difficult situation. So I want you to lean forward."

"What? Are you crazy?"

"No. I am not. I simply have Asperger's. Lean forward."

Rocks trickle past the tires, clattering down the mountainside and into the valley far below.

Chris begins to hyperventilate.

"You are panicking," I say. "You need to inhale big, deep breaths."

His eyes go wide at me, but he does it; he starts to breathe at a steadier rate.

"Good. Now ..." I look at the guardrail; it is stable but crumpled. I am going to count to three. On *three*, I want you to lean forward; then, when I say so, I want you to lean back in your seat as hard as you can." I look at him. "Do you understand?"

He nods, breathing hard. Satisfied that he comprehends what is required of him, I unbuckle my seat belt and begin to clamber over my seat and into the back of the car. It lurches. A loud crack echoes in the air, and rubble and dust tumble over into the sky.

"Shit," Chris says. "Shit, shit, shit!"

I make it into the back and slide around so I am facing forward. My heart rockets, but I feel calm and in control, training from the past kicking in now to the present. I check the windshield. The hood is teetering now, the guardrail bent outward a few more degrees, causing the balance point of the car to shift.

"We're going to fall!"

"Negative," I say. "By initial calculation, we will not fall immediately. If we remain as we are, it will be one, perhaps two, minutes before we completely slide over the edge."

"Oh, holy crap!"

I scan every corner of the car and do my final sums. It can work, but only if Chris complies. "I am going to count now. Are you ready?"

He nods. "Uh-huh. Mmmmm."

I glance to his arm. It is bleeding quite a bit, staining his T-shirt and the cloth of the car seat. I look forward. The sun strains up from behind black clouds, casting a weak orange glow over our crisis.

"I am going to count now."

He nods and grits his teeth.

"One."

The car lurches. Chris swears. "Two." A bird of prey wheels in the sky, passing a long shadow over us.

"Three! Lean back!"

Chris cries out, slamming himself as hard as he can into his seat, the force of it juddering the vehicle. As he does, I throw the whole weight of my body into the very rear crease of the car, where the back window sits cracked and broken, ramming my arms and hips and legs into the area so that every ounce of me is weighted in one point.

The car begins to rock.

"Do … do I stay back?" Chris yells.

"Yes. Remain where you are, putting on as much pressure as you can."

"Okay!"

The car keeps moving. I glance out to the side and see the guardrail begin to bend more, sagging slightly outward.

"Is it working?"

I shove my shoulder into the corner. "Yes. Stay in the seat."

Maneuvering my elbow now, I start to sway, to rock my body in the small space. At first, nothing really moves, the entire metal casing of the vehicle suspended, creaking and groaning as it seesaws between the road below and the wide-open air beyond. I do the calculation in my head. If we remain like this, we will begin to tip back over the edge and onto the road again, but we need momentum.

"I want you to lean forward again, then back once more."

"What?"

"You said 'what' again."

"I know what I said!"

I go quiet at Chris' raised voice, the sound ringing in my brain and mixing with the creaking and clattering of the car.

"I … I'm sorry," he says, exhaling. "I … Sorry. I'm just … I'm just scared."

I look up at him and press my lips together. "I don't like it when people shout at me."

"I'm sorry. Just tell me what to do. You want me to lean forward again, right?"

"Yes," I say after a second, regaining my composure. "I need you to do exactly as we did before, so the car will tip back to the road."

He gulps. "Got it."

I look forward. "One, two …" The car swings a little. "Three!"

Slam! Chris' back rams into the seat, and my body and arms are raised a little higher than last time as, between us, we teeter the car backward, tipping, swaying, until there is an almighty slam as the back wheels hit the road.

"Whooo!" Chris smiles for the first time. "Fuck!"

"Put the car in gear," I say. "Maneuver it around, back to the road."

"Okay!"

He does as I ask and, hands on the wheel now, spins it through his fingers, back and forth until, gradually, the car veers to the left, then right.

"Holy fucking Jesus!"

"Start driving."

"What, now?"

"Now."

I check that my rucksack and notebook and belongings are safe, then turn back.

"Stop the car," I say.

"Roger that."

"Who is Roger?"

Chris slams on the brakes and we come to an abrupt halt, our bodies flying forward then smashing back.

"Jesus, that was close," he says, exhaling hard and heavy. He wipes his forehead. "I mean, fuck. I could see right over the edge and—God, my arm is killing me and"—I undo my seat belt—"the road was, like, there one minute, gone the next. Shit, is that van we saw anywhere near? I mean—"

I climb onto Chris.

"Hey! What the fuck are you doing?"

I straddle him and, ripping off his sleeve, check his wound. "I am a doctor. You have been shot. I can help you."

He mutters something, but my gaze is fixed on his arm. From his earlier cries of pain, I expect to see a deep, serious wound, but it is simply grazed, the skin peppered with glass shrapnel and with no bullet entry at all. I let my shoulders relax a little and exhale. "You've not been shot. Your dermis is grazed."

"Huh?" He looks to his arm.

I immediately drop to the floor, search for the bullet, and find it lodged in the footwell by Chris' running shoe.

"Hey!" he says.

I pick up the bullet and, clambering back over him, drag out my notebook and check my data. I locate the make of the bullet in three seconds, holding it into the fading sunshine as I understand completely what I am looking at: it is Project ammunition. I have used it before; I just do not know when or where.

Chris leans over. "Hey—your drawing is the same as the bullet.

How the fuck is that possible?"

I slap my notebook shut and, pocketing the bullet, slip over a protesting Chris, open his car door, and jump to the ground. I am immediately hit by the heavy, rain-threatening air. It is warm on my skin, soothing silk after the rough chaos, the wet, pungent aroma of vegetation from the mountains hitting my nose, calming me for some reason, and even though I know I shouldn't, that we could be followed again, I allow my three seconds' rest against the hood of the dusty car, as I close my eyes, images of the Project, Dr. Andersson and my ransacked villa, with SIM cards and iron bars whipping through my mind. In the distance, in the earthly, majestic presence of the Montserrat Mountain, wild goats snort and mew, bats click and squeal in their dark roosts, geckos squawk. Life, carrying on, oblivious.

I reach into the car and start to pull Chris out. "I will drive."

"Hey! Maria, what are you doing?"

I pause. This is the first time he has used my name since we met. "I am helping you. You are injured. I will drive."

"Yeah, but you don't have to drag me. I can get myself out."

I step back, uncertain what to do. He is injured; he can't drive; I can. It is logical, simple, so why did he push me away?

"You are hurt," I say after a moment. "I am … I am trying to help."

He blows out air. "Yeah, well," he says, dusting himself down, "dragging me out of the damn car without actually saying a word to me isn't my idea of helping. You're supposed to ask first."

"Oh." I remain very still, unsure what to do. *Think.* In prison, Patricia told me that people like to hear the word "please." Could that work now? I make myself look at Chris. "Christopher …" I pause. "Chris. Please would you vacate the driver's seat so I can drive? I would be a better driver than you at this current moment given your minor injury and mild shock from our near-death fall. Plus, I am faster."

At first, I do not believe he will move, so solid is his body in the seat. But then he does the Goofy stare and smile combination again, frowns and tuts, muttering, "For Chrissake," under his breath, and he jumps down from the car.

I slip into the driver's seat as Chris takes the opposite side, go to switch on the ignition, then pause, keys dangling in midair. "I have trouble conversing with people."

He looks at me. "You don't say." His hair slips into his eyes, and I can feel the gentle warmth of him, hear the one-two rhythm of his breath.

"So," he says after a moment, "it's just, you know, a shrapnel wound in my shoulder?"

"Correct. The wound requires cleaning, but it is not serious."

"And you can drive fast?"

"Of course."

"Good." He slips on his seatbelt. "Because I think the van that was following us is back."

I jerk my eyes to the mirror. On the horizon is a black vehicle approaching at reasonable speed. Slamming my foot flat on the gas pedal, I spin the car around and pull away fast.

The serrated mountain range around us remains unmoved, watching.

# CHAPTER 18

*Present Day*

When I awake, all I see is darkness.

Slowly, the room sways into focus, and as I blink, the bulb above my head swings from the ceiling. I smack my lips together and feel a dry, crumbling sediment around the edges of them—saliva crackled from the effects of the drugs. At first, woozy, I forget where I am, and then, coming to a little, I remember my situation and sit up with a start.

"Ramon?"

"You were out for a while."

I squint to see my brother, the light above casting a pale, sallow glow on his skin. He is sitting on a crate one and a half meters in front of me. His legs are crossed and his arms are folded, and by his side sits a navy-blue box with gold edging that, when the yellow beam passes over it, glows in the dark. I look behind him. The steps to the exit stretch out in the shadows.

"Untie me," I croak.

He bends in, then crouches forward. I immediately recoil. "Hey, hey, it's okay, it's okay." He holds up a hand, in it a plastic bottle. "I just have some water."

I stay pressed back as, gradually, my sight drifts downward. In his hand, I can just see the outline of a clear plastic bottle and cup. He takes the cup, unscrews the bottle cap, and, tipping his head left, pours some liquid and raises it to my lips. "Drink. You'll feel better."

I let Ramon put the cup to my lips, and I sip. The liquid is cooling, and I begin to gulp it down, water dribbling out the corners of my mouth, down past my chin and onto my chest as the coolness of it all calms me where the drugs have raised my temperature.

The cup drained, Ramon moves back, drags the crate nearer to where I am, and, reaching to his side, switches on a flashlight. A shaft of bright white beams into the room, but my eyes are unused to it and I blink over and over, desperate to lift my hand and shield my eyes.

"Do you feel better now?"

"The light is too much for me," I manage to say.

"Oh, of course. I forgot—sorry."

He angles the flashlight to the left, uncrosses his legs, and shifts in his seat. The rope on my wrists digs into me, and there is a sickness in my stomach as the stench of mold takes hold.

"You were talking in your sleep," he says.

"I was not asleep. I was being drugged."

He goes quiet. After a while, he says, "Do you remember how you used to run to me when you had a bad dream?"

"Yes."

"Papa used to help you."

"Ramon," I say, "have the Project said they will hurt you if you don't sit with me like this? Have they said they will hurt you if you take the needle out of my arm?"

"*What?*" He drops his foot to the floor.

"The Project hurt people. They could hurt you. They could hurt Mama."

"M, I don't know what you are talking about, but stop. No one is going to hurt Mama." He leans forward. "Especially not you. Not if I have anything to do with it."

There's a ripple of confusion and something else: fear.

"What do you mean?"

He shakes his head. "Drop it."

"Drop what?"

"This. Here." He exhales. "All of it. Just stop."

"Stop what?"

"All of it!" His voice ricochets in my head as he rounds on me now and gets so close to my face that I can barely take a breath without breathing in his own exhaled carbon dioxide.

"I love you, M, I do, but Jesus!" He steps back now. I gasp out a breath, gulping hard, and my chest feels as if it will burst from the pressure, but before I can really inhale again, Ramon is back, tears streaking down his face.

"I'm sorry," he says. "M, I didn't mean to shout. It's just that ..." He trails off. "I am so worried about you. This"—he gestures to the room—"this is the only answer."

"This ..." I pause, my throat scratchy, the fear in my gut a ball of lead now. "This is not the answer, Ramon. They are lying to you. The Project lies. They—"

"Ssshh. Do you know this song?" And then, out of the blue, he begins to sing. *"At the gate of heaven little shoes they are selling ..."*

A crackle of worry prickles all over me now as I realize what my brother is singing: it is the lullaby Papa used to sing to me when he was alive, the same lullaby I used to hear in my nightmares when I would wake up in a sweat after dreaming about the Project.

*"For the little bare-footed angels there dwelling ..."*

My pulse starts to hammer, and I raise my head and see that my brother has closed his eyes, one hand rested on his chest, the other on the blue box beside him.

*"Slumber, my baby; slumber, my baby; slumber, my baby; arru, arru."*

He ceases singing and keeps his eyes shut. I am shaking. I dart my eyes around the room, see the door shut and bolted with a small, metal touch-pad box, and feel my entire body ripple and crack as

I watch my brother hum now, into the black air, a song that, aside from me, only Papa and Black Eyes knew.

"How do you know that song?" I say, forcing the words out from my brain to my mouth.

But he does not answer, just hums into the air.

"Ramon, how do you know that song?"

He holds up one hand, palm side out, and, opening his eyes so the liquid brown of them flashes in the white light of the torch that beams up in front of him, he ceases humming and places his hand back down on the box beside him and opens the lid.

"I know it from your journal."

## MONTSERRAT MOUNTAIN ROAD, NEAR BARCELONA
*25 Hours and 33 Minutes to Confinement*

I concentrate on the road. It is long and winding, and, to the side, trees stoop buckled by the edge, half-crumbled buildings lying unwanted and forgotten in the dirt. Three minutes and thirteen seconds have passed, and the van is still there, cruising at a normal pace behind us.

"They're still following us," Chris says.

I look. "Yes."

"So let me get this right: this Project has been around for years and you only found out about it with Balthus, when you were in prison?"

Chris has been questioning me about the Project, and I have found myself telling him some of what I know. I do not know why, exactly. Perhaps, despite myself, I trust him. That Balthus recommends him is, for me, an essential reassurance, but it is more than that. I like him, this Chris, and it makes me feel as if I can talk to him, that feeling, that odd emotion of what? Pleasure? Happiness? It is not something I am used to.

Chris falls quiet and clutches his shoulder, and when he loosens his grip, blood oozes between his fingers. I reach over, press his hand into the wound, then glance into the rearview mirror. The van is farther in the distance now. I calculate the time ratio in my head: the vehicle has slowed down.

"It would be optimal to create a diversion now," I say, eyes still on the road behind us.

"Really?" Chris turns, looks back. "They are still following, but shouldn't we just keep driving?"

"Negative. It is too risky."

Ahead, there is a sign for a town two kilometers to the east. "That place," I say, pointing. "Is it in the direction we need to go?"

Chris squints at the sign. "Yes. I think so."

"You either know or do not know."

"All right. Jesus." A pause. "Yes, it's in the direction we need to go."

I shoot one more glance to the rear, then, flipping the car around, screech off toward the town. Chris' phone bleeps.

"Text," he says, "from Balthus. He's there now, waiting for us."

Two minutes later, I park the car down a dark lane and peer out the window. The town is quiet, and in the deserted alleyway to our left, a solitary branch waves languidly in the breeze. The maze of narrow dusty roads has allowed me to backtrack so that when I check, the black van is nowhere to be seen. I pull on the hand brake and scan the area, instinctively calculating ratios and trajectories and routes of escape, but the place is empty. There are no people in view, just shuttered, sand-colored buildings, scorched beige grass rippling in the breeze, crumpled empty Coke cans, and, upon first count, sixty-seven discarded cigarette butts. There is one by the front of the car, and on it I can see an imprint of red lipstick around the circumference, and I find myself wondering who would have smoked it, where they were headed. I imagine a party, perhaps, with friends, all of them laughing as they sway, arms interlocked, along the road, happy, chatting, years of friendship behind and ahead of them. I have seen people do this. From afar.

I unbuckle my seat belt and kick open the door. "We need to go."

"Where?"

I walk seven paces and analyze the area. Neon lights blink on a building eighty yards ahead, and I have to shield my eyes as my brain registers and logs every single bright orange flash. I point to it. "What is that?"

Chris, clutching his arm, walks over. "Hey? Oh, some sort of inn or club, I guess."

My hand stays propped on my brow. "This club place could provide essential cover. It could help us slip out to another exit so we can locate another car, perhaps, but there is a problem."

"What?"

"Do you have any headphones in your car?"

"What?"

"Headphones. They are items placed in or over the ears, often used to listen to—"

"No, no, I know what they are, just wondering why you need them."

I look over to the neon lights, to the club, glance to the lipstick-smeared cigarette butt. "I have trouble with very loud noises, especially when they happen all at once."

Chris smiles, and it reaches his eyes, the smile, creases fanning, but it isn't the Goofy smile. This one is different, more downturned. "I have earbuds in the trunk," he says, and goes to the car.

I watch him for a second, and then my sight locks back on to the lipstick stain on the road.

"Oh, shit."

My head snaps up, expecting from Chris' swearing that his wound is worse, but he is staring down the road, into the distance. I follow his line of sight.

The van—it is back.

"We have to go," I say. "Now."

This time, Chris does not protest. He jumps out of the car, throws me my rucksack and the headphones, and we start to run.

A gunshot rings out. Then another, the sound hammering a hole in my head.

"This way," I yell, pointing to the neon lights, both of us ducking.

One more gunshot cracks into the air. I hear it fly past my head, and pain stings my skin, blood trickling down my neck.

"You okay?" Chris asks, but I do not reply. We negotiate a cluster of trash cans, their height giving us good cover, and reach the neon sign in under twenty seconds, panting for breath. A black spider scuttles past my feet.

I press my fingers to my ear and feel warm, sticky blood—just a nick. Another shot shatters the air.

"What do we do?" Chris yells.

I look at the flashing neon sign, the scrawled black paint of the club's facade, a faint throb of music pumping from inside, the laughter of people partying during the day instead of working. It's going to be too loud for me, almost impossible, but it will provide cover and will scramble the trail for anyone following us.

I grip the earbuds tight and slide them into my ears.

"We are going inside."

As we move, the spider halts then darts away beneath the stone foundations of the building.

# CHAPTER 19

## MONTSERRAT MOUNTAIN VILLAGE, NEAR BARCELONA
*25 Hours and 28 Minutes to Confinement*

The club, once we are inside, is a heaving sea of people—dancing, drinking, talking loudly to be heard over the music—and it does not stop moving. The heat from the bodies is high, and I sweat and stand near the entrance and find that my feet won't work. The earbuds are plugged firmly into my ears, but even so, the music, the deep rhythm of it, penetrates, and every thump of the bass vibrates through the floor and shakes in my legs and bones.

My breathing becomes short. I try to focus, to fix my concentration on something, anything—my hands, the light pressure of the buds against my ear canals—but I can feel myself slipping away, zoning out to deal with the chaos in my mind.

"Whoa," Chris says, "cool! They're playing Nirvana, 'Lithium.'" He stops. "Hey? Hey, are you okay?"

But I cannot answer. Lights are flashing now in all the primary colors of blue, yellow, and red, creating secondary beams of orange, purple, green, and pink. There is intense flashing of neon lights, and I instantly check out, incapable now of making myself focus on anything, and Chris, when I watch him, is speaking and I try to concentrate on what he is saying, but my whole body and my entire head feel infiltrated and assaulted by the noise and the people and the dubstep so much that I struggle to determine the different sounds Chris' words make.

"Pull me away!" I shout to him.

He cups a hand to his ear. "What?"

"I said pull me away. Pull me to the other side of this club. Now." I swallow. "Please."

He hesitates, a frown spreading on his forehead, and then, finally, he grabs my arms, and though I flinch at the touch, he drags me across the throng of people, through the dance floor.

It is awful. Crowds of heads and bodies and arms dance and gather all around me without, it seems, any specific direction to where they are going. It is all random, the movements of the people, the shouting and laughing and screeching setting off all the time around me like fireworks, and as Chris pulls me along, someone bumps into me, then another and another, and each time it makes me jump and I look to them, unsure why they would be touching me, the shock of the sensation temporarily forcing me to lose any flicker of focus I may have. And then I move again and I say to myself, *Get across the room. Get to the exit. Get away from the people firing guns.* I say it over and over, fixate on the verbal process, hoping it will be my thread line out, but the music beat is heavy and I lose the trace of my thought. Desperate as we move, jostled, I start reciting mathematical theory to give my mind even a tiny bit of order and numerical control until, finally, we reach the far exit, where a long metal handle spans the door and where the noise just slightly dissipates.

Chris comes to my side. "Are you okay? You're murmuring."

I watch his lips move, and try to focus. The earbuds are still in, and I take one out and try to slow down.

"I have never been to a club," I say, gulping.

"I … right, right." He pauses, glances around the room, then looks back to me. "Breathe, yeah? Do what you told me to do back when I was shot, and breathe."

I do as he says, and feel the tightness in my chest lighten a little as the music in the club changes to a slower beat.

"Awesome!" Chris says, grinning. "Taylor Swift! This one's called 'Begin Again.' You like it? It's different from her other ones, 'cause this one's about hope, you know, not breaking up and stuff, and …"

Chris talks on as I blink and look around and see that, mercifully, the neon lights have faded, replaced by lower, orange-yellow glows that fall in soft puddles on the floor as couples now, men and women, women and women, men and men, all stand two by two, their arms locked around each other's hips, swaying to the slow tune, to the chorus and words and gently sung melody, and I get a feeling, a sensation in my stomach, of a knot that leaves a hole behind it that I want to fill but don't know how.

Chris stops talking about Taylor Swift and tugs at my arm.

I flinch, and he pulls away.

"Why do people find this kind of environment gratifying?"

He shrugs. "I dunno, it's … it's fun, I guess."

I look around. *Fun.* I consider the word. "Fun," I say, turning now to Chris.

He smiles. "Yeah." He pauses, makes eye contact, and I force my eyes to do the same, not allowing them to look down as they automatically tend to do, but instead direct them at Chris' face, then look away, then back again, trying to mirror what he is doing, without it ending up with me staring at him for too long.

"Are you all right?" he says as I am trying to copy what he does.

"What?"

"You said 'what' again." He grins and shrugs his shoulders. "See? Fun."

Ahead of us is an exit, and as Taylor Swift continues to sing, I shuffle past Chris, stop, and observe the door. For a second, I turn from the door and watch, from the muffling cocoon of the headphones, the swell of arms and legs entangled on the dance floor, the smiles plastered to sweat-drenched twentysomething-year-old faces.

And I think: *Is this what it looks like, fun? Is this what I have missed?*

Chris catches up.

"We are going out this way," I tell him, pointing to the door that, from what I can deduce, should take medium force to pry open.

"This one? Isn't it wired?"

"Negative. There is no alarm or trigger; therefore, no alert can be generated, therefore keeping our cover safe."

"What?"

I point to the door. "We have to go through the exit."

Chris leans in. "What? Did you say you want me to open it?"

"No, I can do—"

"I'll do it. Don't you worry." Stepping in front of me, he pulls at the handle, but nothing budges. Moving back, he smears sweat from his brow and, sizing up the exit, slams his body into the door, his torso lighting up with an orange slow-dance glow as he lunges forward. Yet still the door remains shut.

"*Ow.*" Chris rubs his arm. "Fuck."

"It won't open," he shouts as I barge past him. "We need another way out."

The music has increased in volume, and I can feel myself beginning to zone out again. I have to get out of here.

"Move."

Chris frowns. "What?"

But a neon light flashes, just one, and with the crowd ahead laughing now, shouting, the cacophony of voices rising, I don't want to spend a second longer in here. Taking a run up, I launch myself so hard, so desperate to escape, that the door flies open on the first go and I spill out into the fresh air, coughing as I catch my breath.

Chris runs out behind me, slamming the door shut. "Fuck, you're strong!"

I catch my breath, relieved to be outside in the quiet, the music from the club now a low thrum but nothing else. Spitting out the stale air of the club onto the dirt, I lift my head and scan the alley.

It is dimly lit under the umbrella of dark clouds and weak sunshine, and when I breathe in I get old cigarette smoke, asphalt, and distant damp vegetation.

I check the time. "We need transport."

"Oh. Right. Yeah."

Turning right, I scour the road and spot a lone red car—small, Spanish-made, box-shaped, sturdy. I stride over to it and find myself wondering who left it here. A young university student, perhaps, or a local waitress working the summer in Barcelona who is now on a trip home to see her boyfriend, catching up with old school friends, maybe. I find myself contemplating what that must be like: to be free to move without hiding. How nice that must be.

Chris catches up, and as he looks around, I am already examining the vehicle. I have never, to my knowledge, broken into a car before, but it is possible that I have done so while with the Project, while influenced by drugs or by something or someone. I think through what I need to do, and am so deep in thought that at first, I don't hear the click. It sounds again, and I jump, alert, but when I look inside the car, I get a surprise: Chris is in the passenger seat.

"How did you break in?"

"I didn't." He smiles, all teeth. "The door was open. And look." He holds out his palm. "The keys were in the glove box."

"Oh. Okay."

"So let's hit the road, yeah? Go get Balthus. Don't want to run into, you know, those guns again."

"Yes." I glance up and down the road and check that all is clear. "Yes. Where are we going? Our destination—I do not know it, since I thought it best in case we are captured."

"Huh? Oh, right. We're going to Montserrat Monastery. It's straight on—just take a left at the top, then keep following the road on up. It's only five minutes or so."

Slipping into the driver's seat, I take the keys, watch the mirrors, and start the engine. I throw a sideways glance at Chris. He is checking his shoulder wound and wincing, and as I watch him, a strange thing happens: I smile.

He looks straight at me. I whip my head forward, my features arranging themselves back into a frown.

"Um, Maria?"

"What?" I say, eyes ahead, not daring to look, adrenaline rushing into my bloodstream.

"You've still got my headphones on."

"Oh." I look down at myself. The wire is swinging in front of my abdomen, the bottom of it gathered in a circle in my lap.

Feeling my cheeks flush, I slip off the headphones, hand them to Chris, and, wiping sweat from my face, kick in the clutch and start to drive away. Even though my eyes are focused on the road, I sense Chris staring at me; then he leans his head back and closes his eyes.

In the mirror I see his face, see his chest rise and fall. I drive, counting each breath, and find that the way it moves in time with my own gives me a strange sense of comfort.

# CHAPTER 20

Ramon opens the lid of the blue box by his side and extracts something that, I realize with a gasp, is my journal from my childhood and teenage years. The cover is hard and black, the word JOURNAL embossed in gold lettering on the front, and when Ramon handles it, his fingers sliding over the once-shiny casing, the tips touch two initials that sit tucked in the bottom right corner of the front page.

"Initial 'M. M.,'" Ramon says now, his eyes on the journal and then rising, slowly, to me. "It's in Papa's writing."

I feel suddenly unsafe, vulnerable, but I cannot pinpoint why. I shift in the seat, the rope on my wrists and ankles digging into my skin so I can feel it against my bones. "How did you get my journal?"

His hand glides over the cream pages as he opens the book, and when again he glances upward, his eyes are damp. "It was at Mama's house."

I blink in the semidark, thinking. He is right: I stored my journal along with others at Mama's before I left for England and my secondment in the London hospital. So why can I recall that and not the events in the run-up to my arrival here?

I look over to Ramon, now sitting on the crate, and try to

understand what is happening. The flashlight he has brought shines bright over to the far wall, and I want to look around, study what sits behind me, but each time I move my neck, a sharp pain shoots from my shoulder right down to the base of my spine, and my muscles cry out to be relieved of the stressful position that they have been in now for a long time.

Beside me, the timer ticks. I track it, focusing on the ordered sound of it, getting some small relief from it, from the odd routine in the chaos that the predictability of it provides. If I can determine the space between doses of the drug I am being administered, I can perhaps determine what drug it is, but it will be hard. Many medicines are given at similarly consecutive doses, and the only hope I have is to determine which drug I believe the Project may have used.

Which drug my brother may have used.

"So," Ramon says now, "let's look through your journal."

Panic flies up. "No."

He pauses, looks up. "M, it's okay." He turns to a page and lets his finger trace the words that, even in the weak light, I can see are mine, scribbled years ago when I tracked my thoughts every day, when I was trying to forge a record of what was happening to me, even though I could not fully remember it all. I start to get hot. I start to run through scenarios of possible negative outcomes and eventualities in my head as I imagine what events could happen if anyone could read my private thoughts. There is such a thing as too much information. That's why I don't like to look into people's eyes.

"Let's see," Ramon says now, "if this journal of yours will help you." He breathes out. "If it will help us all understand a little bit more about you."

"Ramon, no."

But, instead of halting, he turns one more page, and as his fingers move, the timer beside me ticks, and a spider scurries along the soot-stone floor and disappears into a hole that the darkness swallows up in a single bite.

## MONTSERRAT MOUNTAIN, NEAR BARCELONA
*25 Hours and 20 Minutes to Confinement*

The clouds are swollen and black, the sun struggling to push past as we drive up the mountain to the abbey.

The car we have taken is old and the tires splashy, so each time I take a bend in the road, we jostle inside the vehicle, and in order to stay calm, I have to make myself focus on what we are doing, where we are going.

I have not detected the black van since we began the last leg of our journey. Chris now checks the road, his head hanging out of the eternally rolled-down window, and as I watch him, I worry that because we have stolen a car, we will be jailed.

"We must return the car," I say, taking a left and then a right as the route winds up toward the mountaintop.

Chris drags his head back into the car. "What did you say?"

I repeat my sentence, and he rakes his fingers through his hair where the wind has shaken it up.

"You're worried, aren't you?"

I do not reply, but instead grip the steering wheel, not wanting to contemplate prison or ever being caught again.

"Look," Chris says now, "think of it as *borrowing*. We are simply borrowing the car, and we will return it. Okay?"

I think about this. "Okay."

The sun bursts through suddenly, casting rays of struggling light onto the car hood, shriveled petals of burnt orange scattering onto the trees by the roadside, onto the rocks and old buildings and onto the birds that swing together in giant pendulums across the marble sky. I roll down the window, and a breeze drifts in. The air is chilled with thick, damp moss, and I shiver. Chris looks over to me but says nothing, and I find myself thinking that I am glad he can cope with my silence. Outside, bats click in the clouds, the ink-swirled sky streaked with their flying shadows, and as we drive upward, near our destination now, the serrated edges of the Montserrat Mountain dominate the skyline—sharp, unforgiving blades slicing into the sky.

The breeze picks up, and goose pimples pop up all over my skin. "I am cold."

"I saw a blanket on the backseat," he says. "You want that?"

"Yes," I say, then hesitate. "Please."

Chris secures the blanket on my lap as I continue to drive. I concentrate. The touch of his fingers on my legs, the smell of him, is distracting—his odd sugary-baking-mixture sweat blending with the damp, pungent vegetation outside. Chris' hair flops all the way down to his eyes. I fight back the urge to brush it away.

When we arrive at Montserrat Monastery, the scalp of the sun peeks out from behind an army of dark clouds, throwing a deep pink glow over the terrain as if it had been dipped in a vat of candy, while behind us, the dust from the road sparkles a phosphorescence of light and color that dances in the wind and swirls ropes of deep orange in the sky.

I let my foot up a little off the gas, and the vehicle slows.

"So," Chris says, craning his neck at the view, "d'you know this area?"

I scan my data banks. "Our destination is Santa Maria de Montserrat," I say. "It is a Benedictine abbey. The mountain it sits on is four thousand fifty-five feet above the valley. The monastery is twenty-eight miles from Barcelona and was founded in AD 1025."

From the corner of my eye, I see Chris' stare. "You're like a human Google."

"I am not."

He smiles. "Google."

I steal a glance.

Pulling the steering wheel around, I inch the car forward by a corner, edging through a small crook until, curving the final bend, we see it: Montserrat Monastery. It rises above the horizon, looming ahead into view, a colossal ancient religious sanctuary of sand-colored stone blocks and arches so high that even the bloated rain clouds behind cannot barge past.

I drive forward, staying slow, searching for a suitable place to park. "Balthus said to meet here, yes?"

"Yeah, yeah," Chris says, nodding. Then, frowning, he leans forward. "Hang on a minute, is that …?"

I follow Chris' gaze and shriek. Slamming on the brakes, I turn off the engine and fling open the car door.

"Hey!" Chris shouts. "Wait!"

But I ignore him and sprint across the open courtyard, stumbling as I run, scraping the heels of my palms against a low wall, the fabric of my jeans chafing my skin. But I don't care, because she is here. Balthus connected with her and brought her, and now she is safe.

I screech to a halt. There, just three steps from me now, standing next to Balthus, is my friend. Relief, joy, happiness all rush up inside my head, the emotions coming fast, all at once, and the only way I can let it out, the only way I can process it, is to whoop and clap over and over, unable to stop the feelings from leaking, neurologically ill equipped to keep a lid on it all.

"Patricia!"

"Doc!" Patricia runs over. "I thought I'd never see you again."

The smile on my face is so wide, my cheeks ache. "You are here! Are you safe? Why did you come?" My words tumble out so fast that my head starts to spin and I have to really concentrate on my breathing to slow down.

"You okay? You good? Doc, I couldn't stay away. I was so worried about you, and Balthus got in touch after everything that happened in London. He said Dr. Andersson was after you."

"The Project have not found you?"

"No." She smiles. "They've not been in touch at all."

I keep my eyes wide open, not wanting to close them, scared that if I do, she may, like a magician's assistant, disappear, and I will be without her again, without my guide. She looks the same as I remember her: the same long limbs, same graceful neck, same skin the color of milk, with tattoos of a blackbird and the Virgin Mary on her arms, and when I sniff the air, her familiar scent of warm baths, soft towels, and talcum powder drifts back to me.

"You are not in prison," I say.

"No." Her shaved head glistens under the sun. "They put me on parole."

"Parole," I say, trying out the word as if for the first time. I sniff her again, the smell of her skin giving me an instant comfort I haven't felt in six months or more.

She raises her hand to mine, and slowly I do the same. They rise, our arms, inch after inch, until finally our fingers fan out—one, two, three, four, five—and touch. Our way of communicating, my safety net. We stand there smiling as I inhale her scent some more, and I think of a tiny bird flying in the sky, and in my heart and head I feel sheer elation. We remain like that, the two of us connected, until, gradually, I turn, vaguely aware of another body close by.

"Erm, hello? Maria?" Someone clears their throat. My hand hovers in the air, touching my friend's, not wanting the moment to pass.

"Maria?"

I reluctantly drop my hand and turn and, this time, speak. "Balthus." I peer at him, inspecting his face and torso. "You look a lot older."

"And hello to you, too." He smiles a wide smile with eye creases, and I count an extra wrinkle on each side. It looks like Balthus, but now there are deeper blue circles under his eyes, and on his head a dark slick of oiled hair sits speckled now with growing gray sides, his skin as brown as an almond. His once taut, wide frame seems smaller now, shrunken but still large, and yet, somehow he seems weaker, more fragile.

"These past few months have been hard, haven't they?" he says, the smile still affixed to his features.

"Yes," I say.

"I miss Harry."

"I miss him, too," I find myself saying, wanting to say more, needing to, but not knowing how. The dust from the courtyard breezes between us, and a strange lump forms in my throat.

Balthus coughs, then inhales. "So, were you followed?"

Chris walks up. "Yes."

Balthus' eyes go wide, and he throws open his arms and laughs. "Chris!"

Chris steps forward, grinning, and greets Balthus with wide-open arms. The two men hug, slapping each other's backs, and I watch, curious at the exchange.

"I'm so glad you're okay," Balthus says, pulling back. "You got a nice tan there."

"Ha, yeah. More than you, Granddad."

"Hey! Who are you calling Granddad?" Balthus says, lightly punching Chris in the stomach, at which Chris actually appears to laugh. "I've tanned pretty good, thanks."

I watch the exchange, not fully understanding it. Are they fighting? I ask, "Are you angry with each other?"

Chris swivels around. "What?"

I turn to Patricia for some reassurance, then realize she does not know Chris, so I try to be social and do what I have seen others do, and introduce him to her.

"Patricia, this is Chris. He is a hacker and has been convicted for such crimes. The USA government wanted to extradite him. He has a Goofy smile, he likes Taylor Swift, and he says 'what' a lot."

There. I step back, satisfied I have contributed to regular social conversation.

Chris stares at me and then shakes his head, bends forward, and holds out a hand to Patricia. "Hi. I'm Chris."

She takes his hand, shakes it. "Hiya. Patricia."

I watch them. I should try to mirror their actions. So, I step toward Chris, hold out my hand, and, taking hold of his, shake it. "Hi."

He smiles. "Um, hi." He nods his head. "You … you do know we know each other already, right?"

I keep shaking. "Of course."

"Right."

Patricia leans in. "Er, Doc, you can stop shaking his hand now."

"Oh." I drop it and step back.

Balthus moves toward us. "Thanks for helping us out, Chris. Maria, what happened when you were followed? Was it the Project or MI5?"

I inform him of everything that has happened to Chris and me since his villa in the village, and Balthus' eyes go wide.

"We'd best get inside, then, and out of sight. The abbot is an old family friend. He's agreed to let us stay here." Balthus searches behind him. "Ah, there he is."

Ahead, by the broad entry to the monastery, a figure looms into view, cloaked in a thick, dark fabric that flaps in the wind as dirt blows over the ground beneath us, snapping at our feet.

"Do you think this is a good idea, staying here?" Chris says, frowning at the apparition ahead.

I look to him. "Throughout history, the monastery has been regarded as a sanctuary for dissidents and political refugees, which is probably why Balthus has chosen it for us to hide in. And during the dictatorship of Franco, when many people hid in the abbey, over twenty monks were executed."

"Oh."

"Well, come on, then," Balthus urges. "We can't be seen out here."

We start to move, but then Chris stops. "Oh, wait." He points to the stolen car. "The keys," he says to me. "Are they in the ignition?"

"Yes."

He smiles. "Then we have just borrowed it, and now …" He runs over to the vehicle and, in the dust on the hood, writes something with his index finger. "… we are returning it as politely as we can."

I cock my head to the left and look as Chris stands back and walks over to us from the car. There on the hood in its sandstone vehicle dust is one word: *Gracias.*

Chris rejoins the group and delivers me an eye-creased smile, and I find myself smiling back. Then Balthus, checking that we are all set, tells us to follow him forward. As I walk, securing my rucksack to my shoulder, I glance to Chris, then to the ground ahead, and notice that the circles of sand that earlier swirled in the breeze have now fallen still, and all that moves where the wind once was is one lone cicada, crawling in the dust as, above us, the clouds finally burst and the rain begins to fall.

# CHAPTER 21

**UNDISCLOSED CONFINEMENT LOCATION**

*Present Day*

Ramon has my journal in his lap, and while he holds it, the timer by my side ticks. I am nervous. I don't know how long it is until the next drug dose, and even though I try to gain some control and trace the time that passes, it is hard because the air is thick and dark and my mind is distracted, not only by all that is in this room, but by my journal and the fact that someone else is reading it.

"You have some days missing," Ramon says, looking up from the page.

I do not reply. For me, it is too hard. Ramon is my brother, but an alarm in my head is telling me that to speak to him too much is dangerous, and yet, that voice—I do not understand it. Days, the recording of their events, are missing from my journal because I was taken by the Project and given Versed, but if Ramon is being coerced by them, how can it be safe to talk to him?

"Papa loved that you taught yourself the piano," he says suddenly. He must be reading my notes, written when I was thirteen, fourteen, and those few years beyond when I played piano to hide from my feelings, from the confusion of death and life and growing up in a world that made no sense.

"How did you do that?" Ramon says now. "You just played the

piano and you didn't even have lessons. I used to sneak in and listen to you when you didn't know I was there, because you didn't like people to watch you. My friends used to laugh about you, call you weird. I hit one of them—did you know that?"

I shake my head, eyes down. Tick, tick, tick goes the timer.

"He called you weird, so I punched him there"—he points to his left cheek—"right on the bone."

Ramon now says something else, but I am distracted. The piano, the thought of it, sparks something in me—a recent memory—and I try to place it, but the rope on my wrists digs into my skin, and the timer rings loud in my head, the two of them colliding to blast any focus I can gain far away.

"He loved you, Papa did," Ramon continues. "He loved the way you knew all the composers' names, all the details of their life. I did, too—I still do. Who's that composer you liked the most?" He shakes his head then clicks his fingers. I flinch at the sharp sound. "Erik Satie, that's it."

I lift my head as a thought springs up. Erik Satie. Erik Satie … I say the composer's name in my head as, somewhere in my short-term recollection, something begins to shift, to move in iceberg fashion from hidden moorings to float into view as, slowly, I begin to remember.

Erik Satie. The composer whose classical talent I admire. The composer whose musical piece, Gymnopédie no. 1, Dr. Andersson played in her office when I was in Goldmouth prison in London after my murder conviction.

Ramon sighs. "I play his pieces sometimes, did you know that? Did you know I play piano now, too?"

But I barely hear him, because shards of images are beginning to come back to me as, bit by bit, the cloak slips down from my memory block and, for the first time since I awoke in this room, I remember an element of the events that led to here, to now.

I remember Dr. Andersson being at my villa.

I remember killing her. I remember Chris, recall going to his house and reciting his name, just as, when I was young, I recited the name of Erik Satie. I remember being followed by a black van. I remember Balthus on my cell, remember his smile and his laughter when he saw me at the abbey, and most of all, I remember seeing Patricia by his side, happy and safe, my hands clapping in the evening sun.

"M, are you okay?"

I jump at Ramon's voice and look at myself. My nails are digging into the wood on the chair, scratching into the groove of it as my brain registers the emotions of happiness and sadness and fear all at the same time.

"Take it easy, M."

I think I nod at him, at my brother—I am unsure—but what I do know is that my mind is beginning to wake up. I have recalled some events, which means, if I have remembered those, I may remember more, and what can trigger it is ... I look up. It is my journal, the pages of my mind that sit now in my brother's lap, that can awaken the events and facts hidden deep in my brain, locked away by the drug in my arm—events and facts that I need to know to help me get out of here. To help us both get out of here.

"Can you read more?" I say now.

"Really?" Ramon smiles. "Of course!" He flicks the page. "See, I told you it would help."

"Yes," I say, trying to keep my mind alight. "It is helping."

He begins to read aloud, and I listen and I focus, and as he speaks the words I wrote more than a decade ago, I will my mind to start recalling every single thing it ever can.

## MONASTERY OF SANTA MARIA DE MONTSERRAT, NEAR BARCELONA
*25 Hours and 13 Minutes to Confinement*

I am sitting by a long wooden table in a room that glows orange. We are in the bowels of the monastery. The walls are sand in color, and the air is chilled, with a scent of incense, and when I look at the lamps on the wall, I count eight on the left and ten on the right. Inside each bulb is a flicker, and even though it is not a flame, it resembles one and I cannot help but watch it, the movement and flow combined with the soft light hypnotizing me into a semitrance state. I yawn. It has been a long time since I last slept, and when I roll my shoulders, they feel tight and solid and ready to drop off me.

Chris works at a laptop in the corner of the room, where he sits on a chair made of wood and red leather, and near him sits Balthus, who is sipping water and watching him. Patricia is to my right, her hands spread in star shapes on the table, so that each time I glance around, I catch sight of them, catch sight of her presence, and, given the new room and space and scent of incense to process, it makes me feel calmer. We have told her now, Patricia, everything that has happened up until this point: the villa, what I found on the SIM card, the flashbacks I had—all of it. Chris, too, listened to the information, and the entire time, he looked at me, and I felt a heat rise to my cheeks and spread to my feet and stomach.

The abbot enters now and sets down water and wine at the table, and behind him a monk in brown burlap carries a metal tray of bread and grapes. We eat, and for a while, no one speaks. Exhaustion appears to have taken over, and as I lift my hands, I feel weary, aches and pains shooting through me, my brain firing, recording every murmur and bite and grind of the teeth made in the room, and each time the incense smell reaches my nose, my brain threatens to tip into overload mode.

Patricia leans in and moves her hand on the table toward mine. "Doc, are you okay? You look pale."

I spread my fingers toward hers and let them touch. The sensation sends tingles up my arm, rippling to my shoulders and chest. I take a bite of bread and breathe a little easier.

"So," she says, "you're really going to try and find this Project facility you had the flashback about?"

"Yes." I sip some wine, but not too much. Alcohol scrambles my ability to focus.

"Do you think it's a good idea?"

"Yes. They had a dossier on you all. They want to find you all. It has to end."

She inhales. "And this other file, the one from your flashback you recall from when you were at the Project—the woman in that said it had details on it that could damage the Project, but you don't know which facility it was at?"

"That is correct."

She chews her lip. "So, the SIM card Dr. Andersson had didn't have anything on it to find this place?"

"It had a grid reference for Switzerland."

"The one in Geneva—could that be where the facility is, do you think?"

I watch Chris tapping on the computer and talking to Balthus. "Perhaps. We need to verify."

"Doc, I'm not going to lie. If you go to the facility, if you try and find this file this woman from your flashback mentioned, you won't be safe."

I pick up my water glass. "I have never been safe. Even in prison I was not safe."

"Okay. True." She pauses. "So it's a case of finding the file, finding out who else is involved, is that right?"

"Balthus says there could be others."

She nods. "The other subject numbers."

"Yes. The Project will not stop. MI5 will not stop. They will not stop going after me and you and Mama and Ramon."

"And so you have to end it."

I break some bread in two. "Yes."

She sits for a moment and sips some wine. She takes a napkin from the plate and, scrunching it up, wipes her face. "Doc, it's important you know that"—she glances to Chris and Balthus—

"you're not on your own now. We can help you with this, yeah?"

The lamps drift gentle brushstrokes of orange and yellow across the room, and I look now at Chris. He hasn't stopped working on the laptop since we arrived, and I don't know what he is doing.

"Do you like him, this Chris bloke?"

Patricia's question takes me by surprise. "Why?"

She throws him a gaze. "He's nice. Seems to be into you. Have you chatted to him?"

"I have asked him some questions inquiring into his family and work particulars, yes. But he has been in prison a lot. I am unsure I can trust him."

"Doc, *you've* been in prison."

Feeling anxious, I fiddle with my bread, begin ripping off tiny crumbs.

"Look, Doc, I know this stuff is hard for you to process, but listen. You've got so much to offer. You're smart, funny—"

"That is what Chris said." I lay the crumbs in neat rows of ten. "He said I was funny."

"Well, he's right!" She lets out a long breath. "If you want something to happen with him—you know, if you like him and want a, well, a relationship with him, say—"

"Sex."

"Okay, um, sure." She bows her head. "Sex," she whispers. "But that, may I point out, is just one small part of it. Then you need to give him a little longer; you need to allow yourself more time for you to get to know him and for him to get to know you. Firing off a line of interview questions is not going to do it."

"Oh. Okay." I fiddle with the bread crumbs I have formed into a neat line as my head tries to make sense of what Patricia means. "Do you mean chitchat?"

"Yeah. You know, things that will help you get to know each other."

"But I have already interviewed him."

"I know, but …" She sighs. "You just, well, keep talking to each other."

I look down. It is all very confusing, not to mention tiring. Then I get an idea. "Can I issue him a questionnaire and that would suffice?"

"Um, no."

"Oh."

I look over at Chris. He is whispering to Balthus now, his hair flopping into his eyes, and yet he doesn't move it out of the way, and I fight the urge to stride over and do it for him.

"Maria," Balthus says, "can you come over here?"

"Why?"

He shoots a glance to Chris. "We've … found something."

# CHAPTER 22

I scrape back the chair and walk over to the corner, and as I do, my hand brushes into the neat lines of crumbs, scattering them randomly across the wood.

I reach Chris, and when I stop, Patricia is right behind me. "What have you found?"

"Well," Chris says, raking a hand through his hair, "you know when you had me hack into that website with that SIM card and the eye came up, and the documents flashed across the screen?"

Balthus looks at me. "What documents?" I tell him. He shakes his head. "Oh, Jesus."

"Well, I found a code," Chris says.

"How?"

"Okay, so, I took the SIM."

"When?"

"From your rucksack as you were walking into the monastery."

"That is stealing."

"Well, no, borrowing—and to help you, see?" He points to the screen. "Here."

I look. A series of numbers and letters and black and white symbols stretch like ticker tape across the screen. "How did you access this?"

"I set up a rock-solid proxy, bypassed the firewall, and released a hack program I wrote in …" He shoots a glance to Balthus, then leans into me. "In prison," he whispers, then raises his volume again. "The files I found have the same stuff on them as the ones we found back at my place: the 1973 Black September reference—your, what is it, subject number, the 375 thing? But see here?" I squint. "There's more detail right there. It's that age click thing, it's going down like before, counting down the time, but, well, does that mean anything to you?"

He points to the screen, and I look to where his finger lies. There is a series of numbers and one special one hidden among it: 115.

"It's the same number we saw back at my place, right?" Chris says.

It has to be Raven. "Yes."

"Thought so. Thing is …" He breathes out. "I think it's connected to something beneath it, to another layer of data, and if we could just—"

Balthus steps forward. "No. No, no, no, no. Guys, leave this."

"Hey?" Chris says. "But we're getting somewhere here."

I look at Balthus and hesitate. I trust him, but this information—it could make a difference. "This data may lead us to the Project facility. It was you who encouraged me to find it. You who said I should find the file Raven talked about, and then, if I did that, we could—"

"End it all. Yes, yes, I remember." He billows out a breath.

"They threatened my family," I say to him. "They threatened you all."

Balthus sighs and rubs his chin. "Do you think it's a code to crack that will uncover something else, this data you think lies beneath?" he says to Chris after a moment.

I go over to my rucksack, pull out my notebook, and return.

I flick the pages.

"Doc," Patricia says, "what are you doing?"

"I am searching for an algorithm." My eyes scan fast, and after three seconds, I find it. There. At the bottom of the page, under some sketches of an intricate iron bridge I dreamed about, is the algorithm I need—one I flashed back to in prison. I show it to Chris. "This can help. Can you feed it in?"

He whistles. "Jeez, that's some code." He begins typing in the data. I instruct him on what it means, but he seems to know already, his brain working fast, and the level of intelligence he displays surprises me. He listens well, responding to my points, and I am surprised at how fast he works. I smell the air, his skin; I like the scent of his sweat.

"I don't think it's going to work," he says after one minute of trying.

I analyze the data. Something is missing. A single numeral, a solitary dash, a dot. I flick again through the notebook, page after page of codes and decryptions and strange sketches.

"Jesus, what is all that?" he says, catching sight of my notebook pages.

"They are fragments of dreams I recall that mirror, I believe, events from my being conditioned by the Project."

"Oh." He shifts in his seat. "Right." He looks at me, his breathing slow, measured, his eyes on my arms and then on my neck and lips.

"Try this code," I say. Seven pages in is a small encryption code I dreamed of during the first traumatic week in prison. I point to it.

Chris peers in. "Okay, yeah, that's cool. There is another idea, though."

"Do this first."

"Okay. No worries." He types, fast, efficient, but still it does not work.

I step back and stamp my foot.

"Y'okay, Doc? Take it easy."

"Maria," Balthus says, "we can't keep at this forever. We have to leave soon. The abbot has a car ready for us."

"Wait!" We look at Chris. He is grinning from ear to ear.

"The code worked?" I say.

"No."

"Oh."

"See, what I was trying to tell you is that the age thing—you know, the clicking-countdown-age odd thing we found?"

"Yes."

"Well—you're gonna love this, right—I changed the last two numbers on it through a small hole in the encryption program used to set it up, and then I was able to go through a different system, and, well ..." He points to the screen. "Voilà! Information uncovered."

"Holy Jesus," Balthus says.

I look at what Chris is now pointing to, and cannot believe what I am seeing. There are multiple times, dates, and locations, all of them listed throughout the 1980s and '90s, leading up to now, to the present day.

"You see that thing at the bottom?" Chris says.

"Yes."

"You can decrypt that code fast, right? I mean, right now? Like I can?"

"Yes."

Patricia leans in. "What does it say?"

Chris looks to her. "It says 'test child.' What is the test child?"

A shiver ripples up my spine. "The test child is me."

"What? You're this test-child chick they're talking about? Have you seen all this they have on you? It's, like, full surveillance."

"Bloody hell!" Balthus says. "They have everything."

I read it all, photograph it to my memory, but find myself shaking slightly as I do. Because the file contains extensive details about me, and as I scan it my heart starts to race. There are details on my handlers, on my test dates with the Project, flights I took with my mother from Madrid as a teenager, my trip on the train to Barcelona when I was twenty, surveillance notes, conditioning documents. They all collide in my head, and when I sniff, the incense in the air fills my nostrils and then my head, and I feel my mind on the verge of zoning out to cope with it all.

"Doc, are you all right?"

I turn to Patricia but keep my eyes down at her shoulders. "They have all the details on my movements recorded."

She spans out her fingers as Balthus scans the information and looks to Chris. "Is this proxy you set up safe?"

"As houses."

"Maria," Balthus says to me now, "I know this is hard, but can you see any link on here that may indicate which facility that woman was at, the one you remembered?"

I make myself look, and focus. There are dates and places, but nothing that, when I correlate all the facts between my head and the screen, connects to formulate an answer. "There is nothing about Switzerland here."

Chris shakes his head. "I searched for that link, too, and you're right: no correlation. But," he says, "look here. Click on this part of the age countdown, just there ..." The cursor hovers over a tiny black dot in the far right corner of the yellow box with my age. "There's another page hidden beneath it—hard to access, but I managed it."

"How?"

He shrugs. "Just used the last segment of your algorithm and adapted it."

I look at him. "Oh."

He grins. "You're welcome."

I read the next level of files, and further facts on my living arrangements are documented. I catch my breath, and my fingers shake a little, because what I am reading is effectively a map of my life. Each person and place has been categorized, and when I cross-reference it all, some elements are hazy due to the Project's drug program, but essentially, the data is correct down to the last second.

"They have been monitoring every step of my movements." There is a tiny tremble in my voice.

I read again and arrive at a file toward the end. The font on this one is smaller but just about readable, and I lean in past Chris' scent.

"Hey, look at that," Chris says. "There's a portion down here that's blacked out in, like, little strips."

Balthus moves in. "Can you get to what's underneath?"

"It's tricky."

I grab my notebook, open it at page seventy-two, and thrust it in front of him. "Use this code."

"Whoa! You know how to do this?"

Somewhere in the monastery, monks begin singing a hymn, and their voices drift into the room and it distracts me. "Can you type it in?"

"Right, yeah, sure." He blinks at me, just nodding for a few seconds and nothing else. "You're pretty neat." He stares at me, and it makes me uneasy.

"The code," I say.

"Oh. Yeah."

Even though Chris' fingers fly fast, the code takes some time to input, but after thirty-seven seconds, the screen begins to change.

"Whoa," Chris says. "It's working. You're a freakin' genius!"

The black strips on the end of the document first turn to gray and then, pixelating, begin to fade entirely. Then they stall. Chris taps two more keys, then stops, a small gasp escaping his lips.

"What?" Balthus looks at him, at me. "Maria, what?"

"The black strips have gone." I look at the screen, at the tiny words revealed, and read them over and over again. "No," I say. "No, no, no!" I stand, and the chair to my left falls over and clatters onto the gray stone floor.

"Doc, what?"

Balthus presses his face to the screen, frantically reading then stumbles back, slaps his hand to his mouth. "Oh, my God."

"What!" Patricia says.

Chris frowns, drags his chair to the laptop. "Okay, so this reads initials 'A' and 'V.' And there's a name, a contact for the Project program: Alarico Villanueva." He swivels around. "Who's he?"

"Their contact," Balthus says, his face pale. "He … he is the contact who's been …" He wipes his face. "Who must have been liaising with the Project to ensure Maria was always accessible."

"Huh? But who *is* the guy?"

Patricia looks from Chris over to me. "It's Maria's dad."

# CHAPTER 23

**MONASTERY OF SANTA MARIA DE MONTSERRAT, NEAR BARCELONA**

*24 Hours and 51 Minutes to Confinement*

I look at the computer and the information on the screen, and it all swirls together in my brain. I step back and wander—I think, to the left, but when I do, I stumble, and the bread from the board on the table falls, scattering crumbs and grapes all over the floor.

I drop down and begin scraping it all up, concerned at the random disorder it has created. Everything is chaotic, the food thrown everywhere. I pick up every fallen piece of bread and place it back on the table in neat, ordered lines, my fingers taking each grape, too, and setting them in rows, shifting each one that moves, so it stays where I need it to.

Patricia comes to my side. "Doc? Doc, breathe."

"How could Alarico be their contact?" Balthus is saying. He is pacing the room, head shaking. "It doesn't make any sense."

It is all too much. I close my eyes, count up in fives, recite some quantum theory, try to remember happy times with Papa: the creases by his eyes, the way he would give me firm, strong hugs because I couldn't bear light ones. But when I open my eyes, there is a lump in my throat and my fingers begin to grab whatever they can on the table—plates, glasses, napkins—and rearrange them into neat, set squares. I reach into my rucksack and pull out the torn photo of the two of us from my villa.

"Doc?"

I look up to Patricia. Her hand is held out with five slim, familiar fingers. I blink at it. I watch her arms and her chest and the way her long neck bends, each movement pressed to my memory.

"Papa gave me to the Project," I say. I trace a finger over the rip in the picture of us.

"The document could be false," she says. "Have you thought about that?"

I hesitate, confused. "It is a Project file."

"Yeah, and the sodding Project could have planted the data deliberately. Think about it—it could be absolutely anything."

But the mixture of the data and Papa's name and the confusion and the smells in the room and even the feel of the denim fabric on my legs all start to overload my mind, and I begin to moan and rock a little to let off the steam of the chaos I feel inside.

"What's she doing?" Chris says.

I sense everyone staring at me, but there is nothing I can do to stop it now. Like an avalanche, it has broken loose.

"She's stimming," Patricia says to Chris, then looks back to me. "It's all been too much for her."

"Can she hear you?"

But Patricia ignores Chris and speaks just to me. "Hold up your hand, Doc."

I raise my eyes. Patricia's fingers are spread out in front of her, and I blink at them, briefly glancing to the blurred faces of Balthus and Chris.

"Is she going to be okay?" Chris whispers to Balthus.

"Doc?" Patricia says, her voice soft, low. "Doc, your hand."

I watch her. I keep my sight fixed on my friend, and slowly my body starts to settle and my humming gets softer, then ceases entirely as I focus on Patricia, on her hand, her fingers, her talcum-powder scent.

"He was my papa," I say. "He worked for the Project."

Patricia tilts her head. "We'll work it all out, okay?"

I look at her—her soft cheeks, wide eyes—as gradually, my hand rises until our fingertips touch, and my breathing begins to slow.

"Er, guys?" Chris steps into view. "There's someone here."

The abbot stands in the doorway, where the room opens out into a dimly lit corridor. He wears black robes that skim the floor in a triangle shape, and around his neck hangs a single silver chain with a thick cross on it.

Balthus turns to him. "Father, what is it?"

"We have visitors."

The abbot holds out a phone, and on it is a photograph. I pull myself up a little now as, ahead, Balthus strides over to the monk, stares at the digital image, and shakes his head. "I don't know them." He turns. "Maria, I know things are difficult for you right now, but do you recognize these two?"

He approaches me, crouches down, and holds out the cell. "Have you seen them before?"

My eyes are blurred from zoning out, and at first it is hard to see, but after two seconds, something in my brain kicks in and memories start to function and connect. I rise a little and take the phone from Balthus. The first face I do not recognize, but the second … Mahogany hair, skin the color of buttermilk, black jeans painted to her legs, a worn leather jacket. A memory slips into my mind. The counseling sessions after my acquittal, the woman who brought coffee, the one who the Project "therapist," Kurt, said was his girlfriend.

Balthus steps forward. "They are with the Project, aren't they?"

"Yes."

He looks to Chris. "Copy those files. We have to leave. Now."

"This way," the abbot says. He turns and sweeps to the left, and as he does, his feet seem to hover over the floor, as if they weren't touching the stone at all.

We gather our belongings and rush out of the room, through the wooden doorway, plunging into ribbons of walkways, my head switched to a focus that earlier I was not sure I could achieve. Staying close to each other, we crisscross left then right, bright lights flickering against walls that are arranged in exposed, raw slabs of stonework splayed out under effigies of Jesus Christ and Mary. Everything hits my senses at once. The lights, smells, sounds, thoughts of Papa with the Project. I document all of it. It is almost too much to handle, but I focus on Patricia, on the heads of Chris and Balthus and the ordered robes of the abbot, and I move on.

We turn a corner, running now, but Chris slips on a polished tile and tumbles into a plastered recess, air billowing out of him as his chest hits the wall. I hesitate. The others have not noticed and are racing ahead. "You go," Chris says. "I'll catch up." He moves to stand but winces, his palm jerking to his injured shoulder.

Unsure what to do, I glance once more to the corridor and catch sight of Patricia's head. They are nearly out of sight. I look back to Chris. We are supposed to be running, leaving—that is the plan, the routine—but the laptop is with Chris and he has a lot of knowledge and … and he helped me.

I drop to the floor. Hooking my arms underneath his shoulders, I heave his body up, but he is heavy and the corridor warm, and sweat seeps through my T-shirt and jacket, and even though it is cotton, the wet fabric irritates my skin and makes the whole thing difficult to deal with. But I keep going. Chris locks eyes with me for one second, and for some reason, I find myself unable to look away.

"They must have found you through me," he says. "Those people on the phone image—they must have tracked you through my laptop."

"Negative." I hoist him upright and tug on his arm. "The higher probability is that they found me by following Balthus or Patricia."

We begin to move again, but progress is slow, the two of us

plodding along until I can barely hear the others ahead at all, and sweat now forms two dark pools under my arms as the thought that they are here, the Project, somewhere near, makes my breathing short and sharp.

After a few seconds, Chris manages to jog again alongside me, and we finally reach a wide arch at the end of the tunnel that stretches out toward the exit beyond. Balthus and Patricia are there, catching their breath as the abbot unlocks a bolt on a heavy plank door strapped with iron. He gestures to Balthus, who goes and talks to him in hushed tones.

"They've arranged a car," Balthus says to us now, walking over, his voice low, a single light beam illuminating every line in his face. "Out toward the far end of this section. We can get to it, but—"

"We cannot go as one group," I say.

Patricia turns to me. "Doc, we have to stay together. We can't let the Project get you on your own."

"I won't come," Chris says. "They may have tracked you all through my laptop."

I turn to him. "It was not your laptop they traced."

Patricia glances between the two of us.

"It is time for you to leave," the abbot whispers.

"Chris," Balthus says, "you're coming with us. End of discussion."

He nods. "Okay." Then he reaches into his pocket and gives something to me. A USB stick. "You should have this. It's got on it all the documents we found just now."

Unsure why he is helping me, I take the memory stick.

"If we get split up at all and you need to contact me, I wrote down my secure e-mail and cell." He gives me a scrap of paper. "The geolocation's off, so they can't find me. Use Text Secure or Signal to contact me—you can send encrypted messages via those."

I read his details, memorize them, then rip the paper up into tiny confetti.

"What, you don't want it?"

"No. I memorized it."

"Oh." He opens his mouth as if to announce something, but instead simply blinks at me and says, "Oh," again.

"Doc?" Patricia says. "Let's go."

"My surname's Johnson, by the way," Chris says, as he goes to move. "You know, 'cause you like names, so I figured, well, you could know all of mine."

"Johnson," I say. "It is a patronymic of the name John, meaning 'son of John.' It is a surname of English origin, yet also an American name meaning 'Jehovah has been gracious.'"

He smiles. "Yep, that's right, Google."

Balthus steps forward. "Okay. It's time to go."

The door ahead is open wide, rain from the broken clouds pouring in, and the abbot is gesturing us over. We start to run.

"Please hurry," the abbot whispers as we reach him. "There are people at the door. We cannot hold them off much longer. You must go."

Reaching into my rucksack, I hand out burner cell phones. "These are nontraceable and all preset with each other's numbers to remain in touch should we get separated." Everyone silently takes one, and I am about to explain at speed how encrypted text messaging works, when a series of shouts erupts in the far distance, then a loud crack.

"Holy shit," Chris says, eyes wide. "Was that a gunshot?"

"This way," the abbot hisses. "Quick!"

The shot rings loud in my head now as we are plunged into a shower of lights, toward the exit, where the car engine growls up ahead. We all run, no words spoken, just a rapid rhythm of breath, the escape vehicle forty yards away, and we are near now, but I trip and fall, and looking down, I see that my shoelace is undone.

"Come on!" Patricia whispers, her arm waving me over.

Annoyance and fear whip through me simultaneously. I can't leave the lace undone, loose, out of place like this, but if I stop and fix it, it will waste us time. Shots ring out again from somewhere in the monastery, and I flinch and try to focus. I calculate the shooters' distance from us using the echoes and vibrations that bounce off the towering stonework, and determine that the people shooting are two hundred to three hundred yards away. I look at Patricia, then at my shoelace.

"Take this!" I throw my rucksack to my friend.

"What? Doc—" It hits her in the abdomen, and she stumbles back a little, like an athlete catching a medicine ball.

"It has the USB stick in it," I say. I drop to my knees.

"Hurry!" Balthus urges up ahead.

My fingers work quickly on the shoelace, but something bothers me—a small chink somewhere, a thin sound that vibrates from outside—but I cannot determine its location. I inch upward. Patricia is standing beside a polished stone wall. But the walls are high, and even though the mounted lamps glow, Balthus and Chris seem too far away. The lights around me are bright, and the noises are loud, and I am sweating from my arms, from my neck, my cheeks, but that is not it. That is not the problem.

A loud crack rips through the air.

We all drop to the ground.

"They're shooting again!" Batlhus yells. "Everyone run. Quick. Maria!"

How did they get here so fast? We sprint across the courtyard. It is hard to hide, and the floodlights bouncing off the sheen of the stone walls dazzle our eyes. Shapes and shadows fly left and right as we sprint across the expanse of ground, cold air slapping our faces, my shoe only loosely tied, and I am acutely aware that I am behind the others. There are two vehicles I see now, and we run past the first, and I am unsure why until we pass it, and I see that the two rear tires have been shot and deflated.

Up ahead, the abbot ushers us to another door at the far end of the courtyard. The door is huge, almost three meters in height, its wood as thick as a tree trunk. It groans open into a vast cave-like space beyond, and I spy the metallic glint of what must the hood of another car, a 4x4, and I am not yet there, but then a thought enters my head and I stop. I cease running and stand alone, chest heaving as I watch my friends race on ahead.

Balthus halts. "Maria, what are you *doing*? Come on!"

The abbot is just ahead, Chris beside him, Balthus by Patricia, my rucksack on her shoulder, USB stick in the front pocket, when another shot sounds, the noise hammering in my head, but I ignore it, clench my jaw.

"The Project is here," I say, my voice raised above the noise.

"I know," Balthus yells. "So move!"

"No."

"Doc," Patricia shouts, "what are you doing?"

I glance to where the gunshots are coming from, then turn back to my friends. "The facility from my flashback was a Project one. Raven pointed me to a file—one that can give me answers."

"Maria, no," Balthus says. "It's too dangerous."

"I have to go. The only way I can get to the file is to *be* there, inside the Project."

Wind and rogue rain slice across our faces, and Chris' hair flicks into his eyes and he brushes it out of the way.

"You know my e-mail, my details," Chris shouts. There is another gunshot, this time from closer, and we run to a large stone column that offers us cover and space to think. "When you're in there, find a phone, get to a computer, set up a proxy, and contact me, okay? I'll see what I can dig up in the meantime, see what ice I can hack."

"Ice," Balthus mumbles. "Ice … *Ice!*" he says. "Maria, I remember now! Remember when you were at the villa and you told me about your flashback with the woman you named Raven?"

"Yes. Of course."

"I said it triggered a memory in me, but I couldn't quite figure out what. Well, I remembered now, when Chris said 'ice.' When

you were in Goldmouth, your mother phoned me, babbling. She
was ill. It was when she was taken to the hospital after visiting you,
do you remember? And she was going on and on about a place
called the *Ice Room*."

On hearing Balthus mention my mother, I feel worried. She has
been ill for a long time, but she has always hidden it well. But the
truth can remain hidden for only so long. "Did she say where it was?"

"No, but she said that if you wanted to keep secrets, you had to
go to the Ice Room, and that the room had a computer that wasn't
connected to a server. I don't know; it may be nothing."

Mama. She thought she was taking me to a help center, not to
the Project. Maybe she overheard something, and when she was ill
with the cancer and worried about me being in prison, she repeated
it to Balthus, my papa's old university friend.

The abbot, black cloak flapping by his feet, urges them to move.
The gunshots are so close, they feel only step away.

"Doc," Patricia shouts, "be safe." And she raises her hand, and
I start to do the same when there is a loud crack, and a searing pain
shoots through me. I fall, screaming out as a fire rips into my body,
and I see two pairs of boots halt in front me and my brain goes into
overdrive. Have I been shot? But I know how that feels, a bullet
stabbing into my body, hot, sickening. But this is different. It must
be a dart—a dart loaded with something.

"Doc!" Patricia yells.

My friend! Not my friend. "Run!" I shout. "Patricia, run!"
Except that I am not shouting, am unable to, because my mouth
has gone numb, spit drooling from between my lips, my body and
legs paralyzed. I try to gain some sight, a visual, but all I see are
shadows that sway, separately at first, and then, as the sedative from
the dart takes hold, they blend together into one large veil of black.

# CHAPTER 24

**UNDISCLOSED CONFINEMENT LOCATION**

*Present Day*

My brother reads from my journal, and I listen very hard. The timer by my side ticks, and he will not tell me how long I have until the drugs speed into my system again. I do not move. The rope in the semidarkness cuts into my wrists and ankles now, but as he talks more, as he reads out the words that sit on the pages of my mind, I start to recall fragments of events.

He pauses and, reaching into the box beside him, pulls out two bags of popcorn and one silver fork. He replaces the lid in one move, careful so my journal remains on his lap, then holds the popcorn bags and fork in the air and smiles.

"You still like this stuff, right? And look! I remembered you used to like eating popcorn with a fork so your fingers wouldn't touch your mouth."

In the oppressive gloom, I can just about see that the popcorn packets are red and yellow, and on the edge and top and bottom are faux-gold strips with the brand-name, which reads *ButterPop*. The lightbulb above swings over the packets as Ramon shifts his crate forward, the flashlight he was holding now placed flat on the dirt floor so it shines outward in a funnel of straw yellow.

I blink. The light is bright, and my eyes have become so accustomed now to the dark that when the bulb shines, the lids flap until they stream tears.

"Have some food," Ramon says, "and I'll continue reading, okay?"

I nod and, following his instructions, open my mouth. He spears three pieces of toffee popcorn with the fork, then slots the fork into my mouth, and the snack melts. It tastes good. I cannot recall the last time I ate, and when he next pulls out a plastic bottle of water, I gulp the liquid down so fast that some of it spurts back up through my nose and Ramon has to come behind me and tap me on the back to dislodge any rogue droplets so I can breathe. While helping me, he knocks the medical stand, and the drug bag swings, causing the needle in my arm to pull at my vein, stinging me with a sharp pain that pierces all the way through to the nub of my elbow.

"Gosh, M, I'm sorry," he says now, coming back around to the front. Are you okay?"

My eyes land on my journal, which he had placed on the lid of the box so he could move. I ignore the needle. I have to keep him reciting my diary entries. "Can you read some more?"

He smiles, and to my surprise, I see eye creases fan out on the corners of his face.

I am recalling more and more details now and I don't want to stop. The urge is strong to ask Ramon again what the Project has asked him to do, as is the desire to demand that he untie me, take out the timer and needle; but if I do that, I worry that he will shout and won't read anything else to me and then I would be stuck, unable to get out of wherever I am. I remember now what happened in the courtyard of the monastery. I recall the gunshots and shouts and how I was knocked out, and I know that I deliberately let myself be taken by the Project, but I need to recollect what happened after that. I need to unfreeze something that will give me a clue—a clue that will ultimately convince Ramon that I should not be kept in here, or perhaps show me what to do, or tell me that help is on the way.

Ramon is reading a section on the Project, in which Black Eyes was testing me to see if I felt pain. When he arrives at the part where I was burned with a cigarette, he stops. I look at him; there are tears in his eyes.

"M, why did you write this?"

"I wrote it because it happened."

He wipes his face dry with a cotton handkerchief. "Why didn't you tell me?"

"Because I thought you would not believe me."

He frowns. "What! You mean this is *real*? When you said it happened, I thought you meant in your head. I thought this was just a nightmare or a bad dream you had recorded."

"No. It is real."

He slams the book shut and I jump. The sound echoes in my ears, making it hard to focus amid the dark and the confusion, but if he doesn't read the journal, where will that leave me?

"You know there is a difference between stories and reality, don't you, M?"

"Yes."

"Then why do you insist on making things up?"

I don't know what to say, am unsure how to act. I have told him it is all true and real, and he has read the details in my own writing, but is it that he has become so used to being fed lies that he can no longer distinguish between truth and deceit, between fact and fiction?

"I liked reading to you when we were little," he says after a moment. "It made me feel as if I was looking after you."

I study his smile and try to mirror it to make him feel comfortable and continue reading aloud from my journal. "Yes. Me, too."

He sighs. "Papa used to read to me, after you went to bed."

*Papa ...*

"He'd read the classics to me, you know: Dickens, Cervantes, a bit of Shakespeare. It says in your journal here Papa would read *Hamlet* to you. I never knew that."

*Papa ...*

"M? Are you listening?"

I look up with a start. Sweat is trickling down my temples, and when I shift in my seat, the shirt on my back sticks to my skin.

"Papa read *Hamlet* to me, yes," I say, but I am not fully focused on the words. Instead, I am fixating on the memory it has dislodged in my brain: a memory of finding some information Chris uncovered.

"Ramon, are there date entries in my journal?"

He looks to the pages. "Yes, mostly. There are some omissions, but, yes, there are dates. Why?"

I look at the gold embossment on my journal, think of Papa and what Ramon said about him, and slowly, like a train arriving at a station, the recent memory comes: Chris found out that Papa was possibly a Project contact, that he was the liaison. It rushes in fast now, the short-term recollection, but Patricia said the data could be unreliable. Could my journal help? The drugs I have been given here have scrambled my photographic data banks, but my journal could reboot them, help me remember. If the dates in it correlate, if Papa could not have been with me on the journal entries when I was at the Project, could that give him an alibi? Could it mean he is innocent or, at the very least, not connected to the Project in that way?

"M, are you okay? Your eyes have spaced out a bit."

I jerk my head straight. I have to figure this out, but at my side, the timer ticks on. "I … I want to hear more from my journal; that is what I was thinking about. I believe it is helping me."

"Helping you feel better?"

"Helping me feel better," I say, mirroring his words. "Yes, but, I think, not having the timer on would help me concentrate on my journal more when you read to me. That would help me greatly. You know I cannot deal with too many noises."

He sits and says nothing, and for a moment I think he is going to be able to see into my head and know what I am really thinking, but then, without warning, he stands.

"M, that's really great news. Yes, of course I can pause the timer.

That's why I'm here. I'm here for you because I love you. Talking is good." He walks to the medical stand. "Talking is really good."

And as he presses a small orange button on the side of the timer face, the ticking stops and the drug stays in the bag, and in front of me Ramon sits and picks up my journal and begins to tell me all the dates that are documented inside.

## DEEP-COVER PROJECT FACILITY
### 18 Hours and 49 Minutes to Confinement

I wake up to see that I am lying in a metal bed, with my body covered in a cornflower-blue hospital gown that hangs loose on my limbs. Dulled, medium-glare stimulus lights line the ceiling, and when I look to the corners of the bed, instead of sharp angles I see rounded corners and a white sheet made of soft handwoven cotton.

I crane my neck to see some more, then wince in pain and flop back. I track back through events. The dart, the monastery, the two people from the Project. I look around, recognize the white of the walls, the blank, empty space, and I know that I am here. I have made it.

I am back in a Project facility—I just don't know which one yet.

I dart my eyes downward and scan myself. There are no straps on my arms, no ropes on my legs, and when I try to sit up, nothing moves, as if I have been frozen, my muscles temporarily suspended or paralyzed. A mild panic begins to rise until I think back to the dart and remember the sedative, and I calm down. It will wear off soon.

The thought of Papa swims into my head, also the information Chris found, and when I contemplate it, I find it hard to cope with the idea that Papa was involved with the Project, but people lie, even people you believe you can trust. Somehow, I need to find out at what facility the flashback happened, and see if it matches where I am now.

I open my eyes and exhale. Unable to move my head and neck fully until the sedative wears off, I take to flicking my eyes around the room to analyze my surroundings in more detail. White anti-climb paint is daubed on every wall of the room, and at the entrance is a gray door made of metal, with a secure air-lock mechanism. To my side is a standard-issue medical cabinet containing one drawer and a shelf with no contents, and next to it is a small stack of fluffed white towels. When I scan for light, I see there is no external window, just the low-stimulus lights on the ceiling above, and a prison-style glass panel on the back internal partition.

I begin to calculate the distance from the bed to the door, when there is a sound, a high-pitched beep. I jump. The beep fades and is followed by something else I did not expect to hear: music— old-style, from the 1930s. It warbles, quiet at first then louder and more distinct, with a tinny, crackled effect that echoes in the air as if it were being played on an old gramophone. When the first segment launches, trumpets dribble out a tune, and a woman's voice wails, linked with jagged jazz notes that slip in and out. Confused, I shiver, goose bumps springing out all over my body as my eyes take in the corner of a speaker that sits bolted up near the ceiling to my left. The music lurches on, and though it is not loud, not booming in my head, the sound still grates on my ears, makes the hairs on my arms stand, pricking my flesh with hundreds of tiny warning shocks. It bothers me. I try to trace the jazz notes, gain some order from it so I can think and focus, and am so wrapped up in it that I don't hear the air lock at the entrance hiss, or see the door swing open into the room.

"You can move, you know. You just have to force it." The voice startles me, and I look up and freeze. "Hello again, Maria." He steps forward. "You took a little while to find this time."

"Get back!" I shout.

But he moves again, so I try to roll off the bed, but my limbs are still weak, and he stalks toward me, the man with the mask, from my nightmares and my flashbacks, the man with the Scottish accent. Dr. Carr. Black Eyes.

"Where am I?"

Black Eyes walks to my right side, drags out a chair, and sits. I press myself backward into the bed, muscles firing as I feel the cold metal of the bedstead on my skin. I knew, when I let them capture me, that I would see him again, but nothing could prepare me for the horror of seeing in the flesh the man who, for the past six months, I have seen only in my nightmares.

"You gave us quite the runaround, didn't you? Oh, but it is so nice to see you again. You look tired, Maria." His skin is pale and rigid, and on his face, pockmarks form craters around his chin and on his cheeks, and his mouth, when he speaks, reveals the tombstone teeth that stalk the corridors of my dreams.

"Where am I?" I repeat.

He crosses one leg over the other. "You are at our Project Facility in Hamburg."

*Hamburg.* My heart races, adrenaline shooting through me. Something about the city clicks and vaguely connects, but what and how? The sedative is still making my cognition fuzzy, and when I attempt to think it through, I keep arriving at an impasse, the music colliding to blur my brain. I talk, focus on buying some time until I am functioning correctly. "Your facility is in Scotland; it is not in Germany."

"Our Scottish facility, Maria—Subject 375—is merely the one we would take you to when you were younger. We are an international program. We have more than a single facility."

"Why have you brought me here?" My eyes flick to the door, the exit … escape.

He follows my gaze. "There's no need to run." He picks up a tiny black remote control with three buttons and points it at the ceiling speaker. The music dies, and the room slips into a loud silence.

"You can't get out," Black Eyes says now, returning his focus to me. "Not yet, anyway. And besides, I've missed seeing you. I'm just sorry we've had to get you over to me—us—in this way."

"Why do you want me?"

He smiles, but nothing happens to the skin around his eyes—no eye wrinkles or creases. I observe him. Without the white mask, I can see his entire face. His lips are thin in a kind of washed-out, pale, dishcloth type of pink, and on his left cheek is a two-centimeter scar. His ears, when I track them, are large elephant affairs that seem to flap when he moves, and on his skull are weeds of black hair, his wiry body attired in a white robe over green surgical trousers and tunic.

There is a plastic file folder in his hand, and he opens it. He consults a document, then looks up, and when he does, a shiver ripples down my limbs, and I realize with anticipation that my muscles are thawing now, some feeling returning, and my mind is gradually beginning to function.

"Black September," he announces. "Do you know of it?"

My brain hits alert. Black September: the organization Chris found data on at his villa. I stay very still while I think, while I try to determine what he is aiming to do.

"Why are you asking me this?"

"You wanted to know why you are here. I am simply trying to explain." He tilts his head, and as he does, it reminds me of the gargoyles chiseled into the stone on Mama's apartment building in Madrid. "Black September was a terrorist organization," he says. "I believe you discovered one of our documents referring to them."

A small stab of panic hits my chest. "The eye on the computer, it was—"

"Me, yes. Well, not actually me, but an image downloaded." He smiles, and I see his murky teeth. "I thought you would appreciate the ... *intelligence* of it, let's say. Some may not. But I know you well, my dear." He sighs. "Oh, it really is so good to see you. I get lonely here, you know. Things have ... well, they've changed. Time moves on."

My panic rises. Patricia. She has my rucksack with the USB stick containing the downloaded files from the computer in Chris' house.

"Anyway, Black September," he says now, "carried out murders and bombings at the Munich Olympics in 1972. There was also an attack on an electrical installation in Hamburg." He pauses, scans my face like a laser, then recommences. "In response to those events and others, professionally trained counterterrorism groups were created. Two of these groups were called GSG9 and GIGN. Another was called Project Callidus. Every organization has a"—he flurries a hand in the air—"a code name, if you will. Ours is Callidus. Project Callidus."

"Callidus," I say automatically, unable to stop myself. "It is a Latin word that means 'astute, clever, or cunning.'"

Black Eyes nods. "Good. Good."

I think now, brain beginning to turn a little faster as some semblance of normal functioning returns in tiny increments. The classified documents I discovered in Balthus' prison office said the Project began in the 1970s, and the ones from Chris' house correlate with the year 1973. Does this mean Black Eyes is telling me the truth? An unease swells in my stomach, and I tap my fingers and clench my teeth as he continues talking.

"Of course, unlike the other groups, no one knows about us." He looks at my rhythmic finger. "I see your original little Asperger's traits are still there." He tilts his head. "No matter. You have been without our chaperoning for a little longer than we'd have liked. It is to be expected." He shuts the file, then looks up. "So, I have been informed that you killed an MI5 officer this week. You knew her as Dr. Andersson, correct?"

I don't reply, fear taking me over now. "How did you know that?"

"Oh, Maria," he sighs. "We have known each other for so long now, so when will you realize, hmmm, that I—we—know everything?" He leans in, and I smell his garlic and tobacco stench, and I almost gag.

"Everything," he whispers.

# CHAPTER 25

**DEEP-COVER PROJECT FACILITY**

*18 Hours and 42 Minutes to Confinement*

Black Eyes moves back from me and sits on his chair. He folds his legs one over the other and delivers me a wide stare. "We want you back in the Project fold, Maria. Back to your surrogate family."

His statement takes me by such surprise that a screech slips from my throat. "No."

"Yes."

"Why?"

He regards me for a moment. "You, Maria, are the one the conditioning program has worked on. You must know this; you have seen the classified files. Did you think we'd spend all the money we have on training you and, what? Give you up, just like that?" He shakes his head. "I don't think so. People can only hide for so long." He pauses. "My own daughter used to like to hide. Peek-a-boo. Isn't that what they call it?"

Something fires in me. I jump at it. "You said I am the only one the conditioning has worked on, which implies you have tested on others. Who else have you used the program training on?"

He smiles. "A good question." He shifts in his seat, and his surgical scrubs rise up to show mud-brown socks on white, wiry ankles.

He sighs and, without saying a word, scrapes his chair nearer me, so that when I look to him, I can see the pockmarks on his face so clearly my brain can count each one.

"I want you to know something, Maria."

My arms press flat and hard into the mattress. "I said, who else have you used the program training on?"

He narrows his eyes. "You think we are the bad guys, is that right?" I open my mouth to speak, but he wags a finger. "No, no. No need to answer. I know your response." He leans back a little in the chair. I barely breathe. "But what you may not be aware of is that we are also known as Cranes. It's a … nickname, if you will." He waves a hand. "Oh, I know, nicknames are childish, and I doubt, given your atypical neurological patterns, that they are something you deal in. But this one, well, we are affectionate towards it. You, naturally, know of the country of Japan, yes?"

I do not respond, instead calculating how long it would take me to spring to the exit from the edge of the bed.

"I want you to answer, Maria." He sits forward. "Now."

"I know Japan."

"Good." He rests back again, and I feel my jaw tremble. "Now, after World War Two, in Japan, a crane came to symbolize hope and peace. A young girl—her name was Sadako Sasaki—contracted leukemia due to the atomic bombings. She knew she was dying, so she took to making thousands of origami cranes." He tilts his head. "She died aged twelve, and the world held her up as a figurehead for the innocent victims of the war."

"Why are you telling me this?"

He inhales. "The cranes Sadako made symbolized peace, Maria. Peace. We, too, stand for peace." He pauses. "Cranes, our nickname— it means peace because that's what Project Callidus represents. That's what we are about, what we fight for: peace. The National Security Agency scandal was just a red herring that threw us off track."

"The NSA were carrying out unauthorized surveillance on nonpolitical citizens."

"What? And you have a problem with that?" He leans in. "Let me tell you something: the work we do saves lives, Maria, *lives*. Does everyone really think they are protected online?" He tuts. "This is the real world. Terrorists. Cyber hack hits, all of them threatening our infrastructures, our economies—our way of life. We do what we do to protect our security and freedom of speech."

"For the greater good," I find myself saying.

His lips tilt upward. "Ah, you remember our training mantra."

I ease my back into the bedstead and feel the metal screws of the steel frame dig into my skin. "The Project is not a peaceful organization."

He bolts out of his chair. It is so fast, so unexpected, that at first I think I am imagining it, but then his face is in front of mine, almost pressed against my nose, his rough skin on my cheeks and his hot breath on me, sending my brain into spirals of chaos. It makes me gag. It makes my stomach want to convulse and my throat want to vomit, yet I do not move. The file. I need to know where the flashback happened, so I can get to Raven's file.

"Peace!" he spits. "We represent peace, Subject 375. You are a member of Callidus and you will not forget that. Will not! Do you understand?"

"Y-yes."

He remains there for two more heat-filled seconds, then finally peels his face away and returns to his seat. I exhale, hyperventilate, desperate to wipe his stench from my skin, wipe away his slimy spit and breath, but I know that if I do, it will alert him to the fact that the sedative has worn off and I can move. My hospital gown hangs in a tent over my legs, and when I glance to my knees, I see they are trembling.

"I am sorry I have to be so sharp with you at times, Maria, but I cannot stress enough to you the importance of what we do." He leans in. "You are shaking. You must be cold. Here." He drapes the end of my gown over the goose bumps on my legs, and I go so rigid with fear, my bones feel as if they could snap in two.

"So," Black Eyes says, sitting back, "we know you were online, hacking." He smiles—a slit, a sharp spike. "What did you find?"

"I found surveillance data."

"On whom?"

I pause. Do I tell him? "On me."

"On you and your father." He consults his file. "One Alarico Martinez, correct?"

My teeth clench at the sound of Papa's name. "Yes."

"And the information you accessed detailed this man as a contact, yes?"

I don't answer, can't.

"Answer me."

Do it. Buy time. "Yes," I force myself to say. I close my lips as I feel my legs and arms returning to me, the sensation flowing in, and as it does, in my head I can feel my brain finally firing, drug free.

Black Eyes crosses his legs and delivers me a stare. For a moment, I don't know what is happening or what to believe. I want to ask Dr. Carr about Papa, but I am scared to, because when I ask if Papa was the Project's liaison, what will I do if I learn that it is true?

The lights in the room cast a soft glow. They pulsate in the air and fill it with a sun-kissed color, and when I look at the walls, at the whiteness of them, they seem cream now in the light, and the familiarity of it all calms me somewhat and enables me to think.

"Let me tell you something, Maria," Black Eyes says now, his bony face protruding outward, "something you should have been told a very long time ago."

I don't move. I keep my limbs still and try to focus on why I am here and what I need to do.

"You understand," he says now, "what it means to be Basque, yes?"

I press my lips together, unsure why he is asking me this. My mouth is dry and the air is tepid, and I can feel my head rush with nerves and adrenaline.

"I asked you a question."

"I know what it means. Yes."

"Of course you do," he says. "So tell me, Maria, what do you think I have to tell you?"

"I cannot read your mind; therefore, I am unable to give you an answer."

"Come, on," Black Eyes says. "We trained you better than this. You are intelligent. You have an exceptionally high IQ. You tell me what you have deduced from the information you found."

"My father was helping you," I say.

"So that is your conclusion. Hmmm." Black Eyes tilts his head back and looks down at me from under creased eyelids. "It's interesting to see you notice everything, yet you have not noticed what is right under your nose." He pauses. "Fascinating. Peek-a-boo this certainly seems to be."

His eyes flutter briefly shut, and I quickly look to the exit and see the shadow of a person outside.

"Blood," he says now, eyes opening, "is the key here, you see. Your blood, its origins—well, let's say it is special to us."

A vague fear begins to rise toward the surface. "Why would my blood be special?" I speak slowly, carefully, as if speaking the words too fast would topple me over and I would never be able to get up again.

He unclips a pen from his jacket and tips it like a level, lowering it toward the file, which now sits fanned open on his lap. "You are blood type A, yes?"

I nod.

"Aloud!" he shouts.

I jump. Every hair on my body shoots upright. "Yes."

His shoulders soften. "Thank you. My apologies. And you are rhesus negative?" He provides me with one sharp stare.

"Yes," I hear my voice reply. "I am RhD negative."

Dread creeps through me as my brain fires, neurons charging. *Blood*, it whispers. *Blood. Blood. Blood.*

"You recruited me for my blood type," I say quietly, almost

to myself.

He angles his head to the left. "Very good."

"Why?"

He taps the nib of the fountain pen on the file. "Only 15 percent of Europeans are rhesus negative—15 percent—but you see, we have discovered over the decades, that these rhesus-negative types make excellent test sources." He pauses. "In Basque natives, did you know, the number of rhesus-negative types is an unusual 35 percent, and they all tend to be blood types O or A? Perfect subject material."

My brain connects and links. "Why are you telling me this? I am not Basque."

He regards me for a moment. "You like patterns, yes?"

I hesitate. "Yes."

"We discovered the quality of Basque blood via DNA patterns, helixes. That was how the real core of the Project took off."

"The Project used only Basque subjects to test on," I say, worried about my conclusion.

"Precisely, because their blood is perfect for use in our conditioning program, and of course, with a 35 percent ratio, there have been so many of them at our … disposal," he says. His pen hovers in midair by his side. "Once we made this discovery, from then on we used only pure Basque subjects, ideally with some Asperger's, with an autism link, like you. Their blood—your blood and your brain—are really fascinating." He pauses. "Do you understand what I am saying now?"

But I can't speak. My mind is moving fast now, but I want it to stop, want it to halt the course it's hurtling on so fast, it will smash everything I know into tiny, unrecognizable pieces.

"Maria—Subject 375—do you understand?"

And even though I do understand, my lips say, "No."

Black Eyes stays still. He remains in his seat and regards me for a second. Then, inhaling, he lifts the file from his lap and, taking his fountain pen from his pocket, unclips the lid and walks over to me.

"Then let," he says, grabbing my arm, "me enlighten you."

Fear floods me. He holds the fountain pen above me and plunges it down, his talon fingers pinching my upper arm, locking it down as he starts scratching green ink into my skin.

"No!"

He scratches deeper into me. "This has to be so, my dear. I know, I know. *Sssh*, there, there. It hurts me to do this, it truly does, but it must be done. It must."

The sound of my own screaming vibrates around the room until I pass out.

# CHAPTER 26

I come to. Black Eyes watches me, then replaces the lid on his pen, sits down on the metal chair, and crosses his legs. I raise my right arm, my hands and limbs, head trembling as, inch by inch I pull my shoulder around toward my face and view what he has done.

A shriek escapes my lips.

"Rather like your very own custom-made tattoo, hmm? I loved tattoos when I was young. Of course, my father wouldn't allow it." He studies me. "I see the sedative has worn off. Good, good."

The lights glow in the room. With shaking fingers, I touch my skin and wince as the tips touch the ink from Black Eyes' fountain pen, and I see with horror what is now permanently etched into me.

The words *I am Basque.*

I lurch to the side of the bed, haul my head over it, and vomit on the floor, drips of food hanging from my mouth and spritzing up my nostrils. Black Eyes frowns. He slides a beige handkerchief from his pocket, flaps it out whole, then, bending forward, dabs his shoes clean.

"Can't bear the smell of vomit. Are you better now?"

"Why did you do this?" I croak as I pull myself up and peer again at my arm. The skin around the scrawl is red and raw where the pen nib has torn into it, my body bleeding green ink with my blood.

"Sometimes, people need the truth just a little bit closer to, well …" He gestures to my arm. "… home. We call it shock treatment. It's very effective. This way, you will always know who you are."

"I know who I am."

"Really? Do you *really*, Maria?"

His voice is soft and low, and when I look at him, tiny creases fan from his eyes, and I don't understand. Is he feeling kindness toward me? Raven said I could find out who I really am if I locate the file. What did she mean? Pain throbbing through me, I blink again at my biceps, trying to piece it all together. "I cannot be Basque."

"Maria, my dear, you'd be surprised what we really can be if we look hard enough. And yes, you are Basque."

I don't know how long I sit there. I stare at my arm, ten seconds, twenty seconds. I lose track of time as the words blur into one and my brain switches off from the overload—at the smells and the sounds and the ink in my arm and even the whiteness of the walls that stare soullessly back at me. I know what it means, biologically, for me to be Basque, but *how*?

"The only way that I can be Basque is if there is Basque lineage in my father's and/or mother's family," I say after a while.

"Finally," he says, slapping his hand down onto his lap, "a probing thought. But," he says, glancing at his watch, "I have to leave you. Momentarily, you understand."

He rises, clutching his file, inserts his glasses into his top pocket, and turns to leave. But my mind does not focus on that, because something has slipped from his lap and dropped onto a pillow of towels that are stacked just to the right of his chair. I dart my sight straight to Black Eyes. I do not want him to notice what I have seen.

"Tests, Maria," he says now, striding to the door, his fingers resting on the handle. "We need to carry out some tests on you— small ones, just to ensure you are ready for service. Ready to work for us once more, for Cranes." He smiles, and my skin shivers. "For peace. It's lovely to have you back in the fold."

Withdrawing the remote control from his pocket, he directs it to the speaker. The 1930s melody creeps once more into the room, and I wince, the woman's voice warbling again as Black Eyes dwells on me for three seconds and my arm by my side screams in pain. I don't like him looking at me. I divert my sight, keep my eyes low, and quietly count the seconds in time to the melody until he leaves. Finally, on sixteen, he intakes a sharp breath, turns, and leaves the room.

I keep counting. With my sight fixed on the closed door, I count five more seconds, and when, on six, the shadow of the guarding officer outside disappears, I make my move.

First, I scan the room for obvious cameras. I detect none on initial search—no manufactured spiders on the wall, no unusual pictures or points. Yes, they could still be recording me, but the probability is that this is a secure area, a room where people can carry out whatever procedures they need to do—such as tattooing ink messages into someone's arm—completely undetected and unwatched.

I turn, drop my feet to the cold tile floor, and slip off the bed. I am unsteady at first, wobbling, almost falling into the chair, but after a few seconds, I become steady, finding my feet, instructing my limbs to move, and when I do manage to step forward, I peer down and see what I spotted only a minute or so ago. There, on the towels, Black Eyes' fountain pen.

I glance to the words tattooed into my arm; then, taking in a breath, I twist the pen nib loose and tear it from the base flute.

It snaps out with ease. I hold the nib in my palm and, slapping back my matted hair, close my fist around it, trying to push aside the music that lurches in and out of my ears.

And then the door sounds.

It is light at first, the noise, but there is an unmistakable click, followed by silence.

I move fast. Plunging the lid on the pen so it appears as normal,

I drop it to the towels, adjust it to its original position, fly across the room, and, shooting a look to the door, clamber to the bed. I swing my legs up and over it, pulling my knees to my chest, the nib locked in my palm. My heart pummels my ribs as I try to recreate the position I was in when Black Eyes left. As I draw my knees to my chest and clamp my arms around my legs, I realize something. The nib. It can't stay in my palm, or they will find it when they inevitably search me, either here or at the next place. My eyes fly left and right, hunting for a safe hiding space, when the door begins to open.

Panic. The 1930s jazz singer warbles on, the nib pricks my skin, and the door creaks farther into the room. A chill sweeps into the air as the cold from the corridor beyond wafts by, leaving me no time to move, and so I do the only thing I can: I slip the nib under my hair. The point pierces my scalp, but I dare not shift it.

Because, right now, the door is wide open.

Black Eyes enters, abruptly halts, then strides to the far side of the bed and, pausing to stare at me, looks down at the towels. My heart hammers. I try to act as I normally would, keep my eyes set downward, no contact made, and when his hand brushes the mattress near my leg, I make sure I flinch.

"Maria, remember to breathe," he says, the lines wrinkling out from his eyes again. "We're all on the same side here. I'm not going to hurt you."

He resumes looking toward the towels, and the music warbles on. My scalp stings from where the nib lies stuck into it, and every other second, I can feel a tiny trickle of blood weeping from the wound. I try not to move. Will he see it? Will he spot what I have done? The writing on my arm sends a sudden stab of pain, biting and hot, up to my shoulder, and even though it hurts, I don't react, in case the nib should dislodge and I give the whole game away.

Finally, Black Eyes picks up his pen and turns. I press my lips together hard, hoping he does not unclip the lid and find the pen empty, knowing that somehow, here, if they know what I plan to do, I may never get out, and then the file I need may as well not even exist.

Black Eyes cradles the pen in his palm, and I watch it and hold my breath. He exhales, and the tobacco from his lungs filters to my nostrils, sending my stomach into a spin.

"So, Maria, the tests are to begin soon," he says now. "Someone on the team will take you where you need to go."

"Where?" The pen nib jabs me.

"Just somewhere in the facility. It is routine." He pauses, smiles. I shiver. "*Routine.* I know you like that word, yes?"

"Yes."

The door slides open, and an intelligence officer enters. He wears black combat boots, a white T-shirt, gray sweater, and black sneakers. He is one meter and seventy-two centimeters tall, and his chest is as wide as an American football linebacker's, and when he stands in the doorway, he fills the space so much that the cold air from the corridor behind him stops blowing forth. He looks strong. My nerves start to spike.

Black Eyes nods to him and stands to one side. "Please take Subject number 375 to the conditioning area." He directs one more look at me, and without uttering another word, he strides out of the room and out of view.

Panic floods me.

The intelligence officer walks fully into the room now. My eyes dart to the exit. "Stay back," I say, but he ignores me and keeps moving forward, each step robotic, his skin, in this controlled light, glistening with a glossy sheen.

"Stay back," I repeat, yet on he comes. I iron myself into the bed and try to think fast. The nib hidden in my hair starts to make the blood from my scalp flow faster, and I shout at the officer, try one more time to stop him approaching, but still he comes. He halts by my side and arranges his face into a frown.

"Subject 375, you are to come with me for tests."

His voice is beige, no detectable accent, no dance to his words, and when he lifts his arms, his biceps move beneath his sweater. Blood crawls down my neck.

The 1930s music plays on as the man brings his body closer to me, and as he does, his eyes scan every fold and curve of my body. It makes me squirm. I shove myself back along the bed as much as I can, but as I do, my gown rides up on my legs, exposing my flesh, and I am shocked to realize that beneath the gown I am naked.

"You must come with me."

"No." Alarms scream in my head, and I smell the faint odor of metal from my own hemoglobin.

The officer glances to my leg; then, without warning, his hand flicks out and his index finger runs down my thigh.

I recoil. "Get off me!"

But he simply drops his hand, slices a smile across his face, and steps forward.

I bolt off the bed, launching myself to the corner of the room, but the officer strides over, blocking nearly all the light. "There are no cameras in here."

"Go away."

"You have to come with me."

"No."

"Yes."

"No!" I yell, heart smacking me, pulse scorching my arteries. "No!"

And then, without warning, he lunges. He juts out his arm and strikes, but I am ready. I roll to the side, my shoulder smacking into the wall as, to the left, the man jerks his torso around and runs at me, forcing me to heave my whole body in the opposite direction. But even then, he is on me, the heat of his frame pressing down on my chest like a vice, squeezing the oxygen from my lungs. I start to choke. Desperate for air, I smack my fist hard into his back, but he grabs my arms, straddling me, pinning me down so none of my limbs can move or fight.

He spits to the side. "They said you were strong."

"Get. Off. Me."

"I think we'll need the cuffs for you."

He reaches to his hip pocket, and without thinking, without stopping to risk-assess the situation, I take my chance.

# CHAPTER 27

## DEEP-COVER PROJECT FACILITY

*18 Hours and 10 Minutes to Confinement*

With my left arm freed for an instant as the officer goes for his handcuffs, I pluck the fountain pen nib from my scalp and rip it across the Project officer's cheek.

Blood trickles down his jawline, and his eyes dilate from the pain as he tries to sort out what has just happened to him. Driving upward, I plant my right shoulder in his solar plexus, to send him rocking backward.

My body slips free. I roll to the side and bang my head against the leg of the bed, a thump of nausea booting me in the stomach. But I haul myself up, not wanting to lose my narrow advantage. The man lies on the floor, dazed and groaning and holding his torn cheek, but not for long. Within three seconds, he drops his hand from his bleeding face and runs at me.

I dart to the right and smash into the metal cabinet, sending the drawer clattering to the floor. The man jumps on me, wrenching my arm so hard it feels as if the entire limb were being torn off, but I manage to keep the pen nib in my hand, and gash his wrist with the sharp tip.

With a yelp, he recoils, and I jump up. He staggers past the bed, then, spinning around, throws a left hook that catches me on the right cheek. My legs wobble, and I think I am going to fall, when the man lunges at me again. But he doesn't see my foot sticking out and goes flying.

His body falls like a tree, and although I am frantic and scared, I don't give the feelings room to surface, instead moving fast out of the way as he timbers down the side of the bed, smacking his skull on the corner of the bedside cabinet and knocking himself unconscious.

My chest heaves, relief and sweat flooding me as I gulp in huge breaths, the 1930s music still playing above my head. I pull myself up, legs wobbling, and take in the sight of the man sprawled on the floor. At the same time, I see my own body. The gown is ripped and my body exposed, and I want urgently to cover up. But before long, someone will notice we are missing from where we are supposed to be, which means they could be here soon. I have to get out.

I go straight to the door and pause. I need to think through for a moment what my plan is. Balthus mentioned an Ice Room, one Mama told him about with a nonserver-linked computer—possibly the very one Raven spoke of—and if I can find that here and then contact Chris, I may have a chance at locating the files I need. The woman sings her 1930s melody, and I take a moment to think, start to formulate a plan, when a hand grips my ankle. I shriek, look down.

"Fucking bitch!"

The officer. Gripping like a vise, he yanks my foot out from under me, toppling me instantly. My hands fly out, clawing the bedclothes, tearing off the sheets as I tumble forward. Levering himself up off the floor, he comes at me with all his strength, and I know that if I don't act now, if I don't do something drastic, he will take me to a room of sedatives and conditioning and tests against my will, and it will never end, this Project and its hold on me. The cycle will never stop.

The man is shouting now, in danger of alerting help, and this time I do not hesitate. Whether it is training or just my own primal survival response, something inside me kicks in.

I grab the legs of the metal cabinet and lift, and with one muscle-wrenching swipe, I swing it hard against the side of his head. He falls, and this time, instead of running away, I clamber on top of him, pinning him down with my legs and knees, and grab the pillow from the pile of bedclothes on the floor. Clutching the edges of the pillow, half of me horrified at what I am about to do, yet frighteningly focused, I press the pillow down onto the man's face and hold it there. His fists smash into my thighs. They hammer at the pillow, my legs, the floor, but as he squirms and thrashes, I press down harder.

And I don't let go.

From the speaker above, the crackly old jazz record plays on.

## UNDISCLOSED CONFINEMENT LOCATION
*Present Day*

"Would you like some more popcorn?"

I say yes and allow Ramon to feed me. Things are calm. My brother has been talking for a while now, over ten minutes in the semidarkness, and every time he looks at me he smiles a smile that spreads creases across his face and it makes me wonder again why he is here.

Ramon has given me dates. He has given times and events and minute-by-minute breakdowns as he reads my thoughts aloud from my journal. Each time he does, I hope that something will trigger a link to an explanation of Papa's involvement, but nothing has yet arisen.

I am recalling more and more, though, as my brother reads, of what has happened in the lead-up to my being here. It has been hard to contemplate, being in that room at the Project, my naked body in the ripped gown, the officer on top of me and then me holding the pillow on his face, but the mental strain of retrieving it is eclipsed by the elation I feel that my short-term memory is returning.

Ramon shifts the journal from his lap and sets the flashlight to the side to give me one more piece of popcorn from the tines of the fork, and as he moves forward, his hand brushes my shoulder.

"Ow."

"Sorry, M."

He has brushed the fabric against my skin, irritating it more than it should. "It itches," I say.

"Where?"

"On the top of my arm."

"Hang on." The fork still in his fingers, he sets down the popcorn bag, moves forward, pulls up my sleeve to scratch my skin, and gasps. "Maria, what the hell is this?"

I crane my neck to see. There on the outside of my left biceps, are the red, sore, etched-on words that Black Eyes scratched into my skin. It comes back to me then: the fountain pen, Black Eyes holding me down and breathing all over me, the Basque blood, the family lineage.

"M, what have you done to yourself?"

"I did not do it. Black Eyes did. He is from the Project."

Ramon drops my T-shirt, steps back, and shakes his head.

His voice drops. "Don't lie to me."

"I am not lying. This is what they did."

He looks again at my arm. "I mean, I knew you needed help, knew you got confused and even lied, but self-harming? I mean, why would you carve *I am Basque* into your arm?"

"It is not self-harm; it is ..." I stop, taken by a connection that is sparking in my head.

"Before the popcorn," I say, "you were reading an extract from my journal where Papa had a meeting with a man from his office in a café in the Plaza Mayor. You read how I sat at the next table eating ice cream, with the yellow sauce and red sauce on separate sides."

"Maria, I don't think that, given your arm, we should be—"

"This helps me."

He stops. I keep going, hoping it works. "Please," I say now, fast, eager. "I need help."

The light above swings in a buttered glow that smears across the room, and for one small instant, it makes the air seem as if the sun itself were here. Ramon rubs his chin and taps his foot and then, finally, picks up my journal and opens it. "What page?"

I feel relief and try to remain calm. "Thirty-five."

He turns the page and reads my words, and it jolts something. That day when I went for the ice cream—I remember it so well because Papa, unlike Mama, allowed me to have my sauces served separately because Papa knew I couldn't cope back then with red and yellow being mixed together, or even side by side. And I remember that now and recall it because, the next day, Mama took me to the autism facility, and Papa wasn't there. But did I write it down?

"What is the next entry?"

"Wait." Ramon flicks the page, states the date. "It says something about a white room and a computer and a load of weird tests." He looks up, a deep frown fixed to his brow. "M, what on earth would you write all this for? Is it some kind of dream?"

But I barely listen, because all I want to do right now is jump and whoop and clap my hands, because even though the memory in my journal would have been hazy and distorted by Project drugs, it gives me the answer I need: Papa could not have been the Project's contact. The date Ramon gave me kick-starts in my head a domino effect, dates tumbling into one another as I recall the times and days and even the weather on the occasions I went to the Project under the pretext of visiting the autism facility.

Papa did not take me to a single appointment.

So if he wasn't the contact, why were his initials on the file we found? It must have been a ploy, a cybertrail the Project wanted me to follow. That's how they found me—it makes perfect, logical sense now. They knew Dr. Andersson had been to my villa, knew I could kill her, take her SIM as I was trained to do, and so they planted false data in there somehow, via their covert asset in MI5, and that plant must have had a virus on it that—when the false Papa contact details were accessed and read, as they knew I would read them—it would instantly trigger a geolocation tracker for them to find me, right there and again at the monastery.

"Maria?"

I jerk my head up. Ramon is staring at me, the frown on his face even deeper now.

"You have a huge smile on your face," he says. "Does it help, reliving the memories of Papa?"

"Yes."

"Good." He beams.

"Because it means that Papa wasn't in contact with the Project. And the Project is corrupt. They hurt people. They scratched words into my arm with a green ink fountain pen and they use people only for their blood type. Did you know we have Basque lineage somewhere in our family?"

His grin evaporates, and he slams the book shut. "Jesus, M, stop it!"

"Stop what?"

"Talking about the Project like it's some awful, evil thing!"

He stops, chest heaving. I watch him, and slowly, dread and fear rise up inside me as I put together what his words signify.

"What do you mean, Ramon?" I say, scarcely daring to ask. "How do you know the Project?"

He catches his breath. He wipes spit from his chin and levels his gaze at me. "You talk about the Project as if it were bad."

"They *are* bad. They do bad things, and they have done bad things to me. They have made me do bad things, too."

"No."

"Yes."

"No, no, no!" He starts pacing and knocks the light, sending the bulb swinging in the air so the room swims in and out of light and shadow.

I begin to worry. This is not the routine way that my brother normally acts, and when he eventually stops, his eyes are down-turned and his face sweats.

"They said you would say this about them," he says after a moment.

"Who?"

He shakes his head. "The Project does not do bad things. They are there to help you."

I keep steady and force myself to ask the next question. "How do you know this, Ramon?"

He raises his head now and looks to me. "Because I asked them to help me with you," he says, then lifts his head high, jutting out his chin and chest. "Because I contacted them. It was never Papa. It was me."

# CHAPTER 28

**DEEP-COVER PROJECT FACILITY**

*18 Hours and 1 Minute to Confinement*

I let go of the pillow and toss it back onto the floor. The officer does not move.

I check his throat for a pulse. There is nothing, no heartbeat, no pumping of blood in his veins, and when I watch him and wait, expecting to feel the surge of horror and shame I felt at killing Dr. Andersson, I feel nothing—not a shred of upset, not a flicker of doubt. I observe his corpse and tell myself that I have done the right thing. *Prepare, wait, engage.* The phrase circles my head.

I stagger to my feet, wincing at the pain, and glance up to the speaker, where the music still flows. I have to move. Soon, very soon, whoever is expecting me to arrive for tests will question where I am, will wonder where the officer in the sweater is, and when he does not show up, they will come looking for us.

I observe my scratched, naked body, the ripped gown hanging from me, and think. I have to get out, but I can't go dressed like this, unprepared. I look back to the man, to the clothes he wears, to his pockets, and, wiping my mouth with the back of my hand, I hobble over to the corpse and start patting it down for anything that may be of use. From the large combat pocket on the left leg, I extract an item and see that it is a computer floppy disk. This is odd. These have not been used for over a decade, so why does this man have one?

I search the rest of his clothes. Pulling out four more items, I examine them at speed: a swipe card, a cell phone, an opened pack of gum, and a tiny black and silver car fob. I turn the fob in my hand, noting the make of the vehicle. Then, setting the items on the floor, I start shucking the clothes off the dead body and putting them on.

The clothes are baggy but adequate. Slipping the sweater over my head and tightening the belt as much as it will go, I scoop the stolen items back up from the floor and stash them in the cargo pockets. I count to five and step to the door, expecting a lock to unpick or a code to crack, but it is unlocked. I glance at the dead officer—he must have thought I'd be easy to handle.

The bass line, drumbeats, and piano riffs follow me out as I look both ways. The area is clear. The walls, like those in the room, are white, and along the crease between wall and floor is a black strip that runs as far as I can see. There are no windows, just strips of clear Perspex in sections, which, like the bed in the room, have rounded edges and corners. And when I track above me, I see that the lights running the course of the ceiling have a low-stimulus glow as the corridor stretches out in clearly defined, compartmentalized segments.

Scanning one more time for personnel, I clasp the sweater around my abdomen and tiptoe out into the corridor, thinking of the dead officer's cell phone. I can use it to contact Chris via secure text so he knows my location. I pad forward and go as steadily as I can with my bruised limbs and battered face, my eyes scanning every inch of space, and even though at first glance there are no cameras or hidden recording devices, I tread along the walkway, slow and silent, stopping at short, defined intervals to check for any sounds.

I peer around a corner and immediately hit a problem: an officer is standing nearby, his back to me, talking on a phone. Heart slamming against my chest, I watch him and think. The best plan right now is to wait—the officer may finish with his call shortly, and with luck, he will keep walking away and I can move. But as I observe him and scan the area, something on his shirt catches my attention. The shirt seems to be of soft cotton fabric, but what makes me go very still is the black printing just below the right shoulder: the letter "H," followed by a three-digit number.

My mind instantly goes to the flashback. In that memory, when I entered the room where Raven was, an officer was there, with the same lettering and number font as this officer. I risk another look to check in case I am mistaken, but I am not. The two are the same. Black Eyes said this facility is in Hamburg, so is that what the "H" on the shirt signifies? And if so, does that mean the image I recalled of Raven telling me about the room and the files is from here? I look again at the walls and the lights and try to conjure any memory I have of being here, of walking here, and there are some hazy, smudged thoughts, but nothing I can hold tightly to.

An idea strikes. Slipping the stolen cell phone from my pocket and scanning the area before I start, I unclip the SIM and check for bugs. Satisfied there are none, I reseat the SIM, switch on the phone, and, bypassing the PIN code via a fast hack, I enable text encryption. Then, peering around the corner and seeing the officer still there, I text Chris.

**With Project. Injured but ok. In Hamburg. Can u trace my location. Looking for file …**

I hit SEND, and almost immediately a reply pings back.

**Hiya! Was worried. Your cell has GPS. Project can track it. Am disabling Project tracking so only I can track u then u r safe. Doing it now … Patricia says: five fingers (??)**

Patricia's hand sign to me. I clutch the cell, and the nerves I feel subside a little from knowing that my friend is there for me and that for now, she is safe. I wait, anxious for the next reply. I cannot tap my foot, or the officer ahead will hear, so I clench my teeth and count. On five, Chris finally replies.

**Done. Got you. Your location is 7 km outside Hamburg near**

disused factory. I can track u to a walkway in building flagging up as a pharmaceutical company. Balthus says be careful. I say what ;-)

*What.* For some reason, amid all the chaos and anxiety, I find myself smiling just a little at Chris' word. I text back.

Tell Balthus: officer here with same letter (H) & number font as in flashback with Raven. Think this could be the facility with the file. Do u concur?

Five seconds later, a reply:

Balthus here. Yes. Agree. Sounds the same facility. Be careful. Stay in touch. Chris ready to help.

I clutch the cell, breathing much easier now when the officer finally finishes his call and strides away down the corridor, leaving the place empty for now. The lights glow, casting soft yellow lines to the white walls, and when I scan the area, the Perspex shimmers and the rounded edges of the plastic take on a small, gentle glint. I am about to pad down the hall when a message comes in from Chris, and I slip back around the corner for cover and read it.

Balthus said file & computer from flashback may be in ICE room. I have an idea how to locate it.

I try to ascertain how he could do this, and come up blank, I text back:

How? Not possible.

Process of elimination, Google, he texts back immediately. Do most Proj. facility rooms, from your memories, have server computers & internet enabled?

Unsure where he is going with this, I speed through what I can recall.

Yes. 98% probability of server connection/internet. What plan?

Hacking into their system now via geolocation on your cell ... Wait ...

I tap my foot and feel nerves rise inside me. The longer I wait out here, the greater my risk of being found. After four seconds, Chris replies and I allow myself to breathe out.

OK. Process of elimination. Only two rooms without server connection/internet that aren't storage cupboards. One could be the ICE room you need.

I stare at the phone, a little shocked. How did he do that so quickly? But before I can think it through, another text comes in, and this time it links to a live map tracker of the infrastructure of the Project building.

I type straightaway.

Is this secure??

100%. The red dots r the two rooms for you to try. Can u find them? Side note: located two cameras in the area and switched them to static image so you safe.

I look up. He's right. In the corner of the corridor, where the ceiling meets the wall, are two tiny black dots, barely visible, and when I squint my eyes, I can see two microscopic lenses with a glassy sheen. I exhale, wipe a bead of sweat from my brow, and, counting to three to stay calm, look back to the cell phone map from Chris. The rooms are not far away, and when I calculate the time it will take to reach the first room, I realize it is only twenty seconds down the corridor to the right. I look up. The area is clear.

Will go to nearest room now.

As I send this, holding the cell phone out so I can watch my movements on the map on the screen, I sprint along the walkway, my feet padding along the tiles.

I reach the first room in twenty seconds as forecast, stop, and scan the corridor to make sure I am alone. When all seems safe, I text Chris with my status and examine the door that now stands in front of me. It is silver in color. It stands 204 centimeters high, and when I touch it, the stainless steel feels cold. Hinges are mounted on the outside of the frame, and when I look to the handle, I see a scanner entry system pad, with a light under the shaft of metal that lies on top.

The light shines, signaling that the door is locked, the room barred. I take out the swipe card from the dead officer, look at it, then at the door and the scanner, and see instantly that the two will match, meaning the door will open. But that is not what grabs my attention, what makes me now realize that I am standing in front of the room from my flashback—the one Raven was in, the one Mama must have overheard someone talking about and told Balthus of when she was ill.

I look up, scan and listen for anyone approaching, and, satisfied I am alone, text Chris.

**Located ICE room.**

He replies instantly.

**What? You certain? How can you tell?**

I lift my eyes to a brushed-metal panel with black writing in the top left corner of the door. The panel reads ISOLATED COMPUTER ENVIRONMENT.

ICE.

I hold up the cell phone, click a picture of the panel, and, sending it to Chris, text **Track me**. Then, swipe card in hand, I bring it up to the entry system pad.

# CHAPTER 29

**DEEP-COVER PROJECT FACILITY**

*17 Hours and 52 Minutes to Confinement*

My fingers pinch the edge of the swipe card and are about to glide it under the scanner, when a text from Chris flashes on the phone: STOP!!

I pull my hand away and read the next message, worried now that someone will come at any moment and find me.

**Do not enter ICE room yet. Have detected a sensor on the door that alerts a central control room if activated. Will disable alarm now.**

I look at the words and think. Disabling the alarm will enable me to enter the ICE room without triggering the sensor, but there is a huge problem with Chris' suggestion. Palms sweating now, I text back fast, not sure I will be in time to stop him.

**URGENT: Do not disable alarm. Control will detect if alarm disabled. Will flag on system. You must instead bypass system and switch sensor to a permanent "no alert" mode. This will not arouse suspicion.**

I stop and wait. My heart beats hard against my chest, and when I look down the corridor, the lights on the ceiling flicker and the walls shimmer in frostbitten white, and in the air a clinical, detergent smell drifts in and out. After five seconds, Chris finally replies.

OK. Good spot. Hacking into control center system now. Hard.
Will be as quick as can :0

I look at the symbols he has put on the end of the message. I
don't know what they mean, and it bothers me. My foot begins to
tap. I am exposed here in the corridor, and even though the cameras
have been deactivated and the Project cannot trace the cell phone,
I am still vulnerable. I wait. My eyes scan the door, again checking
the panel bearing the name of the ICE room. The words appear
etched on, thick, black, rigid, straight. I risk touching the door and
find it is smooth, and when my index finger runs down the center,
a streak of cold comes up so fast and unexpectedly that I have to
snap my hand away.

I check the cell. Chris has not replied, and it is now hard to
contain the anxiety inside me, so I focus on my breathing and clench
my teeth to contain what panic I can and not alert the Project to my
position. My fingers hover, about to text a request for an immediate
update on progress, when I hear a sound. I freeze. Boots in the
distance at, on initial calculation, one hundred meters away, the
distinct slap of their rubber soles on tiles indicating two, perhaps
three people. And they are coming toward this area at a moderate
walk. I quickly text Chris.

Urgent. Officers approaching. Require update now.

I scan the corridor and listen. They are closer, perhaps fifty
meters down the intersecting corridor, no more, the sound becoming
louder and louder in my ears and my head, and when I stop, voices
whisper out, drifting up through the corridor. I look again at the
phone, but still there is no message.

"Where is she?" I hear a voice somewhere ahead say in clipped,
neat words.

They are only thirty meters from me now. I could enter the ICE
room and take a chance on not triggering the alarm, but this is the
Project, and all areas have a high probability of being monitored
and checked, and if, upon entering, something alerts them, they

will find me. Twenty meters now. I swallow, scan the left side of the corridor. Here, the air is darker, the lights lower, and the glow so muted that the color appears to be lilac and purple rather than orange. I could run that way. I could sprint right now and take a chance at finding a route through, contacting Chris so he could track me on his laptop remotely and help me escape. I think. The boots sound. They must be fifteen meters away now.

The cell vibrates, and I nearly jump at the sensation of it in my hand.

**Done. Go in room NOW.**

The voices are ten meters away. Keeping my nerves as steady as I can, I swipe the entry card under the sensor and, twisting the handle as softly as I can, slip through the door, and as I click it carefully shut, three pairs of boots clomp past outside and walk on by.

## UNDISCLOSED CONFINEMENT LOCATION
*Present Day*

Ramon ceases pacing and rolls his head. I don't know what to do. The light in the room has weakened, and the bulb above us hangs limp from the ceiling, where droplets of moisture now gather and fall.

"Why did you contact the Project?"

My brother inhales. It is long and drawn in, sending his eyes up into his brow, so all I can see in the dimness of the room is the pale white of his eyes.

"You needed help."

Worry and confusion collide in my head. How can Ramon believe the Project could help me? The thought scares me because, in all the time I have known about the Project and the hold it has over me, I never imagined that hold would extend to my brother. The fear that grips me now is more than I have ever felt. It rips into me, tearing open so wide what I held true, that reality is barely recognizable anymore, because it's not just me they are poisoning—my entire family is infected, too, and it is all so painful to contemplate that my brain cannot process the emotions of it. I start to bang my head lightly on the back of the chair.

"The Project is dangerous," I say. "They cannot help me."

"They are doctors. M, stop banging your head—you'll hurt yourself."

"They perform tests on me. They will hurt you." The thought makes me bang my head a little harder.

"No, they won't, and tests can help you." He shifts forward.

"M, please stop."

"No."

"Yes." He tuts. "See, M, this is what I don't understand. You've been seeing the Project for years. Why won't you just accept that all along they have been there to help you?"

I stop hitting my head. His words, my brother's words. *Seeing the Project for years.* A cold shiver runs down me as I connect it all, as one by one, the pieces all slot into place like a puzzle. The files, the ones Chris hacked into at the monastery, turning up the false information about the contact being Papa, when all along, it wasn't Papa at all, just as Ramon said.

"How do you know I have been seeing the Project for years?"

He remains quiet.

"I said, how do you know I have been seeing the Project for years?"

"You know."

"I want you to say it."

He closes his eyes. "Because I'm their contact."

Blood rushes up to my head. I instantly thrust myself forward, rattling my arms and legs to break free. "Let me out."

"M …"

"You sent me to the Project! *You* were the contact, not Papa. You let them test on me! How long have you been with them?"

"M, calm down."

"How long have you been in touch with them?"

He shifts from foot to foot. "Several years."

"How many?" He is thirty-six years old. Two decades of contact would mean he started at sixteen.

"M, stop!" His voice rises, and I slap back into the chair at the sounds, and when I look at my hands, they are red and bulging where my fingers and nails press into the wood.

"Maybe it's ten years?" he says. "More? I got the information on the Project from Mama."

And then, when he utters that, it all makes sense: the Project being able to find me; MI5 discovering my villa; the handlers; the file Chris located at the abbey, with all the surveillance data on me; my locations, actions, full day-by-day whereabouts, right down to the second. "You accessed the details Mama believes are for an autism center and you have contacted the Project, and the Project has turned you. They have convinced you they are helping me, and are now using my own brother to conspire against me."

"Maria, that's not true."

"They are dangerous," I say, urgent now. "You can't trust them. Ramon, whatever they have told you, you cannot believe them."

"He said you'd say that."

I stop at his words. "*Who* said I would say that?"

"Dr. Carr."

"Dr. ... Dr. Carr." I say the words as if in a trance, and when I blink, the room feels as if it is swaying and yet everything remains still and frozen and set in stone and time. Ramon does not move. He hangs his fingers by his side and, tipping his head to the left, observes me as I frown and drop my chin, my mind grappling with the weight of what is real and raw and utterly urgent.

"M? M, say something. You're worrying me."

I lift my head. "You know Black Eyes."

"Black *who*?"

"Black Eyes is Dr. Carr. Which facility are we at?"

"What? What do you mean 'facility'?"

I look at the room again. The walls I recall from my dreams are white, but here there is no light and the walls are black and soot-filled, so what does that mean? What location can that be?

"If Dr. Carr has been contacted," I say now at speed, "or if Project officers are on their way, we have to get out of here. They could arrive soon." I try to pull myself up and out, but the rope drags me back and pins me to the chair. Breathless, I look around. The crate is upturned; my journal sits on it, open to a page where Ramon left it. "We have to get away from them. We all are in danger. Mama, is, too. It says in my journal what they can do. It details everything the Project has done to me that I can remember."

He sighs. "M, Mama is fine."

"How do you know Mama is fine? Have you seen her? We could be anywhere now. The Project has facilities in places I still do not know of. We are not safe."

"M," he says, his voice low and hushed, "Mama is fine because … because she is here."

Mama at the Project? Panic rises up like lava. "No! Mama is not well. If the Project has Mama, it means none of us are safe now. You must understand this. Mama has cancer. This will endanger her health!"

He shakes his head and rubs the bridge of his nose with his fingers. "M, please stop."

"We have to get out!"

He lifts his eyes now to mine. The air is stagnant. When I look to my journal, I see scrawled writing, notes, math equations, and sketched drawings. The fork from the popcorn lies next to the open pages, and when the lightbulb swings, glints of metal prongs catch the ripples of air as, before me, Ramon bends down, shuts my journal, and picks it up, knocking the fork to the floor in front of me. He slides the journal under his arm, and pausing to press his fingers into the cover, he takes one step to the side where the timer and the medical stand are.

"What are you doing?" I ask. "It is vital we get to Mama."

"M, Mama is safe."

"How can you be certain? The Project has her."

"You have to stop talking about the Project like this, M. They do not have her."

"You said she is here," I say. "The Project is dangerous. And if the Project does not harm her, MI5 could take her in order to get to me and kill me, just as they tried to in my villa."

"What? *Kill* you? What the …?" He wipes a palm across his mouth and, for three seconds, does not speak. "They won't get to Mama, just as surely as no one is going to kill you. MI5? Jesus, M. You've always done this, ever since we were kids. Exaggerating, saying you've been taken by people, writing down weird made-up stories about doctors and white masks and needles. You just wanted to be a doctor, that's all, so you could make people better, give you a sense of control over life's events after Papa died. It had nothing to do with the Project. You've got to stop making things up, blaming other people." He stops. "I love you," he says after a moment, his voice soft, low. "I really, really do, but you always make it about you—always. I exist, too. All Papa ever saw was you."

"That is physically illogical, and untrue. Papa was not blind; therefore, he could see you in the same way as he could see me."

He opens his mouth to speak but then shuts it, huffing out a great sigh of breath. "That's not … that's not what I meant."

"How do you know the Project will not get to Mama and hurt her?" I say fast, my mind now calculating every scenario of how Mama could be located and used by either the Project or MI5. "You cannot be 100 percent certain."

"Yes, I can," he says, "because (a) the Project is not who you say it is, and (b) Mama is not with the bloody Project, because Mama is upstairs in her house in Madrid!"

The whole room stands still. All of it, everything. Ramon's words hit my brain, and at first they just hover there, suspended in midair, levitating in my mind.

"Are we in … Mama's city house?"

"Yes."

I keep my eyes down, not daring to look up in case they give away the fear and bewilderment I now feel. The Project has facilities in several locations, but all along, this has not been one of them.

"We are in Madrid," I say aloud after a moment, sounding the phrase out. I try to think through my movements before this room, and small flashes of memories whip by, of an airport and people and noise and a tall apartment building.

"Which part of Mama's house are we in?" My voice shakes.

"The basement."

I compute the information and force myself to scan the room. The dark walls, the damp and the droplets, and the suffocating air that swings on a pendulum between hot and cold. As a child, I would come to Mama's Madrid place many times when she was working on a case in the capital, but I was never allowed into the basement. I was permitted only as far as Papa's study in the room before the entrance to the basement steps below.

"You kept me in Mama's house for the Project. Why?"

He pauses. "Because I was worried about you. You disappeared after prison, and you came here through the window, M, the bloody window, and it scared the shit out of us. I mean, what the hell? So I contacted them about you, to see if they could help calm you down."

He flicks something on the timer now, and a rush of liquid floods the still air. I jerk my head to the right. "What are you doing?"

Ramon turns one more switch, then, securing my journal under his arm, steps into full view. His hair has slid down to his eyes in the heat, and under his arms are two circles of damp.

"Turn off the timer, Ramon."

"They will be coming soon," he says now.

I lunge forward. "No. Ramon, no."

But he simply sighs and shakes his head. "M, it's the right thing to do, it really is. You're out of control. The things you say"—he gestures to my journal—"the things you write. M, you need help. I love you, you are my little sister—and you need help. The Project is there for you. Yes, their recommended methods are a little unorthodox, but at the end of the day, they're on your side." He exhales. There are tears in his eyes. "We all are."

I thrash forward again. "Ramon, no. Do not give me any more drugs. It makes me forget! This is what they do. Do not believe them! Do not tell them anything more about me!" Mama is upstairs. Ramon is with the Project. She is in danger.

"No, M. They said the medicine would do you good, keep you under control until they could get here and help us with you."

I throw my body forward against my restraints. "Ramon, do not leave me here!" And as I say the words, as I lunge toward my brother with all my energy, snapshots of images begin flooding back to me, *click, click, click*, one after another like a camera, as my short-term memory finally starts to expose itself in full. I see the Project and a room and the man on top of me and the ICE room that Chris helped me break into undetected. I see it all, finally, recall every single part, right up until I arrived here.

My brother ascends the steps, opens the door, and turns. "It's okay, M. It's for the greater good."

He leaves, the sound of the closing door vibrating through the room and into the darkness of my ears and head.

The timer by my side ticks.

# CHAPTER 30

**DEEP-COVER PROJECT FACILITY**

*17 Hours and 41 Minutes to Confinement*

I slam my back against the wall and, catching my breath, recite the names and birthplaces of Mozart, Debussy, and Wagner to calm me down. I listen for any officers coming this way. After counting ten seconds, and when all seems clear, I grip the cell phone tight, pad ahead, and observe the area.

The ICE room is six meters by six meters, with no windows or soft furniture, and on the walls is a light pattern of leaves that appear as if they have been stenciled on with a lead pencil. It is cold. A small fog of my breath puffs into the air, and I pull the dead man's sweater close to my chest, and hook the fatigue pants up to my stomach so they don't slip down my hips. The lights in this room, as outside, are low-stimulus, casting small shadows of my frame across the walls, and when I move my arms, their shadows rise across the dimensions of the space, making my body seem bigger than it is.

Over to the right sits a computer. I walk to it now and slowly peer down. It seems to be linked, from first glance, to a modem in the corner, on a shelf table that juts out like an ice sculpture and dominates the room. I remain as I am, and keep my eyes set on it. Could this be it? Could this be the computer Raven informed me of?

I text Chris to update my status, then take two steps toward the computer, but something is not right. I bend forward and realize what is unusual about it: its age. The computer is old, not a modern laptop or a flat-screen update, but a clunky, cumbersome machine—a fat, unwieldy dinosaur of a device, with a modem that sits by the potbellied screen where two green lights flash. It is switched on, ready to be used.

The cell phone vibrates, making me jump a little. I compose myself and read.

Creating a secure line now to speak on. Ready in three. Two. One. OK. You can call me now if safe.

I call Chris' cell, and Balthus picks up.

"Oh, Maria, thank God you're okay. Where are you?"

I tell him, my eyes on the computer.

"Does it look like the one the woman in your memory described?"

"It is possible."

"Doc?"

Patricia. Hearing her voice, I instantly smile. "Are you safe?" I ask.

"What, me? Doc, I'm fine. I'm more worried about *you*. Are you hurt?"

I touch the bruises now appearing on my wrist, where the officer pinned me down, and glance to the phrase that Black Eyes etched in ink on the flesh of my upper arm. "I am hurt, but not to a concerning degree. I am in the ICE room."

"Okay. Okay, good, good. I'm going to pass you on to Chris, okay? But, Doc, be careful. We're all here, yeah? You're not on your own."

I breathe in and let her words sit in my head and stay there.

Chris comes on the line now. "Hey, Google, so what can you see?"

"My name is not Google."

"I know."

I look to the room and describe the computer as I have seen it so far.

"Sounds like a stand-alone, all right. Way old, too. Have you switched it on?"

"It is on standby." I lean in. "Pressing the button now. There is an old hard-drive station to the right." I wait one second, two, until finally a fan inside whirs to life and the screen flashes green once, dies, then reappears with an operating page.

I feel a shiver and wish the Project guard had been wearing a coat over his sweater. To the side is a chair made of gray plastic, with black rubber soles. I pull it out—no sound made on the floor—and keeping the cell phone to my ear so no one passing by will hear any extra voices, I say to Chris, "The screen is fully functional now."

"Cool. Anything on there yet?"

It first appears flat and empty, but then, as the screen flickers and moves, a red and blue icon, with a yellow bar like a vulture's beak, appears in the upper right corner. I describe it to Chris.

"Whoa," he says. "Really?"

"Yes."

"Do you know how to access it then bypass the code?"

I think to my notebook and remember all the images from it, of data and numbers photographed in my head. "I can access the first level and then jump to the second."

"Nice. If there are more levels after that, I can help. Oh, wait— Patricia says 'five fingers' again. What the hell is that?"

I think of Patricia's hands held up to mine, and keeping an ear attuned for any external sounds, I push the overlong sweater sleeves up to my wrists and get to work. The first task is to concentrate on the computer screen and locate the yellow symbol that matches the one from my memory of the notebook and coding. Almost instantly, a series of numbers flashes up, then nothing. The screen plummets into black and my eyes try to dig into the glass, searching for something that is not there. I try to think fast. What have I done? Has clicking on the icon crashed the system? Do they know I am here, and have they alerted Black Eyes?

I tell Chris what has happened, unsure whether he can help, but aware that if I waste any more time, my odds of being found go up.

"Okay, hang on," he says. I hear some rustling, and he's back. "Sorry. Bag of chips. Okay, so you should see a blue square, top left corner. See it?"

He is right. At the edge of the screen is a tiny blue square no more than one millimeter in diameter, and squinting, I see that it is soft at the edges, with round corners. "It is pulsating," I say.

"It is? Ah, okay. Don't touch it, then—it's a trap. Kind of. Okay, now look at the yellow part of the icon instead and hover the cursor over it. I'm trying to access their system now at the same time, so I'll be a sec."

There is a clash of sound outside. I don't move—just wait and listen. It sounds like something metal being tipped over, but in this room it is difficult to determine the exact location. After five seconds, the sound passes and the air returns to quiet. I swallow, look to the screen, and carry on.

The cursor, when it hovers over the yellow of the icon, shimmers, as Chris said it would. I lean in and study it. There are pixels—black, tiny pinprick dots that flash in and out as it moves—and when I sit back, they seem to disappear.

"Hey, Google, you still there?"

I ignore Chris' name for me and instead describe to him the structure of the yellow icon.

"Oh, awesome. Okay. I want you to click on it now, and if I've got my sums right, we should be able to get in."

"How can you be certain?"

"I can't, but it's the best shot we've got, right?"

I hesitate. Mathematical certainty is what I prefer to deal in. It is more reliable than people, more black and white, no gray areas, no hidden meanings. But if Chris is not completely certain, how can I trust him?

"Google, have you done it yet?"

"I am unsure about this route of progress."

"Why? Because it's not a definitive model?"

I watch the cursor blink at me. "Yes."

Chris lets out a breath that I can hear. "Look, the way I see it is that life is a series of choices and you can't always predict the outcome. Even as a mathematician, that's impossible. You deal in numbers, right?"

"Yes."

"Well even numbers are not straightforward, even though they're infinite. I mean, look at the twin prime conjecture."

I sit up, surprised that he knows of this complex theory. "That is the conjecture that there are an infinite number of primes that differ by two."

"Exactly. In 2004, someone proved it was true, and then the paper was retracted because a load of errors were found in it, and so they were all back to the start. So you see, nothing's certain, even when you think it is. So the only answer has to be, well, to carry on anyway, the best you can."

I think about Chris' words, his theory and idea. Could it be so? Could I even try to live a life where the color gray was an unknown quantity I could cope with?

Inhaling a deep breath, I count to four, then move the cursor and click on the yellow logo, and tell Chris. Together we wait. After three seconds, slowly, an image unfolds on the screen and I watch as one pixel, two, then tens upon tens shower down the screen.

"Are the pixels still coming?" Chris says.

My eyes track every single one. "Yes." But then something changes. "It has gone clear now."

"Whoa. Okay, can you see anything? Any different color or another logo of some sort?"

I lean in. "There is a file icon with two dark, black ovals in the far right corner, and a name."

"A name?" It is Balthus now, his voice quick and loud. "Who?"

I lock the cell between my ear and my shoulder and look at the screen. The image of Raven sways in my mind. The flashback, the visual of my fingers compiling a report on a computer, with dates and details and confidential operational data.

"The name is the author of the report." My breath catches. "It is me. Dr. Maria Martinez. And the report concerns two subject numbers."

"Which ones?"

I stare at the screen, almost too fearful to read them aloud, because it means the flashback was real—I compiled this report.

"Subject numbers 115 and 375," I say after a while.

Raven.

And me.

# CHAPTER 31

**DEEP-COVER PROJECT FACILITY**

*17 Hours and 35 Minutes to Confinement*

"This is the file," I say. My hands are shaking, and when I look at the screen, it seems blurred and hazy. I scrunch my eyes shut, then open them and try to gain some focus, but it is hard. This woman has haunted my dreams for a whole year, and now here I am and the answers that she told me existed may actually be real.

"Patricia," I say, the cell phone still wedged on my shoulder.

"Doc, you okay?"

I swallow and blink at the file. "You will remain near the phone, yes?"

"Of course, Doc. Of course. Just breathe, okay?"

I inhale long and deep, and when I look to the lights, I feel grateful that they are low and not bright and glaring. I take a moment to think. The crude tattoo Black Eyes scratched into my forearm feels raw and painful, and so I count to ten and imagine slumbering lines of lavender plants, fragrant orange groves fat with fruit, olive trees swaying in a warm evening breeze, and the fire pit in the small stone courtyard of my Salamancan villa sparking a roasting fire.

Exhaling hard and heavy, I open my eyes. "Shall we?" Chris says.

I set my back straight. "Yes."

"Okay, Google. Tell me what you see."

I start scanning. I follow the curve of each letter on my name first, each digit and line. "It is clear the file is encrypted."

"How do you know?"

"It is steeped in a code that, on first sight, I do not recognize."

"Can you try a basic decryption, see if that works?"

My fingers glide across the keyboard, accessing the next level underneath the file, via the subject numbers on the screen. But the second level comes to a halt, and no matter what I do to enter it, it throws back my access request every time.

"To penetrate the file requires a pass code similar to others I have cracked," I say now to Chris, listening for sounds outside and careful to keep my voice low. "But this document seems harder and most likely requires a password pattern I may not be able to decipher, or an algorithm I do not identify with."

I pause, exhale, and listen for any signs of intruders. When I'm sure all is clear, I squash down my anxiety and think.

"Patterns," Chris says. "Accessing the next level could all be a matter of patterns."

My brain joins in. "Find the pattern and we gain access."

Moving fast, I backtrack on myself and review the numbers that have flashed up in my head, following the patterns that arise and matching them to the decryption required to access the file. But nothing penetrates it—no answer, no code—as if my brain has hit pause.

"Anything?"

"No."

"Okay, let me see what I can do."

Pain shoots up from my wrists, and I wince. Lowering my arms, I look at the skin. Bruises are beginning to emerge in even stronger colors now, blues and purples smeared like paint across my skin, and the pain of it mixes with the sting of the fountain pen scar on my muscle, sending a crackle of spikes into my bones. As I stare at the screen, at the empty password bar, anger surges inside me at the thought of what Black Eyes did to me, the word *black* swarming around my head, thicker, faster, like a plague of locusts, darkening my mind. *Black, black, black* … And as I think of this word, a memory begins to float upward in my brain, but this time, unlike the others, the recollection doesn't hurtle me back in time with a jolt, but instead takes my hand and slowly leads me to see what was always there, locked in my head. It is me at a computer, just as I was in my flashback at the villa, but this time, unlike before, I can see the screen that is in front of me, the one where I was working on the file. There is a pen to my left, and a piece of paper with my notes, and in front of me is a red file folder with the word CONFIDENTIAL printed across it. I see my face, no lines or wrinkles, looking to the screen as it asks me for a password, and there is a name on the file.

My name. And two subject numbers …

"Maria? Maria?"

Balthus' voice comes into my ear from the cell phone, and I come around with a start and sit bolt upright.

"Maria," Balthus says, "what is happening?"

I blink my eyes into focus. "I know the password."

"What?" Chris says. "How? Did you crack the code?"

"No," I say, pulling in the chair now. "I *wrote* the code." I pause. "And I wrote the password."

"You remembered?" Balthus says. "You remembered what was on the screen from your flashback?"

"Yes." My fingers hover over the keyboard.

"What was it?"

I begin typing it into the password bar. "Black Eyes."


## CONFINEMENT LOCATION
*Present Day*

The timer ticks loud, and the clock device turns. I crane my neck as far as I can to see it. It is dark, which is good, the lack of light allowing my brain to remain relatively steady and functional. I think. If I let the drug flow now, I will be drowsy and incoherent, and Ramon could return with the Project in tow and I would be unable to defend myself or protect Mama.

The light above swings, one second, two, illuminating the floor for a fraction of time, and I watch it and try to move my head forward when I spot, in the weak shaft of yellow, the item Ramon knocked to the floor earlier.

The fork.

A plan forms immediately and I concentrate on the fork and don't let it out of my sight. It is silver and pronged with four tines. Its handle is slick and elegant, and when I observe it, I attempt to calculate the distance it lies from my feet, but it is hard—the light flickers and the blackness looms, and each time I reach a close figure, the bulb sways away again and I find I have to guess.

I glance to my feet. They are bare, no socks or shoes, and I start flexing my toes to check that I have enough feeling in them, when a bang sounds from somewhere and I freeze. Is Ramon coming back? When all falls quiet, I allow myself to exhale and resume analyzing the utensil in the light that now dribbles in and allows me to see. If my calculations are correct, I should be able to reach the fork even though my legs are tied at the knees to the chair. I pause for a moment. It is a lot to process: Ramon being with the Project, the fact that we are at Mama's house. My brain's automatic reaction is to struggle with it, and it is exhausting, but I force myself to face the problem immediately in front of me and deal with the fallout after.

Checking the door one more time and listening for any suspect sounds, I start.

I use my left foot first. My toes wriggle as, bit by bit, I push out my calf as far as it will go. The left edge of my foot is approximately five centimeters from the fork's handle, but it is not near enough, and so I have to scuttle my toes out as far as they will go until, eventually, I feel the cool metal of the utensil.

I count, keep steady, and continue. Pulling back slightly, I then stretch my leg again, and my toes crawl spiderlike toward the fork, and I find I have to grip the handle to get the utensil in my grasp, and it is difficult. No matter how hard I try, no matter how furiously I stretch my leg forward, it does not work and the fork remains on the floor.

I flop back in the seat, exhausted, the energy required just to move my toes wearing me out entirely, a vision of Ramon swimming into my head, mixed with a thought of how he could hurt Mama. I close my eyes briefly, counting five seconds of rest, turning my feet in circles to get some circulation to them, when something slips a little. My eyes pop open. I look down and see that the rope around my knees appears different from the one around my wrists. While they are tied tight, the rope hard and coarse, the tether around my legs is softer, smooth, less like wire and more like wool.

I think I can slip it off.

With a new surge of hope, I start to push and push against the rope on my legs, and gradually, it begins to come loose. I stop, catch my breath, check for any sounds of Ramon returning. When all is clear, I blow a stray hair off my cheek, then recommence, my eyes blinking in the darkness of the basement. This time it is easier. My legs are fueled by the memories from the sedative, by the stark recollection of what I now know, by the facts, the details, the data. I remember it all now, every part of my journey here. There is a purpose for my escape; there is a reason.

One tug, two. The rope starts to move, gradually at first, then quicker, but then the needle unexpectedly digs in, and the pain is sharp, stabbing me, but I dare not cry out. I press my lips together. The stinging passes. Finally, the rope slips to the floor and my ankles are free.

I exhale hard, exhausted. My legs throb and my bones ache, and when I move, sweat trickles down my face, dripping into my eyes. I rattle my head, try to shake away as much of it as I can, and refocus, glancing now to where the fork lies only centimeters from my feet. With my legs untethered now, I can try again to reach it, to pull it toward me, but it is difficult to see in the growing darkness. I squint, blink over and over, but the light is poor, washed out, and so, weary, I drop my foot to the floor and then stop. There, beneath my toes. The fork.

Steadying my rapid shallow breathing, I spread out my toes, grit my teeth, and, straining my feet as far as they will go, I pull the fork with the right foot, till the handle is firmly between the first two toes of the left.

I raise my foot, and it works, so I keep going, slowly, creeping it up, the metal dangling from my toes, mindful of the needle as, beside me, the timer ticks. The fork reaches my right knee now, and I pause, unsure what to do next. My wrists are tied, and the needle is in my right arm, and my hips are straining.

I think fast. The only way to do this will be to keep hoisting my left leg upward, toes gripping the fork, so that is what I do. I lift the fork higher until I can almost touch it with my left hand. It is wobbling now almost at my fingertips, the only sound in the room my breathing and the tick of the timer as my hand stretches closer now to the metal. So near … I drop the fork.

I watch as it clatters to the floor, by my right foot, and lies still on the ground as if I had never picked it up at all. I want to cry out, scream at the frustration, yell, holler.

But I do none of that. Instead, I swallow, blow back the sweat that swarms my face, and thrust my leg out once more. I repeat everything I did before, and this time, after two minutes of agony, it works. My left foot lifts the fork high enough to reach my hand, and from there I use it to untie the tethers on my wrists and right leg.

The rope slides off. My wrists ache, and I rub them, elated at the tiny victory I have just scored, but the happiness drains away as I hear a loud click followed by the now-familiar whoosh. The drip, the sedative, is activating.

Panic surfaces hard and fast, and with no time left, I reach with my fingers to the crease in my arm and draw in a large breath. Gritting my teeth, my sights set on getting out of here, I rip the tape away and yank the needle from my arm.

# CHAPTER 32

**DEEP-COVER PROJECT FACILITY**

*17 Hours and 27 Minutes to Confinement*

As soon as I press the enter key on the password access box, a torrent of information flashes onto the screen.

"What can you see?" Chris asks.

"Data," I say. "Reams of data."

I barely breathe as, in front of my eyes, information flies left and right, small icons that represent hundreds upon hundreds of documents popping up and filling the screen. The assault is hard on my senses, but I press on, eager to find out what it is, to see if this really is the file that will give me what I need to end it all.

Once the documents slow down, I can zoom in on one at a time and read at speed, photographing every character and icon in my head.

"Maria," Balthus says. "Have you found anything yet?"

"Yes. The files are full of names." I peer forward. "They are … Basque names." I glance to the fountain-pen tattoo on my arm.

"Anything else?"

Slightly concerned, I read on. "There are what appear to be details of people, of other human beings, listed here."

"Others," Balthus says. "Maria, could they be other subject numbers like you?"

"Perhaps, but there is no definite connection, and …" I stop. There at the top of the file, next to the file-creator section, is my name and subject number. I am the author of the report.

"It is me," I say, almost to myself as I realize exactly what I am staring at.

"What do you mean?"

"In my flashback, Raven said the information was linked to a file I created." I grit my teeth, anxious now as I start to connect the small dots. "This is the file."

"Doc?" Patricia says now, coming on the line. "Doc, it's going to be okay. Keep reading, yeah? Then you'll get to the end of all this once and for all."

I listen to her words and force my eyes and brain to carry on. "My number … It sits alongside the word *Basque*, and near it are other surnames. Mendoza, Zabala, Aritza. Balthus, your parents are from the Basque country—do you recognize any names?"

But he does not answer, and I begin to worry that the line has failed, when he finally speaks. "Yes," he says, clearing his throat. "Yes, they are. They're Basque."

"Doc," Patricia says, "does that mean you are Basque, too, somehow? Your flashback—the woman—said the file would tell you who you are."

I glance to my arm, to the phrase carved into my skin, and I tell them about Black Eyes, about his explanation of the Project's complex use of people with Basque blood—and his tattoo work on my arm.

"Jesus Christ," Balthus gasps. "Maria, I am …" He coughs. "I am so, so sorry."

I touch my upper arm and feel the rough grooves cut by the pen into my red, raw skin. "How is Papa connected in all this? If I have Basque blood, then he must, too."

"Or your mam," Patricia says. "Could she be Basque?"

"Er, Maria?" Chris says now, cutting through my thought. "I'm detecting some movement on a sensor device I hacked into further up the system. You're gonna have to get through this file faster."

The air runs cold, and I tug the sweater tight around me, bite down on my lip, and focus. Fragments of names roll up again, and at first there are just a few, but then the file flips into something else, into what appears to be a new document, but what is strange is that each name disappears, replaced instead by a number, and each number is linked to its own genealogy map. I relay the information aloud to the cell phone and then hesitate as, before me, the entire screen begins to fill with data and family lineage, until, at the bottom of the page, I see a line that makes me go cold.

"There are two thousand, one hundred and thirteen subject numbers," I say, my fingers trembling as they hover over the keyboard. "Balthus, the others in the conditioning program do exist."

"Dear God," he groans. "They've been doing this for years and getting away with it. Jesus."

I read more of the file. "This gives extensive detail on their origins, what tests have been performed, and how the subject has reacted to it all. This is key information we can use to halt the entire Project, and …" I stop. The document, as I move it, seems to scroll across to the right, and as it does, a word emerges, the same word over and over sitting alongside each subject number as my eyes frantically scan it all and a visceral fright takes hold.

"Deceased," I say, swallowing, even though my mouth is dry.

"What?" Balthus says. "Who is deceased?"

I look again to be sure, but there is no doubt. "Against two thousand and five of the subject numbers, the document states they are deceased. They died in the middle of being conditioned." I look down, confused, concerned. I played a part in this. I helped file this document of dead people with extinguished lives and existences, and I don't even remember.

"Doc, oh, my goodness." Patricia's low lilt sifts through my worry. "Breathe, okay? Breathe."

I do breathe and try to stay calm, and read on and see more

data that details what Raven said there would be: pages and pages of confidential information on not only who the Project has tested on, but who they have killed on operations, what targets have been eliminated, details and illegal surveillance of civilians, of covert terrorism operations in Iran, Germany, France, Afghanistan, Belgium, and many other countries.

I tell Patricia what I can see. "How can this be for the greater good?" I say, my eyes swimming a little.

"I don't know, Doc. I don't know. But we'll get them, okay? With all this information now, we can get them."

And as her voice lilts in my head, I see it there, two pages in. "My subject number is listed."

"What does it say?"

I wipe the sweat from my forehead and make my eyes take in what my mind does not want to see. "It lists …" I stop, feel my body rock a little as I struggle to process it all. "It lists the people I have killed. It says I am the test child and that I am the only one who has completed the full training program without … without dying." I stop, horrified at what it all means. "Others have died," I say after a moment. "But I am alive."

"Doc, it's okay. You won't be one of them—you won't die."

"That is not based on fact, though. Your thought is being led by emotions." My mind is gripped by a feeling of horror and shame, but when I read a census of what appears to be ten people I have eliminated through operations, I cannot feel upset. I cannot recall any of what I did, and instead work through the names and try to spot any clues. I see lists of cyberops I have been involved in at various ages, look at data showing the training I have completed and, against all of it, against every data cluster is my age at the time, all culminating in the same countdown device Chris and I discovered on the computer at his house in Montserrat. But what is it counting down to?

"Balthus, she was right," I say.

"Maria?"

"Raven said this file would tell me who I am." I look at the numbers and facts on what I have done. "This is who I am."

"No, Doc," Patricia says, "it's not who you are. You never knew what you were doing."

I want to believe Patricia's words, but something inside me is not convinced. I look at the data. The Project has made all this happen, here in Hamburg and elsewhere, these deaths and crimes, and no one in the world but us seems to know about it.

"Is Chris there?" I say.

His voice pops up. "Yep."

"I want you to access the files on here. There is a modem."

"Already on it. I can duplicate what I see by going around the system. I'm still getting some movement on the sensor somewhere in the facility, but I don't think it's too near you. I'll get this done, then you can shut it down and get the hell out of there."

The temperature of the room drops a few degrees more, and my limbs begin to shake as I realize I have been sitting ramrod straight the entire time. I set down the cell for a second, roll my head, and, stretching my arms, pick up the phone again when Chris' voice crackles in fast and urgent.

"Whoa. Whoa, Maria? I'm getting something odd here. It's linking up to something."

My pulse quickens. "What is it?"

"I don't know. It should be appearing on your screen now. It looks like some kind of ... Wait—is that a list of drugs?"

At first, nothing comes up on the screen, but after three seconds, a report emerges. It has a black border, and on the main body the page is yellow. "This is an eyes-only document."

"Holy shit."

I scan the classified file and see details on drugs, on the names of specific medicines, ones that I know and have seen before, as a doctor. "These are cancer drugs."

"I'm reading the same document now," Chris says. "Is that

what they have been doing all along, d'you reckon? Testing cancer drugs on people?"

I examine the data further and see that each drug is linked to a test subject number, and as my fingers hover above the keyboard, the frightening realization of what I am looking at hits me.

"Have they tested these drugs on … on me?"

"Oh, fuck," Chris says.

My eyes check the information again. I am in a haze, a bubble. It does not add up. "Why would there be a need to test cancer drugs in this way? Is that why I have been ill in the past, because of these trials?"

"Think back to the times when you've been sick," Chris says. "Try to link the symptoms to the drugs on the screen."

I think, but there are no direct correlations to any illness I can recall within the date parameters on this file. "If these drugs are trial phase only, then their effects would not be documented and no one outside the Project would ever be aware of the results."

"Look at the final part of the document," Chris says. "It's got information on specific amounts of money in different denominations, and they're linked directly to a cancer drug, and by each amount of money is a date and time."

He's right. Leaning in, I look at the dates and see that they span three decades. "The dates spread back into the 1970s." I steady my hands and track the dates forward, when something changes and a feeling of dread floods me. "In 1979, the amounts rise substantially and there is a location, a place I know."

"Madrid."

Facts slam into me, forging connections as I talk fast now, thinking aloud, my brain overriding emotions with data to help me cope.

"Three decades ago, Black September began terrorist activities, and the Project was created. These dates stretch back to that time. The cancer drug details spread back to that time, also, as do the money transactions, many of them in Madrid." The conclusion screeches in and knocks me sideways. "Was Papa a part of this?"

"Maria?" It is Balthus. "You can't tell from this who is involved. Alarico may have had nothing to do with it."

"The correlations are clear and linked."

"Yes, but what if it's not linked to the cancer drugs? Which means Alarico is not connected at all. The dates don't match. He was in court a lot at the times this file states. I remember because we used to talk a lot then. He was never ill, either. There's one person who has been ill, though."

"Er, sorry to interrupt," Chris says, "but you've got people approaching. They're reasonably far away, but it's hard to tell—best not risk it."

I look to the screen. "There is one more file unopened. Can you access it?"

"Copy that. I'll download it now."

"Doc," Patricia says, "you've got what you came for, and Chris can help crack open anything else that was on there, so we have the full data. But right now you have to get out, okay?"

"Yes."

I stand, pick up the cell phone, and, with Chris' download finished, start to leave.

An alarm begins to shriek through the air.

# CHAPTER 33

**DEEP-COVER PROJECT FACILITY**

*17 Hours and 13 Minutes to Confinement*

The alarm tears through the air, ripping it apart. I crouch down, one hand covering my head, the cell phone to my ear, my brain desperate to escape the auditory assault.

"On the plans, there's a main exit at the end of the corridor fifty meters to your left," Chris says fast over the siren. "The sensor is hacked and set up for you to leave. When you get out, aim for Hamburg Station. I'll get a contact I know to drop you off a fake passport and cash in a locker there so you can travel on. I'll text the details."

"Maria, go!" shouts Balthus. "Go!"

I run to the door, stop, and listen. The low lights help me think, and I can hear voices shouting, but because the alarm is so loud, it is hard to determine their distance from me. The siren bursts in quick, sharp shocks, and pressing one hand to my ear, I click the door open.

I peer into the corridor. There is a white walkway straight to my right, and when I look both ways, it is clear. No intelligence officers, no sign of Black Eyes. I place my hand on the ice wall outside and, checking one more time in both directions, sprint down the corridor toward what I hope is the exit. After exactly fifty meters, I find a corner and stop to assess the situation.

Drawing in long, deep breaths, I scan the area and locate the exit

Chris identified, then go to calculate a contingency option, when voices shout out ahead. Heart racing, I sprint to the initial exit, then halt, scan it fast, and realize, with a deep pit of dread, that I have nothing to make it through—no key, no access code, no way to contact Chris without alerting whoever is near. The alarm wails on.

I move. With the sound of shoes echoing on tiles, I turn and run, breath heavy, pulse revving. I push against each door I come to, but they are all sealed, and surrounded by a black plastic mesh that is soft and sticky to the touch. Panic rising, I race forward and reach a red double door and brake, the rubber soles of the dead man's sneakers screeching on the floor. I glance to the right of the exit. There is an access keypad by the door handle, but it is unusual—there are no buttons to press, no code to crack. I crouch a little, peer at it until I know what I am looking at: a fingerprint access scanner, one that will admit approved users only.

A shout rings out from my right. I drop to the floor, crawl along to where the adjacent corridor intersects, and look left and right. I know I need to hide, to move fast now, but all I spot is a foot-wide gap to my left that rises all the way to the ceiling, like a crevasse in a glacier. The footsteps stomp closer. I glance to the exit scanner once more, but there is no time to make it back over there, so I squeeze myself into the gap in the wall.

My chest compresses, the air wheezing out as the ice walls lock me in, but despite the immediate discomfort, I cannot move. Because in the corridor, a few feet to my right, are two armed intelligence officers.

I hold my breath as they look around. I count, one second, two, three, four. On five, I hear them turn and walk away, and I breathe out.

I peel my body out of the crevice, sprint back over to the exit, and examine the access sensor. There are prints there, sweat residues from the skin of previous users. If I could replicate prints, if there was something to stick onto the glass, then I could get out. Sweat pouring off me, the fatigue trousers start to slide down, and I pull them up when I feel something in my pocket that makes me stop. The pack of chewing gum.

A vague memory of Raven floats into my head. She is working on an operation and smiling and saying, "The Americans like their gum." But she is not using it to chew. Instead, she is turning to a code pad and pressing the gum into the sensor.

The memory rolls away like a tide going back out to sea, and I breathe in, short and sharp. The woman, her veil, the scent of mint gum mixed with spice and turmeric, drifts away. I look up.

I know what to do.

Moving fast, I stick my hand into the cargo pocket and, feeling for the sharp edge, pull out the floppy disk I took off the dead officer. The floppy disk with the sticky tape on the sides.

With jittery fingers, I peel the tape, and it comes away within a second. Crouching down, I survey the corridor. As certain as I can be that all is clear, I bring the tape over the scanner and, using the light on the cell phone, allow my eyes to track the small, flat screen, locating the best whole, unsmudged fingerprint I can find.

Pinching the tape between my thumb and forefinger, I place the strip over the middle section of the scanner where the print is, press it firmly into the glass, then pause. The gum—what was it she did with the gum? An image of a smile spreading like silk comes to me, of fingers working nimbly, elegantly, gliding in air. My breath catches as I realize I liked her, this woman, whoever she was, as if she was kind to me.

I swallow, slot the image back away in my memory, and pull the stolen pack of gum from my pocket. Not giving myself time to doubt my plan, I pop a stick in my mouth and chew. With the gum softened now, I squeeze it dry on the roof of my mouth and, clamping it between my teeth, peel off the tape from the screen and then take the gum from my mouth. Sweat runs past my left eyebrow now, down along my nose. Lowering the gum, I hold it on the tape and keep it in place, counting fifteen seconds, eyes searching for officers the entire time. Done, taking the greatest care not to stretch the gum, I peel back the tape and allow myself one small smile.

Because there, in front of me, is an authorized fingerprint.

I put all my energy into shutting out the shrill of the alarm and press the gum fingerprint gently into the scanner, using it as a substitute person. I wait and hold my breath.

A buzzer sounds, and I feel a wash of relief as the door clicks open and a whoosh of cold air hits my face, followed by a beam of sunshine on my cheeks. There is more shouting, and from the far left I hear people running this way.

Chest tight, throat dry, I drag open the door and, not looking back, not daring to check how near any intelligence officers may be, I gently click the exit shut and run toward a distant parking deck in the early morning Hamburg sun as, back in the Project facility, the siren wails on.


## CONFINEMENT LOCATION
*Present Day*

The needle is out of me. I stumble to my knees and gulp in large breaths. My arms and legs are throbbing, muscles weak from the ropes, and when I raise my head, my neck aches so much that my shoulders seize up, almost cramping, and blood drips from the crease of my elbow to my wrist and fingers.

I stagger to my feet and observe what I can of the room. Blackness, two crates, padded walls. I feel dirty, unwashed and smelly, and when I run a hand through my hair, my fingers catch in the stringy tangles. Not wanting to remain here a moment longer, and fearful of what may happen next with Ramon, I head for the door to escape, when a dull gleam on the far wall catches my eye. Curious, I hobble over and halt. It is a cross of Jesus Christ, twenty centimeters long. A crucifix. I rub my eyes, weariness rippling across them, and crouch down and

look. Even in the weak light, I can see that something about the wall
is not right. I wipe my fingers free of sweat and, with almost no light
to see by, let my sense of touch do the exploring.

There, to the left of the crucifix, is a stretch of padded wall
the same as I had seen in front of the chair where I was strapped.
I feel my way along it and stop. A corner of the leather fabric is
curling at one edge, and when the light above swings over, I hear a
mechanical tick as if from a controlled device. I notice something
under it. Writing. Kneeling down, I pinch the edge of the leather
and pull. It rips away. It comes free in my hand to reveal numbers
scratched onto the bare brick wall underneath: *31*, *100*, *75*, *13*, *21*,
and *26*, each with a specific town or district in the Basque country
and what seems to be a set of calendar years: *1976*, *1985*, *1989*,
*2001*, *2009*, *2010*, none of which show an obvious relationship or
specific pattern. And even though I am tired and hungry, I look at
them and remember the ICE room in Hamburg and call up the
picture of the numbers and places. And instantly, I know that they
all correlate somehow, that what I am seeing here—the numbers, at
least—all matches what I saw on the file that Raven directed me to.

For a moment, I do not move as my brain tries to compute it
all. Have these been scratched on by others like me? Other subject
numbers? And if so, how? Does that mean Ramon has been keeping
them down here for the Project, as he has with me? But how do
the calendar years relate to my brother? Some of them stretch back
to when Ramon was very young—way before he could ever have
been involved with the Project. I study them again, trying to make
sense of it all.

As my head drops down, my eyes land on the crucifix. A religious symbol that represents not life or caring for others or doing
good, but killing and hurting and retaliation. At the top of the wall,
where the padding is pulled and the subject number etchings lie, I
can see something sticking out from underneath the wood where
the feet of Christ are.

I kneel down and give it a tug. At first it does not move, and so, listening for any sign of Ramon or the Project, I grab the medical stand and, angling it at forty-five degrees, I smash it down hard.

The crucifix comes away in one go, and when I pick it up from the floor, a photograph drops out. Curious, nervous, I unfold it. There in my hands is a photograph of a mother and her newborn baby, and in the top right corner, where the faded color of the image bleeds into the card, is a name and a year:

*Maria. 1980.*

# CHAPTER 34

**DEEP-COVER PROJECT FACILITY**

*16 Hours and 2 Minutes to Confinement*

Floodlights hit my face as, in sight of the building, I duck and sprint the hundred meters to where I think is a hiding place. My arm stings and the bruises ache, but I keep moving until I reach a section of the building where the roof hangs low and offers me a shadow to slip into.

Another alarm shrieks from the internal left flank, and through my peripheral vision I see officers dispersing, prowling the area by the series of outbuildings to the left. In my pocket is the dead officer's car fob, and I intend to use it, but there are no cars immediately near here, and the parking deck is still sixty meters ahead. A figure moves somewhere beyond the parking deck, and I drop to my knees. My legs wobble with exhaustion, and my feet prickle with pain from the shoes, which rub because they are too big.

I do rapid reconnaissance. Farther to the right is another building. The roof is blue and the walls are green, and on the door, black skulls are imprinted onto yellow beaks. A shadow creeps into the right. I count to three, crouch down, and run.

Reaching the far parking deck, I throw my back against the wall. It is warm, almost hot to the touch, but I remain rooted where I am, steady, hidden, watching everything, trying to blink the brightness away. Two shadows are on the very ground where I stood just five seconds ago, which means, at this angle, if I run now they will see me.

I stay put. The shapes ahead move, and I refocus and track them, waiting until my path is in line with the officers', and when I am in their blind spot, I keep my nerves steady and creep along the edge of the green-walled building. I reach the entrance of the parking deck in four seconds. I glance up. No guards are on obvious watch, no surveillance cameras pointing my way. Three silhouettes shift toward the left side of the building I just came from. I calculate their angles. They are facing outward, which means, right now, they cannot detect me. For the moment.

I slip through the entrance of the parking deck and halt. At least one hundred cars stare back at me, my brain assigning each one to my internal inventory. I press the fob, but no lights flash, no indicators tick. Feeling a shiver, I pull the sweater a little tighter and walk farther in, uploading all the registration plates to my memory, noting every make and model until I reach a Volvo. Four-by-four. I look at the fob; the symbol matches. Clicking the button, I hold my breath. The lights flash. The car is open.

Glancing around me, I fling open the door, switch on the engine, and pause. Whichever way I go, there will be a gate, a guard, a gun. I sit there for two seconds thinking, pulling at the thread of cotton that dangles from the T-shirt, when I feel a corner dig into my leg from the trouser pocket: the swipe card.

I take it out and look at it. Could this work? But there is no way. Our faces are different shapes, and our builds conflict between small and large. I get out the cell and call Chris.

"Hey, Google, you okay?"

"I need you to access the database to help me get out of the facility."

"No problem. You got an ID number?"

I look at the swipe card and read it out.

"Doc." Patricia's voice feeds in. "Stay safe. Balthus is here, too."

I cling to her voice, then wait for Chris, tapping my foot. I need to go.

"Okay, you're done. Get to Hamburg Station. I've texted you the locker with what you need: clothes, cash, cell. From there you can catch a flight out. We're gonna scramble our route."

The thought of enduring a train ride, a flight with crowds of people … I push it to one side for the moment.

"Maria," Balthus says. "Get to Madrid. We're headed there now to catch a train to Lisbon and then an evening flight to London so we can do something with these files."

A human shadow floats up ahead. "I have to go."

I slip the cell phone into my pocket and look around the car. Rummaging in the glove compartment, I find what I need: a baseball cap.

I slip on the cap but then almost rip it off because it smells of the dead officer, of his smoke and metal and stale beer. Gulping hard, I count to three and recite the birthdate and birthplace of Mozart. Then, trying desperately to ignore the stench, I pull the car out and drive toward the main exit.

Up ahead, the metal gates are over twenty-five meters tall. In the corner, surveillance cameras stare down. Concertina wire gleams along the top edge. I drive up, pull the cap down as much as I can bear, and, adrenaline shooting through me, pull up to the scanner. Then I reach out with the stolen card in my hand and, holding my breath, swipe. One second passes as I wait, two, and on three, the gates finally swing open, and I drive out, careful not to go fast until I am well away and gone.

I breathe out. The window is down, and the air keeps me alert, and when I swallow I can taste a mix of flowers and metal and mint gum. Forcing myself to keep the sunglasses firmly in place, I set my eyes forward and focus solely on driving the car away from the

Project, toward the road ahead, my mind set on the documents we have found and on revealing every last bit of them to the world.

## CONFINEMENT LOCATION
*Present Day*

I look at the worn image of the woman and baby, and my fingers shake. 1980 is the year I was born. The photograph I am staring at, if the writing in the corner is correct, is of me as a baby, but I do not recognize the woman holding me in her arms.

Confused, I trace the pattern of the baby blanket, as if it might give me a clue or provide me with some much-needed order. The only noise in the room is the sound of my shallow breath as I smooth the snapshot down with my palm and blow away the film of dust that coats it. My body trembles a little from the aftershock of the drugs, and a chill chatters down my limbs, bones, feet, making my hands and arms jitter.

I bring the photo close to my face in the weak light and examine the image as best I can. The woman has long, black, bushy hair that hangs like curled wire across her shoulders and down to her stomach, and above her slim, tanned calves is a long, billowing skirt with a delicate crocheted flower pattern. Perhaps twenty-two years old, she wears a loose brown cotton vest, and underneath is the outline of heavy, unhaltered breasts. I squint, angle the photo in the meager light. She doesn't look like Mama when Mama was younger, but I cannot be certain. To her right is an arm, which belongs to a man—black hair, tanned skin.

Turning it in my hands, I flip the picture over and stop. Words are etched in pencil on the reverse side. Feeling a pang of uncertainty now at what I am looking at, I inspect the scrawl, rubbing it with my forefinger, the soft padding of my skin swirling in tiny circles on the rough paper. At first, with the light dim and the darkness almost overpowering, it is difficult to decipher the words, and so I move closer to the bulb and bring the photograph upward as, gradually, the letters coalesce into a name.

*Isabella Bidarte.*

It is a Basque name. Something inside me stirs. What? A memory? A dream? I think of all the Basque names blacked out on the file in the ICE room at the Project. Is this woman one of them? Another subject number? I run the name through my brain: *Bidarte.* I track the meaning. In Basque, *bide* means "way." *Arte* means "between." *Between the ways.*

I lay the picture on my palm. *Isabella.* It is from the name Isabel, a variation on Elizabeth, which means "devoted to God." Other letters are scratched farther toward the middle, but it is lighter here, as if it has been written in the softest, most buttery pencil, and, when I peer at it, eyes straining, I manage to make out the words. *Weisshorn Psychiatric Hospital, Geneva, Switzerland.* A hospital in Switzerland. And then one more line, with two key dates next to her name. *Born: May 1968. Died: June 1989(?).* But it is the string of characters next to it that makes me almost drop the photo, because there on the flip side, beside Isabella Bidarte's birth and death dates, is a grid reference number. The same grid reference number that I found on Dr. Andersson's cell phone.

I lean back, cortisol levels peaking as I think it through, and for some reason, I raise my fingers to my forearm, where the ink tattoo from Black Eyes sits. "I am Basque," I say aloud, my own voice sounding strange in the lonely silence of the room. I hold up the photograph. Am I looking at a woman who was involved in the Project? Who perhaps knew Mama or Papa when I was a baby? And this hospital—is that where she met them? I think, connect the dots, but keep hitting a wall, not recalling a time when Papa or Mama mentioned a trip to Switzerland.

I begin to analyze who the woman is and why she has hold of me and how it all is connected to Geneva, when there is a sound, a clatter, then silence. I freeze. *Ramon.*

I whirl around to the wall where the crucifix once stood, and thrusting the photograph into my trouser pocket, I get to the medical stand and haul it back up. Pulling it hard, I wrench the pole free from the base.

Logical, smooth, I move toward the steps, ready for Ramon. At least, I think I am ready, when I spot something on the floor: the crucifix. There is a sound of a ring tone: Depeche Mode's "Enjoy the Silence," and it gets nearer, louder, with every second that passes. My eyes surge around the room. Ramon will be here soon, and I have to be ready, because this time I am getting out. I need to get to Mama and get to Patricia and Chris and Balthus, and all I can do right now is hope they have some idea of where I am.

My pulse hammers in my ears as, with the ring tone coming closer, I count to three, dash to the wall, and grab the crucifix. I feel something slip off into my palm: the nail from the foot of the crucifix.

There is a low buzzing sound, followed by a creak of the door. One second, two. With no time left, I drop the nail into my back pocket and, rushing to the steps with the metal pole in my hands, I stand by the door and wait for my brother to enter.

# CHAPTER 35

**MADRID**

*3 Hours and 0 Minutes to Confinement*

Balthus stays on the phone with me the whole time I am going through the airport. I reach the Madrid terminal and try to breathe.

"Are you okay?" Balthus says through the cell phone I hold pinned to my ear.

"No," I say, and carry on. I take out my passport and check my appearance in a walkway mirror between an escalator and a shop. My hair is now copper to match the passport photograph from Chris, and when I blink, my eyes are green from temporary contact lenses that match the dark makeup on my skin. The guard's sneakers are still on my feet after the train journey from Hamburg to Paris, but now I wear a loose khaki shirt and white vest with close-fitting fatigues on my legs, rolled up at the ankles. A seasoned-traveler look, Chris said in the note that he left for me in the Hamburg locker. I do not know what that means.

I can smell multiple scents as I walk toward the nothing-to-declare zone. Coffee, toast, bacon, burgers, flowers, pollen, beer, salmon. It hits me like a tsunami and combines with the sounds and the crowds and the streaming lines of people, some of them brushing me as they walk, making me wince, making me want to run away.

"Just keep walking straight on," Balthus says. "I know airports are hard for you. We'll get you through this."

I want to thank him but am rendered mute by the whole assault of the journey. I hate it. I pull my baseball cap down and walk through customs, where it is busy and loud. I have a small gray rucksack on my back, and when people crisscross the walkways, different sounds, smells, fluorescent lights, blare and blink at me all at once, sweeping my mind up in chaos and fragmenting my sense of self. I think of Papa and how he used to be with me in these situations: always calm, always guiding me through.

"Are you still there?" I ask Balthus.

"Yes," he replies. "Always."

His chocolate voice, the pebbled boom of it, gives me a bit of comfort, and I find, as the minutes pass, that I can continue forward and get through the airport and the noise and the chaos and the people upon people who scurry by without obvious cause, and I make it outside without melting down.

"I am out," I say now to Balthus as I leave the terminal and step into liquid sun that spills down from the sky and bathes the tarmac and the cars and the heads of the people passing by, with a soft sheen of silent sunshine. Outside, I instantly breathe easier, the excess of noise muted slightly, allowing me to continue at medium comfort level. All the while, I scan every inch, crevice, and corridor for any sign that I am being followed.

"You did it. Great. Catch a taxi," Balthus says on the cell. "We'll meet you on the corner of the old post office by the market at the agreed time." My heart drops—a market is good cover, but it means more crowds and noise.

Ducking into a cab, I feel a wash of relief as it pulls away in an air-conditioned bubble that mutes the sound and calms my head.

"Thank you, Balthus," I find myself saying.

"You're welcome, Maria. You are so, so welcome."

One hour later, I arrive at El Rastro market and very nearly do not get out of the car. People mill everywhere, great crowds of them gathering in packs on the streets and in the market stalls and the bars and restaurants that run along the roads and pavements and terraces beyond. I step out of the cab, pay the driver, and am hit by the myriad smells that fire at me all at once. Chorizo sizzling, chocolate churros frying, fresh lemonade, calamari, petrol, exhaust fumes, the wet-feet stench of Serrano ham hanging from hooks under canvas canopies in the shade of the sun.

I duck my head down and scurry to the meeting point by the old post office. The noise is overwhelming. Bodies stand everywhere, chattering, shouting, shopping—all wandering, it seems to me, with no clear sense of destination, stopping then walking then stopping again with no set pattern that I can define, and it scrambles my mind, as it did at the airport, into chaos. The only way I can cope is to set a clear goal in my mind—get to a clearing free of crowds, and wait.

By the time Patricia and Balthus and Chris arrive, I am standing in a corner, hiding behind a pair of cheap sunglasses and trying to keep away from everyone so they will not touch me.

"Doc!"

I put my hand to my brow and see Patricia bounding toward me, followed by Chris and Balthus.

As soon as she reaches me, she holds out her fingers and smiles. I reach my hand up to hers, so relieved to see her that I could flop forward and never get up, but then someone brushes past me and it makes me jump.

"Doc, are you okay?"

"People are in my space. I know they are not being rude, but I do not like it. Why did we meet here?"

Chris comes over, wearing a lopsided straw hat and a white T-shirt that reads *Nerds Rule*. "We're here to give us some cover." He grins, and I see that his stubble has grown. "Hello, Google."

"That is not my name. And nerds do not rule."

"I know. Geeks do." He winks.

"Maria, oh, thank God." Balthus rushes over, sweat trickling down his cheeks. He takes out a white handkerchief from his gray linen shirt and dabs his face. He smiles, and his eye creases fan out. "I cannot tell you how relieved I am that you're okay."

I look at them all. My friends are safe, but I don't know how to express the feeling of happiness, of contentment, that it gives me. "Statistically," I say, "only one of us had a chance of dying. The fact that we are all here is a leap over probability."

Chris nods. "Right. Yep, just what I was thinking." He grins like Goofy, and I ignore him.

The crowd ten meters ahead begins to swell, and the noise levels rise. My shoulders scrunch up in response, my head ducking down at the sudden audio assault, and so, on Patricia's suggestion, we move to a quieter area, where a canopy hangs over bare wooden slats that once housed oranges and lemons. We stand under the canvas for shade, spritzed with a gentle citrus scent, and as we rest, Chris takes out his laptop.

As I lean against the stall, my body suddenly feels exhausted, my mind shattered from the chaos and noise of the train and the flight and, now, the Sunday market. I look to Patricia and to Balthus, and only at the reassuring sight of them do I allow myself to rest a little and let my shoulders soften.

"Ok, so," Chris says. "I managed to make it into that file."

"Ah, yes," Balthus says. "We have everything now to hit the Project where it hurts."

Chris attaches a device to the laptop and boots it up. The screen comes to life quickly.

"Here you go," he chirps, fifteen seconds later. "Unlike the others, this one file that was left had a name."

Feeling oddly nervous, I move in and, brushing back a strand of hair from my wig, peer at the screen. It is immediately clear that the file is about Raven, the woman from my hazy memories. Because there next to what must be her photograph, the one I recall from the flashback of her caramel skin, brown eyes, and black hijab, is her name—finally, the woman's name that, when I tried to recall it, was blocked out in black.

*Sadeqa*, I say to myself, reading the name that sits at the top of the confidential document. A document compiled by me. "It is an Arabic name that means 'truthful, true.'"

"Um, you okay?" Chris says.

"Doc …?"

But I don't reply, because what I am reading, what I am seeing for the first time, is the answer to what I have been seeking since my trial, since the moment I recalled the vague whisper of a memory, in court and then again at my villa. Her face, her liquid eyes, her black, breezing veil. We worked together. We worked together on a covert operation, and I went undercover.

"She was an asset, trading information from a new terrorist cell that was surviving," I say, reading fast. "It was growing through cybernetwork links, via encrypted message codes that not even the NSA, the CIA, or MI5 could crack."

"I know, right?" Chris says. "That's some pretty deep stuff you were involved in."

I scan the file and then look up, a sick feeling in my stomach. "She knew all about the NSA, this woman. It is all here. She knew who they were, what they did. And she could hack."

"Doc, talk more slowly."

I read it all now, my eyes racing across the screen, pressing it all into my memory banks. "Sadeqa had a high IQ, could get into the CIA's system, and they did not like it—the organizations, the Project, the governments. She was a danger, and they wanted her dead. And they assigned me to do it. She said they would make me kill her. But before I did, they made me use her as an asset, get as much intelligence data out of her as possible."

I pause, swallow a little as I read the next section, because what is there, what I now witness in black and white, smacks me hard in the chest. I sway a little, then sag into Chris.

"Whoa, steady."

"What's it say, Doc?"

A solitary tear escapes because the answer, finally, is clear.

"I killed her," I say, a quiet whisper amid the thrum and clamor of the market. "I killed Raven. I killed Sadeqa."

"What?"

Patricia scans the file as my sight swims a little and my brain struggles to process the facts.

"You didn't kill her," Patricia says now.

"I did."

"But, Doc, you didn't, not knowingly."

"What if there was a part of me that really knew? What if, deep down, it is who I am?" I look at the wood of the stall and trace the grain with my finger. "She said the file would tell me who I really am, and it has."

"But, Maria," Balthus says now, "the file has told us what the Project has really done, the atrocities of how they have tested on thousands and blanked out their identities. They took you for tests against your will."

"We can use this stuff, you know," Chris says. "We can e-mail it to the government and show them what's happening right under their noses. We have the definitive files."

"That's what we should do," Balthus says. He ruffles his shirt, billowing the creased linen fabric so cool air flows under it. Nearby, a chicken squawks. "There's a flight out of Lisbon to London tonight. We're all going to catch it and I'll get this file to Harriet."

"Balthus' ex-wife, Harriet, is the UK home secretary," Patricia says to Chris.

"No," I say.

"She actually is," Chris says.

I stand up. "No, I can't go to Lisbon."

"Maria," Balthus says, "we have to stay together."

But I shake my head. "I have killed people. I killed this woman called Sadeqa, and the Project knows everything I have done. MI5 knows everything I have done. The only person in that loop who doesn't know everything I've done is me. I thought this file would prove I haven't killed, but I have." I pause as the sentence sinks in, and a strange wave of sadness passes over me, casting a cloud over any sun that may ever shine. "Being the person I am puts people in danger."

"Doc, no."

"Yes. That is what I needed to know. That is why I had to see this file, the Sadeqa file. You three are in danger near me. And because of me and what I have done, my mama and brother are not safe, either. Now I know I have killed. Now I know I have eliminated major assets. I am a target. My friends and family are targets. That is what I needed to know, and now that I do know, I have to go and see them. I have to make certain they are not in danger from the Project, even if that means hiding them away."

"What? Doc, no," Patricia says. "You have to stay with us now. It's not safe. The Project could be watching."

I turn to Chris. "Keep the files and make copies. When I return from seeing Mama, we will need it. Can you help me with her security?"

"Sure."

"Maria, please, no." Balthus says. "It's dangerous."

"I need to know they are safe. I …" I stop, my throat dry, a strange feeling of unease inside me. I look at my friends: at Chris, who I barely know but feel as if I want to know more; at Patricia, who means the world to me, who calms me; at Balthus, my father's old friend, who I feel an unusual bond with, a bond I have missed for so many years. They want to help me, these people, and I fight it sometimes, because I don't know how to handle it.

We stand there, the four of us, amid the humming and the market rumble and the chorizo and the chickens. We stand there and we think and we contemplate what comes next.

"I have to go to Madrid," I say after a moment, looking up. "I have to see if my family is okay."

Patricia lets out a deep sigh. "I know."

"We'll be close," Chris says. "If we get at all concerned, we can be there."

"Yeah," Patricia says. "We'll follow you over, stay near."

She steps forward and spreads out her fingers. I inhale her talcum powder scent, not wanting to leave her again, wishing the feeling of calm and safety she gives me would last forever.

Balthus steps forward. "Maria, do you really think this is necessary?"

"I have to see them," I say after a moment, eyes downturned, suddenly tired. "I can't keep running and hiding and leave my family open to danger—not now, not when I know what I know."

He smiles, eyes creasing, and nods, and a lump scratches my throat.

"Hey, who's that?" Patricia says.

We prop our hands on our brows and squint into the sun. A dozen paces away are a woman and a man, each dressed in casual day wear of loose linens and leather sandals, scanning the crowd. On their wrists are heavy gray watches. We are out of view where we stand, cloaked by the canopy and the narrow tin roof that juts from the wall next to an old fruit shop.

"Do you think they're from the Project?" Balthus says.

"I don't know," Chris replies, "but I think Maria shouldn't stay to find out."

I watch the two figures as they mingle into the crowd. They look like two tourists out for the day. And yet, something bothers me about the way they constantly look at people, spending an extra second or two looking at each passerby.

I look to Patricia. "Stay out of the way; don't let them see you."

She nods, and perhaps for the last time, I hold my fingers to hers and feel her warm, soft cotton pads of fingertips as, in my peripheral vision, I see the figures moving in. My pulse ramps up.

"Maria," Balthus whispers, "go. Contact us when you get to Ines'. Stay in touch."

I glance to them all, take a photograph of them with my eyes, try to recall every scar, mole, curve, wrinkle, smile, crease.

"Oh, shit," Chris says.

I turn. The black boots are approaching faster now. I spin back to my friends, give them one last look. Then, thrusting my cell phone deep into my pocket, I run to the wall, leap onto a bin, and catapult myself over to the other side.

# CHAPTER 36

**APARTMENT BUILDINGS, CENTRAL MADRID**

*1 Hour and 13 Minutes to Confinement*

Out of breath, I reach the edge of Mama's apartment building in the center of the city.

The early evening sun is sighing down onto the pavements, the cars on the roads having a siesta. I slip behind a tree where I can see clearly across the road and check whether I have been followed. The building where Mama lives when she is in the city shines with bright white marble, and when I scan the vicinity, I spot two figures sitting on a park bench across from the main entrance: a man reading a newspaper, and a young woman in running gear, doing up her laces. Neither looks to the other, but it is clear they are watching—two intelligence officers from either MI5 or the Project, waiting for me to show up. And while that concerns me, what worries me more, what makes me tense and eager to get into the building, is that if the Project is here, what have they done to my family?

Pulling my cap down low, I stride forward along the road, to a department store building made of cream-colored stone, and slip into a hidden side street. I take out my cell phone, text my status to Chris, and look around. To my left, a metal stairway zigzags up the building, to the roof. As I turn to where my mother's apartment building would be, my brain automatically calculates height and distance. If I can get up the steps that snake to the top, I can sprint to the roof of Mama's apartment and enter through her balcony doors without being seen by the Project or MI5 below. It is tight, a risk, but no matter which way I turn it, I cannot see another viable way in. A siren wails from the road beyond, making me jump. Not giving myself any more time to contemplate my options, I slap a stray sweat bead from my face and scramble up.

After 107 steps, thighs burning, I reach the top of the fire escape. The height gives me a clear view of this area of Madrid. I can see the cars circling the city gardens, and people the size of small beetles moving along the walkways, and as I observe, all the noise and activity continues, and yet, here it is relatively quiet and calm. I inhale. I am grateful for small mercies.

I start to move, sight set on Mama's building, and am going so fast that I don't spy the metal flashing that juts out on the route my feet take. I trip and tumble over, smacking my head on the ledge, and almost go over the side. Gasping, I drag myself back from the edge as blood trickles past my brow. I stop and wait. The airport, the market, the chaos of earlier, still rattles in my head, and I think of Patricia and Balthus and what they would tell me to do right now, and I find myself breathing easier, counting to ten, wiping my face and starting over. I move forward six steps and glance down—and halt. There is a gap between the two buildings, broken only by marble and window ledges that jut out at ninety-degree angles. I calculate the size of the gap, and the speed I must reach before I jump. If I am to clear the span, I have to spring precisely from the edge, at top speed.

I count to three, think of Patricia, and run.

I fly off the edge, legs flailing in the air, heart slamming against my chest so hard that it feels as if it will break free. Wind slices through my hair, and when I look down, I can see the drop below. The apartment roof rushes closer, closer … until I land with a thud, rolling to the side and banging my shoulder hard against a long metal conduit. I come to a stop. Everything aches: shoulder, legs, knees, arms. I get up and take stock. Finding no major injuries, I carry on. I have a small cut on my face from sliding on the roof gravel, and a sharp pain in my collarbone that makes me wince. But other than that, I am fine. I step to the ledge and look down. The balcony of Mama's apartment is right there.

I ease myself down onto a ledge of stone that juts out from two meters below the roof, and inch along it. This is more difficult than I anticipated. The loose gravel on the roof's surface above me shifts and crunches under my fingers, and my instinct is to overgrip, but I know this will cause lactic acid to build up in my forearms until I can no longer hold on. But bit by bit, I relax and it starts to work, and eventually, the balcony comes into view. Wrought-iron railings, ornate fixtures. Gilded. Guarded.

I take one step more, two, and my foot slides on a bird's nest and slips off the ledge. Hanging by my fingers from the roof's edge, I flail with both legs to regain my footing, and my cell phone slips out of my pocket. I watch it tumble almost lazily in the air until it smashes on the pavement. My feet find the stone ledge again, and I feel a sense of guarded relief.

Taking a last look at the smashed cell phone below, wondering how I can ever contact my friends again, I breathe deeply and get ready for the next part.

Counting to ten, I take my left hand off the edge of the roof and slowly reach down and left to the wrought-iron rail of Mama's balcony. Not glancing down once, I ease my left foot off the stone ledge and onto the bottom rail. Then the right foot. Now, feeling like a gibbon dangling from a branch, I let go of the roof with my right hand, grab the vertical corner post, and swing my weight over. In the span of fifty-two seconds, I am clinging to the outside of the balcony railing. As carefully as I can, I swing one leg and then the other over the corner of the wrought-iron barrier and plant my feet on the floor of Mama's balcony.

I get my bearings and look around. The French doors to Mama's apartment are yawning open, the heavy patterned curtains swinging in a mild breeze, and from this angle I can see that the room is empty. I enter Mama's house, tiptoeing, looking for where Mama may be, anxious to know that she is okay, that she is safe. And just as I call out for Mama and Ramon, something smashes into my head, sending the rooms swimming to nothing but a tiny black dot.

I wake up with a jolt. It is dark, damp here. I cannot see properly. I have been caught, this much I know, but by whom? The Project? MI5? Someone else?

I don't know how I got here.

I don't know how I am going to escape.

# CHAPTER 37

**APARTMENT BUILDINGS, CENTRAL MADRID**
*Present Day*

Ramon opens the door of the basement, light flooding in all around him, and I charge at him.

Before he can move away or even register what is happening, I smash the metal stand across his shoulders and kick him in the shin.

A second later, I am behind him, with my right arm around his throat. "You are going to take me out of here. *Now.*"

"What are you doing?" Ramon says, choking.

I propel him toward the exit. "I am getting out of here."

"Stop it, M! Stop!" His legs are kicking forward, his heels slipping as if on ice. I tighten my grip around his neck and shove him forward with my knee.

"Move."

We reach the stairs, and Ramon tries to thrust his arms out, but my grasp is so strong, my intention so forceful, that my muscles clamp him like a vise. He staggers up the steps, lopsided in my clench, then trips a little, and I wobble, hands loosening slightly. For a second, I feel Ramon's arms push outward, but by then I have my footing and am hauling him to the door.

"Unlock it."

"M, don't do this."

I squeeze tighter. "I said unlock it."

His hand falls to the side, slipping into his pocket.

I jerk my head, immediately on alert. "What are you doing?"

"The key," he says. "It's in my pocket."

"There is a touch pad."

"I know, I know. It uses both systems." I thrust my hand into his trouser pocket.

"Why are you doing this?" Ramon yells out, yet I barely hear him. My only focus is on getting out of here, on ending what is happening. My whole short-term memory of how I got here, of all the data I uncovered from the Project, from the Sadeqa file, is all fresh in my mind.

"You are with the Project," I say. "You have been helping them for years and somehow implicated Papa in it all, even though he had nothing to do with it."

"What? No! M, this is crazy. Stop and think about what you're saying. The Project—they *help* you."

My fingers touch the key, and I yank it out of his pocket. Pulling Ramon with me, I slip the key into the lock and turn it.

"You're hurting me," he says.

But I ignore him, because there is one more obstacle now: an access code.

Keypads get smudged when they are overused, but it can be hard to define if the code is changed. Keys three and seven are so worn, the numerals are almost gone.

"The access pad—the first two numbers are three and seven. What are the remaining two digits?"

"M, please …"

I squeeze tighter. He chokes. "Nine and … five."

Not wasting a second, worried that the Project or MI5 has gotten to Mama upstairs, I punch in the numbers and click. The door unlocks.

Heart firing at full throttle, I draw the three iron bolts that guard the entrance.

A creak slices into the silence as the door swings open on an ascending flight of stairs. The steps are stone, the walls painted a matte slate gray. When I look at it, the color instantly dulls the air, making it dark and cold, and as I drag Ramon forward, I realize I have never been here before, in this part of Mama's town house. She never allowed it.

"Where does this lead to? Papa's study?"

"M, you can't. Please, just stop."

"You are with the Project. It has to end."

"Do you even know what the Project is? M, I think you—"

But I ignore him and, with his throat in the crook of my arm, walk my brother up the steps.

We stop at another door. It is white and constructed of metal. There is no lock or alarm system, and so, eager not to waste time and knowing that Balthus, Chris, and Patricia will be concerned, I flex my arm and feel Ramon swallow. "How long have you had me down here?"

"What?" he sputters.

"How long have you kept me in the basement?"

"Twenty-three … hours."

Nearly a whole day. "How many others have you held down there?"

"Huh? *What?* No one."

"Do not lie. I have seen the other subject numbers etched on the wall. I have found a photograph."

"I don't know what you're talking about. M, please."

Ignoring his pleas, I push him through. "You first."

But Ramon digs his heels in. I shove him, arching his back and prodding him forward with my knee. "Move. Now."

He still balks. "You won't be able to get out. The Project is set on helping you, M." He coughs. "Let them help you."

"The Project does not want to help me. They want to help themselves. They want to help governments and presidents and generals win wars that they themselves have created. They all lie. No one is allowed to be themselves. No one is allowed to simply live in harmony."

"What are you talking about?"

I am set on opening the white door ahead, on getting out, but Ramon's shoulders are as wide as the opening. There is only one option: I have to get him to do it.

"Open the door," I say.

"No." He resists harder now as my arms begin to tire. "M, I care for you. Please, let me go. Stop this. You're only hurting yourself."

"What did the Project make you do?"

"What?"

"What did the Project instruct you to do? How were you trained?"

"M, this is insane," he croaks. "The Project didn't train me to do *anything*. They just gave me advice on how to help you. M, you came into the house via the balcony, shouting out for us. That's not right. You're not well."

"You knew about the subject numbers on the wall."

He shakes his head. "No. The pencil marks were ..." He stops and seems to stare into space.

My brain begins to make the connections. "The pencil marks were what?"

His body drops, limp and wilting. When he speaks again, his voice is low, scratchy. "I found them a long time ago."

"When?"

He swallows. "I found them one day when I snuck down there when Mama said I couldn't. I used to play down there without her knowing; then, for a long time when Papa was away with a trial, it was all locked up and I couldn't get in, and ... and when I returned, the padding was there covering the pencil marks until you found them just now ... Please, M, let me go."

I consider what he says, unsure what to think. *Mama* was in charge of the basement? "Move."

"What? M, please. I'm telling you the truth!"

"How much time do I have until the Project arrive?"

"Erm-*hmm*. Three, maybe four hours?"

I ponder this. That means one hour at the most.

"We need to sort this out," Ramon says. "M, let me help. I'm not moving."

I look at him. "Yes, you are." And I kick him hard in the back of the knee.

He immediately buckles, legs folding as he cries out in pain. I jab my fingers straight into his throat, my training activating, winding him so he stumbles back, unblocking the exit.

I move quick now, sharp, bolting for the door, but before I can roll out of the way, Ramon flies at me. It is so quick, so unexpected, that at first I do not dive. I manage to grip the door handle, but Ramon hooks my legs, and my hand slips off the metal. I feel a twinge, the sharp snap of a punch, then a heavier blow as Ramon drives his fist into my back. I crumple forward, pain radiating down my spine, the confined space giving me no room to swing around, to maneuver into a fighting position.

I focus on what I have been trained to do. Ramon throws a jab at my head, and I duck, hooking his left ankle with my right. He staggers backward and seems to hang there for a moment, balanced on one foot above the stairs.

His eyes go wide. "M! Help!"

I start to move and then, for some reason, stop and watch the inevitable effect of gravity and momentum. After all, he is the Project, and the Project is not good. And then another thought: this is my brother, and he just wants to help me. He loves me. What am I *thinking?*

I thrust out my arm to catch him. "Ramon, grab on to me." But his mouth shrieks in silence as his body tilts backward into space.

I lunge, grasping for him. "Ramon!"

His head smacks audibly on the stone steps as his legs swing over, their inertia carrying him in a slow descending cartwheel.

"Ramon!"

I don't move, chest gasping for air, eyes locked on the broken heap at the foot of the stairs. What have I done? The impulse to check on him, to know that he is alive, is almost too overwhelming to resist, but I stop myself, because what if he grabs me, hurts me, keeps me here for the Project to reclaim?

Heart pounding, I look to my brother, then to the door, to the white metal handle. Without turning, without allowing myself one more glance down, I swallow and, pressing down hard on the handle, swing open the door into Mama's apartment.

# CHAPTER 38

**APARTMENT BUILDINGS, CENTRAL MADRID**
*Present Day*

I stumble into a side room, out of breath. Slamming the door shut behind me, slapping my back to the wall, try to steady myself as the image of Ramon, in a pile on the basement floor, stalks me.

I left him there, my own brother, probably bleeding internally. A small moan escapes my lips. I cannot bear to think about what I have done. And yet, my brother was with the Project, a part of it, so none of us were safe.

Pulling myself up, I smear the snot and sweat from my face and take in the small room before me. As my eyes adjust, I see a lamp glowing in the corner, carving my shadow against the opposite wall. There is a feeling of familiarity, of déjà vu, that I cannot place.

I brush my fingers along the wall. A mahogany cabinet containing wineglasses stands to my right, beside it a dark wooden side table with a silver tray and coffeepot on top. I look at it in the buttered lamplight and feel a stab of something, a memory that comes in a wave and crashes into my head. I have been here before. I spin around, gathering as much as I can, my head growing dizzy as the picture emerges, switching on as I remember. I am young, no more than ten, my limbs skinny and bony. I am with Papa, and it is the week before he died. I see him.

He takes the silver coffeepot and pours coffee into a cup, holding it out to me.

"Here you go, my little bright spark."

I take the cup in my thin, small fingers.

"Careful, now," Papa says. Then he smiles, soft at the edges. "Your white cup, my baby. I know you can't drink out of anything else."

I feel a surge of gratitude toward him, but I am in my emotional cage and don't know how to express what I feel.

Papa sets down the coffeepot now, and I watch him. "Papa," I say, my voice small like a bird's, "don't go down there to the basement without me. Let me come this time."

He turns, eyes drooped, no smile or creases. He crouches down to me and takes my arms in his hands—the only person I will allow to touch me. "I can't let you come with me, sweetheart."

"Why?"

He sighs, heavy and long. "There are things there that …" He pauses then smiles wide, with creases this time. "You run along upstairs now to Mama."

"No."

"Maria, please." And he stands, walks away, and opens the door into the room I am never allowed to enter.

The image blows away, and my eyelids flicker as now, in the present day, I look at the room and try to grasp the vision. To my surprise, tears streak my face, and I lift my fingers to wipe them away. I turn to the wall, skim my hand along it, and locate the light switch. Flicking it on, I understand now where I am.

Papa's study.

Could Ramon have kept anything connected to the Project in here? I trace my palms along every piece of furniture, every wall and corner and curve, as if each one contains memories of Papa. My feet feel the plush carpet fibers beneath my soles as the thick strands ooze between my toes. I drop to my knees and inhale the scent of the carpet, the familiar comfort of wool and musk and lavender, just as when I was ten and Papa was still with me. I lie there, sniffing and breathing, rocking a little, and for a sweet split second, I pretend that none of this ever happened at all: not Papa dying, not the Project being founded, not Mama falling ill or Ramon betraying me—none of it. I inhale the scent of the whole room one more time. Then, standing, I lock my sight on Papa's desk in the corner and, walking over to it, open it up.

The desk is just as it was in my memory. It is flat and rectangular, and the mahogany bears light scuff marks on the rounded edges. There is a wooden chair with a curved backrest and a leather seat, and the smell reminds me of Papa and the cigars he used to smoke.

Pulling the chair out of the way, careful not to bump the wood, I lean in and scan the old-fashioned bureau desk. In the top are six small drawers, three on each side. I slide open each one, quietly, softly. Nothing there, just empty wooden shells and the wistful scent of sandalwood, but what catches my attention most is the long drawer that stretches across the middle, beneath the writing surface. It is shallow, perhaps ten centimeters deep, and when I open it and click on the low lamp that sits on a side cabinet, beside a vase of silk lilies, I start to get a better look.

The drawer still appears empty, until I run my hand underneath and feel something bumpy at the right end. It is a tiny bolt latch. Stopping to check for any sounds of movement from Ramon or anyone else, I release the bolt, and a twelve-centimeter panel swings down from the bottom of the drawer, onto my lap. A false bottom, two centimeters in depth, extends the entire length and breadth of the drawer. Above the hinged section released by the bolt latch, I feel something crisp, starched, like heavy paper or card stock.

*Odd.* Sliding it carefully out from its hidey-hole, I place it on the desktop above and read the name on the top page: *Garcia Building Company S. L.* Turning it, I find myself staring at some sort of detailed technical documents. The first few pages are simply construction notes and calculations for a building project Mama must have commissioned, because her name and signature are at the foot of each page. Not wanting to waste any time, I am about to close the report and search for other information that may be stashed away in the bureau, when a number catches my eye. The date on the file: 1976.

Mildly wary, I flip all the way to the end of the file, check the address for the building plans, and see that it matches here, this address where I now sit: Mama's Madrid house. A strange lump begins to form in my stomach as I reopen the document and take a closer look.

The first technical drawings detail an extension to the rear of the property, but then, farther in, they switch to the basement. With rising unease, I read on, the lamp casting an eerie orange glow over my hands and the paper in front of them. There are measurements, calculations, numbers, all in great detail, all appearing normal, natural. And yet, as I delve a little deeper, they are anything but.

Because what I am looking at now are complex plans to widen and strengthen the wall in the basement, to create a soundproof room. My pulse quickening, I read further and learn that later, in 2001 and then again in 2010, both the cellar walls and the window were replaced and reinforced using some of the most expensive materials available, including one notable feature: padded walls. The new material was installed in 2009, replacing original padding installed in … 1985.

They are all the same calendar years that were scratched onto the brickwork by the subject numbers in the basement. The same calendar years and subject numbers that correlated with the data found on the file in the ICE room in Hamburg.

I grip the desktop with both hands as I read on to the very last page. Near the bottom, just above where the builder has signed on behalf of his company, is another name, another signature agreeing on the work to be carried out.

And it is not Papa's. It is not Ramon's name or the Project's.

It is Ines Villanueva.

My mother.

"Hello, Maria, dear."

# CHAPTER 39

**APARTMENT BUILDINGS, CENTRAL MADRID**

*Present Day*

My mother leans on the door frame, dripping with jewelry and draped in Chanel. She smells of jasmine and orange and caramel dipped in cream, and in her left hand is a shiny wooden walking stick. I don't move. She raises a skeletal hand to her smooth scalp and delivers me a thin smile. "My dear, if I had known you were coming, I would have popped my wig on."

I am alarmed at her appearance: thin, translucent, a pencil drawing of her former self. The cancer must have taken hold. I don't know what to think. I am so glad she is safe, and yet, something holds me back from feeling any joy.

"Mama," I say, my hand on the file I have just seen. "You look ill."

"Always direct," she sighs, and glances to the documents on the bureau desk. "So you found them. Ah, my clever, clever girl. Come." She beckons me with her finger. "I have things to tell you."

I feel my confusion turning to fear. "What is happening?"

She gestures toward the twinkling ceiling of the next room. "Let's go somewhere cozier, my dear. I need to sit."

She looks at me, waiting, brown eyes piercing and with no creases at the corners, and I am paralyzed. This is my mama, yet I feel not myself when she is near me. Instead, I feel doubtful, withdrawn, and when I think of it, this has always been so, but I do not know why. Her fingernails clack on the wood of the door frame, her pointed chin held high, her gaze rippling over me, appraising my attire and my face and my hair.

"My dearest," she says now, "you do look a fright." She leans on her walking stick. "Come."

She leads me to a drawing room with soft yellow light, and embers glowing from a fireplace in the center of the room. I suddenly recall it from my childhood. Along the wall, locked cabinets of rich mahogany stand at attention between ornate window frames graced with sumptuous woolen drapes that sweep the floor. This is a place of bookcases, decanters, crystal chandeliers, antique rugs, all oozing with the hushed flutter of money. Of wealth and power.

My mother lowers herself into a high-backed chair, the brown of the leather overpowering her pale, almost translucent skin. Her rich bronze tan is now gone, along with her glorious black tresses. She is a whisper of her former self.

"Maria, my dear, would you like some water?"

Unable to speak, I shake my head as my brain connects the dots with what I have found in the drawer. She pours a glass of water from a crystal decanter and, letting out a mew of a sigh, takes a sip.

"Did you know Ramon was holding me here?" I say.

"Pardon, my dear?"

"He held me in the basement for twenty-three hours. I was tied up and drugged. He said he was keeping me there because he was helping me." It occurs to me that I am shaking. "Did you know I was in the basement?"

Mama's knuckles go white where they grip the glass, but she does not say anything—just dabs her cheek with one hand and sets the glass back down on the table. "Yes," she says eventually. "I knew."

Her answer blindsides me. I sway a little to the side, as if the words hitting me had physical weight.

"Why?" I say after I have regained my footing.

"Oh, Maria," my mother says, "do you not remember?"

"I … you …" I halt, suddenly realizing that I don't know what she means.

"You came to us off the *balcony*, of all places." Her voice is soft, a warm blanket of words. "You were erratic. Upset. My dearest, we didn't know what to do. You were, well, a little out of control. I gave the number of the Project to Ramon, and he called them."

I go quiet as my brain begins to fire and connect, but seeing Mama shakes me, makes me nervous. "Mama, do you know what the Project is?"

"Well, yes. They've helped you for a long while, my dear. They are the clinic people I used to take you to when you were little."

"So Ramon is the contact now for the Project?"

"He is. They are there to help, aren't they? I haven't dealt with them for a while—it's all Ramon now. That's their name—the Project."

I go dizzy, not sure what to do or think. Nothing is making sense. Ramon knew about the Project; that's what he said. And now Mama is saying she knows them, too, but that she thinks they are someone else, affiliated with my old Asperger's clinic she used to believe she was taking me to. I have to tell her the truth.

"Mama," I say now, making myself speak even though just looking at her makes me doubt my own mind, "the Project is a covert conditioning program. It is part of the UK intelligence services operation and has been ongoing for three decades. It is not an Asperger's clinic, as you thought it was."

She lifts her hand to her mouth. "Oh, my goodness. Maria, this … this sounds so far-fetched. Are you sure?"

"Quite. How did they contact you originally, Mama, when I was young?"

She hesitates, touches her neck with fingers frail as twigs. "Well, my dear, you had … troubles. The Project said they could help you. I took you to the doctor's appointments. They were quite ground-breaking, I was told. It was just for your Asperger's, really, for when you had certain issues. We traveled a lot with you because of it—they had facilities all over the world. Father Reznik—do you remember him? He helped enormously when Papa was away on business."

"Mama," I start to say, but it is hard to speak, the uncertainty hitting me. Hearing Father Reznik's name spoken aloud destabilizes me. "It was not simply a doctor's appointment or a visit to the priest," I say. "I was being tested on. Father Reznik was a handler for the Project. For MI5."

"*What?*" She laughs, a crumpled laugh like a piece of paper being scrunched up, and it tears me inside, that laugh, rips my confidence in one swipe. "Oh, my dearest, surely not. I used to take you there! Well, no wonder Ramon was concerned about you and … and …"

I begin to worry, start to think, as she laughs at me, that perhaps I have made a huge mistake, when her shoulders visibly drop. She shakes her head on that scrawny neck.

"Mama?"

"I'm sorry, I can't keep up this pretense," she says after a second, her voice barely a whisper. The lights glow and the fire crackles. "Ramon drugged you, my baby." A small sob slips out. "He took you down into that cellar, saying you needed help." She shoots a hand to her mouth. "Oh, my goodness, was he not telling me the truth? Should you not have been in the basement? I told him I didn't like it one bit, but he said the Project insisted, said it was some new, radical treatment."

She lifts her gaze now, eyes moist, and I don't know what to say or think as I hear her speak.

"Oh, I was so worried. Ramon was acting crazy, and I was scared. I didn't know what to do. I knew he had you in the cellar and he was becoming increasingly erratic. I didn't know this Project was really what you are saying they are. If it is true, then, dear Lord, forgive me." She pauses, dabs her cheek with her fingers. "Your brother's been … different recently. Distracted, preoccupied. I thought it was simply work, the busy legal circuit, but then he started talking about this Project more and more—even mentioned Balthus. Yes, I believe he mentioned Balthus. Oh, my, is he involved, too?"

My fingers scratch into my leg for control as my mind tries to connect what Mama is saying, but it doesn't make sense—mostly because I don't want to believe it. Because if Ramon was in contact with Balthus about the Project, then Balthus is their contact, too, and has been all along.

The smells in the air now collide with the glitter of crystal and the confusion of the words spoken, and I struggle to impose some order on it all.

There is a loud crack. My head jerks to the left.

Mama jumps. "What was that?" she says, hand on her chest.

There is a rattling sound—sharp, piercing, like a rod of metal being thrust down hard on concrete—then nothing. Silence. My whole body is on high alert. The Project—are they coming?

Mama stays in her seat as I turn to the door and listen. There is a tap, then another—soft at first, then louder, until it is nearer, closer, outside.

"Maria, my dear, I am worried. Please see what that is."

Uncertain, I take seven steps to the door, stop, and listen. There is a rustling outside, a scrape, and then, without warning, the door bursts open, sending me flying backward to land in a heap on the floor. My brother stands there looking like a walking corpse, blood smeared on his skull and cheeks and throat, and his hair is soaked and matted where he hit the stone steps.

"Ramon!" my mother shrieks.

I dart back, and at first I think my brother is going to run at me, to throw himself on me, but he turns and, staring straight at my mother, screams, "You liar! You fucking liar!"

# CHAPTER 40

Ramon lunges at my mother, knocking her cane to the floor, the metal head clanking on the air vent and sending a sharp snap vibrating through the air.

"You liar!" he shouts again, trying to drag her up out of her chair and onto the floor.

I run, grab him by the shoulders, yank him backward. His fists fly out, teeth snarl, but then Mama begins to cough and sputter, and Ramon suddenly deflates, dropping in front of me like a stone, hauling in great gulps of oxygen.

I slap back my hair. "Why did you attack Mama?"

He doesn't look at me, just stares at our mother as she clutches her throat, gasping for breath. I run over and help Mama back to her seat.

Ramon stands, stumbles a little, then slaps his hand against the cabinet to his right and pulls himself up. "Mama's a liar," he says, blood seeping from his lip. He spits red flecks onto the antique Bokhara rug.

Mama's eyes go wide. "Ramon! Manners!"

He laughs, but it comes out more as a low, feral growl. I step back. I do not understand what is happening.

"You manipulated me to do what I did," my brother says to Mama, "and it's *me* you call the liar? I heard you, heard everything you said to Maria just now."

Mama looks from him to me, then back again. "My son, I don't know what you're talking about." Her voice is low, hushed. "What did you do to your own sister?"

"What did *I* do?" He paces. "What did *you* do? It was you who told me to put Maria down there in the cellar. You who told me all about this Project thing. You said it would help her. You convinced me! So I did it. I did what you asked. But I found out, Mama. These Project people of yours—they have DNA. Oh, yeah, I did some digging and found out." He turns to me. "M, you have a photo, don't you? I found it, too, but I didn't know what to do about it."

My hand reaches into my back pocket, as if of its own volition, and pulls out the picture from the crucifix. I look at my name and year of birth scratched into the corner.

"I found some information on you," Ramon says to me. "Something on some documents the Project sent to Mama's e-mail, and I read it, thinking it was just standard advice regarding you, M, but it wasn't—it was a DNA report. M ..." his shoulders drop. "You're adopted." He exhales. "You're not my sister. And *she*"—pointing to Mama—"has lied about who you are and what she's done all along."

*Adopted.* The floor feels as if it were slipping out from under me. I stagger back, eyes down, unable to make contact or see in their eyes what they see of me. "Mama, is ... is what Ramon says correct?"

She looks now to the photograph I hold in my fingers. "I said I had something to tell you." She nods at the image. "That is it."

I stare at the photograph, and I think I begin to shake, but I am unsure. I look at Ramon. "You are not with the Project?"

He shakes his head. "No, not the one you describe, and definitely not in the way Mama described. M, she set you up. She set us both up. I thought it was a specialist doctor's clinic, that's all. That's what Mama told me. M, I meant it down there when I said I loved you." Tears streak down his face now, past his cheeks, falling from the tip of his chin. "I didn't mean to hurt you, I'm so sorry."

"Ramon!" Mama says. "Enough tears. Real men don't cry."

"Like hell they don't!" Ramon yells, rounding on her, and I wince at his volume, at the chaos that is setting in. "Tell her! Tell Maria about the knee-deep shit you've got our lives into!"

Mama does not move. Her hair sways, and her skin is pale even in the glow of the embers. She picks at a cotton fiber on the corner of the chair, then sighs.

"Maria, my sweet, you are not …" She searches the air. "You are not our biological child."

The words drive a knife right through me, and when I fall back, Ramon catches me. "I am not Papa's daughter," I say to him. "I am not your sister."

"Oh, M."

The room swirls, and it feels as if my whole world has been snatched away from me. *Papa.* He was everything to me, and that fact throbs now in my head and I can't stand it. I can't stand the sadness that forces its way through me, clashing with the smells in the room, with the colors and with the traffic noise outside, and even with the messy wisps of Mama's hair.

I blink past tears that flow down my cheeks and past my chin, and a surge of anger and despair rises up, and I stamp my feet into the carpet and scream. "Tell me!" I yell to Mama. "Tell me now how this happened! Tell me what you did!"

Mama sniffs and dabs her nose. When she eventually speaks, her voice is low and measured.

"Balthazar came to me," she says. "It was in 1979. He was engaged to be married to Harriet, but, well, he had a wandering eye, as men do. He met some young girl named Isabella when he was visiting his parents in San Sebastian. She got pregnant, and Balthus panicked. He was on a political career trajectory, his fiancée, of course, even more so. She is currently making a fine British home secretary. So a rogue pregnancy would not do. I helped out. I took Maria off his hands. Alarico, well, we had you, Ramon, and we loved you, but your Papa was desperate for a daughter, so when you came along, Maria, well, he was delighted. He could help out an old friend and gain a child." She holds her head up high and, inhaling, narrows her eyes to me. "My dear Maria, Balthazar—Balthus—is your biological father. And the woman in the photograph is your real mother."

"No."

"M? M, it's okay."

But I push him away. "No, no, no." The bellows, fire tongs, shovel, and poker in the hearth stand are all in disarray, and I slump over to them now, drop to my knees, and begin to set the fire items out in neat order, first by length, then by weight, then by shades of blackness—anything to feel order, to stop my thoughts and being from becoming utterly fragmented. Order after order after order.

I stop, fingers dark from the ash, and look at the photograph in my hand, but it all blurs into one, and all I can think of is the fact that Papa is not my papa. Not my real, biological papa. Balthus is. I stamp my foot, unable to contain the confusion and upset. Why did he never tell me? All that time we were in Goldmouth, and he never said a thing.

I round on Mama. "You lied to me. You *all* lied to me!" I point to the woman in the picture. "Tell me again her name."

"Isabella," she says. "Isabella Bidarte."

The name on the reverse of the photograph. Isabella Bidarte. Mama is telling the truth. The truth.

I wipe spit from my mouth, tears from my cheeks. "Where is she from? Is she alive?"

"The Basque country. Like Balthazar. And, well, I think she died, my dear."

Dead, like Papa. I fall back. The Basque blood data, the information Black Eyes told me on why Basque blood was so important to the conditioning program. It all dazes me, disorients me, and without thinking, I raise my shirtsleeve, inch by inch, until the fountain pen tattoo on my arm is exposed. *I am Basque.* I am Basque, not because Papa has Basque roots, but because I am not in his bloodline at all.

I hear Mama gasp at the green ink tattoo. As she does, bile shoots up my throat and I swallow it back, throwing out my hand and finding Ramon's to steady myself.

"You made me feel like I was not myself. You never went near me, never tried to hold me like …" I stop, wanting to say "like Papa did," but finding now that those words no longer have the same meaning. "Who let the Project have me? Was it Balthus and … and this Isabella?"

Mama regards me for two seconds, then emits a small lemon-scented sigh. "My dear girl, I have been ill with cancer for a long time. Longer than you think." She pauses to wheeze in a sharp breath. "I was at Cambridge University when MI5 was recruiting people—bright, intelligent people." She shrugs. "It wasn't something I wanted to get involved with, but I made contacts. Valuable contacts. I knew about a trial project they were developing following the airport atrocities in Athens in 1973—this was just a year after the Munich massacre and Black September. It was just after that I began to get ill, the cancer was diagnosed, and my contact at the Project told me about experimental cancer drugs they were developing. The drugs were a miracle, but weren't licensed. Nothing else was working for me, so when they offered me the medicine, with conditions, I did what anyone would do: I took the chance. They were looking for Basque people for the program, and I had you, so it was a straight exchange."

"You gave them Maria," Ramon says, "to test on in exchange for medicine."

I stand still. I cannot move.

"My boy," Mama says, "I only did what anyone would do. The Project had not really had a child before, so it really was a very exciting opportunity for everyone. And the program directors thought it best if the child was brought up in a normal, natural environment. They suspected Maria could develop Asperger's—Isabella was on the spectrum, dear—and so I kindly offered to keep Maria, house her in a normal developmental environment so they could put her on the program and help her … achieve her potential."

The shock is so much I can barely speak. "Did Papa know about this?"

"Oh, no. Alarico didn't know."

"And what about Balthus and … Isabella?"

She pops in a breath. "Ah, no. He didn't know. It might have complicated things, what with him being engaged and then married to a government official."

Ramon shakes his head. "You selfish bitch."

She waves a hand. "Don't be so naive, my dear. I had a career. I had a life. And the drugs worked. It is self-preservation. This is called life."

"And what about Maria's life?"

"My boy, I had cancer. I wanted to keep my life."

I do not move, because now, in my mind, I can see him. Black Eyes. Dr. Carr. His explanation of Project Callidus being called "Cranes." Black September, the secret government files I discovered in Hamburg, about the cancer drugs. It all links now and explodes in my head.

"It was you," I say, almost to myself, barely recognizing my own voice. "I saw the classified files about the cancer medicine. There were dates tracking back three whole decades, right into the 1970s, with cash amounts linked to each one. In 1979, the money amounts rose substantially, the cash wired to Madrid. The Project began when you gave me to them."

"The Project began, young lady, when Balthus and Isabella gave you up because they didn't want you!"

"1979?" Ramon says. "M, that was the year before you were born. You took cash in exchange for looking after Maria?"

"So they paid me to keep you. Sue me." She sits back, twirls a bony finger on the edge of the glass.

I force my eyes up now, make myself look Mama in the eye. "Why are you telling me all this now?"

But she doesn't reply.

"Tell her!" Ramon shouts.

Mama picks up the glass, takes one sip, then lowers it. "When Maria was acquitted, she hid. No one could find her, which meant the Project could not get to her."

"And if they don't have her, you don't get your drugs." Ramon shakes his head. "This is fucked up. You lied and got me to imprison my own sister in a basement so you could get your medicine? You want to sacrifice Maria so you can be well enough to run for fucking prime minister of Spain."

"I sacrifice Maria so I can live!" she yells. She stays still, glaring at Ramon, her blouse low on her shoulder from the scuffle, and flecks of spit in the corners of her mouth. She sits back, takes a breath, then smooths down her skirt and dabs her lips.

"Jesus Christ," Ramon says now. "Jesus fucking Christ."

I swallow, breathe hard, every part of me wanting to run now, desperately needing to rock and moan as the emotions force their way into me. Nothing I knew to be true is anymore. The family I thought I had does not exist, and without knowing where we are from, without having that foundation a family provides, how can we grow to be the people we were meant to be?

"You … you knew why I was in prison," I say after a moment. "You knew all along that I didn't murder the priest. You knew the Project set me up. You knew because you were working for them, letting them use me right from the start. You told Balthus about the ICE Room."

"Ah, yes. That was a mistake. I had been pumped too full of morphine that day. There was a time, you see, when I used to confide in Balthus about everything."

"Except the Project," Ramon says.

Mama slowly tilts her head. "The Project is doing great things, Maria. *You* are doing great things."

"No. No …" Memories flood in, a torrent of them, rushing forward in quick succession. "You took me to the Project's facilities," I say. "The flashbacks I had with you at my bedside while Dr. Carr tested on me. Black Eyes …" My voice trails off as the memories slash into me, one after another. My mother standing as Black Eyes cut into my stomach to see if I could feel pain. "I was only a child," I say now. "I was only a child."

"Mama, how could you do all this?" Ramon says, but she ignores him, her focus totally on me.

"Dr. Carr said you would be helping people, my dear, that you were so intelligent, so unique, that only good could come of what they were doing with you."

"For the greater good," I say, and turning from her, I begin to rock as a tsunami of emotions rages inside me. "My handlers—did you help to arrange them? Father Reznik? My university professor? My hospital bosses? Did you know they were all working under-cover for the Project? Was Balthus involved?"

Mama angles her head back so her eyes can look down on me. "I knew about your handlers," she says. "Balthus wasn't involved." A small sigh slips out. "I helped arrange the handlers' positions, of course, helped ensure they would have access to you. It was for your own good." She dabs her cheeks. "You needed to be monitored so they knew that the tests and the conditioning they were carrying out on you were safe, controlled. And it helped. Look how well you've done! You're so sharp, so intelligent, my little angel."

"This has to stop." Ramon shakes his head. "This all has to stop."

# CHAPTER 41

## APARTMENT BUILDINGS, CENTRAL MADRID
*Present Day*

I stand by the fireplace now and rearrange the fire tools one way and then another, then another, putting them in defined patterns, in order. Ramon stands near me, looking at Mama, her arms and legs arranged in an elegant bag of bones in the armchair.

"You've called them, haven't you?" he says. "The Project."

She sighs. "They may be on their way, yes. The cancer is taking hold now, my dear. I need help."

"We have to go," I say. "I do not want the Project to find me." I dig my nail into my thumb at the thought of the Project arriving.

"Wait." Ramon paces three steps, then stops. "You told Maria it was me who had the room soundproofed—I heard you. But that paperwork Maria found—it was all you. Why?" he says. "Why did you get all the work done?"

She looks away over to the window and watches the curtain billow in and out. "I would ... look after people sometimes for the Project."

"Subject numbers," I say, finding my voice. "There are numbers etched to the wall. I have seen them. The years correlate with your documentation that I found in the desk. They have your signature."

"Why did you install the padding and the reinforced walls?" Ramon says.

She shrugs. "They would be loud sometimes, the subjects, before the Project collected them. For many, the drugs they were given didn't quite work as planned. There were … complications. We had to keep them safe from themselves, you understand."

Ramon stares at her. "And you didn't want anyone to hear. You didn't want Papa to hear." He drops his head. "Oh, my God."

She smiles. "What is it, dear?"

"He found out, didn't he?"

I put down the wrought-iron ash broom and listen. A dark, heavy fear begins to build in the base of my throat. It mixes with the pungent jasmine and orange-blossom scent that seeps from Mama's skin, and as Ramon stares at Mama, I find myself slowly walking to her, and before I can fully understand what I am doing, I thrust the photograph of Isabella and me in her face. "Who put this in the cellar?"

She frowns, shakes her head, finally glancing to the picture. "I, I don't know, my dear."

"Yes, you do," Ramon says. "Tell her."

"No, I don't—"

A surge of anger and loss and sheer, overwhelming sadness engulfs me, and before I can stop myself, I have Mama by the throat. "I said. Tell. Me."

"Al … Alarico," she finally croaks. "Alarico put it there." I release her and she rubs her throat, eyes wide.

I force myself to ask the next question. "Why did Papa put this picture in the cellar all those years ago?"

Ramon stands tall as we both look to our mother now, waiting. She shifts a little in her seat, tries to cough, then stops, chest sinking backward.

"I put him in there," she says after a moment.

"You did *what*?" Ramon says.

She looks up now, eyes narrow, a strange smile slicing her face, as the glow of the lamps and the embers casts faint shadows across her face. "I put him there; he gave me no choice."

My mind fires; connections fuse. "You got the room sound-proofed and you put him in there and he hid this photograph."

Ramon jerks his head. "Why did Papa hide the photo, Mama? Why did he feel he had to do that?"

Mama coughs, levels a stare at my brother. "Ramon, my boy, you don't understand."

"Try me."

"He didn't realize …" She coughs. "He didn't realize what he had stumbled onto," she says finally. Ramon and I fall still. "Alarico discovered some documents I had about your conditioning, Maria—about the tests I took you for. Well, as you can imagine, it was all highly confidential back then, very hush-hush."

"Jesus Christ …"

"And, well, one day he found some conditioning documents and, well, the Project directors advised me to keep Alarico down there for a while until they could decide how to handle the information leak. We made it look like … like a robbery."

Ramon drops his head. "Except Papa knew it was you, didn't he? He'd figured it out by then. That's why he hid the photo there. He'd found out about it all, thought he could hide it, come back for it, and expose it all."

"You have to understand, my dear, I loved him so much."

"But what did they do to him, Mama?" Ramon says.

"My boy …"

He hammers the wall with his fist. "Tell us!"

"My children, please! I did it for you; you must understand that. I had no choice. I was ill. I *am* ill. They are not giving me the drugs anymore until I give you to them, my dear Maria. Without the medicine, I have only three months left to live." Then she stops, sighs. "My dear, he loved you so much, your papa, Alarico."

"What did they do to him?" I find myself saying, though it doesn't feel like me, as if I were somehow detached from my own voice.

Mama pulls herself up to her feet, her whole body shaking, and takes two tiny steps forward.

"What did they do to Papa?" I say again.

"They killed him," Ramon says.

I turn to my brother, confused. "How do you know?"

He glances to Mama, then gazes back to me. "Because I did it, M." He stops, smears his damp face with his sleeve. "I think I killed Papa."

I stare at my brother now, not understanding what he means. "You could not have killed Papa. He died in a car accident."

Ramon glances to Mama and back to me. "She asked me to do something to his car."

My head starts to spin. "Do what? Do what to his car?"

"My dear boy," Mama says now, hobbling nearer, her knuckles as knobbly as her walking stick, and I think of the witch in the Hansel and Gretel fable Papa used to read to me. "Please, don't."

But Ramon wipes his eyes and keeps his gaze on me. "It was in the morning. I remember it as if it were yesterday. Father Reznik had been teaching me how to work on cars." He shakes his head and smears snot from his nose. "Father Reznik was your handler for this fucked-up Project, but I didn't know, and there he was, teaching me how to fix a car—or so I thought." He spins around to Mama and steps back. She is closer now, so close Ramon can almost touch her.

"Ramon, my dear, do not say any more."

"Why?" he says, spit flying from his mouth. "Scared I'll say something you don't want anyone to hear?"

She takes one more step forward. "Stop. Please, my son."

But Ramon just smiles and, gritting his teeth, leans in to mama so his face is almost touching hers. "Fuck. You."

Stepping back, he says to me, "The morning of Papa's death, Mama asked me to fix something on his car."

Cogs begin to spin in my head, but I don't want them to, don't want to face the reality of what Ramon is about to say.

"She asked me if Father Reznik had taught me what she needed me to do on the car, and he had, only the week before. I was excited. I was getting to fix Papa's Jaguar all by myself."

"Ramon. Son. Stop."

But he continues, talking fast. "The bleeder screws—they were rusted. I remember now. I was going to clean them with some brake fluid, fix them up like Father Reznik taught me, but Mama came in and talked to Father Reznik, and he and Mama—they told me to just loosen them instead. Father Reznik said it would 'give the screws room to seat properly.' It didn't make sense at the time, but I trusted him, and I trusted Mama. I thought it would be okay. Father Reznik was a priest." He looks straight at Mama now. "Except he wasn't a fucking priest, was he? And he knew that a loosened brake screw would go undetected, that it would mean that Papa could get off the drive and onto the road without suspecting anything. And then, on the downhill where the road bends left, the loose screw would eventually leak out the hydraulic fluid, and the brakes would fail."

"Father Reznik was working with the Project," I say to myself, in a bubble of shock.

"Children," Mama says, eyes slicing into us both, "I think you are getting too excitable, inventing stories that have no basis."

"Bullshit!" Ramon snaps. "I did what I did to Papa's car, and that morning, on the way to work, he crashed. The car—the car that I altered, doing what *you* told me to do—veered off the road and he died." Ramon sniffs. "Papa died. And you made me do it—and for what?" He searches her eyes. "Because he found something out that uncovered it all—your drugs, your illegal payments—didn't he?" Ramon laughs now, head nodding. "He found out what you were doing with my sister, and he confronted you."

"Ramon, you will stop this at once and—"

"Don't you dare!" His hands clench into fists by his side. "Don't you dare tell me to stop. I have seen you, manipulating, plotting. But I loved you, made excuses for you, protected you, because that's what families are supposed to do. Except that you don't, do you?"

The door to the side swings back a little, half closing. Mama shuffles forward.

"Son, calm down. We can work this out." She reaches out a frail hand. Ramon smacks it away.

"You lied about me to Maria," he says, tears flowing down his cheeks. "You said it was all my idea to put her down there. I am your son! Your own son, and yet, you would do that to me, despite everything I have done for you. For what? Power? Money?"

Exhaustion washes over me. Confusion, fear—every emotion I feel—courses through my bloodstream. But there is something in my mind, something clear, present. Dangerous. "Ramon, the Project. When you contacted them, when did they say they would arrive?"

He turns to me. "Oh, God."

"When, Ramon?"

He stops, checks his watch. "Shit, in about an hour now, maybe less."

I swallow back the panic. "We have to go."

"No." Mama has picked up her cane and is holding it across the doorway. "You cannot go. And anyway, I have contacted them, too. They need you, Maria, my dear. You are one of them now. The Project is good for you."

"Rubbish," Ramon says. "You just want your drugs so you can rule the fucking world in parliament. It's nothing to do with what's good for Maria, and everything to do with what's good for you. That's all politics ever fucking is—everyone in it for themselves. You even got me, your own son—a child—to rig a car so your own husband would be killed. What wouldn't you do, Mother, to get what you want? Hmm? Where the fuck is it all going to stop? The whole world is not about you!"

The cane still blocks the door. "You cannot keep us here," I say. "We are going to leave."

Mama holds out a spindly arm, frail fingers gripping the cane.

"I can't, my dear. I cannot let you go. I am so ill."

Ramon lunges at Mother. He does it so quickly, slips his fingers around Mama's bone china throat so fast, that I don't have time to stop him, to shout for him to step back.

"Be ill, then, bitch," he spits. "And when we get out, I'm going to tell everyone about this. I'm going to go to the press, to the government, to your precious cronies on the political circuit, and tell them what a lying, selfish, conniving old harpy you really are."

He drops his hand, and Mama drops the cane on the floor and gasps for breath.

Ramon turns to me. "You ready to go?"

I glance once to Mama, a coldness forming inside me as I look at her, feel the enormity of what she has done to me, to my brother, to Balthus … to Papa. "I am ready," I say, and rush to the door. In that moment, there is a crack that vibrates in my head and sends shock waves down my entire body.

"Ramon?" My eyes go wide as Ramon slumps against the wall, hands clutching his chest. Between his fingers, blood oozes out at an alarming speed.

"No!"

I run to him, dropping to my knees, desperately trying to stem the blood loss, but there is so much of it, I can't see his chest properly.

"Step away from Ramon, Maria, dear."

I twist my head around. Mama stands holding a gun. And it is pointed at me.

"Why did you shoot him?" Frantic, I watch my brother as he goes into shock, his eyes wide. I press down on the wound with the heels of my hands, take his pulse, but nothing makes any difference. His body is going cold; his heart rate is slowing fast.

"Maria, dear, I said come away from your brother." The gun is pointed at me. I glance to the door; it is open. I see Ramon's eyes fall to it, too, his body weak now, heart failing, and then, silently, his fingers find mine, squeezing them. I look at him now, my brother.

I thought he was with the Project, assumed he was lying to me just like everyone else, but he was the one being lied to. He was just doing what he thought would help me, because he loves me.

"Move now, my dear," Mama says. "You can't help him."

I glance to the door, and Ramon squeezes my fingers one more time, then lets go, hands falling like feathers to the floor.

Slowly I rise, eyes on the door as, behind me, Mama still points the gun.

"That's it," she says. "Good girl. You know it's the right thing to do, to stay. It's who you are. You can't run from that."

I breathe in and, glancing one more time to Ramon, to my brother dying on the floor, bolt for the exit.

# CHAPTER 42

**APARTMENT BUILDINGS, CENTRAL MADRID**

*Present Day*

A gunshot rings out now as I sprint down the hallway, past the gilded mirrors and art deco paintings. The entrance hall is up ahead, the main door, the exit. I hear Mama scream as she moves, faster than I expected her to, out of the drawing room.

I dash through the door to my left, to the lounge, hoping to find a new route out, but the windows are locked and there is no other exit. My heart slams against my rib cage as I dart out, back into the hallway, then stop dead. My mother is standing at the foot of the stairs, gun pointed, arms shaking.

"You can't leave, Maria, dear."

I look down the barrel, then back to Mama. "You killed Ramon. You made him do something to Papa's car."

"I didn't know what would happen."

"I don't believe you."

She sighs. "My darling, I can understand that. I can. But right now I don't have time for this conversation, because I need you to go into that room and stay there until the Project comes. What will everyone think if you keep making this racket, hmmm? So please," she says, leveling the gun at my chest, a slip of a smile on her lips, "be a dear and pop in the lounge, hmmm?"

"No."

Her smile drops. She angles the gun toward my leg. "I don't want to kill you, my dear—naturally. But I will shoot you so you cannot run. So please, cooperate for Mama, yes? I'm really very tired."

I stay still, not a muscle moving, every nerve ending in my body on fire. "You are not my mama."

There is a knock on the front door.

We both freeze. Mama frowns. I peer at the pane of frosted glass that is cut into the wooden door. Three shadows.

"The Project," Mama says. She waves the gun at me. "Well, what are you waiting for, my dearest? Open it."

The weapon is directed right at me, and no matter what flight calculations I do in my head, no matter how many times I try to formulate a fresh plan, nothing sticks, because I am trapped. The Project is here, Ramon is dead, and Mama has a gun to my head.

The knock comes again, louder this time. I take one step, two, sweat trickling down my back, my body spent and beat, mind washed away. I reach the front door and rest my palm on the handle. Mama waves the gun and mouths, *Open it*, and I turn. Drawing in a deep breath, I pull back the lock and swing open the heavy black door.

"Doc! Thank God you're okay!"

My mouth hangs open as I stare at the people in front of me now. They are not the Project or MI5.

They are Balthus, Chris, and Patricia.

"Oh, Maria!" Balthus says, "Thank goodness! And, Ines … I was worried." He falters. "What is …?"

Mama points the weapon at him. "All of you, in the lounge. Now."

"What? Ines?"

Patricia looks at me, eyes wide.

Mama moves toward us, looking at Patricia and Chris. "And whoever you two are, into the lounge. Now."

We enter the lounge, Mama behind us as she shuts the door.

She switches on a ceiling chandelier, and the room shimmers in a twinkling array of little rainbows.

We halt by the empty fireplace. "Mama is with the Project," I say.

"Ines?" Balthus says, mouth dropping open. "*What on earth?*"

Mama shuts the door, leans back on her chair, and smiles. "Balthus, dear, you of all people should not be surprised that someone has had to do what was necessary to survive."

Balthus frowns. "Ines, I ... I don't know what you mean."

She laughs, the gun surprisingly firm in her skeletal hand. "Maria knows."

"I don't understand what you mean."

I glance to Patricia, to Chris. They lower their eyes.

My hand slides to my pocket, and Mama raises her gun to me. "What are you doing?"

Almost in a trance, I take out the photograph and spread it out in my palm.

Balthus gasps, his shoulder shaking, as I pinch the edge of the picture between my fingers and hold it out to him. "Isabella," he says, his voice barely audible.

Tears well in his eyes as he looks at the photograph that I hold in front of him, unable to speak the words of sorrow and loss and confusion that I feel, locked in my emotional cage.

Tears slide down his face. "Maria, I'm so sorry."

"Oh, dear me," Mama says. "Balthus, you have got yourself into a pickle, haven't you?"

Balthus raises his head, eyes narrowed at Mama. "Ines, I asked you for help. You agreed to take Maria in when Isabella couldn't look after her. And are you saying you gave Maria to the Project? You fucking heartless wretch." He wipes his eyes, jaw locked, cheeks flushed.

Chris throws his eyes to me and mouths, "Are you okay?" but before I respond, the lights flicker and the air turns to a chill as Mama holds the gun out at us.

"Maria," Balthus says, tears streaming down his face now. "I didn't mean for you to find out this way. I was young and stupid. I …" He drops his head into his hands, his shoulders shuddering.

Mama tuts. "What, that's it? No explanation?" She sighs.

"I didn't know about the Project," Balthus says to me now. "Maria, when I saw you were in trouble—the conviction, the murder—I had to try and help you. You were—are—my daughter. I spoke to Harriet and she secured you a place at Goldmouth."

I blink back tears that I didn't know were there as, inside my head, everything seems to be happening at once. "Does she …" I swallow. "Does your wife know that I am your daughter?"

"No," he whispers. He raises his eyes to mine. "Maria, that first time I saw you in prison on the day you arrived, I couldn't stop staring at you. You were so beautiful."

I blink over and over, confused, sad, angry, happy. All these feelings at once and no way to express them. "You have been …" I stop, struggling to find the words amid the chaos. "You have been a friend to me. And I don't have many of those."

My finger starts to tap my thigh.

Patricia looks at me. She shuffles a tiny amount, barely noticeable, nearer to me, when Mama suddenly lets out a long sigh.

"Not that this hasn't been touching," she says, "but I think we've all said enough for one day. The Project will be here soon. They know how to deal with Maria."

"Deal with her?" Balthus snaps, stepping forward. "*Deal with her?* She's not a piece of fucking machinery, Ines—a fucking robot for you to use and discard at your whim."

Mama stares at Balthus, then smiles. "Oh, really? You dumped her just to save your own career. You dumped her mother in some Swiss nuthouse to die, and it's *me* you get cross with? Well, it's good your precious daughter sounds like a robot most of the time, my dear Balthus, isn't it? Because she's perfect for the Project. She always has been and she always will."

"Balthus launches himself at her and smashes his fist into her fragile face. "She was my daughter! She was my beautiful baby daughter! And you gave her to those fucking butchers!"

"Balthus, stop!" Chris shouts.

Chris tries to drag him away, but Balthus is too quick and knocks her to the floor. She slams against the floor, smacking her head and crying out, but Balthus springs up, and Chris goes again to grab him, all of us shouting at him to calm down, the noise like a hammer in my head. Then comes a loud blast. We all freeze as, almost in slow motion, Balthus slumps to the floor.

Mama stands holding the gun in both shaking hands.

Blood pools under Balthus' head, and immediately I drop to my knees, rip open his shirt, and begin CPR, interlocking my fingers and pressing the heel of my left hand on his sternum. After thirty compressions, I pinch his nose and breathe twice into his mouth, my own tears mixing with his blood until I cannot tell one from the other.

"Come on!" I shout, starting the chest compressions again. I repeat the procedure over and over again, oblivious of everyone around me, tears streaking my cheeks and chin, blood in stripes on my arms and legs and hands. One minute passes, two, three.

"Doc," Patricia says after four minutes. "Doc, he's gone."

My eyes lift to hers, sweat streaming down my face, blood speckling my arms.

"He's gone, Doc."

I pause the compressions, my lungs heaving, and look at Balthus' lifeless body. Everything becomes a blur, a wash of color and darkness merging into one deep, cavernous hole as I stagger to my feet, Patricia and Chris steadying me. "Balthus was my friend," I cry. "He was my friend."

I look at all the blood and blink as it pools on the wooden floor, seeping into the joints. I smear the snot and tears from my face and touch my arm, feeling the faint bumps of the words that Black Eyes scratched into me: *I am Basque.* Balthus, his blood, his DNA. My papa. Ramon. My brother who loved me.

All the thoughts colliding in my head at once, I spin around, blinded by a sadness so powerful that I hardly know what to do. Mama is leaning against the chair now, all bones and angles.

"You killed him," I say now, my hand slipping into my pocket, feeling for what I need. "You killed Balthus. You killed Ramon. And you killed Papa."

"Doc? Doc, take a breath."

Mama takes a step back. "Maria, dear, let's talk. Balthus would only have messed the whole thing up anyway. You're better off without him. After all, he gave you up, abandoned you, hmm? There is a solution here, sweetheart. You have to look at the bigger picture, at what can be achieved through the Project: peace, global harmony. It's all for the greater good. I can't let you run. And if you do"—she points the gun at Patricia and Chris—"I'm afraid I will be forced to shoot your friends. Needs must." She levels the gun directly at them.

Without thinking, I jump on Mama, shielding my friends from the gun, clawing at her gaunt face and scalp. She cries out, and the gun goes off at an oblique angle. "You don't hurt my friends!"

I have fallen, and feel panic as the gun swings toward Patricia. Ducking, I spring at Mama from the side and jab my hand against her neck. Now blood is spurting from her, and she gurgles and grabs at her neck.

Mama slumps to the floor, so much blood coming from such a small body.

Patricia catches me as I stagger backward.

"She would have killed you both," I say to them. "She killed Ramon because he was going to go to the press about her. She killed Balthus, and she would have killed you both next." I look at Balthus' body, then at Mama's. She seems to be staring at the little rainbow bars dancing on the ceiling. "I'm sorry," I sob, and start to rock. "I'm so sorry."

I collapse, and Patricia kneels down, gathering me in her arms and rocking me back and forth. "*Sssh. Sssh.*"

Chris kneels beside us, grasps my hand, and uncurls my fingers. Something falls out and clinks on the floor.

It is the nail that I took from my pocket and drove into Mama's neck. The nail from the foot of the crucifix where Papa hid the photograph.

# CHAPTER 43

**MADRID-BARAJAS AIRPORT, SPAIN**

*Present Day*

We sit in a dark corner of the airport, as far away from the noise and the passengers and the smells as we can possibly get.

None of us speak. The television in a nearby café delivers a steady patter of news as we sip our hot takeout coffee. Even with sugar and cream, it is too hot, but I barely notice as numbness spreads its tentacles over me. I welcome the dulling of my senses after what we witnessed just hours ago at Mama's house—after what I did there. After what she did.

We have cleaned ourselves up, but still I feel shaky. The images of Ramon, Balthus, and Mama swirl in my mind in a red-tinted whirlpool. When I think of Balthus' face, I see his black hair, his white teeth, and I find myself thinking about how he would check on me, often without my realizing it, so he could be reassured I was okay. He is gone, but I don't know how I feel, because Papa will always be my father, and yet Balthus was connected to me. He was my friend.

"Doc?" says Patricia. "You okay?"

I look down—her fingers are spread in a star shape. I touch mine to hers and breathe out, and without saying anything, I feel a connection that, only a year ago, I could never have imagined I would have with anyone.

Chris is working on his laptop. He has secured us flight tickets, in new names, to Zurich, where we can hide out at a place he knows through his hacking contacts. He has arranged passports for us all, and cash that will last us until we get low-profile jobs in a faraway place where we can easily go unnoticed. Chris has dyed his hair light blond. He wears a smart navy-blue suit with a white shirt and a yellow tie. Patricia wears a wavy brown wig, black slacks, cream blouse, and matching black jacket, while I have a new long blond do with an emerald skirt suit. We hope to pass as coworkers traveling through Europe on business. Chris has said that since he's now on MI5's and the Project's watch list, he may as well take his chances hiding out with us.

"Hey," he says now, "heads up. Isn't that your mom's house?"

We glance up as, on the screen above, the news anchor reads a breaking-news bulletin in Spanish.

"A triple homicide was reported in Madrid, in what is being cited as a cartel crime. Spanish lawyer and member of parliament Ines Villanueva, her lawyer son Ramon Martinez, and a British prison chief, Balthus Ochoa, have all been implicated in what sources are saying is a decadelong fraud ring stretching into millions of dollars and which includes trafficking in illegal medical drugs. The bodies of the three were found at Villanueva's central Madrid house this afternoon. Villanueva, who was a likely pick to become the next leader of the right wing, and prime minister ..."

"Fuck," Chris says. "They've covered it all up."

"They are lying." I spin around to Patricia. "Why are they lying? Balthus was not involved in any cartel."

"The Project must have got to the scene and rewired the story. And in the meantime, this Project bollocks continues to exist and there's fuck all we can do about it."

"Oh, I don't know about that." Chris sits forward, scratching his chin.

I turn to him. "What do you mean?"

"Well, I still have a copy of all those files, right? The ones we—you—hacked in Hamburg and the one I got into at the monastery." He taps his laptop. "So how about we send those files to someone who can blast hellfire out of the Project's ass?"

I pause. "Does that mean expose what the Project does?"

"Yep."

"If we expose the Project," Patricia says, "it all stops. They won't be able to chase Maria and use her, because the public profile of the whole scandal will be so high, just like with Snowden and the NSA Prism files."

"The trick," Chris says, "is knowing who to send the documents to. It has to be someone who can really do something about it. Do you know anyone?"

"Harriet," I say immediately. "Harriet Alexander—the UK home secretary." I pause. "Balthus' wife."

"Do you have her e-mail?" Chris asks.

"No."

Without standing up, he gives a little theatrical bow. "Then allow me to hack into the British government system and get it for you."

With the flight due to board soon, Chris works fast until, hacking straight into their system, he locates the right address, uploads all the encrypted files, and prepares the message. He looks to me. "Okay, so it's on an anonymous proxy and I've encrypted it to your e-mail, uploaded the files, so all it needs now is a message from you about what's been happening with all this Project shit, and we're good to go."

Hesitating, I glance to Patricia, then tap out a detailed message on the keyboard, including all the facts, dates, and details I can use to make the communication as authentic and believable as possible. Done, I lean back and exhale.

Chris looks up. "Ready?"

I nod, thinking of Balthus, Papa, Ramon. A family, though not in the normal sense. But then, what is normal these days? Has the concept ever really existed? Normal is not necessarily safe. "Yes," I say to Chris. "I am ready."

We all glance to each other as Chris' index finger hovers over the enter button.

"Wait!" I say. Chris looks to me. "I did not ask her about Isabella. I did not ask where her grave is, if she knows anything about it."

"Doc, you know she could be alive."

"No. We saw the documents from the files. So many died. She would be old now, too. If the Project subjected her to unregulated tests, she has died like the others."

Patricia and Chris throw each other a glance as I tap my inquiry into the keyboard and step back. I look at the words on the screen, at the finality of them, and want them somehow to make me feel better, to fill the new hole that has gaped open inside me. But no matter how much I stare at them and read the words *gravestone* and *Isabella*, nothing changes, and the empty feeling still sloshes around inside me, untethered and unassuaged.

"You all done?" Chris says. I nod, and he hits send. "Then bye-bye, Project."

We all stand staring at the laptop for a moment, and then, while Patricia and Chris head over to the departures board, I stop. Something is digging into me through my back pocket. I reach my hand behind me and pull out the photograph. It is the picture of Isabella and me, the one hidden by my papa, hidden by him so the truth would always exist. I flip it over and read the name of the hospital in Switzerland.

Patricia comes to my side as I blink at the image in my hands.

"Don't you want to find her?" she says. "See if she's still alive?"

We look at the photograph together. "She is dead. Mama said she is dead, and the dates of her life and death are written down here."

"But your mam, Ines, well, Doc, you can't very well trust what she said, can you?"

My sight swims at the image in my fingers. "I might go to her grave if Balthus' wife knows of it."

Patricia sighs. "I'm sorry for all of this, Doc."

"Why are you sorry? It is not your fault."

She smiles at me.

"Your eyes are downturned."

"I know," she says, her voice heavy. "I know."

Up ahead, Chris calls our names, jabbing a finger at the departures board. Patricia nods to him, then, turning to me, holds out her hand, and I hold out mine. Our fingers touch, just for three seconds, and a wave of calm spreads over me.

"Ready to go?"

I look at the image of Isabella one last time, at the dates and the details. Then, folding the picture in two, I slip it back into my pocket.

We catch up with Chris, the Zurich flight notice flashing on the screen behind him. He hands me his iPod and earbuds, and we walk away, away from Madrid and away from the Project, until all that remains to prove our existence is an e-mail. One e-mail among the millions of miles of fiber optics that cover the globe and are tracked every day without our knowledge.

An e-mail that will expose the entire Project and put an end to it all. For the greater good.

# ACKNOWLEDGMENTS

Thanks to everyone in getting *The Killing Files* out into the world. Thanks to all my editing team and the whole gang at Blackstone. Also, thanks to my previous agency gang at PFD and my new one at Curtis Brown. Big up to the supportive, beautiful book bloggers and Facebookers who make this such fun. And a super shout-out (once again) to Kelly Duke for reading this novel when, well, it wasn't really one, and to my mum, too, for giving it the thumbs-up. Hugs to Marg and Brian for being the best friends and neighbors—Bri, you will always be in our hearts. And to Barry and Wendy for being the most amazing parents-in-law (and gardeners). But, as ever, my biggest thanks have to go to my beautiful little family: Dave, Abi, and Hattie, without whom I could never, ever write. DJ—you and me against the world, babe.

And finally, to you now, holding this book—yep, *you*. Thank you for reading *The Killing Files*! Without you, this book lark simply couldn't exist. I am mighty, mighty grateful.

**NIKKI OWEN** is an award-winning writer and columnist. As part of her degree, she studied at the acclaimed University of Salamanca—the same city where her protagonist in the Project trilogy, Dr. Maria Martinez, hails from. Born in Dublin, Nikki now lives in Gloucestershire, England, with her family.